# Summer OF Joy

A NOVEL

## Ann H. Gabhart

Revell
Grand Rapids, Michigan

© 2008 by Ann H. Gabhart

Published by Revell
a division of Baker Publishing Group
P.O. Box 6287, Grand Rapids, MI 49516-6287
www.revellbooks.com

Printed in the United States of America

Library of Congress Cataloging-in-Publication Data
Gabhart, Ann H., 1947–
   Summer of joy / Ann H. Gabhart.
      p.   cm.
   ISBN 978-0-8007-3170-0 (pbk. : alk. paper)
   1. Clergy—Fiction. 2. Newspaper editors—Fiction. 3. Children of clergy—Fiction. 4. Fathers and daughters—Fiction. 5. Teenage girls—Fiction. 6. Remarriage—Fiction. 7. Weddings—Fiction. 8. Kentucky—Fiction.  I. Title.
PS3607.A23S86  2008
813'.6—dc22                                                    2007037012

Scripture is taken from the King James Version of the Bible.

To Sarah, Austin, Fiona, Ashley, Katie, and Jillian
who always bring me joy.

# 1

The diamond was small. Even smaller than he remembered. David Brooke sat at his desk in his office at the *Hollyhill Banner* and stared at his mother's ring. Out in the front office Zella was banging on her typewriter, and in the back the press was spitting out pages of ads and filler items for the next *Banner* issue.

The rumble of the press was a good sound. It meant nothing was broken. Praises be, Wes was able to work again and keep the cantankerous thing running. Jocie shouted something to Wes in the back room over the noise of the press and then laughed. David couldn't hear what she said, but that too was a good sound. Jocie laughing, happy, being herself.

She'd be laughing at him if she caught him staring at the diamond, wishing it bigger. He was supposed to be working on his editorial. That was the excuse he'd given for shutting his office door, but he wasn't really worried about the editorial. He could crank out a couple of paragraphs about the new Christmas decorations the city council had finally approved and that had just been hung on the light poles along Main Street. Plastic green wreaths with red berries. At night under the streetlights, they were almost pretty. Then if that wasn't enough words, he could throw in something about the Christmas parade coming up on Saturday.

The parade was supposed to kick off the 1964 Christmas shopping season in Hollyhill. The Main Street merchants were having sales and giving away peppermint sticks and sugar cookies to entice the townspeople to buy from them instead of driving to Grundy or Lexington to shop in the big stores. At least the town had waited until after Thanksgiving to start pushing the gift buying.

Not that everybody had waited. Zella had informed him last week she'd had her shopping done for weeks. Weeks. Then she'd given him that look that made him feel like a goofy ten-year-old, and asked, "What are you getting Leigh?"

When he stammered something about having plenty of time to go shopping, she narrowed her eyes even more and said, "Honestly, David. Sometimes I think you're hopeless. You can't just go out on Christmas Eve and buy Leigh a box of those awful chocolates you have to stick your fingernail in to see if they're even eatable and expect her to be happy. After all, you've been dating for months. If going to church or out to eat at the Family Diner can count as dating."

"We went on a picnic once." David didn't want Zella to forget his one attempt at a romantic outing.

"Right." Zella rolled her eyes at him. "In the cow pasture behind your house. That had to be the highlight of the poor girl's year."

"Tabitha's baby was due any minute. We had to stay close."

"And Tabitha's baby is how old now?"

"Three months next week."

"Exactly." Zella glared at him.

"Leigh hasn't complained. She says she likes walking in the park and watching the Hollyhill Tigers play basketball."

"And taking Jocelyn shopping or babysitting Stephen Lee. Of course she doesn't complain. She's too nice for that. Maybe too nice for her own good. But I tell you, David, she's a treasure. And it's time you opened your eyes and saw that. She deserves something especially nice for Christmas." Zella poked her finger toward his chest. "From you."

"You're right." Agreeing with Zella was sometimes the quickest way to get her off his case. "I'll go shopping next week."

"None of those knit gloves and hat sets. Something romantic." Zella's face changed from stern to dreamy as if maybe she was mentally leafing through the last romance novel she'd read for ideas. "Some perfume. Not that cheap stuff, but the kind they have behind the counter at the drugstore. Chanel Number 5, maybe. Or a gold locket. Ooh, that would be even better. Real gold, mind you."

"How about some gold-colored house shoes? Leigh says the floor in her apartment is always cold." David tried to make a joke.

Zella hadn't been in a joking mood as she looked at him with disgust. "You are hopeless. I don't know what Leigh sees in you."

"Neither do I," David had agreed.

But Leigh did see something in him, and he was glad. He wanted her to keep seeing something in him in spite of the fact that he was too old for her and hopelessly impaired when it came to being romantic. That was the reason he was staring down at the ring between his thumb and forefinger. He shined the top of the diamond on his sweater sleeve. That made it glisten a little more, but it didn't make the stone one bit bigger.

David hadn't thought it looked all that small the last time he'd seen it on his mother's finger before Gordon Hazelton had closed the casket to take her body to the cemetery six years ago. He'd thought they would bury the ring with her, but later Gordon had handed him his mother's rings and watch in a small brown envelope and told him not to worry about the bill for the funeral until the next week. As if one more week could make that much difference in how much money David had in the bank.

Money. The Bible said a man wasn't supposed to worry about money. David had preached sermons on how Christians were supposed to trust the Lord to take care of their needs. And hadn't Paul told Timothy in the Bible the love of money was the root of all evil? Not money, but the love of money. Enough money to keep a man and his family out of the poorhouse was a good thing. A blessed thing.

David looked at the stack of bills on the corner of his desk. Hospital and doctor bills for getting Stephen Lee into the world. A bill from Gary's Garage to fix the brakes that had gone out on his car. And then they'd gotten up last week to find a puddle of water in front of the refrigerator. Wilson at the Appliance Center down the street said it was past fixing with no chance for any kind of thirty-dollar patch-up repair. David had let Wilson talk him into a new two-door model instead of waiting and trying to find a used refrigerator. They had to have a way to keep Stephen Lee's milk cold. So somewhere he'd have to find money to pay for that.

Aunt Love had told David not to worry about Christmas,

that a new refrigerator could be all their gifts. But naturally enough, Tabitha wanted to buy her baby something, and Jocie at fourteen might have outgrown believing in Santa Claus, but she hadn't outgrown Christmas presents under the tree on Christmas morning. He doubted Leigh had either. She might say she had, if he asked her. She'd say that awful box of chocolates or those gold house shoes would be perfect. She was that kind of woman.

That was why he wanted to surprise her with a ring. Surprise everybody, he supposed. Nobody thought he'd be ready to plunge into an engagement yet. He wasn't sure he was ready. They'd only been dating a few months. She claimed to have had her eyes on him longer than that, but David hadn't been paying attention. He'd been resigned to living out life alone after Adrienne had left him years ago. But then he'd already been living life alone before she left. They'd never had any kind of real marriage of the mind or soul.

Now if indeed the Lord was giving David a second chance at love and a happy marriage, he didn't want to drag his feet and let Leigh slip away. For weeks he'd been praying about it every morning on his prayer walks. Was it right for a man into his forties with two daughters, a just-born grandson, and an elderly going-senile aunt to ask a young woman like Leigh to share his life and take on those kind of responsibilities?

The Lord hadn't made things easy for David by saying yes, it's okay, or no, it's not. Or maybe David was afraid to listen too closely in case it was an answer he didn't want to hear. He wanted to climb up the stairs to Leigh's apartment and have her throw open the door and give him that smile that made him feel like a teenager again. He wanted to smell the fresh apple scent of her shampoo when she leaned her head on his shoulder while they watched some silly show on television. He wanted her beside him for the rest of his life. He loved her. He hadn't told her that yet, but he was going to just as soon as he figured out how and when.

So he'd driven all the way to Grundy to go to a jewelry store there. He couldn't very well walk up the street to the Jewelry Center on Main and ask Rollin Caruthers about engagement rings. The news would be all over Holly County before the hour was gone. And he wanted to be the one to give Leigh the news, not some guy off the street leaning on the counter in the county clerk's office where she worked.

It had been a long time since he'd been in a jewelry store to buy anything. He'd had his watch repaired by Rollin, but he hadn't looked at any prices. Rings had gone up since he'd bought Adrienne the one she'd picked out after he came home from the war. He had more money then with his accumulated soldier's pay and his mother supplying room and board for Adrienne and Tabitha. He'd hoped the ring would make Adrienne happy, but he never was able to do anything to accomplish that.

That diamond had been twice, maybe three times, as big as the one in his mother's ring. Adrienne had stopped wearing it after a couple of years. She said it didn't fit right and that she would get it sized sometime. That had never happened, but she took the ring with her when she left Hollyhill and him behind. She probably hocked it first thing. Tabitha might know, but what difference did it make now? That ring had never meant anything.

David wanted the ring he bought now to mean something, but the clerk in the Grundy jewelry store had sized him up on sight. A middle-aged man without much money in his pockets. "We have payment plans," the clerk had suggested when David asked him the price of one of the rings. "You'd have to be approved for credit, of course."

"I didn't ask about a credit application. I asked how much this ring cost." David had stared straight at the man until he had to uncurl his upper lip and give David some prices. All of them completely out of David's range.

"And is this ring for your own fiancée?" the clerk asked as if he was having a hard time believing any woman would be interested in marrying David.

"A man usually buys an engagement ring for his own fiancée," David answered.

"That is the customary practice." The man slid his glass case shut, locked it, and dropped the key in his pocket almost as if daring David to ask for another price. "Perhaps I could make a suggestion. Many of our older couples come in together to allow the lady to choose her own ring." The corners of the man's mouth curled up in another fake smile as he looked at David and went on. "After all, we're not exactly teenagers, are we? We don't have to get carried away by the moment."

David stared down at the rings in the case a moment longer before saying, "You could be right." He didn't get the man's name. He didn't want the man's name. As he'd driven back to Hollyhill, he wondered if he could call Rollin Caruthers and arrange for him to show him some rings in the back room where nobody could see David ring shopping.

But that wouldn't solve the not-enough-money part of the problem. He could wait, try to save up some money before Valentine's Day or whenever, but he didn't want to wait. His mother would be glad he took her ring out of the envelope and put it to use. She'd have liked Leigh. The diamond wasn't big, but it was a diamond. And it had

11

symbolized a good marriage for his mother and father. He could get it reset. Not in that store in Grundy. That snooty clerk would probably whip out a magnifying glass to see if he could locate the diamond. No, he'd just have to swear Rollin to secrecy.

Jocie knocked on his door and called, "Hey, Dad. You got that editorial ready?"

David jumped as if he'd been caught napping. He tried to drop the ring down into his shirt pocket, but missed. The ring hit the floor and bounced. He dove under his desk after it as Jocie pushed open the door. His chair crashed into the wall and his shoulder banged against the side of the desk. A fat file of newspaper clippings slid off onto the floor, scattering papers everywhere. Then somehow his foot got tangled up in the telephone cord, and the telephone knocked his coffee cup over on its way off the desk. Coffee started dripping down onto his legs. At least it wasn't too hot.

"Oh my gosh!" Jocie said. "Are we having an earthquake?"

# 2

ocie had never been in an earthquake. She'd lived through a tornado going over her head and had been right in the middle of a house burning down, but she didn't have any experience with an earthquake. At least not yet. The way her year was going, anything was possible.

She touched the doorframe. The building didn't seem to be shaking. But why else would her father be diving under his desk while everything on top of it was falling off on the floor?

"Don't be silly." Her father's voice coming from under the desk sounded cross. He backed out of the kneehole of the desk to peer over it at her. His hair was mussed and his cheeks were red. He grabbed his coffee cup to set it up, but the coffee was already spilt and streaming across his desk toward some letters. "We're not having an earthquake. I just dropped something."

Zella came up behind Jocie. "That has to be the understatement of the year. What in the world, David?"

"I just knocked off a couple of things. No need to get in a panic." Still on his knees behind the desk, Jocie's father tried to corral the coffee with his hand. "It might help if one of you would go get some paper towels."

Jocie put her hand over her mouth to keep from giggling. Her father looked so funny trying to hold back the coffee with his hand, but he wasn't smiling. Not even close. Jocie decided to run for the towels and let Zella ask what was going on.

Her father must not have been in a question-answering mood. When Jocie got back with the towels, he was chasing Zella out of his office before she could pick up even one of the papers scattered all over the floor. "I made the mess. I'll clean it up." He grabbed the paper towels out of Jocie's hand.

"Well, fine and dandy. I've got more than enough to do without picking up after you anyway." Zella straightened her dark-rimmed glasses and stomped back to her desk.

"You okay, Dad?" Jocie asked as she watched him mop up the coffee. While Jocie and Wes sometimes made a game of getting Zella steamed up, her father never did. He said he owed her too much for helping keep the paper out of the red when he first took over as editor of the *Hollyhill Banner*.

"I'm fine. Clumsy, but fine." He looked up at Jocie. "Now get out of here and let me get this mess cleaned up."

"You don't want any help?"

"No."

"What about the editorial?"

"I'll bring it back when I get it finished."

"Sure, Dad. Whatever you say." Jocie backed toward the door.

"And watch where you step."

"Yes sir." Jocie carefully stepped between the papers on the floor.

"And shut the door when you go out."

When Jocie pulled the door shut behind her, Zella looked up from her typewriter to say, "He's certainly in a mood." She sniffed and jerked a pink tissue out of the box on the corner of her desk to blot against her nose. Then she patted the black sausage curls on her head to be sure they were all in perfect order as usual.

"Yeah. You think him and Leigh had a fight or something?"

"No, Leigh would have told me," Zella said, but she looked worried. She took almost total credit for finally getting Jocie's father to notice Leigh Jacobson. In return, she expected Leigh to keep her up-to-date on whatever was happening between them. Zella still hadn't gotten over finding out that Wes had caught the couple kissing before she knew the romance had progressed that far. The first real tiff was something she definitely should know about. She reached for her phone.

Poor Leigh. If there had been a fight, Zella would badger her for every detail. Jocie started to run out the door and down the street to the courthouse to warn Leigh, but Zella would already have Leigh cornered on the telephone by the time Jocie got there.

Besides, even though Leigh was definitely a softie, she had a way of handling nosy people. She'd had plenty of practice out at Mt. Pleasant. Church people thought whatever their preacher or his family did was their business and they didn't mind grilling his new girlfriend about anything and everything. Leigh spent the better part of some Sundays blushing, but Jocie had noticed Leigh didn't answer any questions she didn't want to answer. So maybe she could handle Zella's third degree. Jocie went on through the door back into the pressroom.

Wes looked up from moving some papers off the press. His white hair was sticking up in all directions as usual and he had an ink smudge on the side of his nose. Every time Jocie saw him in the pressroom, a thankful prayer took wing in her heart. For weeks after he'd used his body to shield her in the middle of that tornado last summer and ended up with a tree crushing his leg, she hadn't been sure he'd ever be back to his old self, helping with the paper, riding his motorcycle, telling zany Jupiter stories. But he'd finally gotten the last cast off his leg the week before. He was still limping. But he could walk. He could climb on his motorcycle. He could ride. He could keep the press running and Jocie laughing.

"What's going on up there?" Wes asked. "The Martians invading?"

"Martians? Where did you come up with that? It was your Jupiterians come after you, but we refused to let them have you."

"They wouldn't have took me now anyhow," Wes said with a sad shake of his head. "They'd have took one look at me and seen I've done been earthed."

"Earthed?"

"That's right. It's the number one most dangerous threat to space travelers, especially us guys from Jupiter. Old Mr. Jupiter, he wants to find out all about earth and what makes the gravity so strong down here that folks stick to the ground so good. So he lets some of us come on down here to try to figure things out and send back reports, and by jumping juppie, that gravity sometimes reaches right out and grabs us too. Then we're earthed. Stuck tight to the ground. Mr. Jupiter can't transport us up no more."

"Good," Jocie said. "I don't want you transporting up anywhere."

"You don't have to worry." Wes leaned over and tapped on the shin of his leg. "This here rod in my leg would set off all the transporting alarms. Earth metals mess up the Jupiter magnets that hold the ship together. Why, once when this guy tried to carry home an Earth penny as a souvenir for his kids, you know, we pretty near fell out of the sky before he owned up to it and threw that penny out a window. Now it could be they've come up with better magnets since I fell out of the spaceship all them years ago, so they might be able to transport me up—leg and all. That is, if I hadn't been earthed."

"Do earth people ever get jupitered?" Jocie asked.

"Sure," Wes said. "That's what's happened to those people down at your space center. The ones trying to figure out how to go to the moon and all. Course they've got a long way to go before they get things figured out, so I don't think Mr. Jupiter has anything to worry about for a while. Or the man in the moon."

Wes had been telling Jocie Jupiter stories ever since he'd landed in Hollyhill when she was three. She used to believe them. Now she just loved to hear him tell them. Someday she planned to write them down in one of her notebooks.

"But where's your daddy's editorial?" Wes asked. "Did the Jupiterians steal it for their earth news column or something?"

"I don't think he's written it yet. He's acting really strange." Jocie glanced over her shoulder toward the front office and then looked back at Wes. "I knocked on his door and he nearly turned his desk upside down diving under it. Said he'd dropped something."

"He has been a mite jumpy lately," Wes agreed. "Oh, the things love will do to a man."

"Do you think he's really in love with Leigh? I mean *really* in love."

"Could be. But maybe that's a question you should ask him and not me." Wes sat down, put his foot up on a box, and peered over at Jocie. "Would it bother you if he was?"

"I don't think so." Jocie frowned a little as she gave his question some thought. "Tabitha says Dad's not really all that old even if he is a grandfather now. She thinks he should get married again. She said she thinks she should get married too, but that she doesn't figure there's much chance of that happening as long as she's in Hollyhill. What with having Stephen Lee and all."

"She thinking about leaving?" Wes asked.

"Gosh, I hope not. It would kill Aunt Love if she took Stephen Lee off somewhere. You've seen how Aunt Love is with him. She sings verses out of Psalms to him when she rocks him to sleep. I don't think she ever loved me like that."

"Well, you weren't quite so loveable as baby Stephen Lee when she came on the scene. You were already what? Maybe eight. A lot of difference between an itsy sweet baby and a smart-mouthed eight-year-old. And a lot has happened since then."

"You can say that again."

"And a lot has happened since then." Wes smiled at her.

"Is that why you're earthed now? All that's happened lately?" Now it was Jocie's turn to peer over at Wes and wait for his answer.

"I've been giving that very thing a lot of thought ever since the doctors took the last plaster anchor off my foot." Wes stared down at his foot and worked it back and forth. "A man don't realize how nice a shoe looks on his foot until he hasn't worn one for a good long spell."

Jocie sat down on the stool in front of the composing table. They had more pages to run, but there was no hurry. The paper didn't go out until Wednesday and this was only Monday. She'd raced through all her homework earlier in study hall, so she didn't have to worry about that. Maybe she'd even have time to work on a new idea for the Christmas program at church. They'd probably done the nativity scene bit every year since Mt. Pleasant had been established back in eighteen whatever. That was a lot of shepherds in bathrobes and angels in sheets and garland halos.

It would have to be something simple. Their first practice was Sunday afternoon. Miss Sally normally had the play organized and well on the way by this time of the year, but this had been a hard year for her what with her house burning down and Mr. Harvey having a heart attack. Miss Sally had tried to get someone else to take over planning the Christmas program, but everybody insisted she had to do it the same as always. Jocie's dad said Miss Sally needed to keep working with the kids at church so that she'd have a reason to keep smiling because Mt. Pleasant needed Miss Sally to keep smiling.

Jocie looked over at Wes and asked, "You want to be in the Christmas program at church?"

"And what would I be?"

"I don't know. How about one of the wise men? It might be neat if the adults did the manger scene this year instead of us kids."

Wes frowned a little. "I think you'd better find a wiser man than me for that job. I haven't even gotten officially dunked yet." Wes had joined the church back in September, but they'd put off his baptismal service until he got his cast off.

"The wise men came seeking knowledge. That sounds

19

like you. You're always reading to find out something new. And you look like somebody who might ride a camel across the desert." Jocie leaned forward and studied Wes as if measuring him for a wise man costume.

"I don't know, Jo," he said with a half shake of his head. "I think I'll stick to motorcycles. Besides, I'm doubting the folks out at the church would take to a Jupiterian wise man. From what I've seen, most church folks don't like anybody messing with their traditions at Christmastime."

"I'm a church folk and I'm wanting to do something new." Jocie leaned back against the composing table and made a face. "Something different. Anything different."

"Fact is, it could be enough different has already hit Mt. Pleasant, what with your daddy being the preacher and you the preacher's daughter and Tabitha and little Stevie and me joining up with them to make things interesting."

"Everybody's happy you and Tabitha are coming to church now, and I haven't heard anybody talking about Stephen Lee."

"They're afraid Lovella might hear them. She'd be quoting them something out of the Bible about flapping tongues causing problems. She wouldn't stand for anybody talking bad about little Stevie."

"None of us would. It's not his fault his father wasn't ready to settle down and be a daddy." Jocie's hands curled into fists. She knew what it was like to have a parent who didn't care if you were born or not. She wouldn't let Stephen Lee be mistreated. "And what difference does it make that his father was black? He's cuter than the average baby. Tabitha says out in California people don't pay as much attention to color."

"Hollyhill's a long way from California," Wes said.

"You can say that again." Jocie looked at him and held up her hand. "But please don't."

"Make up your mind. You either want me to say it again or you don't."

"Say what again?" Jocie's dad asked as he came in the pressroom.

"That Hollyhill is a long way from California." Wes grinned over at Jocie.

"And I hope it stays that way." Jocie's father handed Wes his editorial. "Sounds like the press is running okay."

"Betsy Lou is doing just fine." Wes stood up and patted the press. "We were just giving her a little break. Sounds like things were running a little rougher up front in the editor's office."

Jocie's father looked embarrassed. "I guess you could say that, but everything's under control now."

"Good. I wouldn't want you breaking no legs and having to get a cast before Sunday. You have to step out into the water too to dunk me."

"Don't worry. That's happening this Sunday for sure, God willing and the creek doesn't rise. And it might be good if the creek did rise. Make things easier. You haven't changed your mind about going to the river, have you? It's supposed to be pretty cold Sunday. We can probably still arrange to use the baptistery at First Baptist."

"You don't think the ice on the river will be too thick to break, do you?" Wes asked.

Jocie's father laughed. "I don't think there will be any ice. Just lots of very cold water."

"Then we'll go to the river," Wes said. "That's how it was done in the Bible."

# 3

Wes looked at the group of people on the bank of the river and was amazed. He'd been pretty amazed every Sunday since he'd asked the good people at Mt. Pleasant to accept him into their family of believers. They hadn't done so grudgingly just because it wouldn't be Christian to deny anybody entrance into the kingdom of God. Instead, they had invited him right into their hearts, even if a goodly portion of them did think he might really be from Jupiter or, failing that, had surely escaped from some insane asylum before he found his way to Hollyhill. When Wes told David how surprised he was to be so welcomed by the church, David laughed and said every family, even a church family, needed a weird old uncle or two.

Wes didn't have any problem fitting the bill on that one. He encouraged his weirdness, even celebrated it. He thought maybe the Lord did too. After all, the Bible had plenty of weird characters. Take old Elijah going up in a whirlwind to jump into that chariot of fire and move on up to heaven. Or John the Baptist eating locusts. Nothing normal or regular about that. Fact was, the more Wes came to really know the folks at Mt. Pleasant Church, the more he was noticing that plenty of them had a few weird quirks of their own.

And now twenty-five or thirty faithful souls had followed him out to the river to stand in the brisk early December air and watch their weird old uncle get baptized. Wes felt a little guilty for turning down the warm confines of First Baptist Church in Hollyhill when he saw how Tabitha was trying to keep little Stevie's arms inside the quilt she had wrapped around him, and how Lovella was having to hold on to her hat to keep it from flying into the river. But it was too late to change his mind now. They were at the river. It was almost time to wade into the chilly waters.

The deacons and their families had shown up in force. Their Christian duty, Wes supposed. The McDermotts, the Jacksons, even the Martins—although Ogden Martin's face was frozen in its usual scowl.

Sometimes Wes wanted to sidle up next to the deacon and say, "Smile, brother. Rejoice and be glad in the Lord." It might not be written exactly like that in the Bible, but close enough. A man should be happy at church. But Wes bit his lip and kept quiet. David and Ogden Martin had prayed down some peace between them, and Wes wasn't about to do anything to spoil that for David.

And of course Sally McMurtry was there with the Hearndon children clustered around her. She had hold of the little girl twin while Noah had a vise grip on the boy. Little Cassidy was standing close against Sally same as always since the day she'd claimed Sally for her grandmother. Alex Hearndon stepped up behind Sally to use his big body to shield her and his babies from the wind. Sally's face was a white smiling circle in among all those dark-skinned faces.

It was funny how the Lord gave people family if a person let him. Like the Lord had gifted Wes with Jo. Wes looked over at her. She'd normally have hold of one of the babies, either little Elise Hearndon or Murray McDermott, but today she was right down by the river with nothing on her mind but seeing Wes go under the water. She had her camera in hand ready to catch the moment. He was hoping she wasn't thinking the *Banner* needed to run that shot.

Jo was turning into a pretty thing. She didn't know it. Might never know it, but she had a glow about her that made face shape and eye color inconsequential. Wes had seen that glow the very first time he'd laid eyes on her when she wasn't but three years old. His heart, shriveled up by years of grief, had come back to life in the warmth of that glow. She'd become his family. And she'd never given up on making him part of her family of God.

She had to have asked him to go to church with her fifty million times over the years, but he always had an excuse. Too cold, too hot. Too tired, too lazy. Too mean, too crazy. Too scared. He hadn't ever told her that last one, but it was the truest one. He'd been too scared to turn his face toward the Lord. He'd been afraid he would have to see things about himself he didn't want to see. Remember things he didn't want to remember.

As if he could ever forget Rosa and Lydia nodding off to sleep in the car, trusting him to keep them safe. Some things a man couldn't live with. Some things a man had to run away from. It was easier to keep his eyes turned away and to become someone else. Someone from Jupiter with no past, no hope of a future.

But through all the excuses, Jo had kept loving him. The Lord had kept loving him. Had made him run out of gas and money in Hollyhill. Had made a little child take his hand and offer him unconditional love. Had dropped a tree on his leg so he'd have to pick up that Gideon Bible in the hospital room to keep from going bonkers. *And let him return unto the Lord, and he will have mercy upon him; and to our God, for he will abundantly pardon.* Wes had found a lot about forgiveness scattered through the book of Isaiah. Through the whole Bible. Amazing grace. How sweet the sound.

Myra Hearndon had sung that song in the morning service. She had such a beautiful voice that sometimes the rest of the church just stopped singing and listened to her. That's how it had been that morning. She'd sung the way the rest of them would surely be able to sing once they reached the golden shores of heaven.

Now she was leading the little group of shivering Christians in "Shall We Gather at the River." No country church could have a baptism without singing that song. Especially not when they were gathering at the river, even if the song did deal more with crossing over the Jordan River than getting dunked for Jesus. But then again baptism symbolized death. Death to the old life and being raised up a new man.

Wes wasn't all that sure he was going to be a new man, but he'd felt the need to walk the aisle and turn over his life to the Lord. So now he'd just follow along with whatever the Lord laid out there for him. The Lord said be baptized. So that was what he was doing, even though he'd already parted the waters of baptism when he was a boy. His mother had taken great joy in seeing her youngest baptized. She'd already been sick then, and it had seemed the least he could do for a dying mother.

It had worked well enough in his other life, but it hadn't been something he took with him when he went on the road after Rosa and Lydia died. So it was only right that this new person he'd become start fresh with the Lord. Maybe that would be enough. Maybe his old life wouldn't come back to haunt him.

Myra was winding down the song, and beside Wes, David opened his Bible. The wind ruffled the pages as David tried to hold open his place with hands shaking in the cold. Wes looked at the gray-green river behind them. No ice out on the flowing water, but he could see the frosty beginnings of ice clinging to the frozen mud on the bank. They were both going to freeze. No doubt about it. Maybe the Lord would be kind enough to protect them from catching pneumonia.

After the services, if his teeth weren't frozen shut, he'd have to tell Jo to say a no-pneumonia prayer. The girl sometimes seemed to have a direct line up to heaven what with the way her dog prayer and sister prayer and Wes-getting-enough-use-of-his-leg-again-to-climb-on-his-motorcycle prayer had all been answered, just to mention a few. Who knew? She'd never said so, but she'd probably had a "save Wes" prayer.

Up on the road above the river, a car door slammed and Zell came hustling down the hill. "Wait! Wait!" she shouted down at them. "Don't start without me."

Zell showing up was a real surprise. She'd told Wes in no uncertain terms that a person had to be crazy to be baptized in the river any time, much less in the middle of winter when that person could go up to her church in town and have it done right, in comfort, with proper white robes on and everything. Plus she'd make sure the church didn't charge anything for heating up their water. She'd stood uneasily just inside the pressroom door to make the offer.

"That's kind and all of you," Wes told her. "But I've got my heart set on doing it like in the Bible. The way Jesus did. In the river."

"But that was then. If the Lord was here now and getting

26

baptized, he'd have the good sense to come to First Baptist," she said. When David came in the back door of the pressroom, she pulled him into the conversation. "Isn't that right, David?"

"Could be, Zella," David said. "One thing for sure, he'll be there for the baptism no matter where we have it. And it doesn't really matter where as much as what it means to the person being baptized. If your heart's right, any place is good."

"Even if your heart is in the right place, your feet won't be," Zell said with a little huff. "You'll probably both catch your death of pneumonia or who knows what in that dirty river water. Just don't expect any sympathy from me if you do and don't be crying about hiring somebody else to do your work. There's no money for that."

"Noah would come help us out again," David said.

"Did you turn off your ears before you heard the part about no money?" Zell looked like she might like to box David's ears to be sure he was paying attention. "Besides, Jocelyn says Noah's playing on the basketball team. He won't have time to work here till March."

"Then I guess we'll just have to ask the Lord to keep us healthy," David said.

"He did give us brains to use, you know," Zell said before slamming the pressroom door and going back to her desk.

So Zell had been the last person Wes expected to see on the riverbank this morning. But the fact was that lately Zell had been acting even more peculiar than usual. One day she'd almost jump out of her skin if he so much as looked her way and the next day she'd be asking after his health as though she really wanted to know. She'd been too much for Wes to figure out.

27

Then again Zell was Zell. She sometimes came up with her own plans for people, the way she had getting David to notice Leigh Jacobson. While that had turned out pretty good, Wes didn't want Zell making any plans about him. Especially not the romantic kind.

Seeing Zell running down the bank in her dress shoes with the tails flapping on her Sunday-go-to-meeting coat with the mink collar and not paying one bit of attention to the muddy spots struck a chill through Wes even before he stepped out into the river. Something was going on besides just a friend come to wish him well. And he wasn't sure he wanted to find out what.

Leigh went to meet her and ushered her over to stand in the front with Jocie and Lovella. With the family.

Wes turned his mind away from Zell's ulterior motives and back to why he was standing on the riverbank in the first place. David was reading from Acts. "Then they that gladly received his word were baptized."

David handed Matt McDermott his Bible and stepped into the water. He gasped but kept walking. Wes followed him. The cold water squished up over his shoe tops, but Wes didn't pay it much mind. Once he'd made up his mind what the Lord wanted him to do, he wasn't about to let a little cold water stop him.

David's lips were blue as he lifted his hand and said, "I baptize you, Wesley Green, in the name of the Father, and of the Son, and of the Holy Ghost."

Wes took hold of David's arm and let him lower him into the cold water, but he didn't feel the first chill. The Lord was warming him through and through, and while he was under the water, he saw Rosa. She was smiling at him the way she had the day they got married.

# 4

When David brought Wes up out of the cold river water, the people on the bank began clapping their hands as if they'd just seen somebody score the go-ahead bucket at a Hollyhill High basketball game. They didn't make much noise since nearly all of them were wearing gloves, but it was still a joyous sound. David couldn't remember ever being as proud of a congregation of believers as he was at that moment. Even Ogden Martin was almost smiling. Almost.

There wasn't any doubt about whether Jocie was smiling. She looked about to explode with happiness. She'd knelt down on the cold ground next to the river to snap a picture of Wes coming up out of the water. It would probably turn out to be a prizewinner. Jocie had a knack for snapping the shutter at just the right instant. David wished he had a camera to take her picture, but since he didn't, he just captured the image of her joy in his mind. Her hair was blowing in her face. Her nose was red from the cold, and she had muddy knee prints on her good dress that would get

29

her into trouble with Aunt Love. But she wasn't worrying about any of that. She was too busy rejoicing with Wes.

The day she'd been born into his life had surely been one of his sweetest blessings. And now she was surrounded by other blessings standing on the riverbank watching him, but he couldn't stop to count them right then. He wasn't even sure he still had feet down on the cold river bottom, and his nearly frozen fingers were aching. Wes looked even colder as water dripped off his gray hair and eyebrows. Icicles would be forming on the poor man's nose and ears if they didn't get somewhere warm fast. The next person who wanted a river baptism would just have to wait till spring.

Matt McDermott and Whit Jackson were waiting with blankets to wrap around David and Wes when they stepped back up on the riverbank. It kept the wind off but didn't stop their shivering as the icy cold was clinging to them in their wet clothes under the blankets. David hadn't been this cold since he'd been down in the submarine in the Pacific Ocean during World War II and they'd lost all but their emergency power.

"You holding up, David?" Wes asked through chattering teeth.

"I don't know. I'll tell you when I thaw out," David said. "How about you?"

"I'm sure I've been colder, but my brain's too froze right now to remember when," Wes said. "But it was the right thing. I'm beholden to you for wading out there in the river with me."

When Jocie came running to hug Wes, he put out a hand to push her back. "No sense you getting wet and turning into an ice cube like us, Jo. We'll have a Jupiter hugging party later."

Everybody was smiling but nobody was stopping to talk as they scrambled back up the hill to the road and their cars and heaters. Not only was the wind frigid, they'd come to the Redbone River for the baptizing right after morning services, so their Sunday dinners were calling to them at home.

Matt McDermott followed David up toward his car. "You remember you're coming to our house for dinner, right?"

"I'll be there as soon as I get changed into dry clothes back at the church," David said.

Matt looked over at Wes. "Dorothy fixed plenty, Wesley, so come on over to the house with Brother David."

"I'm not one to turn down good cooking," Wes said. "Especially today if it's hot."

"Don't worry. It'll be hot and I'll throw another log on the fire while Dorothy sets an extra plate." Matt turned his eyes back to David. "And of course we're expecting Leigh too."

"She told me she's looking forward to it. Dorothy asked her last week." David looked past Matt to where Leigh was helping Zella back up the hill. She must have felt his eyes on her because she looked up, wrapped her arms tight around herself, and shook in an exaggerated shiver before she smiled at him. David forgot about his frozen toes squishing water out of his wet socks with every step and felt warmer even before he climbed into the car and turned the heater on full blast.

His mother's diamond ring in the folded up envelope was still tucked in his wallet back at the church. He'd have to take it up to the Jewelry Center next week for sure if he wanted to have the diamond reset by Christmas. He'd take in his watch to be cleaned and get Rollin Caruthers to vow secrecy before he pulled out the ring. After that, all he'd have to do was figure out a time and place special enough to pop the question to Leigh.

Jocie climbed in the backseat behind David and Wes. Normally she'd have ridden on to the McDermotts with Leigh to play with little Matt, Molly, and baby Murray, but today she was sticking close to Wes. She scooted up on the edge of the backseat and put her hands over his ears. "I think maybe Zella was right and we should have gone to her church."

"Why's that?" Wes asked.

"Your ears are purple."

"That's what happens when a Jupiterian puts his head under ice water. Makes his true colors show through," Wes said. "Just be careful you don't break them off."

"I thought you said you'd been earthed," Jocie said.

"That don't change what color a body's ears turn when they get cold. Or how long it takes said ears to thaw out, but you can be sure my heart's nice and warm and earthed," Wes said. "You just send up a no-pneumonia prayer for me and your daddy, and we'll be right as rain come Monday. I figure it'll take us that long to warm up."

"I've already been praying that," Jocie said. "And that your fingers and toes don't fall off from frostbite. Can you believe Zella came?"

"Zell's been hard to figure lately," Wes said as he looked over at David. "You got any idea what's wrong with her, boss?"

"Maybe she needs to start reading a new brand of romance novels," David said.

"No, I don't think that's it." Wes gave his head a little shake. "Her matchmaking plans have been going good. Better than good. You and Leigh don't hardly need her to do any conspiring to get you two together these days."

"Well then, maybe that's what's wrong. She's ready to move on to a new challenge. Maybe she's decided you need a woman in your life, Wes." David smiled over at Wes.

"Maybe she's decided she's that woman," Jocie added.

Wes put his hand over his heart. "You two are trying to do what that cold water didn't do. Give me a heart attack. Could be you should forget about that no-pneumonia prayer for me, Jo, so I'll have a reason to hide out in my apartment for a spell."

"I don't think you have to worry about that," David said with a laugh. "Zella may read about romance. She may plan romances for other people, but she's not about to invite romance to her own breakfast table."

"I hope you're right, because neither am I," Wes said with an extra shiver. "I like chugging down my coffee with nothing but a bowl of cornflakes and a good book to keep me company."

David couldn't remember the last time he'd eaten breakfast alone. Not that he especially wanted to. He liked eating Aunt Love's biscuits and listening to what Jocie had going on at the high school that day. Even Tabitha who couldn't bear the sight of food that early in the morning was sometimes in the kitchen now, fixing Stephen Lee's morning bottle. If David wanted peace and quiet in the morning, he took a prayer walk in Herman Crutcher's cow pasture back behind the house as the sun was coming up.

There certainly wasn't any peace and quiet at the Mc-Dermotts' dinner table when they finally gathered to eat. Dorothy McDermott seemed unfazed by the noise as she set up a card table in one end of her big kitchen for her kids and Jocie while everybody else gathered around the oak table at the other end. Dorothy made sure Leigh was sitting next to David.

The Mt. Pleasant women had embraced the idea of Leigh and their pastor being a couple once they'd examined and discussed in detail how much older David was than Leigh. David had overheard some of the discussions and had been informed by those who thought he should know about some of the others. And he and Leigh had laughed about the many ways the ladies had come up with to try to find out her age without asking straight out. Through it all, Leigh had been graceful and kind and caring. Something Adrienne had never been in the years she'd been his wife. She'd searched for ways to insult his church members simply because it entertained her and upset him.

David rarely ever thought about Adrienne anymore. For years he'd carried around the guilt of their failed marriage. He should have done this or he should have said that. He still thought he should have been able to find some way to reach Adrienne's heart before she ran away from him and her life in Hollyhill, but he'd finally forgiven himself for his failure as a husband and turned loose of his resentment of her failure as his wife.

Tabitha coming home had made him face that wounded place inside him. David looked across the table at Tabitha who was hooking a strand of her long hair back behind her ear and laughing at something Matt McDermott was saying. She was so pretty, just like Adrienne, and yet in another way she didn't look a bit like her mother. While the nose and mouth and eyes might be the same shape and color, they weren't the same. Smiles sat easily on Tabitha's face, especially now when she looked at her baby.

But Tabitha didn't save all her smiles and love for Stephen Lee. She wanted people to like her. She cared whether the people around her were happy. Something she definitely hadn't learned from the Adrienne David remembered.

David's eyes touched on the tiny rose on Tabitha's cheek. She'd been part of the love movement out in California before she'd ridden the bus across country back to Hollyhill. But what real difference did a tiny tattoo and long hair make? It was what was inside that was important, and his beautiful daughter who had disappeared in the middle of the night with her mother when she was thirteen hadn't forgotten how to laugh and love. David couldn't remember ever seeing happiness sit so easily on Adrienne's face. Maybe after she'd left Hollyhill she found reasons to laugh and smile. He hoped so.

He had plenty of reasons for smiling himself. He leaned a little in his chair until his shoulder brushed against Leigh's, and he could smell the fresh scent of her blonde hair curled down around her shoulders. Across the table Aunt Love was holding his healthy grandson. Wes, his best friend in the world, had entered into the family of God so he could be his best friend in eternity too. At the kids' table, Jocie was feeding Murray mashed potatoes while little Matt and Mollie clamored for her attention. David was beginning to know he had toes again, and Dorothy was passing him a plate of hot rolls fresh from the oven. Life was good.

He didn't even have to worry about the Christmas play at church. Miss Sally had told him that morning she had everything under control.

# 5

abitha sat on the back pew and fed Stephen Lee while that bratty little Martin kid chased a couple of little girls up the aisle. Miss Sally ought to make him be the donkey in the play since he was so good at acting like one. But no, Miss Sally just grabbed and hugged him before she told him he'd have to sit on the front pew beside her while they decided who was going to do what.

Tabitha hadn't wanted to come to the play practice. She'd wanted to stay at the McDermott house and fold and refold the baby clothes Mrs. McDermott had given her. Stuff Murray had outgrown. There had been tiny denim overalls and corduroy pants and red and blue shirts with snaps on the shoulders. She must have given her a dozen pairs of socks and a pair of white tennis shoes with a red stripe.

As if Stephen Lee needed shoes yet. But they were so cute. Tabitha had taken Stephen Lee's footed sleeper off on the spot and put the pants and a shirt on him so he could wear the shoes. Mrs. McDermott got her camera out and took some pictures. She promised to give Tabitha copies as soon as she sent them off to be developed.

Jocie had taken pictures of Stephen Lee with the *Banner* camera, but she always had black-and-white film. Tabitha wanted the pictures in color. She was wishing for her own camera for Christmas so she could have it at hand to capture Stephen Lee smiling or yawning or doing whatever cute thing he was doing. But cameras cost money, and film and flashbulbs cost money, and having the pictures developed cost money, and money was something she didn't have.

Her father would give her whatever she wanted if she asked him, but she didn't feel right asking him for anything more. He'd already given her so much without the first hint of reluctance or regret. He'd welcomed her home and kept loving her even after he found out the baby was on the way. Best of all, he loved Stephen Lee without reservation and didn't pay the first bit of attention to the Hollyhill holier-than-thous.

He hadn't told her about the rash of canceled subscriptions to the *Banner* after Stephen Lee was born. Zella had. Not with malice. Zella's eyes had opened a little wider than usual on her first sight of Stephen Lee as she'd sniffed and dabbed her nose with one of her ever-present tissues before stammering out something about how healthy he looked. But honestly, Tabitha thought Zella had had a harder time getting used to the rose tattooed on Tabitha's cheek than Stephen Lee's skin color.

So Tabitha didn't think Zella had told her about the problems at the *Banner* out of meanness of spirit, but just so Tabitha would be aware of the sacrifices her father was being forced to make because of her. As if Tabitha could shut her eyes and go back in time a year and make better choices. Not that she would even want to do that.

Her arms tightened around Stephen Lee. While she had been absolutely certain she was going to have a girl and had been calling her unborn baby Stephanie Grace for weeks before she went into labor and gave birth, she couldn't imagine not having Stephen Lee now. There was no way she would ever wish away the moment in time that had led to his birth no matter how right or wrong her actions had been or what problems she or anybody else might face now because of them.

Stephen Lee was too precious, too perfect to wish changed in any way. She let the baby wrap his hand around her finger and played a gentle game of tug with him as, up in the front of the church, Miss Sally began picking angels for the play.

Besides, her father hadn't spoken the first word of complaint about any of the problems Stephen Lee's birth had caused for him. Thank goodness the people at Mt. Pleasant hadn't taken one look at Stephen Lee and shown her father the door. Of course it had helped that Myra Hearndon had already forced the church members to break their color barrier, and it had helped even more that most of the church people loved her father so much that they didn't hold the sins of his daughter against him. Or against Stephen Lee. There were always eager arms reaching out to hold Stephen Lee every Sunday.

Still, that didn't put extra money in the bank or pay the hospital and doctor bills for Stephen Lee's birth. Tabitha stared down into the baby's brown eyes. She had decisions to make. She wasn't a child anymore. She had a child. Somebody who depended on her for his life. She didn't want to fail him.

Leigh had told her about a part-time job at the courthouse. Mostly filing with a little typing, but Tabitha had taken business courses in high school. She could do the job, but what would she do with Stephen Lee? Aunt Love would be happy to keep him, but what if she sat down and took a nap and forgot about him? Tabitha didn't think she would. Aunt Love doted on Stephen Lee, but she did forget things all the time. Tabitha made regular trips through the kitchen to be sure Aunt Love hadn't started cooking something on the stove before going off and leaving the burner turned on high. And she sometimes told the same stories three or four times a day.

Tabitha looked at Aunt Love sitting patiently in one of the pews reading her Bible and ignoring the commotion at the front of the church as Miss Sally and some of the mothers tried to get the kids to sit still and pay attention. Tabitha couldn't hurt Aunt Love's feelings by taking Stephen Lee to some other babysitter. Besides, Tabitha wanted to be the one to take care of him. But there was the money problem.

Tabitha could barely remember any time when she didn't have to worry about the money problem. She and her mother had never had enough money after they left Hollyhill. Plenty of times they had packed up in the middle of the night and left town when they didn't have money to catch up on the rent. DeeDee said it was good to make a fresh start every so often, that a place got stale after a while.

They'd never really stayed long anywhere until they got to California. Then DeeDee had settled, had been happy, had fallen in love with Eddie even though Eddie mostly hung with them because he needed somebody to pay his rent while he got his band going.

Tabitha wondered about DeeDee now and again. She'd written to her a few times since Stephen Lee had been born, but she hadn't heard the first word back. DeeDee hadn't wanted to be a grandmother. DeeDee hadn't wanted to be a mother. Whether or not she wanted to be, though, she was.

If Mrs. McDermott gave her those pictures, Tabitha would send one of them to her mother in a Christmas card.

Up in the front of the church, Tabitha heard Jocie say Stephen Lee's name. "He could be the baby Jesus," she was saying.

There was a moment of absolute silence as if even the rowdy kids in the front pews knew Jocie had said something weird. Lela Martin opened her mouth, then looked at Miss Sally and shut it again. Behind her, Myra Hearndon smiled and Leigh looked worried as her cheeks turned red. Miss Sally held her head to the side a moment as if considering what Jocie had suggested before she said, "We always use a baby doll for Jesus. I think that might work best."

Aunt Love saved the day as she looked up from her Bible to say, "Of course it will. All churches use a baby doll for Jesus. Nobody can step in and play the part of the Lord. Not even an innocent little baby. Besides, Stephen Lee is too big. Don't be trying to cause problems, Jocelyn."

"I'm not." Jocie turned to stare back at Aunt Love. "I just can't see why we have to do everything the way it's always been done. There could be a better way."

"There's no better way than the Bible," Aunt Love said. "In a Christmas play, you need shepherds and angels and wise men. You have to tell the Christmas story the way it's written." She looked back down at her Bible as if the discussion was over.

Jocie sighed. "We could tell the story the way it's written in the Bible and somehow do it different. Like letting the adults take a turn at being shepherds and wise men."

"That might be a fun idea. If we could get enough adults to agree to do it. We might try that next year." Miss Sally reached out and patted Jocie's arm. "And we do want you to finish your poem about Christmas so you can read it to us that night."

"Sure, all right. I'll go work on it." Jocie picked up her notebook and walked back to scoot into the pew beside Tabitha.

"It's okay, Jocie. Stephen Lee might not be ready to be a star yet anyhow. He'd probably spoil the scene by screaming bloody murder if you put him down in a manger stuffed with hay," Tabitha whispered to her. "And Aunt Love's right. He is too big to be a newborn."

"Whoever they pick for Mary could have held him, and Dad says the wise men didn't show up until two years later anyway."

"Well, I know Stephen Lee would have never laid still in the manger that long." Tabitha laughed a little and squeezed Jocie's hand. "You just can't mess with tradition, kid. Baby Jesus is a doll, has always been a doll, and will be a doll again this year. I mean, the poor people will have enough to get used to with Cassidy being an angel."

"You don't think heaven has black angels?"

"I don't know. Does the Bible say it does?"

"I'm not sure. I'll have to ask Dad. All I remember it saying is they had glowing faces or sometimes in the Old Testament they looked just like everybody else at least until the Lord decided to let the Bible people know they were talking to angels. Do you think you've ever talked to an angel?"

"I hope not."

"Why? Shouldn't we want to talk to angels?" Jocie looked over at her.

"Not me. It would scare the socks off me, and angels don't generally show up for an everyday how-are-you talk. They always show up making some kind of big pronouncement

41

like you're going to have a baby. I have a baby." Tabitha ran her finger across Stephen Lee's cheek. He smiled up at her. "I'm not planning on having any more anytime soon."

"But they might come with some other kind of message. Something not so big and dramatic, like maybe it's okay to do something different in church every once in a while." Jocie slumped against the back of the pew and stared toward the front of the church where three little girls were lining up to be measured for their angel halos.

Tabitha laughed. "That angel shows up here and now and tells them that, you might have a chance. Otherwise, forget it. Tradition is going to rule. They've done it this way a hundred years and they're going to do it this way a hundred more, give or take a year here and there."

# 6

Zella scraped a hunk of mud off the bottom of her good shoes with an old table knife she'd dug out of the back of her utensil drawer. If she didn't hurry, she was going to be late for choir practice. She was never late. Brother Charles, who directed the choir, would think she was sick or something and send somebody to check on her.

After all, she did live alone and she wasn't as young as she used to be, although she wasn't nearly as old as some of those young people at church thought she was. People had no relativity. No, that wasn't the word she needed. Relationshipness. Reactivity. She shook her head and frowned at the shoe she was holding as she tried to pull up the right word, but it slipped out of reach.

She wiped the mud off her knife with a piece of newspaper as her irritation grew. She hadn't only muddied her shoes, she must have muddied her thinking, not even being able to come up with the right word. She never had problems coming up with the right words. It had been years since she'd had to peek at more than two or three of the answers to work the crossword puzzle in the Sunday paper.

At any rate, whatever the word was, it just meant people didn't think straight when they thought about how old somebody was. Just because a person was on the far side of sixty didn't mean she was going to sit down and die in her chair or something. Not if that person was hale and healthy and went to work Monday through Friday and showed up at church twice on Sunday the same as she had every livelong week for years.

At least David didn't treat her as though she had one foot in the grave and a head emptied out by age. He listened to her when she said something about what they should do at the *Banner*, and well he should. After all, she had years more experience there than he did. Than any of them did. Even Wesley, though he was older than Zella.

She didn't know what in the world had possessed her to go to the river that morning. She hadn't intended to. There was absolutely no reason for Wesley to be baptized out there in that dirty old Redbone River instead of at First Baptist. It would serve him right if he did catch his death of something.

She dampened an old rag and began scrubbing mud off the top of her shoe. She looked at the clock. Maybe she should find some other shoes to wear. But these were the ones she always wore to church in the winter. They were warm and sturdy and comfortable. She wasn't the type to be a slave to fashion with pointed toes or spiky heels. And she'd never seen the need of having two pair of good shoes when one would do. But then before today, she'd never seen the need to walk down a muddy riverbank to see somebody get baptized.

Of course, it wasn't something that was apt to happen often. In fact, with Wesley, it was honestly something she'd never thought would happen ever. She still wasn't sure he

44

wasn't a fugitive from the law, even if she didn't have any proof except that the man had obviously been hiding out in Hollyhill for years now.

Hollyhill would be a good place for somebody to hide out. Randy Simmons, the chief of police, didn't have a suspicious bone in his body. Hollyhill could be full of fugitives, and as long as they kept nickels in the parking meters and didn't disturb the man's morning coffee at the Hollyhill Grill, he could care less.

Zella plopped one shoe down on a sheet of newspaper to dry and picked up the other one. She wondered if every Mt. Pleasant Church member was having to do the same shoe cleaning job before church. She sniffed a little and rubbed her nose with the back of her hand. The people out there were country. They probably didn't think twice about scraping mud off their good shoes or finding clumps of mud on the church floor.

But it had been nice how the people at Mt. Pleasant had welcomed Wesley into their church. Zella wasn't sure he'd have found that kind of welcome at First Baptist. Of course she'd have welcomed him into the church. She believed everybody should go to church no matter how odd they might happen to be. The Bible was plain about that. Nobody was supposed to be left out. Love your neighbor didn't just mean the person who happened to live next door. Else you could just move to some other, nicer neighborhood when one of your neighbors started getting on your nerves.

She supposed that was why she'd gone out to the river. To prove that to herself and to Wesley. After all, they were all members of the same family of God even if they didn't sit in the same pews under the same roof.

It didn't have the first thing to do with the letter that had come in the mail on Friday. She'd recognized the writing on the envelope right away, even though it had been months since she'd gotten the first letter. So long in fact that she'd about decided the Greens in Pelphrey, Ohio, had forgotten about it all, and she wouldn't have to worry about how she was going to tell Wesley she'd poked around in his apartment to find out where he was really from, while he was laid up with his broken leg.

Certainly not from the planet Jupiter the way he was always telling Jocelyn. That silly girl had believed Wesley's outlandish stories for years. Some of these days she was going to have to get her head out of the clouds and grow up. Zella had told David that very thing just the other day, and he'd looked as if she'd smacked him with a rolled-up newspaper or something.

"Oh, I hope not for a few more years at least," he'd said. "I like Jocie just the way she is."

"A bit more respectful and responsible couldn't hurt," Zella said. David had just gotten a call from one of Jocelyn's teachers about her speaking out of turn and contradicting what the teacher said.

"Well, tact might not be her strong suit, but how much more responsible could a fourteen-year-old be? She's here helping us every day or home helping Aunt Love. Sometimes I wish she were less responsible. I'm afraid I've stolen her little girl times by having her work so much with us here at the *Banner*," David said. "Besides, she was right and Mr. Hammond was wrong. 'God helps those who help themselves' isn't in the Bible. It was Benjamin Franklin who wrote something like that. A teacher should be open to the truth, don't you think?"

The truth. That was something David had never wanted to examine too closely when it came to Jocelyn. Some truths were just too hard to face. Or to tell to others.

Zella put down her other shoe and took another look at the clock on the stove. She had time to let them dry a couple of minutes before she put them on to walk to church. She supposed she could drive, but she wanted to walk. She needed to think about what to do about the letter.

She went across the room and picked up the half-unfolded sheet of notebook paper off the table.

*Dear Mrs. Curtsinger.* Still calling her Mrs., as if every woman over the age of consent had to be married to somebody. Of course, she hadn't answered his first letter so there was no way for him to know he'd addressed her wrong in that one. She was going to write back to him. Eventually. When the time was right, but that time hadn't gotten here yet.

Evidently the boy on the other end of the letter didn't care whether the time was right or not. She held his letter up and read it again for the fiftieth time. The words were emblazoned on her mind, but she read them anyway.

> Dear Mrs. Curtsinger,
>
> It has been some time since I first responded to your inquiry concerning my grandfather, Wesley Green, who has been missing for over twenty years. In your letter to us, you stated that you thought you might be acquainted with a man who could be my grandfather. I have eagerly awaited a reply from you that might shed more light on the whereabouts of my grandfather, but have yet to receive any kind of response from you or from the Wesley Green you know.
>
> You wrote in your first letter that he had been gravely injured. I pray he has recovered and hasn't passed on. It would be a sad blow to think I might be this close to actually meeting my grandfather only to find out that he had died.

Zella looked up and out the window at her rose garden. Some leaves still clung to the vines, but they were shriveled and brown. After the terrible summer they'd had when the whole town had practically dried up and blown away, they hadn't put on their usual beautiful fall blooming show. She was worried about them making it through the winter. Her mother had planted most of them, and Zella considered it her duty to keep them alive and healthy.

Just as it had been her duty to find out the truth about Wesley when it looked as if he might really pass on into eternity. His family would have needed to know then. His real family and not just David and Jocelyn who claimed Wesley was the same as family. But now that he didn't appear to be in any immediate danger of expiring unless he caught his death of something from being so stubborn about being baptized in Redbone River instead of at First Baptist, she wasn't sure what to do. She started reading again.

> I am hoping to make a trip to Hollyhill as soon as I have a break from my studies. Could you send me directions to your house so that I might talk to you about the Wesley Green you know? I wouldn't want to show up on his doorstep without warning and cause him to have a health relapse of any kind from the surprise. As far as I know, he doesn't know I exist.
>
> I think this man could really be my grandfather. I don't know why. I'm sure there are many Wesley Greens in this world, but I have a feeling about the Wesley Green in your town. I am very anxious to find out if that feeling turns out to be correct. Please respond to my letter at your earliest convenience.
>
> Respectfully yours,
> Robert Wesley Green II

Zella folded the letter and stuck it back in the envelope. The boy had even sent a self-addressed stamped envelope. As if she wouldn't answer if she had to buy her own stamp. She didn't know why he thought that. She'd bought the first stamp that had plummeted her into this dilemma.

Zella put on her slightly damp shoes and got her coat out of the closet. She'd think about writing him when she got home from church. She could tell him to wait a few more months while she found a way to tell Wesley about him. She could say that the shock might be too much for Wesley if she didn't have time to properly prepare him, and that it could be she'd made a terrible mistake and this Wesley Green wasn't the boy's grandfather at all.

But that wouldn't be true. The boy had sent a school picture along with his letter. No mistake about it. Wesley's eyes had stared out of the photograph at her. Younger, happier eyes, but Wesley's eyes nevertheless.

As she went out the door, she was glad she'd gone to see David baptize Wesley even if it did mean she'd have to buy new shoes months before she might have had to do normally. Wesley was a Christian now. She'd seen proof of it. And Christians had to forgive one another.

Not that she had done anything that needed all that much forgiveness. She'd just done what needed to be done. What Wesley should have done himself years ago. And she'd tell him so just as soon as she figured out how.

# 7

**B**ut why does everything always have to be the same every year?" Jocie asked Wes on Monday afternoon as they blocked out the ads for that week's *Banner* issue. "Even these ads. Same every week. Why even bother with ads if everything's going to be the same? Everybody already knows a loaf of bread costs twenty-nine cents."

Wes looked up from the composing table. "But it's not twenty-nine cents this week. It's four loaves for a dollar."

"Four cents. Whoopee!"

"A penny saved is a penny earned," Wes said.

"You sound like Aunt Love."

"That's not in the Bible, is it?" Wes looked up at her with a little frown. "I thought old Abe or maybe Ben Franklin said that."

"I didn't say it was in the Bible. Aunt Love quotes stuff besides Bible verses sometimes. She's been doing that 'penny saved, penny earned' a bunch lately since the refrigerator died on us and *Banner* sales have been down. Do you really believe it's because of Stephen Lee, like Zella says? Not the refrigerator but people canceling their subscriptions."

Wes made a clicking noise out of the side of his mouth before he said, "Hard to believe for sure, but then old Zell usually has a finger on the pulse of what's happening in Hollyhill."

"But that's just so silly." Jocie stepped back from the composing table and threw out her hands. "Daddy didn't have anything to do with Tabitha falling in love with that guy out in California or at least thinking she was in love with him. She says now that she must not have known what real love was and now she probably never will."

"Why's that?" Wes turned to look at her. He leaned back against the table and waited for her to answer.

"Because of Stephen Lee, she says."

"Poor little tyke. He seems to be getting blamed for a lot not to be no bigger than he is. How old is he now?"

"Three months this weekend. He's trying to turn over. We can't lay him on the couch anymore. He might just plop right off on the floor if somebody isn't holding on to him." Jocie almost smiled thinking about Stephen Lee.

"How about that? Next thing you know he'll be crawling." Wes did smile with a little shake of his head. "He seems a happy little fellow every time I see him. Chewing on his fingers and drooling all over himself. I guess he doesn't know he's causing problems all around."

"He's just a baby. It's everybody else that has the problem." Jocie frowned and sat down on a pile of newsprint paper. "I mean, even as much as they act like they love him out at church, I thought some of them were going to faint when I suggested he could be baby Jesus in the Christmas manger scene. Just because they'd never used a real baby before didn't mean they couldn't this year. The doll they have doesn't even look real."

51

"Could be they thought a baby might be too real. Afraid he might exercise his lungs at the wrong time."

"Yeah, well, I still thought it was a good idea even if Aunt Love says nobody, not even an innocent little baby, can play Jesus. It looks like we could do something different. Anything different."

"You aren't paying attention if you don't think anything's different out there, Jo. Your daddy preaching every Sunday. Me sitting in one of the pews. Myra Hearndon leading the singing. That church out there has been floating on the sea of change for months now."

"I guess." Jocie put her elbows on her knees and stared down at the floor. "Maybe it's just me, Wes. Maybe there's something wrong with me. Sometimes I feel like I've got a bunch of spiders inside me making me feel all jumpy and weird."

"Spiders, huh?" Wes stepped over closer to her.

"Spiders. Or maybe hummingbirds fluttering their wings."

"That sounds better than spiders spinning webs on your rib cage. 'Cept for their pointy beaks."

"I guess." Jocie didn't smile.

Wes put his hand on her head for a second. "It's just an age problem, Jo. All them crawly legs and fluttering wings just mean you're growing up."

"Well, I don't like it. It's almost Christmas. I'm always happy at Christmas."

"You're not happy?" Wes asked. "You could have fooled me yesterday."

"I was happy yesterday."

"And you must have prayed the no-pneumonia prayer and the Lord must have heard you, because I'm here without sneeze one and your daddy looked in fine fettle when he left out of here to take his watch to be cleaned." Wes sat down in his chair and put his foot up on a box.

"That's good, I guess," Jocie said.

"Of course it's good. If your daddy's watch isn't working, then we might have to depend on my Jupiter sense of time and never meet the paper deadlines."

Jocie knew Wes expected her to pick up on the Jupiter talk, that he was probably ready to spin some wild story about how Jupiter days were a year long or something. But instead she just sighed and wished she could open her mouth real wide and let those hummingbirds fly out of her insides so she could go back to being happy all the time. But that was before this year. Before she started high school. Before some of the kids started taunting her because she was friends with Charissa and Noah. Before she had to have Mr. Hammond for her English teacher. Before Charissa had called her moody.

Charissa was supposed to understand. Charissa was a preacher's kid too. But Charissa didn't let it bother her when somebody was being mean to her. She just turned her dark brown eyes on whoever was picking on her and stared holes into him until the other kid suddenly remembered he was late for class or whatever. Jocie had tried to do the same thing, had even practiced her glare in the mirror at home, but it never worked for her at school.

Her father had told her to pray about it. To pray every morning before she walked into the school, and she'd done that. Short and to the point prayers. *All right, Lord, I'm going into the school. If Sammy Sparrow is in the hall, make him trip on his shoelaces before he can say anything mean to me.*

But so far Sammy Sparrow hadn't tripped on his shoelaces once, even though he never tied his sneakers. She really wasn't all that worried about Sammy Sparrow and what he said, although it would be great if he fell down so everybody would laugh at him for a change. Still, she could just walk away from Sammy Sparrow and whatever he was saying.

She couldn't walk away from English class. She had to go in there every day and sit through a whole hour of Mr. Hammond. She'd never had a teacher who didn't like her. She'd had some who told her she talked too much and that she should pay more attention. But they'd never put her name on their bad list and left it there the way Mr. Hammond was doing. Jocie didn't just pray before she went into English class. She circled a little prayer constantly inside her head. *Lord, let me be invisible today.*

It wasn't one of the prayers the Lord had decided to answer for her. At least not with a yes answer. Her father said no was an answer too, or not yet, and that they had to trust the Lord to pick the right answer for each of their prayers, even if it wasn't the answer they wanted.

Jocie wasn't complaining about that. She'd probably had her share of prayers answered this year already anyway, what with finding Zeb out in the woods to answer her dog prayer and Tabitha coming home from California to answer her sister prayer and Wes throwing away his crutches to answer her let-Wes-walk-again prayer. And that was just a few of the prayers.

When she thought about it, she'd kept the Lord pretty busy all year helping her out of first one mess and then another. So if the Lord decided she should find her own way out of the mess English class had become, then she couldn't really complain. Not after he'd kept her safe during the tornado and had helped her find a way out of Miss Sally's burning house.

English class wasn't going to kill her. It might make her

unhappy. No "might" about it. It *was* making her unhappy. But Aunt Love was always telling her that nobody had to be happy all the time. That rain fell in everybody's life. Something like that was in the Bible somewhere. Of course at the end of last summer everybody had been praying for rain to fall on them in Hollyhill. Everything had been drying up.

But that was the good kind of rain. The rain Aunt Love was talking about was troubles, and there was plenty about troubles in the Bible. Everybody had troubles. Even King David. Jocie's father had preached on that just a couple of weeks ago. And King David had been a man after the Lord's own heart. If the Lord let him have troubles, then Jocie shouldn't expect not to have things go wrong for her now and again. Or lately every day she had to go to school.

Beside her, Wes was being so quiet that Jocie thought maybe he'd dozed off in his chair, but when she peeked up at him, he was just sitting there waiting for her to be ready to talk again. "You think Daddy would let me quit school? Not forever. Just for a few weeks?" she asked.

"It's not likely," Wes said. "You want to talk about it? Tell me what the teacher from Neptune did today that's got you so low?"

Wes always knew. Some kind of invisible thought line ran between them. That's how Wes had found her when the tornado was coming. That's why she could talk to Wes about almost anything.

"I guess it really wasn't all that bad. He just made me stand in front of the class and repeat ten times that I'd quit daydreaming and pay attention." Jocie's face felt hot just thinking about it. "I wasn't daydreaming. I heard every word he said. I just wasn't looking at him."

"But that didn't keep him from seeing you."

"No." Jocie looked down at her hands. "Everybody laughed at me. Even Charissa." After class, Charissa had told Jocie she was sorry, but that it was just so funny she couldn't help it. Jocie hadn't cried then. She'd been too mad. But now a few tears pushed out of the corners of her eyes.

"You want me to go to school with you tomorrow and give him a Jupiter sock in the nose?" Wes asked.

"Yes. No. Maybe." Jocie imagined Wes going into the school and cornering Mr. Hammond in his room and popping the man in the nose. "He wears glasses."

"I'll make him take them off," Wes said.

"He's bigger than you."

"That don't matter to me. No Neptunian could ever hold his own against a Jupiterian."

Jocie couldn't keep from smiling. "But you've forgotten. You've been earthed, remember? And not just that. You've joined the church. Become a card-carrying Christian. You have to turn the other cheek now."

"My cheek. Not yours."

Jocie got up and hugged Wes. "Thanks, Wes. I'm the luckiest girl in the world to have a granddaddy like you."

"Yeah. One who can still fight." He stood up and moved over to shadowbox the press. He stumbled over a pile of papers and almost fell down.

Jocie laughed as she reached out to steady him. "Maybe you better be careful about picking your battles."

"Okay. So Betsy Lou won that round." Wes patted the side of the press. "But I'll win the next one."

"Shh." Jocie put her finger against her lips. "She might hear you and throw a cog on purpose, and then we'll never get the paper out on time."

# 8

Wes could always make Jocie feel better. He didn't tell her what she should be doing. How she should be feeling. He didn't tell her Edwin Hammond was right just because he was a teacher. That's the way most grown-ups thought. If there was a problem between a teacher and a student, then it had to be the kid's fault. Nobody ever thought the teacher might be doing something he wasn't supposed to be doing. Like trying to teach when it was obvious he couldn't.

When she had tried to tell her father that, he'd given her his stern look and said she should be worrying less about what Mr. Hammond might be doing wrong and more about what she might be doing wrong. That was after Mr. Hammond called to complain about her setting him straight on the "God helps those who help themselves" thing. You'd think a teacher would appreciate knowing how something really was, instead of teaching it the wrong way.

It didn't matter all that much who started that thing about God helping them, though. The Lord did help you. A lot of times whether you helped yourself or not. And maybe her father was right. Maybe she should think about what she'd done wrong to get on Mr. Hammond's bad side.

She wasn't perfect in school. She talked out of turn. She sometimes forgot to hide her yawns when a teacher droned on and on about something that everybody had known since second grade. She couldn't keep from giggling when one of the boys acted up in class. But she didn't act up. She did what she was told. She behaved properly. But Mr. Hammond said she didn't.

As Jocie helped Wes and her father finish printing the pages of ads and fillers, she tried to remember the first time Mr. Hammond had given her that evil eye. It was before the "God helps those who help themselves" thing. But it wasn't right at first, when he'd come to finish out the year for Mrs. Wickers after she'd had to take time off because she was expecting a baby. That was in October.

He'd seemed nice enough then. An exciting change. Paulette said he was a dreamboat, and some of the girls clapped their hands over their hearts and practically swooned when he walked past them in the hall. He did look like somebody out of a book. Mysterious. Exotic. Not at all like the other teachers. He wore black all the time, even on warm days, and he never wore a tie. The other men teachers did. But Mr. Hammond wore T-shirts under his suit jackets.

She'd asked him about that in the new-teacher interview for the *Banner* the second week he was at Hollyhill High. He said a tie was a noose some depraved person had designed to keep a man from being able to soar free and realize his potential. She had the whole idiotic answer written down word for word in her notes somewhere. Maybe that's where she'd gone wrong. Writing the new-teacher article. When she thought about it, it was after the article came out in the *Banner* that he'd started marking up her papers and inventing things she'd done wrong.

Later, back at the house after she helped Aunt Love wash the supper dishes, Jocie dug through the stack of old papers out on the porch and found the one with Mr. Hammond's new-teacher article. Her father had put the piece on the bottom fold of the front page. The picture she'd taken of the man wasn't bad. He looked sort of like a young Sherlock Holmes without the pipe or the hat. It was the most flattering picture of the four she'd taken. She remembered.

She skimmed through the words in the article under the picture. He'd taught in Cincinnati last year. Spent some time in New York City before that. Planned to write literary novels someday. Was sure being part of a small town like Hollyhill would expand his horizons. Maybe someday he'd put them all in a book. Hoped to marry and have children in the near future. His mother was in the Peace Corps. Jocie had left out the part about the tie. She'd left out a lot. She hadn't written anything that could upset anybody.

Of course Mr. Hammond hadn't wanted to answer her questions at all. When she'd asked him about doing the interview, he let out a weary sigh and said, "A necessary evil, I suppose. I'll give you fifteen minutes after school today, so have your questions ready. I could probably write out the answers and give them to you without even hearing your questions, but we'll carry through the usual farce."

Jocie had written out her questions in history class. And they were the usual, but that was what people wanted to know. Where he was from. Why he had taken the job at Hollyhill High. Et cetera.

After the last bell rang that day and all the other kids had exploded out the doors toward home, Jocie had hurried back to Mr. Hammond's classroom. The hallways seemed twice as big and spooky quiet without all the kids pushing toward their classes. Earlier at her locker, she had heard the muffled sounds of bouncing basketballs and the coach's whistle from back in the gym where the boys were practicing, but even those sounds faded away as she went down the hall past all the closed classroom doors. Her footsteps echoed on the tile floor. She should have asked Charissa to stay with her and keep her company while she talked to Mr. Hammond.

He looked up from his desk at her when she knocked on his open door and motioned her in with a long slender finger. "I've got the questions ready," she told him holding up her notebook. "But if it's okay, we can do the pictures first."

"Whatever." He looked bored with the whole idea, but he sat still while she snapped four pictures.

"Great," she said as she dropped the camera back against her chest and scooted into the student's desk right in front of his desk. She didn't know why she was nervous. She'd interviewed a half dozen of the teachers in the school for this or that story in the *Banner* already this year. Interviews weren't hard. She just asked the questions and wrote down the answers.

"I wasn't aware the school had a student paper," he said.

"We don't. This is for the local paper. The *Hollyhill Banner*." Jocie opened up her notebook and pulled her pencil out of her purse.

He frowned. "You work for the local paper?"

"I don't really work for the paper. I just help out. My father is the editor, so he lets me do the school news." She gave Mr. Hammond what she hoped was a dazzling smile.

He didn't smile back. "I thought you said your father was a preacher."

"Right. That too." Their first assignment from Mr. Hammond had been to write a page about themselves. She'd written that her father was a preacher and an editor, but a teacher couldn't be expected to remember every word every student wrote.

"Interesting." Mr. Hammond leaned back in his chair, made a steeple with his long index fingers, and studied Jocie over them. "Are you sure you are capable of doing a proper interview?"

"I've done a lot of interviews." Jocie let her smile drain away and plastered her best serious look on her face as she gripped her pencil until her fingers hurt. The man's eyes bored into her as if he didn't believe a word she was saying. "You can read the final copy before it comes out in the *Banner* if you want."

"Oh well, it won't matter all that much. Your news rag is hardly the *New York Times*." He waved his hands in a dismissive gesture before he picked up a pen and began twirling it back and forth between his fingers. "So on with it. Ask."

When she started reading her first question about where he was from, he stopped her. "Wait. Let's shorten this. Please. I'll give you the capsule info. I was born in Pittsburgh, Pennsylvania. My mother taught eighth grade math. My father was a policeman. He was killed in the line of duty when I was fifteen. My mother joined the Peace Corps last year and is somewhere in South America helping the poor unfortunates there learn how to add and subtract, I suppose. No brothers or sisters."

He paused to take a breath, and Jocie said, "I'm sorry."

When he looked at her as if he didn't know what she was talking about, she added, "For your father dying."

"Why? Nobody else was. Certainly not me. He wasn't a nice man." He didn't miss a twirl.

"Oh." Jocie thought about saying she was sorry again—this time because his father wasn't a nice man—but she decided against it. Instead she concentrated on writing down what he'd said while the silence in the room pushed against her ears. Finally she looked up and said, "And you say your mother is in the Peace Corps."

"Oh yes. Inspired by our late president's fiery oratory about asking what we can do for our country. God and country. I can almost hear the national anthem playing, can't you? My dear mother always committed to the greater good. She never worried a lot about what the greater good was for those closest to her."

"Oh," Jocie said, not sure what he expected her to say to that. "Well, it must be pretty neat, though, having a mother in the Peace Corps."

"Neat. That's as good a word as any." He looked bored as he went on. "And what else do you want to know? Let's see. People usually want to know where I taught before, as if last year had anything to do with this year. Different schools. Different reluctant minds to pry open. Same parts of speech to pour in." He let out an elaborate sigh. "At any rate, last year I taught in Cincinnati. My first position was in New York. I don't like staying in one place for long."

Jocie asked, "Why?"

"Why what?" He stopped twirling his pen and stared at her.

"Why don't you like staying in one place for long?"

"I am a writer. A writer needs to experience new things, fill his mind with characters in all sorts of situations to people his stories. No doubt Hollyhill will help fill my reservoir of odd characters to the brim."

"Is that why you are an English teacher—because you like to write?" Jocie glanced up at him from her scribbled notes. He was looking at her as if she'd just asked the dumbest question ever.

"I don't *like* to write. I *do* write." He sounded insulted as his eyes narrowed on her.

"Oh, okay. Sorry." Jocie looked down at her notepad, but she could still feel him frowning at her. "What do you write?"

"Whatever my muse suggests. I doubt you even know what a muse is."

"Your inspiration to write?" Jocie said.

"Go to the head of the class." His frown was replaced with an amused look. "I'll wager you have dreamed of being a writer yourself someday. Oh, the somedays that we might have."

Jocie's cheeks felt warm. She ducked her head and scribbled some notes as she answered, "I write for the newspaper already." She wasn't about to tell him about her journals and how she liked to write down people's stories. He'd laugh for sure.

"So you do. Does your father give you bylines?"

"He probably will for this story," Jocie said.

"Amazing. I'm the reason for a byline for a child of what? Thirteen? Fourteen?"

"Fourteen." Jocie searched through her notes for a question to get the interview back to business. His business. She cleared her throat and asked, "So are you inspired to write stories? Or maybe poems?"

"Literature. I write literature." He leaned forward in his chair and hit the end of his pen down hard on the pile of papers on his desk in front of him. Jocie couldn't keep from jumping. "Shakespeare. Hemingway. Fitzgerald. Poe. They surely didn't have to start out this way—marking papers. Alas, what depths a man must sink to before he reaches his destiny!"

For a moment Jocie thought he might leap up and start reciting Shakespeare or something. She shrank back in her seat. The man was strange. Plain and simple. Or not so simple. She licked her lips and managed to say, "Right." Her eyes strayed over to the door.

"Right?" he shot back at her. "What do you know about destiny?"

"I guess everybody has one," Jocie ventured.

"Again you have an answer." Mr. Hammond pointed his pen toward her. "But have you thought about your destiny? Whether you are destined for greatness or destined to grow up, live out your life in this small hamlet, and never do anything of note. I believe a person can plan out his own destiny. Shape his life. Not that a detour doesn't occur at times. Such as this year in Hollyhill. But perhaps even here destiny awaits. Perhaps I will find the love of my life or write my first literary masterpiece. Do you think that's possible?"

"I guess so." Jocie grabbed at his last remark as a way to get back to a semblance of a normal interview. "So you aren't married?"

"You knew that already." He looked smug now as if he'd caught her in some mistake and it pleased him. "Every girl in the school knew I wasn't married before the end of the first day I was here. Single and available. Be sure to put that in your article. Who knows? The love of my life might be one of your subscribers. And it could be that I want to get married."

"Why?" Jocie was sorry she asked as soon as the word

was out of her mouth. She should have just mumbled "right" again and said thank you before making her escape out the door. That's what it was feeling more and more like. As if she needed to make an escape.

"Vietnam." He looked angry for a moment. Then he took a deep breath and started twirling his pen again as he said, "Our noble president is allowing our country to be sucked into that conflict on the other side of the world. In the name of freedom, he says. But there is little freedom for draft-age men. Uncle Sam says go, then go you must. But Uncle Sam is less demanding of married men with children."

"I see."

"Do you?"

"Maybe. Sort of." Jocie glanced up at the clock over the chalkboard. Her fifteen minutes were up and then some. She had enough to write her piece. Leigh would be out front waiting for her. Leigh was taking off work early so they could make Christmas cookies to take to church.

"In a hurry?" Mr. Hammond asked, his amused look back in place.

"You told me I only had fifteen minutes. I was trying to keep to your schedule."

"But you haven't asked me your questions."

"You answered some of them already." Jocie looked down her list.

"But surely you had some personal questions. Perhaps my favorite writer. Or about my mode of dress."

"So who is your favorite writer?"

"Hemingway, both on the page and off the page. He knew how to live. And die."

Jocie looked up at the teacher with a puzzled frown. "I thought you told us he killed himself."

"That he did. In control of his destiny till the end." He

made a gun with his finger and thumb and pretended to fire it toward his own head. "Admirable."

"Oh." Jocie stared down at her notes before she licked her lips and made herself ask one last question. "And how come you don't wear a tie?"

So he had given her his ridiculous "tie is a noose" reason. That had seemed a good time to close her notebook and thank him profusely for talking to her as she backed out of the room. She hadn't been happy when he stood up and followed her into the hall. Neither of them said a word as they walked toward the front door. Jocie had to force herself not to run. Once outside on the steps, she was relieved to see Leigh parked on the street waiting for her. Leigh got out of the car and waved.

"Is that your mother?" Mr. Hammond asked.

"No. My dad's girlfriend." Jocie edged away from him down the steps.

"Girlfriend. Interesting. Where's your mother?"

"California, last we heard," Jocie said.

"Indeed." Mr. Hammond was staring at Leigh. "Your father's friend is very attractive. Perhaps you could introduce me."

"I'd love to, but we're in a big hurry. Maybe next time," Jocie said before she ran down the sidewalk to Leigh's car. She hoped Mr. Hammond wasn't running behind her.

"Thanks for coming to pick me up," she told Leigh as she jumped in the car and slammed the door. "Let's go."

Leigh got in and started the car. "What's the hurry?" she said. "Your teacher looked like he wanted to talk."

"I've already talked to him enough today. He's not your normal Hollyhill English teacher. Trust me."

"Interview didn't go well, then?" Leigh pulled out on the road.

"I escaped in one piece." Jocie looked back at the school. Mr. Hammond was still standing on the sidewalk watching them drive away.

"Escaped?" Leigh looked over at her with a sympathetic smile. "That bad, huh?"

"Yeah. I don't know. Just kind of weird." Jocie rubbed her finger up and down the wire coil on her notebook.

"He's the guy that took over for Mrs. Wickers, isn't he?" Leigh didn't wait for Jocie to answer. "I've heard some people talking about him. They say he lived in New York City for a while. Was a writer there before he started teaching."

"That's what he said." Jocie tried to change the subject. "What kind of cookies are we making?"

Leigh had laughed again. "I don't think you want to talk about Mr. New Teacher. I guess I'll just have to wait and read about him in the *Banner*."

The *Banner* article had come out the next week. Jocie didn't know if Mr. Hammond read it or not. He had never said the first word about it to her.

Jocie looked at the teacher's picture one more time before she folded the paper and stuck it back in the stack of old papers. That was definitely when things started going bad for her in English class, but she still had no idea how to make it better. None at all. All she could do was look forward to Christmas break and not having to see the man's face for two whole wonderful weeks.

## 9

Leigh couldn't remember when she'd ever been so excited about Christmas coming. Certainly not since she was a little kid wondering how she'd get anything from Santa Claus since her house didn't have a chimney, and maybe not even then, because Santa Claus had always ended up putting stuff she needed instead of stuff she wanted under the tree.

But this year she was getting to play Santa Claus. She'd already bought Stephen Lee a footed sleeper with trains on it, a pair of the cutest blue jeans, and a set of brightly colored wooden blocks. Not that he would care what he got for Christmas this year, but it was fun having a little one to buy for, and not only the baby but Jocie too. While Jocie was several years beyond the Santa Claus age, she was still a kid who believed in the magic of Christmas. Or at least needed to.

Leigh herself was grabbing on to that magic this year. That feeling of love everywhere as the world celebrated the greatest gift ever given in the form of a tiny baby. People were smiling more. Even the people coming into the clerk's office to buy their car licenses didn't grumble quite so much about having to fork over their money to the government in order to keep their cars legal.

And that morning in the park when a few snowflakes had drifted down, the very air had seemed to be sparkling. "Look," she'd told David who had been waiting at the park to walk with her the way he was every Saturday morning now. She hardly ever even wondered if he'd be there. She expected him to be there. "There must be glitter on the snow. It's sparkling."

She held out her hand to catch one of the snowflakes to show David, but instead of looking at the snowflake on her glove, he kept his eyes on her face as he said, "You're what's sparkling. You're beautiful this morning."

Her heart melted faster than the tiny snowflake on her palm, and she felt as if she were spinning in sparkles just like Cinderella after the Fairy Godmother touched her with her wand. She had never dreamed in her sweetest daydreams that being in love would feel so good. For years she'd been afraid it was a feeling she'd never know, but now no matter what else happened, she did know how it felt to be in love.

And even though no words had been exchanged between them to admit love on either side, she was hoping—no, more than hoping. She was praying that David was feeling some of that same thing. He liked being with her. Else he wouldn't get up hours early on a Saturday morning to come walk with her around a deserted baseball field in the park as the sun came up.

She'd wanted to stand there with David in the park all day and enjoy the feeling, but of course she hadn't. They'd kept walking until they made their usual rounds and then had gone their separate ways. David headed to the *Banner* offices to put in a few hours on next week's issue before he went home to work on his sermon for Sunday, and she came home to shower and get ready to drive to Grundy to take her mother Christmas shopping.

It was a tradition. Every year since Leigh was twelve, she'd gone shopping with her mother the first Saturday in December to pick out all their presents. That first Christmas Leigh had hid in her room and cried after she opened her presents and there wasn't one surprise. She thought her mother would go out and get her one thing she hadn't already known she was getting. Some small something to keep the fun in the gift opening ritual, but no, there were no surprises then and none in the years since.

But this year just climbing out of bed every morning seemed to promise surprises. Glittering surprises. She sang "Joy to the World" at the top of her voice in her shower and didn't worry about cranky old Mrs. Simpson who lived below her apartment. She planned to throw caution to the wind and buy three rolls of that expensive shiny foil paper and some curling ribbon to use when she started wrapping her presents.

A whole stack of boxes sat on the end of her kitchen table and she had more to buy. She'd bought David a tie with red stripes, but she wanted to find something better. Something special, though she had no idea what. She'd been racking her brain for the perfect gift for days.

She'd thought about a new watch, but the one he had seemed to keep time fine. Or a transistor radio he could listen to as he went around visiting since his car didn't have a radio, but he said he used that time to catch up on his praying. Maybe a book of sermons, but then he might think she thought his own sermons weren't good enough. A new Bible, but that was more the kind of gift a grandmother might give him. She certainly didn't want him to confuse her with his grandmother. A new shirt to go with the tie, but it wasn't really proper to give a man you weren't married to an article of clothing other than a tie or gloves. If they were engaged, that might be different.

If they were engaged, everything might be different. And wonderful. Leigh looked down at her left hand on the steering wheel and could almost see a ring there. Then she laughed at herself as she reined in her imagination and reminded herself she needed to pay attention to the traffic and not get so carried away.

She and David had gone on a few dates. He came out to the park to walk with her. She drove out to his church every Sunday morning and felt more than welcome. But all that was a long way from an engagement. A long way. And so she had to think up a gift that was proper and perfect.

What he needed was shoes. Poor man had worn holes in the soles of his shoes, but she couldn't get him shoes. Not even if she knew what size he wore. Besides, that would be entirely too sensible and practical. She was tired of being sensible and practical all the time and especially at Christmas.

Every Christmas she gave her parents sensible and practical gifts like house shoes and robes, aftershave and hand lotion. For years she had sat in the same chair in her mother's living room on Christmas morning and opened up gifts of sweaters and gloves and sometimes underwear. Every Christmas since she could remember, before they could pick up all the gift wrapping her parents had found some reason to start sniping at one another.

Something always turned out to be wrong. The doughnuts her father had brought in for breakfast weren't fresh enough. The oranges weren't juicy enough. The thermostat was set too high or too low. Her father didn't want to go

71

to her mother's sister's house for dinner. Every year the same presents. Every year the same arguments.

But this year was going to be different. This year Leigh was going to put the joy back into Christmas. Gifts didn't matter. Stale doughnuts didn't matter. When they celebrated didn't matter. Leigh hadn't figured out exactly how she was going to break that last one to her mother, but she knew in her heart that if she had even a hint of an invitation, she wanted to be at David's house with a whole new family on Christmas morning.

And she was going to insist her mother and father meet David. Her mother kept making excuses. She didn't feel well. The house wasn't clean enough. And heavens no, she couldn't go out to eat. Her feet were too swollen to wear anything but house shoes. Her father was playing golf or his favorite team was playing basketball on television.

Her mother didn't want to meet David. She didn't want to like him. She didn't want him to be real. She didn't want Leigh to be in love. She gave the excuse that David was too old for Leigh, but the truth was that she wanted Leigh to move back home, and how could that ever happen if Leigh found a man to love. A man to love her.

Could it be true, Leigh wondered as she turned down the street to her parents' house. Had she found a man to love her? No doubt she'd found a man to love. She felt the song "Joy to the World" swelling up inside her again. She loved Christmas. At Christmas anything was possible. A baby was born to a virgin. Angels sang to shepherds. Wise men followed a star to Bethlehem. The world rejoiced as salvation was born.

Anything was possible. She could get something besides a sensible beige cardigan for Christmas. She could resist all the Christmas candy people kept pushing in front of her.

She could keep from gaining back the weight she'd lost. A good man like David could fall in love with her. Her mother could smile and be happy for her.

Leigh knew just as soon as her mother met her at the door with her coat already on and carrying her big black purse that the being happy for Leigh wasn't going to be possible that day.

"You're late," her mother said without even saying hello.

"Not much," Leigh answered as she gave her mother a little peck on her cheek. "Are you ready to go get some shopping done?"

"Just a week late," her mother said. "We always go shopping the first Saturday in December. Not the second Saturday."

"I was busy last week. I explained that to you. Hollyhill was having its Christmas parade."

"So you said, and you had to take that preacher's daughter and that baby she has to the parade. Looks like he could have taken her himself." Her mother pulled the door shut behind her as she stepped outside.

"He was taking pictures for the paper. And I didn't have to—I wanted to. Parades are fun. Don't you remember when we used to go to the Christmas parade downtown here?"

"I can't even imagine standing on a street, watching a parade now. Not with the way my legs are. I don't know how I'll make it shopping today."

Leigh looked at her mother's feet. They were swollen but didn't look too bad. Her mother was too heavy, had always been too heavy ever since Leigh could remember. She'd told Leigh it ran in her side of the family and so Leigh shouldn't worry about being too heavy herself. That there wasn't anything she could do about genetics.

But of course, there was, and Leigh had done it finally. She'd stopped eating everything in sight and started walking every day. And she looked the other way when she went past the potato chips at the grocery store. Even though she wasn't skinny, probably would never be skinny, she was a lot closer to the "pleasingly" part on pleasingly plump. She didn't look bad. She kept being surprised whenever she saw her reflection in a window.

"Have you been putting your feet up the way the doctor told you?" Leigh asked her mother as she helped her get into the car.

"How do you think anybody could sit around with their feet up this close to Christmas with everything still to do and no presents bought?"

"We'll get the shopping done today," Leigh said. "One week won't make that much difference."

"Not if you don't mind everything being picked over," her mother said glumly as she put her hands on top of her purse in her lap and let Leigh close the car door.

"Maybe there will be more sales," Leigh said as she slid in the car behind the wheel and started the motor. She was determined to stay cheerful and to hang on to the joy no matter what her mother said.

"I doubt it. They just put the prices up the closer you get to Christmas. They know you're going to be desperate to buy something, anything then."

Leigh pulled in a deep breath and let it out slowly. She loved her mother. She really did, but loving her and enjoying being with her were two different things. It was as if her mother had a grudge against the world, and she nursed that grudge like a favorite child.

"I'm sorry, Mother," Leigh said, and she meant it. She might not be sorry she was a week late, but she was sorry her mother was upset. She was sorry her mother didn't feel well. She had gotten out of breath just walking to the car, and no doubt, her feet did hurt. "Maybe it would be better if you just gave me your list and let me do your shopping for you."

"You think I can't do my own shopping?" She sounded insulted.

"I didn't say that. I was just thinking about how you said your feet were hurting."

"Well, of course my feet are hurting. They've been hurting for years," her mother said. "But you weren't too worried about that when you decided to move off to Hollyhill when you had a perfectly good job right here in Grundy and could have lived at home and wouldn't have had to spend all that money on an apartment."

"You didn't want me to be a child all my life, did you?" Leigh asked softly.

"You are my child all your life."

"Your child, but not *a* child. I'm an adult, Mother. I need to try my own wings just as you did when you left home and got married."

"Married?" Her mother almost choked on the word. She pulled a handkerchief out of her purse and fanned her face with it. "You aren't thinking about marrying that preacher, are you? Your father and I haven't even met him yet and you're talking about getting married!"

"I'm not talking about getting married," Leigh said. But she'd like to be. She couldn't think of anything she'd rather be talking about. "And I want you to meet David. You'll like him. I know you will."

"Does he want to meet us? That's the question."

"I told you he did. He does. Christmas is on Friday this year. I'll get David to come up with me sometime that weekend."

"But you'll already be home on Christmas Day and you always spend the night on Christmas after we go to Stella's."

Leigh opened her mouth to say maybe not this year, but then shut it again. She felt cowardly letting her mother take her silence as agreement, but they had to get through the day shopping. And Leigh didn't know what she was going to be doing on Christmas Day for sure. She just had hopes. No plans. But oh, what hopes.

# 10

The church was nearly full. A children's Christmas program always brought the people in. Mothers and daddies, grandparents, aunts and uncles packed the pews to see their little shepherd, angel, or wise man in his or her moment of glory. The only other time David saw the church pews any fuller was at Easter, but he didn't believe in lambasting people for not coming more often when they did show up at church. That was the time to welcome and embrace them. Show them the Lord's love. He'd never found anything in the Bible about only loving the faithful who came to church every Sunday. The Lord received all who came to him.

Up front Miss Sally and Lela Martin shooed three shepherds in bathrobes out from behind the white sheets that served as stage curtains. The little boys peeked out from under their towel head wraps and headed toward the red construction paper flames sticking up out of a circle of sticks in front of the podium. The pulpit had been moved to make room for the hill where the shepherds were keeping watch over their flocks

On the other side of the stage, Dorothy McDermott and

Myra Hearndon pushed four little sheep out into the lime-light. They crawled toward the shepherds slowly to keep from losing their cotton ball fleeces and ears. Two of the sheep—the Hearndon twins, at two and half—had been prone to wander from the flock in practices. Myra had tried to talk Miss Sally out of putting them in the play, but Miss Sally insisted every child needed a part.

Myra couldn't argue with Miss Sally. Nobody in the church could. Not this year after she'd lost her brother and her house to the fire in September. Not that anybody ever wanted to argue with Miss Sally. She might not step out and be in the play. She might stay behind the scenes, but her part in the program, her part in the church, was to represent Christ with his arms outstretched. She played her part well, but with Miss Sally it wasn't acting. She radiated love.

So when Myra had worried about her twins wandering down the aisles or crawling under the pews or who knew where, Miss Sally said that was why there were shepherds. To keep their sheep from wandering. And because those shepherds were out on that hill that night doing their job and keeping their sheep safe, they were blessed. David was thinking about using that thought for his sermon next Sunday.

Of course the little shepherds tripping on their bathrobes and stumbling over their wooden staffs toward the fire weren't much older than the little lambs. Two of the little shepherds made it to the fire and sat down without a glance at the sheep milling around behind them. The other little shepherd, Jeremy Sanderson, shoved at the towel that had slipped down over his eyes and fell right over top of Eli Hearndon who was doing some kind of spinning sheep moves in the middle of the aisle with a full chorus of baas.

Jeremy fell into the campfire. He jumped back as though the construction paper flames were real, and the towel fell off his head. The other two shepherds tried to help him put it back on, because it was a well-known fact that nobody could be a shepherd without a towel on his head.

Meanwhile the sheep, seeing their chance, took off crawling up the center aisle. One of the little shepherds, looked around at the escaping sheep, put his hands on his hips, and announced, "I told Miss Sally we should've had cows instead of sheep."

The congregation let out a roar of laughter, and Miss Sally, who had come out from behind the curtain to be sure Jeremy was okay, laughed so hard she had to sit down on the front pew and wipe her eyes. The little sheep might have made it to the door if Jocie hadn't put down her camera to give chase. She herded them back to the front, settled them into position while Miss Sally got the shepherds situated around the fire. The rest of the church folk, still smiling, caught their breath and waited for the angels to appear.

Leigh leaned over and whispered in David's ear. "I don't see how the rest of the play can top this."

"You never can tell with kids," David whispered back. Her hair brushed against his cheek, and he was glad he'd come back two rows to sit beside her, Tabitha, and Aunt Love who was holding Stephen Lee. The baby had jerked awake at the burst of laughter but had settled back to sleep when Aunt Love started patting his bottom.

David reached over and took Leigh's hand and thought about how the ring he had picked up the day before from Rollin Caruthers would look on her finger. It had turned out better than David had expected. The diamond was small, but the setting made it look bigger. Rollin had known exactly who to send it to, and he'd gotten them to rush the order.

"For you, Brother David, we'll get it done. Wouldn't want Miss Leigh to be disappointed on Christmas Day, now would we?" he'd said and then grinned at David. But he'd kept David's secret. Had promised not even to tell Mrs. Caruthers, although he said he'd probably be in the doghouse when she found out.

He'd also been understanding when David told him he couldn't pay him the whole amount until sometime after the first of the year. "That's okay, son. I know things are tight for you right now. You should tell that church out there to up your pay. I'd wager they're not paying you half what you're worth. If they're like most churches, they think preachers don't have bills the same as regular folks."

"They've been good to me at Mt. Pleasant." David had taken up for his people. "They're always giving me things."

"I'm sure. Cabbages and green beans and turnip greens, no doubt. They need to bless you with some other green stuff." Rollin had rubbed his fingers together as though feeling for dollar bills. "But don't concern yourself. You just pay me whenever you get the money."

David didn't like being in debt. Paul spoke against it in Romans. *Owe no man any thing, but to love one another.* Then again, weren't they all debtors to the love of the Lord and to one another? David owed a big debt to this church, to his family, to his town. And the Lord would supply David and his family their needs. But did the Lord think David needed to be engaged? Did David need to be engaged? Married again?

He'd been wearing that prayer out as he searched for assurance that he wasn't about to ruin Leigh's life by asking her to share his. He'd allowed himself to be carried away by impulse when he married Adrienne. That had obviously turned out to be wrong. He shifted a little in his pew as the older kids sang a verse of "It Came Upon a Midnight Clear." He brushed against Leigh's shoulder and she turned to smile at him.

And suddenly a verse from Psalms was playing through his head as though he was hearing Aunt Love quoting it to Jocie. *Delight thyself also in the Lord; and he shall give thee the desires of thine heart.* Psalm 37:4.

Was this beautiful woman sitting next to him a gift from the Lord? She was definitely becoming a desire of his heart. If only he could come up with a way to tell her that. He wondered what would happen if he just pulled the ring out of his pocket right then and there and handed it to her. But no, she deserved more thought than that. She deserved better than he could ever give her.

"Here come the angels," she whispered as the singers finished the carol.

Cassidy Hearndon, Sandy Wilson, and Mollie McDermott stepped out from behind the sheet curtains up onto the back of the podium. Mollie started proclaiming the Good News. "Fear not: for behold I bring you good tidings of great joy, which shall be to all people." She stopped to swallow, and for a minute it looked as if she might have forgotten the good tidings.

Cassidy leaned over close to Mollie and loudly whispered, "Jesus. Tell them about baby Jesus getting born."

Mollie picked up the angelic message. "For unto you is born this day in the city of David a Savior, which is Christ the Lord. And this shall be a sign unto you. Ye shall find the babe wrapped in swaddling clothes, lying in a manger."

Then the multitude of the three angels, the singers in

the front pew, and the mothers behind the curtain said, "Glory to God in the highest, and on earth peace, good will toward men." For a minute even the sheep stayed still as the angels held out their hands to sprinkle blessings down on the shepherds before they disappeared behind the curtains again.

Chad Everts, the shepherd who'd wished for cows earlier, stood up and said, "Wow! We've got to go see this. God told us to." He turned to look at the sheep. "Come on, sheep. You can't stay out here by yourselves. You'll have to go too."

Not exactly the way it was written or the way they'd practiced, but Chad had found an audience and was enjoying it. Dorothy McDermott and Lela Martin pulled the sheets together to set up the manger scene behind the curtains while the older kids sang "O Little Town of Bethlehem."

Improvise. Maybe that was what David needed to do as he tried to figure out when and where to pop the question. At the park on the ball field where they'd had their first kiss? Another picnic in Herman Crutcher's cow pasture? At least there wouldn't be mosquitoes in December. Snow maybe, but no mosquitoes. After a night out at the Family Diner? At the *Banner*'s offices after Tuesday night's newspaper folding session? None of those passed the romance test.

Maybe he needed to sneak a look at one of Zella's romance novels to come up with a romantic scene. Zella would tell him a candlelight dinner for two where they served roast duck and had men with violins playing beside your table. The violins might be too much to ask, but David was sure Grundy had restaurants with candles on the tables, but he didn't know where they were. Plus that led him back to the no-money problem.

Maybe he'd just wrap the ring up in a big shoe box and

put it under the Christmas tree and invite Leigh over to open presents. Not very private, but maybe he was afraid to be too private.

Chad the shepherd didn't try to steal any more scenes as he and his fellow shepherds and the two sheep that had made the journey settled down to worship the baby Jesus. The two baby sheep, Eli and Elise Hearndon, had been sent out from behind the curtain to their father. The wise men brought in their gifts and laid them before the baby in the manger.

Behind the curtain, Myra Hearndon started singing "What Child Is This?" Her voice was so true and beautiful that David felt shivers up his spine. What a blessing she and her family had turned out to be to the congregation. Proof that the Lord answered prayers his people didn't even know to pray.

Blessings sometimes brought with them special challenges, though. The church had received threatening letters, and many of the members feared another fire. Every prayer meeting someone stood up and made a special appeal for the Lord to watch over their church building. They also put feet to their prayers, and the deacons and some of the other men took turns driving by the church several times every night.

As Ogden Martin had told David last week, "We're glad and all that Myra and her family are in the church. She has a fine voice and Alex is a good man. Being colored doesn't make a bit of difference in how the Lord blesses a person with talents, but the Lord didn't tell us to bury our heads in the sand. Them being part of our church could make trouble for us because some people just can't accept coloreds and whites worshiping together in the same church."

"Praise the Lord that we can here at Mt. Pleasant," David

had said. David prayed every day that he was speaking the truth.

It seemed true as Myra finished up the song and then came out from behind the curtains to lead the congregation in "Silent Night, Holy Night."

So many prayers. So many blessed answers. The privilege of leading this church. Leigh beside him. Little Stephen Lee in Aunt Love's arms. Jocie snapping pictures and radiating the joy of Christmas. Wes walking. This Christmas play and the baby in the manger. He felt ashamed to have spent so much time worrying about money. Hadn't the Lord always supplied? Hadn't the Lord always been right there beside him in good times and bad?

David stepped forward on the last line of the song to lead the congregation in prayer before they went to the basement where one of the men was going to play Santa Claus and hand out sacks of candy to the children. Maybe David should put the ring in a sack of candy and let Santa Claus deliver it to Leigh.

# 11

Mrs. Brooke." The nurse stepped half out the door that led to the examination rooms and waited for Adrienne to stand up and run to her like an obedient dog.

Instead, Adrienne looked around as if hoping some other woman would look up from leafing through a tattered six-month-old magazine to answer the call. After all, she hadn't been Mrs. Brooke for years. She told everybody she met she was Adrienne Mason as if she'd never been married, but she'd never made the name change official.

Her social security card read Adrienne Mason Brooke and that's the name they'd used when she'd moved up into the manager's position at the restaurant and been eligible for the health insurance coverage. She'd never had health insurance before. Hadn't been to a doctor more than five times since she'd left Hollyhill. Waitresses didn't have benefits. They just had to work their tails off and smile and act as if they weren't waiting on idiots. Then if they were lucky and the idiots felt generous, they might get enough tips to pay the rent.

Now she was managing the restaurant. Now she had

insurance. And the gods that be must have decided to punish her for getting so middle-class. Of course Francine, the only person she'd let know she was going to the doctor at all, told her she was lucky that she'd gotten on the insurance before she found the lump. As if "lucky" and "cancer" could be in the same sentence.

Francine had been careful not to say the C-word out loud. Nobody had yet. That's why Adrienne wanted to stay in the plastic waiting room chair with the California sunshine streaming in the window behind her, making her too hot. Making the sweat pop out on her forehead while her hands, clasped tightly in her lap, felt clammy cold.

But the woman in the nurse's white stayed in the door, looked straight across the room at Adrienne, and spoke again. "Adrienne Brooke." Almost as if saying you're going to have to hide better than that. The woman was smiling as though she were holding out a prize to Adrienne that she just had to walk through the door to claim. Here, entrance to one lucky person.

That word again. Lucky. Adrienne was suddenly too aware of her left breast as though the lump in it had ballooned and was ready to blow a hole through her chest.

Adrienne stood up. The eyes of the two men who had brought their wives to their doctors' appointments followed her as she moved across the room. She still had it even if she was knocking on the door to forty. Everybody guessed her closer to thirty. Sometimes that's how old she said she was.

Actually she looked better now than she had when she was thirty. When she was thirty she was still stuck in Hollyhill, still the preacher's wife. But she had changed that. Changed everything. Reinvented herself the way she should have when she was eighteen. The way she'd thought she was doing when she'd ambushed David Brooke when he came home on leave for his father's funeral. She'd been so sure she could get David to leave Hollyhill after the war. She thought once he'd seen the great wide world, he'd want to be out where people lived. Where they didn't just vegetate the way they did in Hollyhill.

But no, he came home from the war a man of God. A preacher. How could she fight that? Even if she had been in love with him. He'd always been praying for her. Praying she'd change. Whole churches had prayed for her as though she had some kind of terrible disease that needed a miracle cure. She'd found her own cure. Out on the road. Away from Hollyhill.

She watched the pudgy nurse's hips bounce up and down as she followed her down the hall to the examining room. She sat in the chair as told and let the woman take her blood pressure. Perfect as always. She was in perfect health. Perfect shape.

"The doctor will be in to see you in just a few minutes." The woman was no longer smiling now that she only had an audience of one. Nurses didn't have to depend on tips to pay their rent.

The nurse waddled out of the room, shutting the door behind her. Adrienne shivered in the cold air streaming down on her from a ceiling vent. She felt as if she'd been shut up inside a refrigerator. Everything was white or stainless steel. She was the only color in her red scoop neck top that showed cleavage and clung to her body. A catsup bottle left behind and forgotten in the sterile cold.

No, that wasn't the right color red. The red she was wearing was more like a tomato fresh off the vine. She liked to wear red. It made a statement. The blonde in the red dress.

She'd gone California blonde the week after she crossed the border into the state and knew she'd finally arrived at the place she'd left Hollyhill to find.

Hollyhill. She shook her head. Why was Hollyhill popping into her head over and over today? She never thought about Hollyhill. Or what she'd left behind there. She'd been glad to shake free. She'd given up Jocie at birth— or really, before. She'd have never carried her to term if David hadn't practically locked her up in the house so she couldn't do anything about it. Tabitha had tagged along with her when she finally drove away from Hollyhill. She hadn't been invited. She just caught Adrienne leaving in the middle of the night and refused to get out of the car.

Adrienne hadn't wanted Tabitha along. She wanted to shake free of everything about Hollyhill and being a preacher's wife. But once they were in Chicago and Tabitha was calling her DeeDee instead of Mother, it was sort of nice having her there. She never caused Adrienne any trouble. At least not until California and she fell for that drummer in Eddie's band. Got knocked up and refused to fix the problem even though it wasn't that hard to do in California. Not like in Hollyhill.

Back in Hollyhill a woman just had to jump on one foot for an hour and pray that she could shake the baby seed loose. Adrienne didn't remember who had told her that. Probably her mother. Her mother had always said the weirdest things. Still did on the rare occasions she called from her retirement village somewhere in Florida. She'd left Hollyhill even before Adrienne had.

It hadn't worked anyway. Just made your leg and foot sore. Neither had prayer. Babies weren't that easy to lose. But Tabitha hadn't wanted to lose hers. Seemed to be thoroughly enraptured by the kid now that he'd been born even with his brown skin like his father's. That had surely shaken up the good folks in Hollyhill.

Tabitha had sent a picture last week. Adrienne had peeked at it in the envelope, but she hadn't pulled it out. She didn't know what Tabitha wanted from her. She'd told her from day one that she couldn't be a grandmother.

She couldn't have cancer either. Not breast cancer. Women who had breast cancer had to have their breasts cut off. She looked down at the two perfectly matched mounds stretching the material of her red top. Maybe that's why she kept thinking about Hollyhill and all those churches that used to pray for her when she didn't need it. Maybe now she needed it.

The doctor came into the room and sat down on the stainless steel stool with rollers. He said hello before he opened up the folder he was carrying and looked at it. He was young, nice looking. Nothing like she'd expected when she'd made the first appointment. She'd almost enjoyed being examined by him. Not that he wasn't professional. He was. She just sort of wished he wasn't. That they were meeting somewhere besides a sterile refrigerator.

His eyes touched on her breasts before he looked at her face. "I'm afraid I don't have good news. I told you when you opted for the biopsy instead of the surgery that if the lump did turn out to be malignant, that you were just delaying your treatment and the faster we get on these tumors, the better."

"And so the lump was malignant?" She asked it as a question, but it wasn't. She'd known from the first instant she'd felt that foreign pebble-sized knot in her breast that it was not going to be benign.

"Yes, I'm afraid so." He did really look sorry as his eyes

touched on her breasts again. "Not only that, but it's an aggressive strain."

"Aggressive? What does that mean?" Of course she knew what aggressive meant. She dealt with aggressive people all the time. She was an aggressive person, but how could a lump in her breast be aggressive?

"Fast growing. The cancer is the fast-growing type. You need to have surgery right away. Tomorrow."

"Surgery." She felt like an idiot repeating everything he said. But she needed to absorb it. "You mean to remove the lump?"

"Not just the lump. With this kind of malignancy, we can't do anything less than a radical mastectomy."

She refused to let the words land in her brain. "It's just three days until Christmas."

"I know. That's why you will need to check into the hospital tonight."

"No."

The young doctor looked up from scribbling something on her chart. Obviously very few people said no to him. He pushed his stool back until he was leaning against the white wall and stared at her. He wore a white doctor's coat, but a red tie peeked out at the neck. Coordinated. It was good they were all so coordinated. It would have been better if he'd been blond, but he had plain brown hair a bit long over the ears as if he hadn't wanted to completely give up his youthful hippie ways when he had to start following his calling to slice off women's breasts. To save their lives, of course.

"No is not an answer you can afford to give, Mrs. Brooke. This isn't cosmetic surgery we're talking about. It's a matter of life and death. Your life and death."

"Call me Adrienne please. I never cared for the name

90

Mrs. Brooke. It belonged to my ex-mother-in-law." Adrienne flashed him her brightest smile. He'd think she was a dizzy blonde, but she didn't care. While she might not be a real blonde, she was definitely dizzy right now.

"All right, Adrienne," he said, speaking slowly as if weighing every word for the proper impact. "I don't think you realize the seriousness of your condition. You have breast cancer. The malignancy has more than likely already spread to your lymph nodes. Without aggressive treatment, your survival chance is not only not good. It's nonexistent. Without surgery, you'll die."

"Unless there is a miracle cure." She didn't know why she said that. Probably all the Hollyhill thoughts about churches praying. As well as she could remember, none of those prayers back then had been answered in a miracle. Certainly not the ones asking the Lord to make her the perfect preacher's wife.

"Are you expecting a miracle?"

"No."

"Then I'd suggest you follow the recommended treatment."

"And what are my chances if I do agree to the recommended treatment?"

He looked down at her chart again as if unable to look her in the eyes while he answered. "You're relatively young. In good health otherwise. You should have no problem recovering from the surgery."

"But my chances? What percentage of women with this, ah . . . ," she hesitated on the word, ". . . this aggressive strain of cancer live those five magical years after surgery?"

"You have an excellent chance of being in the 30 percent of women who live through this."

"Disfigured and maimed."

"But alive. With a good prosthesis, no one will ever know you've had surgery."

"I will. The man I love will."

"If he doesn't love you for more than your breast, he's not worthy of you." He looked up from her chart and fastened his eyes on her.

She thought about pointing out to him that she hadn't said the man who loved her, but instead she stayed quiet as she met his eyes. He waited a long moment and then asked, "Are you refusing treatment?"

"No. But I need a little time first. To get used to the idea. I'll come back in January. A couple of weeks can't make that much difference, can it?"

"Perhaps the difference between 30 and 15 percent," the doctor said softly. "I don't advise it."

"I understand," Adrienne said.

"I fear you don't, but I can't force you to make the right decision." He glanced at his watch, no doubt thinking of other patients stuck inside other refrigerator rooms, readier to listen to him or who might have already listened to him and sat waiting with their chests scraped clean for him to admire their scars.

Adrienne drove home, aware each time she took a breath and pushed her breasts out against her bra. The apartment was empty when she went in. Her eyes went to the old flat top guitar hanging on the wall over the television. Eddie had taught himself to play on that guitar when he was thirteen. Adrienne looked for it every time she came home and Eddie was gone. As long as the guitar was still there, he'd be back.

She checked the clock. It was already nearly five. He'd be at the club getting ready for his set that night. Maybe she'd stay home. Let the pretty young things make eyes at him while he sang. She was tired and she needed to put up the Christmas tree.

Eddie had asked last night why she hadn't decorated yet. She'd almost told him then about the doctor and the C-word, but she hadn't. He would split. They'd been together three years. Love on her side. Convenience on his. It wouldn't be convenient to have a girlfriend with cancer.

Adrienne dropped her keys down on the table. They hit Tabitha's letter and jarred the picture she'd sent halfway out of the envelope. Adrienne picked the photo up and stared at Tabitha's baby grinning up at her. He had Tabitha's eyes. Not just Tabitha's, but her own eyes.

Adrienne ripped the picture across once and then put the pieces together and ripped it again before she dropped it in the wastebasket. She got a glass out of the cabinet and filled it with ice. The diet soda she poured had that nasty artificial sweetener taste, but she couldn't afford the calories of the regular soda. She caught her reflection in the window over the sink. She had to look good in her coffin.

She poured the drink down the sink. Then she dumped three drawers looking for a roll of transparent tape. She had to have some tape somewhere. She finally found a roll on top of the refrigerator still there from when Tabitha used to tape notes to the fridge to let Adrienne know where she was. Adrienne had never told her to. She just had.

Adrienne was already crying as she picked the pieces of the picture of Tabitha's baby out of the trashcan. She blinked away the tears so she could see where the torn edges of the picture pieces matched up. It took her a long time to get them taped back together just right because of the way her hands were shaking. Then she looked into the baby's eyes and let the tears roll unchecked down her cheeks.

# 12

Leigh stared at the presents spread out on her kitchen table with dismay. The blue Hollyhill Tigers sweatshirt for Jocie. Three rolls of film and some flashbulbs to go with the camera David was buying for Tabitha. The navy blue purse for Aunt Love. The tie and tie clasp for David. All practical, sensible gifts. Even the wooden blocks for Stephen Lee shouted sensible.

Leigh had vowed not to be sensible. She had determined to be extravagant and generous this Christmas. To buy things nobody needed. To only buy things people wanted. She thought she had been, but now looking at the presents in their boxes ready to be wrapped, she realized she hadn't been able to shake free of her practical bent.

It was no wonder she hadn't once been able to find a way to tell David out loud that she loved him. Three little words shouldn't be all that hard to say. *I love you.* All she had to do was open her mouth and let them out. There was no written-down rule that said the man had to say the words first, and even if there was, she could break it. But now looking at her practical presents she knew her problem. She couldn't be daring. It wasn't in her makeup. She couldn't even buy a daring Christmas gift.

A tie, for heaven's sake. What kind of gift was that for the man she loved? What difference did it make that she wasn't sure he loved her back? She could still love him. She could still tell him so in words. She could still show him so with a real Christmas gift. But not with a tie. Even if it was red.

Leigh put the tops on the boxes and set all of them aside except Jocie's gift. She measured out the wrapping paper for the box holding the sweatshirt. She wasn't wrapping any of the other gifts. Jocie was coming Thursday morning to make chocolate fudge and wrap presents. Since Leigh was off work because it was Christmas Eve and Jocie was out of school till the New Year rolled around, Leigh had told Jocie they might as well join forces and have some fun. Besides, Leigh wanted to ask Jocie her opinion of the tie. To see if she thought it was too bright for David to wear. Now Leigh wanted to just throw the tie away.

She wanted to throw all the gifts away and start all over. Except for her parents' gifts that were already wrapped and under her tree in the next room. They would be upset by anything other than sensible and practical. Her mother would be happy with the soft house shoes and the pink, flowered snap-up-the-front housedress. As well she should be since she'd picked them out when they went shopping. Her father really didn't care what he got for Christmas as long as the day got over with quickly so he could go back to playing golf whenever the sun pushed back winter a bit or, if the weather kept him off the course, then sitting around out at the club drinking coffee and talking about playing golf with his buddies.

She finished taping the red foil paper around Jocie's gift.

Of course she couldn't throw the gifts away. Not and be who she was. She couldn't even throw away her stockings when they got a runner in them. She had to save them to wear under her slacks, or if the runner was too bad for that, to stuff pillows or something. She'd never made the first pillow, but when and if she did, she had plenty of old stockings for stuffing.

Leigh curled a long piece of white ribbon to fasten on top of Jocie's present and then made herself a cup of tea. Her throat was feeling scratchy and her head hurt. She hoped she wasn't catching something. Not now. Not with Christmas Eve on Thursday and here it was already Tuesday. Earlier that night after they had finished folding the *Banner* for delivery the next day, David had told her he was planning something special for them on Thursday night. He wouldn't say what. Said it was a surprise.

She wouldn't allow a cold to surprise her. Not that it would be all that much of a surprise. People had been coming in to the clerk's office all week hacking and sneezing while they leaned on the counter and waited for her to handle whatever business they had.

She didn't have time for a cold. Christmas was almost here. She and Zella were exchanging gifts over lunch tomorrow. At least Zella's present wasn't a bit practical. Four romance novels with covers showing heroes in white cotton shirts unbuttoned to reveal their chests as they clutched the beautiful long-haired heroines. Before she'd wrapped them last week, Leigh had leafed through a couple of the books and wondered how it would feel to be so beautiful that men fought for your favor.

Never, even in her wildest dreams, had she ever imagined men fighting over her. Maybe that was her problem. Maybe she should have wilder dreams. Then she wouldn't be too sensible. Too practical. Still single into her thirties. Past the age of wildest dreams.

But who said a girl couldn't keep dreaming? She was still dreaming and hadn't her dreams gotten wilder every month since July until now she had a date with a wonderful man on Christmas Eve? Until now she was thinking—no, planning a way to say *I love you*.

She put her finger under her nose to stifle a sneeze. She would not catch a cold. She would take an extra hour for lunch tomorrow. She had some vacation time built up. She had money in the bank. She could still go shopping.

The next day Leigh took off at eleven and headed uptown. She passed up the hardware store and the ten-cent store. She didn't even look toward the shoe store or Pelham's Men's Store. She headed straight for the Jewelry Center, the only store in Hollyhill that held out any promise of frivolous spending.

When she stepped through the door and set off the bell, Rollin Caruthers looked up at her and smiled clear across his face. "Miss Leigh, what a pleasure," he said as if he already knew she had frivolous spending on her mind. "What can I help you with? Perhaps size a ring for you?"

Leigh frowned a little and looked at the class ring on her right hand. "You mean because I've lost weight?"

Rollin looked sort of flustered as he waved his hands in the air at her. "Oh yes, of course. Losing weight can make rings too loose. Make them slip right off your fingers."

Leigh held up her hand and shook it. The ring slipped up to her knuckle but didn't come off. "I think it's okay, but it's nice of you to notice I've lost weight."

"Yes, indeed. You are looking especially nice these days," Rollin said and that seemed to fluster him even more. "I mean that's what the missus said."

"How sweet of her! Please be sure to tell her thank you for me," Leigh said before she looked down into the jewelry cases. "No, I'm just doing some last-minute shopping."

"Oh, wonderful. Did you have anything in mind? Perhaps something for a certain gentleman I know?"

Leigh blushed as it was her turn to feel flustered. Then she laughed and said, "How did you guess?"

Thirty minutes later she walked out of the Jewelry Center with a charm bracelet for Jocie, a locket for Tabitha, and a watch for David. A watch wasn't exactly frivolous, but it was the closest she could come. After all, he didn't need one. Rollin had told her David had just brought his watch in to be cleaned and it was in perfect working order, but Leigh didn't care. She'd looked straight at Rollin and said, "Well, now he'll have two."

"Yes, yes, indeed. And such a fine watch too. Would you like to have something engraved on the back? The date perhaps? His initials?" Rollin had raised his eyebrows a little at her. "Both your initials?"

And so she'd had the chance to be wild and crazy after all. "How much can you put on there?" she'd asked.

Rollin had turned the watch over and looked at its smooth silver back. "Whatever you want. Do you know his favorite Bible verse? You could put the Scripture reference."

"Initials. DB. Then 'love always' followed by the initials LJ."

She had hardly even blushed as Rollin had said, "That should work fine. I'll stay open a few minutes late so you can pick it up when you get off work today."

Leigh had wanted to kiss him. She thought maybe she should have as she went back out on the street and headed to the Grill for her luncheon date with Zella. If she was going to start being wild and crazy, she might as well go whole hog.

At the Grill, Zella was settled in their usual booth with coffee cups and menus already on the table in front of her. As Leigh smiled and headed toward her, a man stepped into her path.

"Leigh. How are you?" the man said as if they were old friends.

He looked familiar, but then everybody in Hollyhill looked familiar. They all had to come into the courthouse several times a year to conduct some sort of business. No name came to mind, but he'd called her Leigh. It must be somebody she was supposed to know. She smiled and said, "I'm fine. And you?"

"I'm absolutely great. School let out for Christmas vacation yesterday." He pushed black-framed glasses up closer to his face and smiled. "People don't think we should be glad about that, but the truth is, most teachers are happier even than our students when we get some days away from the enfants terribles."

"I guess everybody likes a few days off." Now Leigh remembered him. He was the teacher who'd been with Jocie the day Leigh picked her up to make cookies. Edwin Hammond. The new English teacher who was giving Jocie fits. Leigh smiled back at him. He was tall and slim, probably around Leigh's age. Perhaps even younger. And handsome in an offbeat way.

There had been a lot of talk about him ever since he'd been hired to fill in for Janice Wickers after the doctors made her go to bed to keep from losing her baby. He was always telling everybody he was going to write the next great American novel and an author could never have too much material stored up. Who knew? Perhaps one of these days they could be reading about themselves. Somehow, after meeting Edwin Hammond, few of Hollyhill's citizens expected to like what they might read.

Leigh hadn't actually ever officially met him. Just seen him that day on the steps of the school. Jocie didn't like him. She said the man was strange. And unfair, mean, unfeeling, callous, malicious. She'd gone through a whole thesaurus list of unattractive traits. After Jocie's article about him came out in the *Banner*, the teacher had started tearing her papers apart. She said the man could probably even find fault with Shakespeare or the writers of the Bible, and the only kids he liked at school were the cute girls.

Jocie didn't put herself in that category, although Leigh thought she could. Jocie was sure the teacher had it in for her, whatever *it* was. And Leigh couldn't say she was wrong since Mr. Hammond had already called David twice about Jocie's behavior in his class. Zella had reported that to Leigh with a good measure of satisfaction since Zella had long thought Jocie needed more discipline.

So now, although Leigh couldn't imagine why the man had stepped so purposely into her path, she took the chance to study him. With his black hair combed back from his face and his angular features, he could have stepped off the cover of one of Zella's gothic romances. Half the girls at the high school probably had a crush on him.

Maybe that was Jocie's problem. Maybe she did have a crush on him, and that was what kept getting her into trouble with him. But it hadn't sounded like that. It had sounded more as if Jocie thought the man had horns sprouting under his black hair.

"You do know who I am, don't you, Leigh?" The teacher smiled down at her and put his hand on her arm.

100

Leigh wasn't sure if it was the smile or his touching her that made her uncomfortable, but something did. She shifted her arm away from his hand and forced herself to keep smiling back at him. "Of course. The new English teacher at the high school. Mr. Hammond."

"Please call me Edwin or even Ed. I hear Mr. Hammond this and Mr. Hammond that way too much at school."

"Well then, Edwin," she said. Behind him Zella was peering at them over the top of her glasses. "It's been nice talking to you, but I'm late for my luncheon date. So if you'll excuse me."

"Excuse you?" Edwin laughed. "That's what the little girls at school are always saying when they need to go wee wee. They wave their hands in the air and bounce up and down in their seats, saying 'Can I be excused, Mr. Hammond?' It's hilarious."

Leigh's polite smile disappeared as she started to step past him. "As I said, I'm late."

He reached out to stop her, but she stepped back out of his reach. "Do forgive me, Leigh. I didn't mean to offend your sensibilities. I keep forgetting that you people out here in the boonies don't have much sense of humor."

"I'm sure I'll laugh later. Goodbye, Mr. Hammond." She moved on past him to slip into the booth across from Zella.

"What was that all about?" Zella asked.

"Who knows? He's that new English teacher."

"I know who he is," Zella said. "But what did he want?"

"Beats me. To talk, I guess."

"About Jocelyn?"

"No. He didn't mention Jocie." Leigh unfolded her napkin and put it in her lap.

"Hmph." Zella mashed her mouth together and her eyes

narrowed as she stared past Leigh toward the front of the restaurant.

Leigh took a quick glance over her shoulder to where Edwin Hammond was sitting back down at his table. He caught her looking at him and smiled and waved a little. Leigh pretended she didn't see him as she turned back to Zella.

"He must have been flirting with you," Zella was saying. "He's single, you know."

"Flirting with me? That's ridiculous."

Zella looked at Leigh. "Not so ridiculous. You're looking very nice today. Practically glowing."

"Yeah, like Rudolph. I'm afraid I'm catching a cold." Leigh sneezed to prove it. She sat her gift up on the table to make Zella quit talking about Edwin Hammond flirting with her. Surely that wasn't true. For sure, she didn't want it to be true. Jocie was right. The man was just too strange.

# 13

ocie's father dropped her off at Leigh's apartment Thursday morning before he went on to the *Banner* offices. Jocie would have just as soon gone on to the office to help him and Wes work on some of the pages for next week's *Banner*, but Leigh had wanted her to come so much. And she owed Leigh some time. Leigh was always doing stuff for her. Taking her shopping. Helping her cook something. Listening to her complain about school.

At least Jocie didn't have to worry about Mr. Hammond giving her the evil eye until after Christmas break. Jocie wasn't going to think about him at all. He was just too weird. The last day of school he'd even smacked her on the shoulder with a rolled-up sheaf of papers. His excuse was that she looked as if she was about to fall asleep. She hadn't even been slouching in her seat. She'd started to ask him if aliens from Neptune had trouble seeing, but she bit her tongue and stopped herself in time.

She had to survive English. She couldn't drop out of school and the school said she had to take English. Mr. Hammond taught the only freshman English class. If you could call it teaching. Sometimes Jocie wasn't sure he knew the difference between a noun and a verb. The last day before break, he'd read them a story he'd written. It was awful. Didn't half make sense and was way too wordy. He needed some practice writing for a newspaper so he could figure out the value of a word.

Not that she was going to tell him that. She wasn't going to tell him anything. She was going to wipe him completely out of her mind at least until she went back to school, and then she'd figure out a way to endure the rest of the year. Praying for him the way her father had suggested hadn't worked.

She knew what Jesus had said in the Sermon on the Mount. Her father preached about it, and Aunt Love was always quoting that part about loving your enemies. *Pray for them which despitefully use you, and persecute you.* And there was something about doing good for people who hated you. She didn't want to do anything good for Mr. Hammond. She wanted him to fall in a hole and disappear. Forever. She didn't want to even think about him, much less pray for him. The best she could do was pray he'd be called back to Neptune and soon. Before January.

As she ran up the steps to Leigh's apartment, she did whisper a little prayer. "Help me not to think about the teacher from Neptune once until after Christmas."

Leigh opened the door a few inches and peeked out. "Oh, Jocie. I tried to call you. I don't think you should come in. I've got a cold." She sneezed a couple of times to prove it.

"You sound awful," Jocie said.

"I know. I feel like crying."

"Did you get your presents wrapped?"

"Not yet. I can't quit sneezing long enough. I can't believe

I caught a cold right here at Christmastime. It's going to mess up everything." Leigh mashed her lips together, sniffed a couple of times, and blinked her eyes. Tears slid down her flushed cheeks.

"You might feel better by tomorrow."

"But your dad had something planned for us tonight. There's no way I'll be better by tonight, and even if I do get better by tomorrow, I couldn't come to your house and be around Stephen Lee."

"He's going to catch a cold sooner or later. Everybody does."

"But I don't want to give him his first cold. That wouldn't be much of a Christmas gift."

"I never catch anything. Let me come in and help you finish wrapping your presents." Jocie held up the sack of presents she'd brought with her to wrap. "And I need to wrap mine too."

Leigh looked as if she wanted to open the door and let Jocie come in, but then she had a sneezing fit. After she mopped up her nose, she said, "No, no sense in you getting sick and not being able to enjoy your break from school. But wait a minute. I'll give you some wrapping paper and ribbon and you can wrap your presents at the *Banner* offices before you go home. Okay?"

"I promise I wouldn't catch anything," Jocie said.

"I know, but we need to be sensible," Leigh said and then looked as if she was going to cry again. She mashed her mouth together and fought off the tears. "Wait here."

Leigh left the door open as she headed toward the kitchen. Jocie peeked in at Leigh's Christmas tree in front of her living room window next to the street. Jocie had helped Leigh decorate the tree the first week of December. It wasn't a live tree. They'd had to fit it together branch by branch, but it looked beautiful adorned with shiny gold garlands, red and blue satin balls, and miniature wooden toys.

The lights were on even though it was daylight. Aunt Love never let Jocie turn the Christmas lights on during the daytime except on Christmas morning. Several shining red packages with ribbons cascading down their sides sat under the tree on the white felt tree skirt.

That's what Jocie liked best about Leigh. That she was so extravagant. She bought things just because she liked them, not because she had to have them. She had a whole stack of records. She bought grapes even when they weren't on sale. About as extravagant as the Brooke household ever got was buying a frozen can of orange juice every now and again. Aunt Love might have forgotten a lot of things, but she hadn't forgotten how to pinch a penny.

Leigh came back to the door and handed Jocie an unopened roll of red foil paper and a spool of white ribbon. "You have tape at the *Banner*, don't you?"

"Yeah. Gee thanks, Leigh. This stuff is beautiful." Jocie shoved the paper down in her sack of presents before she smiled at Leigh and said, "You're the best."

"I wish I felt the best." She tried to cough and sneeze at the same time. "You want me to call your father to come get you?"

"I can walk. It's not that far. I hope you feel better. Rub some of that stinky salve on your chest or something. That's what Aunt Love always makes me do if I sneeze even once, and like I said, I never catch anything."

"I hate the smell of that stuff, but I guess it's worth a try," Leigh said with a weak smile.

Before Jocie could start down the steps, the Hollyhill Flower Shop van stopped in front of Leigh's house. "Looks like somebody has sent you flowers."

"They might be for Mrs. Simpson downstairs." Leigh opened her door a little wider to peer out at Blanche Baker lifting a vase filled with at least a dozen red roses out of the van.

"Wow," Jocie said as Mrs. Baker started up the stairs to Leigh's door. She couldn't believe her father had been so extravagant. Roses had to cost a mint this time of the year.

"Oh, Jocie. I wasn't expecting you to be here." Mrs. Baker frowned as she carefully edged past Jocie on the narrow landing as if she thought Jocie might stick her foot out to trip her or something. Then she smiled at Leigh still standing in the doorway. "I've got roses for you, Leigh."

"My heavens, they're gorgeous," Leigh said. "Where's the card?"

"Right there in the middle, but maybe you should take them inside before you read it," Mrs. Baker said as she held the vase out toward Leigh. Then with a pointed look at Jocie, she added, "It might be private."

Leigh didn't pay any attention and neither did Jocie as she peered over Mrs. Baker's shoulder at the words on the card. "With great affection, Your Secret Admirer."

"A secret admirer," Jocie said. "Oh shoot. Then they must not be from Dad. Nothing secret about his admiration."

Leigh was staring at the card as if she was as surprised as Jocie. Mrs. Baker thrust the vase into Leigh's hands. "Merry Christmas, Leigh. I've got other deliveries. Make sure you keep the water in the vase fresh." Then she gave Jocie a hard look as she said, "And you, Jocie Brooke, don't be so nosy. They're not your roses."

"I can still smell them before I leave, can't I?" Jocie said.

"I guess that's up to Leigh," Mrs. Baker said before she went down the stairs.

"What's the matter with her?" Jocie asked.

"I think she thought it might be awkward for me to get the roses with you here."

"Why?" Jocie looked at Leigh.

"Because, as you said, the roses must not be from your father."

"Oh," Jocie said. "So who's your secret admirer?"

"I'm afraid to hazard a guess," Leigh said as she studied the roses. She wasn't smiling. That might have been because her cold was making her miserable as she sneezed again so hard that she almost dropped the vase.

Jocie put down her sack of presents and took the vase from Leigh until she got over her sneezing fit. "You want me to carry them in for you?"

Leigh blew her nose and then shook her head. "No, I can take them now." She reached for the vase and stared down at the flowers. "A girl loses a little weight and things get crazy."

"And you really don't know who they're from?"

"How could I? There was no name."

"You think Mrs. Baker would tell you?"

"Maybe. If I asked," Leigh said.

"Don't you want to know? Aren't you curious? I mean, this is the kind of thing you read about in books. Books like Zella reads. Flowers from a secret admirer. You think Zella sent them to get Dad motivated?"

Leigh laughed. "That's an idea, but I don't think so. Not unless she could somehow charge them to your father."

# 14

David pulled away from the curb back out on the street as soon as Jocie was on the first step up to Leigh's apartment. He wanted to sit there and wait until Leigh opened the door. He wanted to see her smile and wave at him, but he couldn't take the chance that she might run down the steps to ask him about the special date he'd promised her that night.

As usual he'd promised more than he was going to be able to deliver. He kept hoping for this great idea to rise up out of some subconscious romantic reservoir in his head or that maybe the Lord would grab him, give him a shake, and say do this or do that. But all he'd ended up with was a big question: Do what?

He wanted to give Leigh the ring. He wanted to tell her he loved her. He wanted to ask her to marry him. The want-to was swelling inside him until he thought he might burst. But at the same time the words were hanging up in his mouth. So much so that he was beginning to wonder if maybe the Lord had grabbed him and was giving him a shake and telling him not to be such an idiot as to think a young woman like Leigh would want to spend the rest of her life with him.

And not just with him. He came with plenty of baggage. Two daughters. A grandson. An elderly aunt. The ugliest dog in the county. A newspaper barely breaking even. A whole church full of lambs he was trying to shepherd.

Leigh would have to be out of her mind to want to jump into all that. David knew that with his head, but in his heart he was praying she might just be willing to give it a try. He was praying that if this gift, this blessing, was his to receive, then he wouldn't ruin it by his ineptness at romance.

The truth was, he felt like a sweaty-palmed high school kid trying to work up the nerve to ask a pretty girl to the prom. Except there was no prom. He was supposed to come up with the prom. Some special event. Some special evening. Some special way to tell Leigh he loved her. He'd promised.

He'd thought up and rejected a dozen ideas. He'd even considered going down on his knees after the services last Sunday morning and asking her in front of his whole congregation, but then he worried that she might want to say no and wouldn't feel she could in front of all those people wanting her to say yes. The church people already had them the same as married just because Leigh had moved her membership to Mt. Pleasant. And he didn't think she'd say no, but he didn't want to force her to say yes by surrounding her with fifty or sixty pairs of expectant eyes.

He'd thought about hiding the ring in the community section where the engagement notices were printed when they'd folded the *Banner* on Tuesday night, but he could imagine what Zella would think of that. She already thought he didn't have a romantic bone in his body and that Leigh deserved better. Trouble was, Zella was right on both counts.

At last he'd settled on something simple. Dinner out somewhere. He'd bring his own candles from home if he had to. But that was before he started trying to make reservations. Every place was closed. It was Christmas Eve, after all. People wanted to be home with their families.

Now he was nearly desperate. He should have gone on and proposed last Saturday morning at the ball field with the sun coming up and their breath frosty in the air. Leigh might have thought that was romantic. But he hadn't. And now there wasn't another Saturday morning before Christmas. This was Christmas Eve. This was the day he'd promised something special.

He looked over at the Hollyhill Flower Shop as he turned in to the street behind the *Banner* offices. It was open. He could still get some flowers. A couple of roses to carry with him when he showed up at her door that night without a plan. That might be almost romantic, or at least as close as he was going to get. He'd taken Leigh a rose once when he'd gone to the park to walk with her. The first time they'd kissed. The first time he'd admitted to himself, even if he hadn't admitted it to her, that he didn't want to be alone anymore.

As he got out of his car, he felt in his pocket for the envelope of money the people at Mt. Pleasant had taken up for his Christmas gift. He was planning to go down to the Appliance Center at lunch and pay off the refrigerator, but he could keep out a few dollars for a couple of roses.

"What's up, boss?" Wes asked him when he came through the back door into the pressroom. "You're looking sort of down in the mouth this morning. Don't you know it's Christmas Eve?"

111

"I guess that's my problem, Wes."

"You afraid Santy Claus has lost your address?" Wes gave him a quizzical look.

"We haven't put out any cookies and milk for a long time." David pushed a smile out on his face. He fingered the ring box that had become a permanent fixture in his coat pocket so he could have it close to hand in case he got a sudden romantic inspiration. He'd about rubbed the felt off the box.

"Then I guess it's a good thing the Lord don't have to have cookies and milk to send down the blessings."

David looked over at Wes. "You trying to preach at the preacher?"

"Sometimes the preacher needs it."

"A lot of the times the preacher needs it." David's smile disappeared as he sank down on one of the wooden stools by the composing tables.

"Aren't Christians supposed to be extra happy at Christmastime? You know, with the birth of Christ and all." Wes limped over to sit in one of the chairs they kept in the pressroom now for him to rest his leg.

David looked at the man's ankle above his shoe top. It didn't look swollen today, but it was early. "Leg doing okay?"

"It's holding me up."

"I'll have to be honest. That's more than I thought it would ever do again when I pulled that limb off you last summer."

"You prayed me through. You and Jo." Wes gave him a hard look. "You're looking like somebody might need to pray you through something. Did you forget to go shopping for Miss Leigh or something?"

"No, the problem is, I did go shopping."

"How's that a problem?"

David felt the box in his pocket again and looked at the pressroom door. Zella was out at her desk in the front office. He could hear her typewriter. But she generally stayed clear of the pressroom except when she had to help fold papers. David pulled the box out and flipped it open to show Wes.

Wes lit up like a Christmas tree. "I didn't think you had it in you, son."

"I'm not sure I do. I've been carrying this thing around for over a week. I can't seem to get it out of my pocket when Leigh's around."

"You got cold feet?" Wes said. His smile faded.

"No, nothing like that. I want to give it to her, but I'm not sure I should."

"You should," Wes said.

"I'm old for her."

"Not that old."

"I'm a preacher. Preachers' wives have a hard job."

"Miss Leigh's up to it. If ever I saw a girl up to it, it's her. And she wants the job."

"Do you think so?" David stared down at the ring.

"I don't have the first doubt about that. The girl's been after you for months, and once she got you to notice her, she's bloomed like a flower. Oh yeah, she wants the job."

David wished he could be half as sure of that as Wes sounded. "But sometimes we want things that aren't good for us."

Wes frowned over at him. "Are you trying to shoot down this blessing? That ain't like you, David."

"I don't have a very good track record with love and marriage." David closed the ring box and slipped it back in his pocket.

113

"You've never had love and marriage. I don't know what you had with Adrienne, but it wasn't that."

David was quiet as he stared at the press across the room. Wes was right. David had tried to manufacture love between him and Adrienne. He'd tried to pray up love between them, but it had never happened. Passion on his side. Then when that faded, responsibility and duty. But never love. And who knew what on Adrienne's side? Nothing, as far as David had ever been able to tell.

"Do you love the girl?" Wes interrupted his thoughts to ask.

"I do."

"Then give her the ring and tell her so."

David looked back at Wes. "I don't know how."

"What do you mean, you don't know how?" Wes had his frown back.

"I wanted to do something special. She deserves something special. What did you do when you asked your wife to marry you?" Asking that surely showed how desperate David was. Wes didn't talk about his past. Had never mentioned his wife and family to David but the one time when Wes had told him about the wreck. About living when his wife and daughter died.

Now Wes turned his eyes to stare at the press, and for a minute David thought the gloom of the memory was going to swallow him. David reached over and touched his arm. "I'm sorry, Wes. I shouldn't have asked that."

"No, maybe you should have," Wes said with a little shake of his head. "You know, for years I've blocked out all the memories because I just wanted to forget, so losing her and Lydia wouldn't hurt so bad, but that wasn't right. Isn't right. We had some good times, Rosa and me. But I wasn't no Don Juan. We were so young. I was barely twenty and

114

she was eighteen. I didn't have money for a ring, so I just asked her. We were in the swing on the front porch at her house. It was spring and I can still hear the way the birds were singing in the trees and how I couldn't breathe until she whispered yes." Wes leaned forward and fixed David with his eyes. "It's Christmas Eve. You've got a gift for the girl you love. Give it to her. Trust me. It'll be that easy."

"Except for not being able to breathe until she says yes."

Wes sat back in his chair and smiled at David. "Yeah, except for that."

In the front the bell jangled as somebody came into the office and the sound of voices drifted back to them. David frowned as he stood up. "That sounds like Jocie. She's supposed to be at Leigh's."

Jocie looked up at him as he came out into the front office. "Leigh's sick."

"Sick?" David said.

"Don't look so worried. Just a cold, but she's sneezing all over. Tawking like dis. I told her I never caught stuff, but she wouldn't let me come in."

"Oh, dear." Zella snatched a tissue out of the box on her desk. "We had lunch together yesterday. I'll catch it for sure." She held the tissue up to her nose as if to be ready.

"You want me to go get you another box of tissues?" Jocie said as she rolled her eyes at Zella. "You might run out."

"Jocie!" David called her down. The last thing he needed was Zella on a rampage about Jocie's lack of respect for her elders, namely Zella.

"Sorry, Zella. I really will run get you some tissues if you need them." Jocie ducked her head a moment before she looked back at David. "Dad, you ought to call Leigh. She was feeling blue about not getting to come out to the house tomorrow. Just talking about it made her cry. I told

115

her Stephen Lee was bound to catch a cold sooner or later. I mean, Christmastime is special. You can't just stay home by yourself. You don't, do you, Zella? You go to your cousin's house or something, don't you?"

"I have family to celebrate with." Zella's voice was a little huffy. "And so does Leigh. Her parents in Grundy."

"Yeah, but she's supposed to come to our house first in the morning. Wes too same as always. We're going to have a crowd." Jocie looked satisfied that everybody was taken care of for Christmas. "I told her she might feel better by morning. But she said you guys had planned to do something special tonight and that she couldn't get better that fast. That made her cry too."

"I'll call her," David said. At least now it wouldn't matter that no restaurants were open. He'd have to come up with a new plan.

"But the roses should have cheered her up," Jocie said.

"Roses?" Zella's head jerked up. "What roses?"

"Mrs. Baker brought them as I was leaving. They were those deep velvety red kind people put on casket tops when somebody dies. Of course these were in a vase. Probably a dozen of them."

"A dozen roses?" David couldn't even guess how much that might cost.

"Yeah, at least. Maybe more. Did you send them, Dad?" Jocie looked at him. "I told Leigh you didn't. I mean, you would have signed your name, wouldn't you? And the card on these just read Your Secret Admirer. But who else would that be?"

"I don't know," David said. He had a funny sick feeling in the pit of his stomach. He had theorized that Leigh could do better than hook up with him, but he hadn't thought there was actual competition on the scene. "But it wasn't me."

116

Zella gasped, and they all looked at her.

"You didn't send them, did you, Zella?" Jocie asked.

"Of course not. Don't be silly. But I know who did." She paused for effect.

"Well, don't just sit there. Tell us," Jocie said.

"Edwin Hammond. He was flirting with Leigh yesterday at the Grill."

"Mr. Hammond?" Jocie almost squawked. "The teacher from you know where."

"Pittsburgh, I think he said," David said with a stern look at Jocie even though at that moment he was agreeing with her all the way. He'd met Edwin Hammond. He was good-looking in a bookish way. And young. Young like Leigh. David's heart sank into that sick feeling.

"Now wait a minute." Wes stepped up to put his hand on David's shoulder. "No need in everybody going over the edge here. This mystery admirer might or might not be the teacher from Neptune. We don't know since whoever it was didn't have nerve enough to sign his name. But even if it turns out to be him, Zell here says he was flirting with Miss Leigh, not the other way around. We know who Miss Leigh's wanting to flirt with, cold or no cold."

"True." Zella sounded relieved. "Leigh didn't seem particularly impressed with the man's attentions."

"I hope she breathed germs all over him," Jocie growled. Then she looked at David. "And she really didn't look all that glad to get the roses either."

"But he's so young," David said.

"For mercy sakes, David. You don't exactly have a foot in the grave or anything," Zella said.

"And faint heart never won fair maiden," Wes said.

"Dad doesn't have a faint heart." Jocie looked from Wes to David. "Do you, Dad?"

# 15

At first Leigh set the roses on her kitchen table. Then she moved them to the kitchen sink. She needed the table cleared off so she could wrap presents. Just in case she had a miraculous recovery before morning.

Miracles did happen. Somebody had just sent her a dozen roses. The funny thing was, she wanted to pitch them in the garbage can. She stared at the roses sticking up out of the old white sink with its chipped enamel. Hardly the proper place for such beautiful roses, but she didn't put down her teacup to go move them to a more worthy spot.

Edwin Hammond. She'd known he sent them as soon as she saw the card. She just didn't know why. Maybe he did simply admire her the way the card said. What was wrong with her that she couldn't believe that? What was wrong with him that she didn't want him to admire her?

She sneezed and grabbed another tissue out of the box she'd been carrying around with her all morning. She was beginning to feel like Zella with a tissue constantly under her nose. At least Leigh's weren't pink. The way she was sneezing and blowing, she was going to run out of tissues.

Then what? She didn't feel like going to the store. No problem. She could always carry around a roll of toilet paper. Tissue was tissue. And besides, she already felt like her day was going down the toilet. Maybe she'd try that menthol salve the way Jocie had suggested.

What a rotten time to catch a cold. She went to the bathroom to look in the medicine cabinet for the salve and something to take for her head. It was throbbing, and she couldn't breathe through her nose.

James Robertson. He was the one. He'd come into the office last week looking just the way she felt and had proceeded to sneeze all over the twenty-dollar bill he'd handed her to pay for transferring some old truck he'd sold. He could have waited another day, but no, he had to come in and shower them all with cold germs. She had half a mind to call him up and tell him how he'd ruined her Christmas.

Maybe she was wrong about Edwin Hammond. Maybe James was her secret admirer. Leigh almost giggled at the thought. James was sixty-five if he was a day, and since he'd lost his wife to cancer a couple of years ago, he seemed to have forgotten why people bought soap. That gave him a certain distinctive air, but it didn't keep him from making eyes at anybody in a skirt. He always had a thick roll of bills in his pocket, so he had the money to buy the roses. But he wouldn't.

That was the thing. There probably weren't five men in all of Holly County who would spend that kind of money on roses. Not as long as their wives were still breathing anyway. That's why it had to be Edwin Hammond. He wasn't from Hollyhill. He had practically waylaid her in the Grill. He'd tried to poke holes right through her with his eyes. He'd sent the roses.

Leigh got the aspirin out of the medicine chest and

shut the door. She stared at her reflection and almost laughed. Her nose was red. Her hair was flat. Her eyes were watering and bloodshot. She looked horrible. If Edwin Hammond could see her now, he might change his mind about that secret admiration thing.

She didn't care what Edwin Hammond thought about her. She did care what David Brooke thought. Desperately. And she'd been so sure that this night, this first Christmas they were celebrating as a couple, was going to be something wonderful, and now she was going to be home sneezing alone.

She'd already talked to David. He'd called after Jocie got to the *Banner* to see how she was feeling. She told him she couldn't go anywhere that night barring a miracle and nobody would want to waste a miracle on a cold that would go away in a few days. She hadn't called her mother yet. She'd wait till tomorrow morning for that. She hadn't planned to drive to Grundy till late Christmas Day anyway. And then David was going to drive up for dinner with her parents on the day after Christmas.

She'd had plans. All kinds of plans that were going down the drain. She yanked off a piece of toilet tissue and blew her nose with a loud honk. She rubbed that horrible smelling salve all over her chest, took two aspirins, and crawled under the covers on her bed. The Christmas presents would just have to wait.

She lay there feeling extra miserable for a long time before she dozed off. Then she dreamed she was running. She had to keep running. Somebody was chasing her. She wasn't really afraid. More worried that whoever it was might catch up with her. She kept looking over her shoulder, but she couldn't see anybody. She knew somebody was there, though. Knew somebody was coming after her.

She turned her eyes back to the dim path in front of her, and there in the distance was David, smiling and holding his hand out toward her. Relief exploded inside her. It was going to be okay. David was waiting for her. But then roses started raining down around her, landing on her shoulders and in her hair. David stopped smiling and dropped his hand. She tried to run faster to get to him, but she slipped on the rose petals. She couldn't move. She couldn't get to him. He looked so sad as he began turning away. She yelled his name, but he didn't hear her. The roses piled up around her feet and behind her someone was reaching for her. She screamed.

Leigh jerked awake, not sure whether she'd actually screamed out loud or not. She was soaking wet. Her fever must have broken. She lay still while her heart slowed its gallop as she pulled herself out of the molasses of the dream. She surely must be the only woman in the universe who could have a nightmare about getting roses.

But even awake the roses scared her. Not the actual roses, but what David might think when Jocie told him about them. He might remember his worries about being too old for Leigh. He might feel bad that he couldn't buy her roses. He might think she needed roses. He might think he shouldn't encourage her to love him. He might not believe that in fact there was nothing he could do to discourage her from loving him. A thousand secret admirers and a million roses couldn't change that one way or another. He had her heart already.

She got out of bed and headed for the bathroom. She needed a shower. The hot water pounded down on her head as she breathed in the steam. Once she thought she heard the phone ringing, but she didn't turn the shower off to be sure. Whoever it was could call back.

# 16

David walked down the street to the Appliance Center and paid off the refrigerator at noon. He didn't save out money for the flower shop. How could two roses compete with a dozen? Even Jocie had been impressed before Zella had said who must have sent them to Leigh.

Edwin Hammond. The teacher from Neptune. He was making Jocie's life miserable at school. No doubt about that. David hadn't figured out why. He'd talked to the man, listened patiently to his complaints about Jocie, but David hadn't understood the problem. He knew Jocie could talk out of turn at times. He knew Jocie didn't mind pointing out when people were wrong about something. He knew Jocie sometimes thought she didn't need to learn anything else when it came to writing, and in truth, the girl had a gift for words.

Most of her teachers praised and encouraged her gift. Not Edwin Hammond. He marked up Jocie's writing assignments with a red pen until it looked as if the papers were bleeding. Nitpicking things about a comma here or there and her o's not being round enough and not enough spacing after punctuation marks. Then after Jocie had used a ruler to make the spaces after the periods in her next paper, he'd marked them as too wide. If the idea wasn't so far out in left field, David might believe Mr. Hammond picked on Jocie because he was envious of her natural writing ability.

Zella said that same Edwin Hammond was Leigh's secret admirer. Now it was somebody else's turn to be envious. Envious of the man's age. Of the man's flare. Roses from a secret admirer, indeed. It sounded like something straight out of one of Zella's romance novels.

How could he fight youth and romantic flare? Should he even try? If a person truly loved another person, he wanted the best for her. Maybe Edwin Hammond was the best man for Leigh. Maybe David was wrong to stand in the way of a man who might make Leigh happier than he ever could. A man more her age. Not someone tied down with family responsibilities. And a calling as a man of God.

As he walked up the street back to the *Banner* offices, he slipped his hand in his pocket and felt the ring box. The words Wes had said echoed in his ears. *Faint heart never won fair maiden.* Is that what he was? Faint of heart? A verse from Psalms popped into his mind. *Be of good courage, and he shall strengthen your heart, all ye that hope in the Lord.*

That was what he needed. His heart strengthened. His courage boosted. He did hope in the Lord. And trust in him. If the Lord had sent Leigh as a blessing to David and his family, another man sending her roses wasn't going to change that. Didn't he think Leigh was capable of making the choice that was best for her? If her heart had been touched by another man's attentions, by another man's roses, she'd tell him.

And a cold wasn't going to keep him from letting her make that choice. He had the ring in his pocket. The Lord was going to give him the courage to lay his heart out in front of her. David didn't know exactly how, but somehow before the end of the day, he was going to pull the ring out of his pocket and give it to Leigh. Maybe her getting the roses was a good thing.

They shut down the office officially for Christmas at three. David took Jocie home. Aunt Love and Tabitha were baking cookies while Stephen Lee lay on a blanket on the living room floor staring at the Christmas tree. When Jocie knelt down beside him to put her wrapped presents under the tree, the baby smiled and kicked and threw out his arms as if trying to propel himself off the floor into her arms.

It worked. Jocie grabbed up the baby and bounced him up and down in the air in front of her face. "Look here. Santa Claus has already come and left this very best Christmas present." The baby squealed as Jocie kissed his cheeks. Jocie smiled over his head at David. "I can't wait until morning. It's going to be so much fun with everybody here. You've got to talk Leigh into coming even if she is still sneezing."

"Do you want her here that much?" David asked.

"Sure. Don't you?" Jocie kept her eyes on him. "I mean, you are in love with her, aren't you?"

"You do have a way of getting straight to the point."

"That's what newspaper reporters are supposed to do, aren't they?" Jocie didn't wait for him to answer her as she started swinging the baby back and forth. "Me and Stephen Lee could write a story for you. Who? You and Leigh. What? A big date. When? Tonight. Where? Leigh's place. Why?" Jocie grinned at him. "Maybe me and Stephen Lee should let you answer that one."

"That might be best." David put his hand in his pocket and rubbed the ring box.

Jocie danced Stephen Lee across the room to David. "Give your granddaddy a hug so he can go out and slay dragons and win fair maiden." She held the baby up to David.

David took the baby and kissed the curls on top of his head. Jocie was right about the baby. He was a gift, just as she had been. He stroked Stephen Lee's back as he looked at Jocie and said, "You don't mind?"

"Mind what?"

"Leigh." David hesitated, then added, "And me."

"Leigh and me. Hey, that rhymes. Say, Dad, maybe you should write a poem. I'll bet even Zella would say that was romantic," Jocie said. "But why should I mind?"

"I don't know. I mean, we've pretty much held down the fort around here alone for a long time. Along with Aunt Love."

"But now Tabitha is home. And we have Stephen Lee. Not to mention a whole church full of people who are always wanting you to do something. Maybe that's why the Lord picked this year for Leigh to decide she liked you." Stephen Lee reached for Jocie and she took him back while she kept her eyes on David. "Maybe he could tell we needed help. What's that verse about Adam and Eve? You know the one about why Adam needed Eve."

"'And the Lord God said, It is not good that the man should be alone; I will make him an help meet for him.'"

"That's the one. Tabitha told me that the same was true about you. That it wasn't good that you were alone." Jocie peeked toward the kitchen to see if Tabitha was listening and lowered her voice. "I told her you weren't alone. That you had me and Aunt Love and her and like I said, the whole church, but she said there were all different ways of being alone. And that you'd been alone one of those ways way too long."

David looked over Jocie's head toward the kitchen where Tabitha was taking up cookies. When she raised her head to meet his eyes, her cheeks were red, maybe from the heat of the oven and maybe because she'd overheard Jocie telling him what she'd said. She looked relieved when he smiled at her. The poor girl. She knew about him being alone because she was feeling very alone as she faced raising Stephen Lee as a single mother. He'd been praying for her even though he had no idea what to pray. The Lord knew her needs, knew all their needs.

David drove back to town. The wind was picking up and turning colder. Now and then a few flakes of snow hit his windshield as if to remind him it was Christmas Eve, but then the snow was gone on the wind as quickly as it had come. The weathermen weren't forecasting a white Christmas.

He didn't call Leigh. She'd already told him she was too sick to go anywhere. He stopped at the market on Model Street, making it in the door minutes before Harold locked up to go home. David bought three cans of chicken soup, the fanciest crackers Harold had, some cheese, two big chocolate bars, a box of tissues, some cough drops, and a bunch of grapes.

"That's an odd assortment on Christmas Eve," Harold said as he rang up the groceries.

"Not all Christmas Eves are the same." David began sacking up the groceries while Harold got his change out of the cash register.

"True enough," Harold said. "True enough. I've seen my share. A couple of them I was overseas during the war. I guess you were too."

"Not overseas. In the sea."

"That's right, you were one of those submarine guys.

I never envied that tour of duty. I'd rather see the bomb coming at me." Harold handed him his change. Then he went around the counter to pick up one of two poinsettias sitting in the window. "Here, Merry Christmas, Reverend. Take this home with you. I'll never sell it after Christmas anyway."

David's heart started doing a strange fluttering dance as he carried the groceries and the poinsettia across the yard to the stairs leading to Leigh's door. This was it. He was going to pull the ring out of his pocket and give it to Leigh before he left. One way or another.

He still didn't have a plan, but he was going to do it. He was going to ask Leigh to share the craziness of his life, to jump into being a preacher's wife and a stepmother. He wasn't going to think about how he was too old or how Leigh was too young. He wasn't going to think about Edwin Hammond. He was just going to think about how he felt when he looked into Leigh's eyes. His heart did another strange dance in his chest.

He hoped he was just having an attack of nerves and not a heart attack. His father had died of a heart attack, but he'd been seventy-three. Thirty years older than David was now. He'd already been in his late fifties when David was born. A late blessing, David's mother always said. David could still have his own late blessings. The thought nearly froze him in place as he reached the bottom of the steps. What in the world was he doing?

He took a deep breath to steady himself. Bits and jumbles of verses played through his mind. *Be of good courage. Desires of your heart. Knock and it shall be opened unto you. There shall be showers of blessings.* Hadn't he always been showered with blessings? Hadn't the Lord helped him recognize those blessings one by one? He would not turn away from those blessings just because he was getting weak in the knees. He started up the steps.

Mrs. Simpson peeked out the window to watch him as usual. He'd stopped waving when he realized the woman thought she was hidden behind her curtains. Leigh said Mrs. Simpson kept a log of his visits including arrival and departure times to share with Leigh's mother. One thing for sure, in Hollyhill somebody was always watching.

David shifted the groceries and poinsettia to one arm and knocked on Leigh's door. He couldn't hear anything from inside. Maybe he should have called. Maybe her parents had come after her so she wouldn't be sick and home alone on Christmas. Maybe Edwin Hammond had ridden his white stead up the steps to carry her away with him.

David shook that thought away and knocked again, a bit harder this time. She had to be home.

# 17

Leigh's teakettle was heating up and her refrigerator was making its usual assortment of rattles and hums as she folded the wrapping paper around the box holding Stephen Lee's blocks. She had to stop and blow her nose twice, but she wasn't sneezing as much. Coughing a little more, but the aspirin had dulled her headache. She was better, but not enough better.

If she were enough better, she wouldn't be alone eating crackers and drinking hot tea on Christmas Eve. She'd be with David doing whatever special thing he'd planned for them. She blinked back tears as she yanked off another length of toilet paper. She thought she heard something as she blew her nose. She stopped to listen but all she could hear was the popping in her ears and the teakettle starting to whistle. It sounded a little as if it had a stuffy nose too.

She picked the kettle up off the stove and poured it over the tea bag in her cup. This time there was definitely knocking. On her door. She glanced quickly at the roses still sitting in her sink and whispered, "Please, Lord. Not Edwin Hammond."

Without making a sound, she very carefully set the teakettle down on one of the cold burners. She could pretend she wasn't at home. Nobody stayed home alone on Christmas Eve. Maybe he'd go away if she could keep from coughing and making any noise. But then he knocked again. Louder. Mrs. Simpson would be coming outside to see what all the racket was about, and she knew Leigh was at home. She kept watch from her downstairs window. Leigh would have to go to the door.

At least she wasn't wearing her ratty old robe the way she had been that morning when Jocie came. She'd dressed after her shower. Nothing fancy. Her most comfortable putter pants and a red sweater to match her red nose in honor of Christmas Eve. Why was it red had come to symbolize Christmas? Santa's suit maybe or poinsettias or lights. Not roses, certainly. Even if there were a dozen of the red things sitting in her sink on Christmas Eve leering at her. Making her feel like a coward.

Another knock. She'd go to the door. Tell him thanks but no thanks. She didn't need roses from secret admirers. She happened to already be in love and would he kindly get lost? Forever. Before he messed things up. Her cold was doing a fine enough job of that already, and she didn't really need Mrs. Simpson spreading the news of his visit all over Hollyhill. She couldn't quite block out the image from her dream of David backing away. Letting her go.

Of course it wasn't smart to just open the door to anybody. It might not be her secret admirer. It might be an encyclopedia salesman or some psycho pretending to be an encyclopedia salesman. No real salesman would be trying to sell anything on Christmas Eve.

Leigh put her hand on her forehead. She must still be

feverish to be having such crazy thoughts. Psycho sales-man? In Hollyhill?

She felt like Mrs. Simpson as she inched back the curtain to peek out at whoever was standing outside her door. She had been so prepared to see Edwin Hammond there that for a minute she couldn't believe her eyes. David. Of course it was David. Just because she'd told him not to come didn't mean he wouldn't.

She thought about running back to the kitchen to shove the roses into the broom closet. But no, he knew she had them. Jocie would have told him.

Besides, she'd already made him stand out on the land-ing so long he had to be half frozen while she imagined secret admirers and psycho salesmen at the door. She pulled open the door.

"David. I wasn't expecting you." She had to look hor-rible with her watery eyes, her hair barely combed after her shower, and her Rudolf nose, but at the same time just seeing him standing there made a smile run through her clear down to her toes.

"We had a date," David said as he stepped inside.

"We did, but I told you I have a terrible cold. You might catch it."

"I'll take my chances." He held up his sack. "I brought supper for the sick and a beautiful flower for a beautiful lady."

Leigh took the plant with a laugh that turned into a cough. "No beautiful ladies around here tonight," she said when she could quit coughing. She set the poinsettia down on the floor and fished a piece of toilet paper out of her pocket to blow her nose. "I must look horrible."

David reached out and put his hand on her cheek. "No, you could never look horrible. You're always beautiful."

She almost melted into his hand. "Even with a red nose?"

"Even with a red nose," he said.

For a minute she thought he was going to kiss her, red nose and all, but then he pulled his hand away and shifted the grocery bag. "Point the way to the can opener and get ready for a feast fit for a queen. At least one who has a cold."

Leigh positioned herself in front of the sink, but David still saw the roses. "Funny place to set such a beautiful bouquet," he said.

"Oh." Leigh looked around at the roses as if surprised to see them there. "I was wrapping presents on the table and they didn't seem to go with the Christmas tree in the other room. I guess Jocie told you I got them."

"Yes. A secret admirer. I'm not surprised."

"You aren't? I am."

"You shouldn't be. And the roses are very nice," David said, but he didn't look as if he really meant it.

"They make the place smell like a funeral home." Leigh wrinkled her nose. "I like roses fresh out of a garden better." She was remembering a particular rose David had brought her last summer. She had it pressed in her dictionary on the page of "l" words right below the word *love*.

"Too cold out there for that right now. Harold at the grocery said they were predicting it might get down to fifteen tonight. And it's spitting snow now and again." David pulled some cans out of the grocery sack. "Do you have a pan I can heat this up in?"

"Chicken soup. Perfect." Leigh said as she got the can opener out of the drawer and pulled a pan out of one of the cabinets. "And I love snow at Christmas."

They'd stopped talking about the roses, but there seemed

to be things still unsaid causing uneasiness between them. Maybe she should say the wretched roses were making her sneeze and shove them in the closet.

"What don't you love at Christmas?" David asked as he dumped the soup into the pan.

"That's easy. Colds and red noses except on Rudolf." She tore off some toilet paper to wipe her drippy nose. "How about you? What don't you love at Christmas?"

He set the pan on the stove and turned on the burner before he looked at her. "Roses in your sink that I didn't send. Being of faint heart."

"Faint heart?"

"Just something Wes said. I'll tell you all about it later, but right now I think our soup is almost warm enough. Where do you want to eat your feast, fair maiden?"

"By the Christmas tree," Leigh said. Anything to get away from those infernal roses. "We can have a picnic by the Christmas tree."

"Our last picnic didn't turn out too well."

"Oh, it wasn't that bad," Leigh said.

"Not bad?" David smiled. "You mean except for the mosquitoes and the pungent odor drifting over from Herman's cow pasture and that it had to be about a hundred degrees in the shade?"

"You forgot the hard ground," Leigh said with a laugh. "But there aren't any mosquitoes here and we can put the couch cushions on the floor and pretend the coffee table is a tree stump to hold our food."

"A tree stump?"

"Well, you might take blankets and you might take cushions, but you'd never take a coffee table on a picnic."

So David carried their soup into the living room on a tray. The lights on the Christmas tree gave the room a cheery

133

glow. Leigh started to turn on a lamp, but David stopped her. He produced a candle from somewhere. He lit it and dripped enough wax onto a saucer to hold it up before he set it in the middle of the tray. He brought in the poinsettia and placed it beside the tray.

After they ate their soup, David carried their bowls to the kitchen and brought back grapes and two huge chocolate bars.

"Wow," Leigh said. "My favorite diet breaker."

"I promised you something special tonight, didn't I? We'll walk twice as far next Saturday to make up for it." David smiled at her, but didn't sit back down on the couch cushion. He looked almost nervous as he said, "I'll put on some music."

"I probably don't have anything you like," Leigh said.

"I'm sure I'll find something." He carried the candle over to look through her records.

"You want me to help?" she asked when he started fumbling with the controls.

"I think I've about gotten it figured out."

The record clicked into place and Elvis started singing, "Love me tender. Love me true."

Leigh's heart was beating double fast even before David scooted his cushion closer to hers and sat back down. She was glad the light was dim so he couldn't see how her cheeks were surely now as red as her nose.

He reached into his sack and pulled out a box of tissues. "For you, fair maiden." His hand seemed to tremble as he handed it to her.

"You surely knew just what I needed." Leigh laughed a little. The box was already open with a tissue sticking out. She pulled on the tissue and a little black ring box fell out in her lap. She was almost afraid to reach for it for fear it might disappear, that this all might be a dream and she was going to wake up and be alone. She held her breath while somewhere Elvis was singing "Love me tender."

Beside her, David slid off the cushion to kneel beside her. She could feel his eyes on her as she picked up the ring box. She made herself breathe in and out as time seemed to stand still. She was acutely aware of the lights on her Christmas tree, of the flickering candle flame, of David's breathing. She tipped open the top of the ring box and a diamond glittered up at her. Again she lost her breath.

David reached over and put his fingers under her chin to raise her face up to look into his eyes. "I love you, Leigh Jacobson. Will you marry me?"

She couldn't help it. She began sobbing. She was that happy.

## 18

For a second David's heart plummeted like a stone pitched in a lake when Leigh started crying. The roses in her sink had meant something. He was too late. Too old. Too inept at romance. Maybe he should just take the ring box back and slink away out of her life.

But then she was laughing along with her tears. "Yes. Oh very definitely yes!" she almost shouted as she jumped forward to hug him.

He held out his arms to catch her, but it wasn't like in the movies where the hero and heroine embrace smoothly and easily while the music plays. Instead David lost his balance and they both tumbled over, knocking against the coffee table. The poinsettia bounced off onto the floor, and grapes and candy bars went flying. Elvis stopped singing as the needle got stuck on the end of the record and didn't lift off the way it was supposed to. It just sat there and kept slipping in the groove with no music.

All of the sudden there was a knocking noise somewhere. It didn't sound like the door, but rather as if it was below them. Right below them.

Leigh giggled. "I think Mrs. Simpson is trying to tell us we're making too much noise."

She started to disentangle herself from his embrace to sit up, but he tightened his arms around her. "She'll get over it," David said. Leigh was laying half on top of him wedged between the sofa and the coffee table. He shifted a little so they could get more comfortable and he could see her face in the glow of the Christmas lights. Her cheeks glistened with tears. He pulled out his handkerchief and gently dabbed her cheeks. "I didn't want to make you cry."

She took the handkerchief from him and mopped up her face. "But I'm so happy I can't help it. That sounds silly, doesn't it?" She lifted herself up on one elbow to blow her nose.

David sniffed the air. "Do you smell smoke?"

"I can't smell anything with this cold," Leigh said, but she raised her head up a little higher. "Oh my gosh! The candle! The napkins are on fire."

David sat up. The blazing napkins were on a metal tray, but the flames were rising perilously close to the Christmas tree. He slapped a magazine down on the flames to smother them. Black papery ashes floated up in the air when David carefully lifted the slightly scorched magazine off the tray, but the fire was out. The Christmas tree was safe.

Leigh had her hands over her mouth. Her blue eyes were open wide as she watched him.

"So much for candlelit picnics by the Christmas tree," David said. "Maybe we should just forget about picnics altogether."

"Oh no," Leigh said. "I love picnics."

David reached over to hold her hand. "What do you love about picnics?"

"Eating grapes." She picked up a grape and popped it

in her mouth and then picked up another one to put in his mouth.

"Even off the floor?"

"The floor, the ground, whatever."

"Eating grapes. Is that all?"

"Oh no." She smiled at him. "I love chocolate bars. And campfires."

"The fire might be better at outdoor picnics," David said.

"Wait. I'm not through yet." She put her finger over his lips. "Rings in boxes. You."

He pulled her close then and kissed her. This woman who had agreed to be his wife. This woman he loved. He didn't know what he'd done to deserve her love, but he thanked the Lord he had it. Then again, when was love ever given because it was deserved? Respect and honor were earned. Awards were deserved. But love was a gift from one heart to another.

Her lips felt incredibly soft under his and for a minute he thought his heart might explode from the feeling. Even after she had to pull back to catch her breath because of her stuffy nose, he held her close and kissed her hair that smelled like apples.

"Maybe we should start over from the beginning and this time try to keep from setting the place on fire," he said. When she suddenly stiffened against him, he was afraid she was having second thoughts. "What's wrong?"

"The ring. Where's the ring?" She pulled away from him and began frantically feeling around on the floor. "I can't have lost it before I even got to put it on."

"It's bound to be here somewhere among the grapes." David picked up a bunch of grapes and put them on the coffee table. "And here are the chocolate bars."

Leigh had her face flat against the floor peering under the couch as she ran her hand under it. "I can't see anything under here. What if it fell out of the box and I never find it?"

"I'll get you another one," David said, then laughed. "When I save up enough money in a few years. You did realize you weren't saying yes to a rich man?"

She raised her head up to look straight at him. "You're the richest man I know. In the riches that count."

"Maybe now that you've been added to my riches," David said. He lifted up one of the couch cushions. "Violà! Here it is." He picked up the little velvet box and checked to be sure the ring was still inside. "Let's try this over again without the fireworks."

"Why? Fireworks are fun. Exciting. We want exciting, don't we?"

"Okay. Without the fire."

"All right. We can skip the fire," Leigh said as she sat up.

David put the cushions on the couch. "You sit there."

"Wait," Leigh said. "Let me go fix the record player. That noise is getting annoying." She jumped up and started Elvis singing "Love Me Tender" again. Then she came over and sat on the couch as directed.

David knelt in front of her and handed her the ring box. "Leigh Jacobson, will you marry me?"

This time she stayed sitting demurely as she answered, "Yes, David Brooke, I will marry you."

He kept his eyes intently on hers. "Are you sure in your heart that you want to marry me for better or worse, in sickness and in health, till death do us part?" He'd said the words many times as he'd married other couples. Better or worse. Sickness and health. He supposed he'd said them when he and Adrienne married although no echo of those words came to mind when he tried to remember. They had stood up in front of a judge in Tennessee. Perhaps judges had a different ceremony. Legally binding without the spiritual promises.

Leigh's eyes didn't waver on his. "For better or worse. In sickness and in health. Till death do us part. And even then. Forever and ever through eternity I am yours."

He took the ring out of the box and slipped it on her finger. It fit. Rollin had made a good guess on the size.

She held her hand up and looked at it. "It's beautiful." Then she burst into tears again.

He found the tissue box and handed it to her as he sat down on the couch and put his arm around her. "We're not going to do this again if you're going to keep crying on me."

"Happy tears," she choked out.

He pulled her close to him and let her cry. He'd never seen Adrienne cry. In all the years they'd been married. She didn't care enough about anything to cry. He mentally shook his head and pushed Adrienne out of his thoughts. Adrienne was out of his life forever. He was giving himself completely, heart and soul, to this wonderful loving girl beside him who cried when she was happy. She cried when she was sad. She cared. She loved.

After a few minutes, Leigh raised her head off his shoulder and mopped up her tears. "I'm sorry I'm such a weeper," she said and smiled at him. "My nose is probably glowing like a Christmas tree light now."

"You're glowing, all right. A perfect glow."

"Hush, you'll make me start crying again." She took a deep breath. "I don't know why people are always saying there won't be any tears in heaven. What about tears of joy?"

"I don't know about tears, but the Bible promises joy. Greater joy than anything we can imagine."

"Then I'll have to cry."

"The Lord will understand. He always does."

"He does, doesn't he? When I was just out of high school, I wondered why I couldn't fall in love. Why no one wanted to marry me when all my girlfriends were getting married. Now I know." Leigh looked up at him. "The Lord was waiting for the time to be right. He knew I was going to find you."

"I'm glad you did," David said. "And I'm glad he knocked open my eyes so I didn't miss out."

"You might have to thank Zella on that one."

"The Lord sometimes works in mysterious ways," David said. Elvis had stopped singing some time ago, but Leigh had fixed the record player right and the needle had lifted off the record. Now a peaceful quiet settled around them.

"She's going to be surprised," Leigh said, holding out her hand to admire the ring again. "I'm surprised. Really surprised. I figured I'd have to keep chasing you awhile longer."

"I quit running weeks ago."

"I'm glad."

"Do you want to pick a date?" David asked. "Or do you want to talk to your parents first? I guess I should have waited until after they met me to see if they approved before I gave you the ring."

"No. I'm not a child." Leigh's voice sounded a little tight all of the sudden. "I approve. That's what's important. And they'll be happy for me once they get to know you." She sounded as if she were trying to convince herself more than him.

"So you want to get married next week?"

"You're kidding?" She leaned forward to stare straight into his face.

"Only a little. I'm not getting any younger, you know."

"June," she said as she sat back. "I've always wanted to be a June bride. And that will give the church time to have showers for us. You know they'll want to be in on it all."

David groaned a little. "It'll be like having fifty extra aunts and uncles at the wedding."

"No, more like fifty brothers and sisters, but it's going to be so much fun."

"Did you ever hear a voice telling you to be a preacher's wife?"

"Yes, as a matter of fact I have."

David was surprised by her words. David believed being a preacher's wife was a calling, but he hadn't really expected her to say the Lord had actually spoken to her to say she should marry David. "You have?"

"Of course. Just now when you proposed. The very voice I most wanted to hear." She laughed and gave him a little hug. "Jocie is never going to believe you played Elvis as background music."

## 19

ocie was surprised the next morning. Not just by the Elvis music, but by the ring. By everything. But she was glad Leigh showed up on Christmas morning. Leigh's nose was still red and she had tissues tucked up the sleeves of her sweater to keep them handy, but she wasn't sneezing so much. She wouldn't pick up Stephen Lee even when he reached for her. Jocie figured Leigh might as well go ahead and love on him because Jocie's dad wasn't staying away from the baby. And it was pretty evident by the way her father kept looking at Leigh with that goofy grin on his face that if there were any germs to exchange, they'd been exchanged already.

After the flurry of present opening, they sat around and ate the sweet rolls Aunt Love always made for Christmas morning. Jocie had practically camped in the kitchen while they were baking to make sure Aunt Love didn't forget and let them burn. It wouldn't be Christmas morning without Aunt Love's sweet rolls. She only made them Christmas and Easter. They were for special times.

And it had been a special morning, extra special even

for Christmas. When her father had read the Christmas story out of the Bible, Jocie had almost been able to see the wondrously clear sky and hear the angels singing the good tidings. They sounded something like Myra Hearndon in her head. Jocie had smelled the hay and straw in the stable and heard the donkey braying. She'd shut her eyes and imagined how Mary must have traced the eyes, nose, and mouth of her baby with her finger and been amazed afresh at the miracle of his birth. And over the stable the new star had shone so brightly in the sky, it had surely cast shadows off the camels plodding across the desert to bring the wise men and their gifts of gold, frankincense, and myrrh.

While everybody settled down to quiet talk, Jocie got out her new ink pen and notebook. She could write and listen at the same time. And she wanted to get on paper some of what was happening, some of what she was feeling. It was a funny thing about feelings. Things happened that a person thought she'd never forget. Then something else would happen, something not half as important, but it would just jump in a person's head and push the other right out. Not all of it, but sometimes the best parts. Jocie didn't want to forget the best parts.

Up at the top of the first page, she wrote *Christmas Morning 1964*. Then she placed her hand flat on the blank page for a moment as if she could just transfer her thoughts to the paper without using ink. She looked around at everybody still sitting around the Christmas tree. On the couch, her dad had his arm around Leigh. Leigh kept sneaking looks at the diamond shining on her left hand. Aunt Love was feeding Stephen Lee his bottle, and Tabitha was yawning behind her hand. She didn't usually get up so early. Wes caught Jocie looking at him and winked.

Jocie didn't know where to start. So many good things

to write about. So many Christmas blessings. She put the point of her pen on the paper and started forming letters. Her hand could hardly keep up with the words spilling out of her head.

This is the best Christmas ever. I know. I've been saying that every year. At least the last few years and I did think they were best. Well, not the Christmas after Mama Mae died. That one was the worst. The one when I was eight. Lots worse than the one after DeeDee left with Tabitha. Although that one wasn't so good either.

I missed Mama Mae. Mama Mae was Christmas. I guess when Mama Mae died, so did Santa Claus. At least for me. But another Christmas came around and another and now I'm old enough to know Christmas is more than what's under the tree. More even than who's sitting around the tree with you. Although, boy, am I glad this year for who's sitting around the tree with me. Especially Wes. After that tree fell on him back in July this could have been another worst Christmas ever like the one after Mama Mae died. A person just can't keep from missing people they've lost at Christmas.

I said a prayer for Miss Sally today when I woke up since she lost Mr. Harvey last September. But she told us at Sunday school last week not to worry about her or be too sad about Mr. Harvey. That he would surely have the best Christmas a Christian could ever have up in heaven this year. I wonder do the angels sing up in heaven every year the way they did on that first Christmas when Jesus was born? Of course, Miss Sally won't really have time to be too sad since she'll be having Christmas with the Hearndons. The twins and Cassidy will keep her more than busy. Eli and Elise are sweet as they can be, but they'd try to climb the Christmas tree if you didn't watch them.

But back to my best Christmas ever. Last year there was just me and Dad and Aunt Love and Wes. That was good, but we've almost doubled our number this year with Tabitha here and baby Stephen Lee and Leigh.

I'm so happy I'm about to burst. Of course I'm not as happy as Leigh.

Jocie stopped writing for a minute and looked up at Leigh. She was laughing at something Wes was telling her. If a girl had to have a stepmother it was good to have one who laughed. The wicked stepmothers in the fairy tales never laughed except for that evil witches' laugh. But then again, no way could "wicked" and "Leigh" go together.

Dad popped the question. To Elvis music. To "Love Me Tender." Can you believe that? Me either. I guess, as Tabitha keeps telling me, there's more to a dad than meets the eye.

They've already set a date. The first Saturday in June. Leigh wants to be a June bride. She followed me into the kitchen awhile ago when I went to get Wes some coffee to make sure I wasn't upset. I don't know why everybody thinks I'm going to be upset about Dad being in love. I'm happy Dad's in love. I know how much love Dad's got in his heart and there's plenty to go around. I mean someday when I'm all grown up I might meet somebody and fall in love.

I can't imagine that happening right now. Boys are mostly just yucky. Paulette says I'm weird, that she loves boys in general and Ronnie Martin in particular. She says they're going to get married when she graduates in four years. But who knows with Paulette? Of course Ronnie has lasted longer than most of her boyfriends. Three months now. And Ronnie's not quite as obnoxious as he used to be. We even speak to each other sometimes when Paulette's not around.

But anyway if I ever do meet a boy who makes me go gaga the way Paulette is over Ronnie, I won't stop loving my father. I could never stop loving Dad. Ever.

But back to Leigh and the wedding. She wants me to help her with it. With making plans and stuff. Help her decide on the best dress. The colors the bridesmaids should wear since I'll be one. That kind of thing. I guess nobody's going to worry too much about Dad having been married before. I mean people say you shouldn't have fancy church weddings when you've been married before, but Leigh's never been married before. And it's her wedding too. Besides we've

146

been breaking all the usual rules lately anyway. What with Tabitha not married and her keeping Stephen Lee without even thinking about letting some couple adopt him.

That makes my heart hurt just thinking about it. Not that it isn't great when people do adopt babies. It is. But we love Stephen Lee too much now. Even if the whole town turns against us, it won't matter. Stephen Lee is ours. Besides, a few extra requests for gift subscriptions for the *Banner* came in. Maybe people are going to quit blackballing us and start renewing their subscriptions again. After all, if they want to know what's going on in Hollyhill, we're the only game in town. Dad's been printing extra pictures of the kids at the elementary school. And then he put in a whole section of kids talking to Santa Claus at the parade a few weeks ago. We sold all our extra issues that week. Zella says things will come around, and whatever else you say about Zella, she usually knows how many papers we're going to sell.

Leigh called her and told her about being engaged this morning before she came to our house. Got her up, but Leigh didn't want Zella to get mad because Wes found out before she did. I'll bet Zella's about worn out her fingers calling people to tell them how well her matchmaking worked. We won't even have to put an announcement in the paper. Maybe somebody has already told a certain Mr. Somebody who I'm not saying his name until 1965. I hope so. Him and his funeral home red roses. I don't care if they were pretty. Leigh says she took them and dropped them off at the nursing home this morning. I hope she left the card on them so all the old ladies there will think they have a secret admirer. Maybe I can figure out a way to tell them who so he'll have to run every time he sees a wheelchair coming.

"Hey, what are you writing about, Jo?" Wes limped over to sit beside her. "One minute you're frowning. The next you're grinning ear to ear. If it's that entertaining, maybe we should put it in the *Banner* to up circulation."

Jocie looked up at Wes and laughed. "It might be worth a shot. One week I can do a column called Main Street Gossip and the next you can do your Hollyhill Book of the Strange."

"The first person I'd have to write about would be me," Wes said. "I'm about as strange as they come."

"And I'd have to write about Dad and Leigh, and you shouldn't gossip about your family."

"And everybody in Hollyhill is family except me," Wes said.

"That's not true. You're family now. My granddaddy, remember."

"No way in Jupiter I could forget that. And looks like your family—"

Jocie interrupted him by clearing her throat and leaning over to stare right into his face. "Excuse me. Whose family?"

"Oh yeah, I mean our family." Wes grinned. "Our family is growing."

"Almost double from last Christmas," Jocie said.

"And who knows? In another couple of years it might be double again."

"How's that? You getting married?"

"No way. That'd take a miracle. Course this time last year I might have said it would take a miracle to get your pappy in the romantic mood."

"So see, you never know," Jocie said. "Zella may start using her matchmaking talents on you. She's been acting pretty funny lately, so she's bound to have something up her sleeve."

"Zell always acts funny," Wes said. "It's her nature. But if she's wanting to matchmake again, maybe she can order in a feller for Tabby. Or for you. You're getting nigh on old enough to set some boy on his ear."

"Yeah, right."

"It'll happen one of these days. But I ain't rushing you. I sort of like you unattached so you still have time for your Jupiter grandpappy. You start making goggly eyes at boys, then I'll have to chase after you on my cycle to get you to say hello. And to keep the boys straight."

Jocie thought about Wes on his motorcycle chasing after her and some yet-to-be-named boy out on a date and laughed. "A lot is going to have to change before that happens."

Wes was still smiling but something about his smile looked almost sad. "Well, I guess that's something we can be sure of. Everything changes."

"What's going on over there?" Jocie's dad looked at them.

"We were just talking about how things change," Jocie said. "And Wes said everything changes. It does, doesn't it?"

"Maybe not everything," her father said. "And certainly not the Lord. We can count on that. The Bible says so. Right, Aunt Love?"

Aunt Love looked up from patting Stephen Lee's back to get him to burp and came out with the Bible verse. "Hebrews 13:8. Jesus Christ the same yesterday, and today, and for ever."

Later Jocie finished writing in her notebook.

I'm glad some things change. I'm glad we have more people around our Christmas tree. I'm glad Dad and Leigh look so happy. I'm glad Wes is still telling me Jupiter stories. I'm glad Tabitha and Stephen Lee are here. I'm glad Aunt Love's smiling more. I'm glad Zeb curls up on my feet to keep me warm when I sleep out on the back porch.

But I'm glad some things don't change. Like the Lord. Like people loving other people a little extra at Christmastime. Like Dad and Wes loving me a little extra all the time. Like the Lord blessing people even when they don't know what blessings they need.

Happy birthday, Jesus!

## 20

Leigh couldn't remember ever being so happy. It could be she had never been this happy. Even coughing her head off until she had to sit up to try to sleep, she was happy. Nothing could make her unhappy tonight. Barring tragedy, and she certainly wasn't going to think about tragedy tonight.

She was going to lie or rather sit there propped up in her bed on four pillows and let the good things that had happened in the last two days play over and over in her head. Maybe this was why she'd never gotten those wished-for gifts from Santa Claus when she was a little girl, so that she could save all her wishes come true for this one wonderful Christmas.

She was floating on a cloud of happiness. She'd stayed at David's house all day. Had helped Aunt Love and Tabitha and Jocie put their midafternoon dinner on the table. Really had mostly just watched, since it seemed wise to stay away from everybody's forks and spoons the way she had to be leaking cold germs. But it had been good to be in the kitchen with them. To see how Tabitha and even Jocie protected

151

Aunt Love from her fading memory. To see the peace among them.

She'd sat at the table and peeked around at them while David was saying grace. Such an odd assortment. Every one of them so different and yet they all belonged. Even Wes. They were family. And now she was part of that family. She belonged with them. Nothing could spoil that. Nothing.

Not even her mother telling her she was an ungrateful child that morning when Leigh had called to tell her she was too sick to come go to Aunt Wilma's house for Christmas dinner. She'd tried to sound as sick and pitiful as she could, but her mother hadn't bought it.

"I'll bet you're not too sick to go to that preacher's house."

"Really I shouldn't," Leigh had said and coughed to prove it. She hadn't said she wasn't going. Just that she shouldn't. She hadn't told her mother about the ring either. She'd sworn Zella to secrecy for a day at least and hoped Zella was keeping her promise because if Mrs. Simpson heard the news, Leigh's mother would know in minutes. And it would be better if Leigh could break the news in person.

Break the news? That was a funny way to think about it. Leigh pulled one of the pillows higher behind her head. You'd think somebody had died or something. And maybe for her mother, it would be like that. Her idea of Leigh would have to die and be reborn. Surely her mother would be able to see how happy Leigh was. Surely she could see that nothing but good for all of them could come from Leigh being in love and getting married.

That morning her mother had sounded near tears. "It's a daughter's place to come home and be with her parents on Christmas."

"I'll come Sunday. I'll be less contagious by then. David and I will come after church." She hadn't been able to keep the tinkle of joy out of her voice as she said David's name.

"I didn't buy him a present," her mother said. "I didn't think he'd be here when we opened up our gifts."

"He won't care. He just wants to meet you. I want him to meet you. I want you to meet him."

"It's supposed to snow Sunday," her mother said.

"They're only calling for flurries, and I'm really sorry I can't be there today."

"No, you're not." Her mother sounded cross. "You want to be with that preacher's family. You act like you don't even have family of your own anymore. I never thought I'd have such an ungrateful daughter."

Leigh's hand tightened on the telephone receiver as she pulled in a long breath. She shut her eyes and reminded herself it was Christmas morning, that in a half hour she would be at David's house, that her mother did love her, and that she loved her mother. Then she said, "I don't think you do, Mother, and I'll see you Sunday after church."

"You could come early and go to church with me here. You know your father won't." Her mother didn't give up easily.

"Aunt Wilma will come by and get you. I'm coming with David after church," Leigh said patiently. She held out her hand and looked at the ring glittering on her finger and wondered about David's mother who had once worn the diamond on her hand. Would she have liked Leigh? Would she have been happy for her son? "Merry Christmas, Mother. I'll see you and Dad Sunday."

Her mother hadn't said Merry Christmas back. She'd just hung up. Leigh had felt sorry for a few minutes, but then the wonder of her happiness had swept her up on

153

cloud nine again. Cloud nine wasn't a bad place to be and one nobody at Brooke Central Station, as Wes sometimes called David's house, begrudged. They were all glad she was there. All glad David had given her his mother's diamond set in a new ring. It had been a nearly perfect day except for not getting to hold Stephen Lee.

She'd come home before dark. She was exhausted since, even if she hadn't been coughing and sneezing all night Christmas Eve, she'd been too excited to sleep. She kept reaching over to touch the other side of the bed and thinking that next Christmas Eve, she'd be able to reach over and touch David lying there beside her.

She must have finally drifted off to sleep when the telephone rang and jerked her back awake. Her heart jumped up in her throat as she spilled out of bed and ran to the kitchen to stop its shrill ringing. She took a quick look at the clock when she turned on the light. It wasn't really that late. Only eleven. Just because she'd already gone to sleep didn't mean somebody was calling with bad news. Maybe it was her mother wanting to say Merry Christmas before the day was gone so they wouldn't end Christmas Day at outs. Or David. That was more likely. David calling to say good night.

She was smiling as she picked up the receiver. "Hello."

"Oh, did I wake you?"

It wasn't David. Leigh didn't recognize the voice. "I'm sorry. I think you must have the wrong number," she said.

"This is Leigh, isn't it? Leigh with eyes as blue as a clear summer sky."

"Who is this?" Leigh was suddenly very awake. There was something about the voice that made her uneasy. Something that made her glance at the dark window over the sink as if she might see eyes staring in at her. There was no

154

curtain over the window. No need for one since she was on the second floor and there was no neighboring house with matching windows. Her reflection stared back at her, pale and distorted by the window.

The man on the other end of the line laughed softly. "Don't you recognize the voice of your secret admirer?"

"No, I don't." It wasn't much of a lie. She hadn't recognized his voice until he'd given her that clue. It was Edwin Hammond. Of course. Calling to claim credit for the roses. "And it's too late at night to be playing games on the telephone."

"I'm not playing games. I never play games. Life is much too serious for that, my dear."

"If you don't say who you are, I'm going to hang up." She shouldn't have warned him. She should have simply hung up. She didn't have to stand there talking to him just because his fingers had dialed her number. Just because he'd spent money sending her roses she didn't want.

"You know who I am. Ed."

"Ed?" She didn't want to admit she knew who he was.

"Edwin Hammond." He sounded irritated to have to say his whole name.

"Oh, Edwin," Leigh said as if she'd just realized who he was.

"Your secret admirer."

"How sweet of you to say such a thing. And the roses were lovely. But really you shouldn't have. As it turns out, I'm already taken."

"Taken?" Edwin laughed. "What an odd word to use. Taken. Taken by that over-the-hill editor-slash-preacher? I doubt very much he's taken you anywhere of note. Certainly not to the places I could take you. The heights of ecstasy. The depths of love."

"Goodbye, Edwin. Don't call again." She kept her voice even and calm, the way she did when one of their customers showed up at the clerk's office to shout about having to pay taxes on this or that car they'd bought.

"Why? Are you afraid to talk to me? Afraid I will awaken some feeling inside of you that will transform your little world? Transform you into the woman you can be."

She took the receiver away from her ear while he was still talking and hung it up. She couldn't remember ever hanging up on anyone before. She stared at the phone for a few seconds until, just as she'd feared, it started ringing again. She counted the rings. When it got to eleven she thought of Mrs. Simpson and picked up the receiver, but she didn't put it to her ear. She simply popped the plunger to disconnect the line and then laid the phone receiver down on the table. No one would call her before morning. And if her mother did need her for any kind of emergency, she'd call Mrs. Simpson first thing if Leigh didn't answer the phone.

The busy signal started beeping, but it would stop. Even if it didn't, she didn't care. She wasn't going to talk to Edwin Hammond again this night.

She caught her reflection in the window over the sink again and a shiver shook through her. It wasn't cold. She'd turned the thermostat up a few degrees as a Christmas present to herself. Even the floor didn't feel cold under her bare feet. This chill came from inside—from the echo of Edwin Hammond's voice in her ear. She didn't know what bothered her about the man. She hardly knew him. Had only talked to him that one time in the Grill. Twice now, counting the phone call. Two times too many.

She flicked the light off and felt better standing in the dark. Hidden from any eyes. She shivered again.

"Don't be stupid." Her voice sounded loud in the

darkness. "No one can see you. You're in your kitchen. In your apartment. You're perfectly safe."

But before she went back to her bed, she checked to see if her door was locked. She couldn't remember the last time she'd been worried about whether her door was locked or not. She was in Hollyhill. Lots of people left their doors unlocked all the time. Probably didn't even know where the keys to their doors were. Leigh turned the lock on her door. And then she propped a chair under the knob.

## 21

Snow flurries whipped across in front of the car as David and Leigh set out for Grundy to her parents' house on Sunday afternoon. Mt. Pleasant had dismissed evening services so David had the afternoon free. Nobody expected or even wanted a visit from the pastor two days after Christmas.

Besides, they knew he had other things on his mind on this day. The church had practically cheered when he told them he'd asked Leigh to marry him. A couple of women had actually said amen. Not a whisper under their breath, but right out loud. David had never heard a woman say amen from the pews before. Miss Sally hadn't said amen out loud, but from the look on her face, she'd surely been shouting it in her heart.

He was glad he hadn't made the announcement before the sermon or nothing he'd said about living for the Lord would have made the first impression. Nothing much had anyway, because most of them had already seen the ring, already knew the news before church started.

He'd asked Leigh to come up front with him after the

invitation was sung and before the final prayer. She blushed, but she looked happy. She looked beautiful. After the benediction, every person in the church came up to hug them. Even Ogden and Lela Martin. And Miss Sally hugged him and laughed and hugged him again.

Now they were headed for Grundy so David could meet Leigh's parents. It was the first time they'd been alone since he'd proposed on Christmas Eve.

As they drove out of Hollyhill, David reached over to take Leigh's hand. "Still want to marry me now that you've gotten a glimpse of life as a preacher's wife?"

"You mean standing up front with you to let everybody in on the news? I'm sure I turned redder than a beet. I blush easy as anything, but really I didn't mind at all. Who in the world could complain about hugs? They were all wonderful. So happy for you. And for me."

"They're good people, but as you said the other night, they'll want to be in on everything about the wedding," David warned.

"That's fine by me. I've always wanted a big family. Of course I already felt like part of your church family. They've been so sweet to me ever since the first Sunday I showed up out there." Leigh squeezed his hand, then laughed. "Do you remember the day I caught my dress in my car door? I felt like such a klutz."

"And I felt like such a lucky man to have a girl like you making eyes at me. Wanting to come be part of my church."

"I love the church now," Leigh said. "But I'm afraid my reason for coming wasn't entirely due to spiritual devotion. I was trying anything I could think of to get you to notice me, and I knew you'd have to shake my hand on the way out the door after the services."

"And what a beautiful hand." David raised her hand up and kissed her fingers.

The snow started coming down thicker with fat snow-flakes plopping against the windshield. David had to let go of Leigh's hand to turn on the wipers to sweep them away. Leigh sounded a little worried as she said, "Do you think the roads will get slick?"

"They weren't calling for much snow. Just flurries."

"Some flurry. The ground's already white."

"But it's not sticking to the road."

"It might start," Leigh said. "Maybe we should go back."

"It's not that bad yet. And we wouldn't want to disappoint your mother."

"It might be too late for that," Leigh said.

David looked over at Leigh. She was frowning. "What do you mean?"

"Oh, I don't know. I guess I shouldn't have said that." She looked away from him, then down at her hands in her lap.

David looked back at the road. All day he'd sensed something was bothering Leigh even though she'd kept smiling, kept telling him everything was fine. He knew she was nervous about him meeting her parents. He was a little nervous about meeting her parents himself, afraid they might not approve of him as a prospective son-in-law, and he could understand why. First off, he was divorced. Undeniable proof he'd failed at marriage once. He didn't think he'd fail again. Not with Leigh as his bride, but her parents had no reason to believe that. Plus he was old for Leigh, already a grandfather. On top of that, preachers didn't make much money. They lived on faith more years than not. All he really had to offer Leigh was his love and steadfast devotion. Maybe for her parents that wouldn't seem like enough.

The windshield wipers sweeping the snow off the windshield sounded loud in the silence building between them. Up ahead David spotted a deserted driveway and pulled off the road.

"So are we turning around?" Leigh asked as she looked out at the snow.

"No. We need to talk."

"Oh." She glanced at David and then looked back down at her hands. "About what?"

"You tell me. Something is bothering you, and if something is bothering you, then something is bothering me." He turned sideways in the seat and took both of her hands, gently pulling her around to face him. "I want us to be as one the way the Bible says. Hearts and souls and minds. That can't happen if we try to hide our problems from one another. So tell me what's wrong."

"Nothing's really wrong." Her eyes came up to meet his. "It's just that my mother isn't too excited about me being in love with you."

"That's understandable. I'm not the ideal candidate for son-in-law."

"You're my ideal candidate for husband." Leigh's face softened for a moment, but then the worry came back. "To be honest, I'm not sure what they might say to you today. I'm never sure what they might say to *me*. I mean I know they love me, but it's sometimes hard to tell when I'm with them. It's not like at your house."

"I hope not. It can be a madhouse there sometimes."

"But a nice madhouse. A happy one." Leigh looked back out at the snow. "My parents are always fussing with one another."

"I'm sorry about that for their sake," David said. "But you don't have to worry about me. I have a tough hide. And they can't be all that bad if they raised a beautiful daughter like you."

Leigh had tears in her eyes when she looked back at him. "Thank you, David."

"For what?"

"For loving me."

"You're welcome." David looked at her. "Now is there anything else you've not been telling me?"

"You haven't told me everything either," Leigh said.

"Not yet, but I will. You'll get so tired of hearing my problems, you'll want to get earplugs." David smiled.

"I doubt it, but okay, there is one other thing." Leigh took a deep breath.

"Uh-uh. This doesn't sound good. You're not backing out on me, are you?"

"No, never. But you have to promise me you won't get too upset."

"How can I promise when I don't know what I'm going to get upset about?"

"Edwin Hammond."

"Edwin Hammond? What about him? Did he send more roses?" He tried to keep the growl out of his voice, but he felt it inside.

"No, he called me."

"What did he want?"

"I don't know. To let me know he sent the roses, I guess. I barely know the man, but something about him gives me the willies. Even over the phone."

"You want me to call him and tell him to leave you alone?" David said. First the man picked on his daughter and now he was chasing after the woman he loved. Was

162

the Lord testing David's ability to control his temper? To turn the other cheek?

"No, no. I already told him not to call me again. And I feel better now that you know he called. Now I can go back to worrying about what awful things my parents are sure to say to you. And about sliding off the road in this snow." She smiled and leaned over to give him a quick kiss. "Promise no matter what that I get to keep the ring."

"It's yours. I'm yours. Forever."

By the time they got to Leigh's parents' house in Grundy, there was at least an inch of snow on the ground. Leigh gripped David's arm as they walked to the door. "Can we just go on back to Hollyhill? Please."

"Not until I meet my future in-laws," David said as he punched the doorbell.

Inside after the flurry of introductions and hellos, Leigh shrugged off her coat and leaned close to David to whisper, "Might as well get it over with."

She turned back to her parents and held her hand out to show the ring. Mrs. Jacobson gave a little shriek that didn't sound a bit joyful and sank down on the couch in a near faint while Mr. Jacobson looked over at David and said, "Well, well. So you popped the question. Just how old are you anyway?"

"Dad!" Leigh said. "Mind your manners."

The man laughed. "You should have warned him that I don't have any manners. But don't worry, I'll let him pray over the food as soon as your mother pulls herself together. Catherine, dinner is going to ruin if we don't eat soon."

David was already doing some praying. Still, he wasn't sure what to say or do first. Leigh was stroking her mother's hair and talking softly to her as the woman half whimpered, half moaned. "Now, Mother, don't take on so. This is wonderful news. You need to be happy for me."

"Should I go get her a glass of water?" David offered.

"That won't do any good unless you're planning to throw it in her face. That might help," Mr. Jacobson said.

David didn't know what to say to that. It might be that he should have gotten Leigh to tell him a little more about her parents. She'd told him that her mother had a weight problem and used guilt as her number one weapon to keep Leigh in line. She'd said her father was retired and played a lot of golf. That was about it except for what she'd told him in the car about them fussing a lot.

Leigh looked over her shoulder at her father. "Dad, stop being so mean."

"I'm not being mean. Just honest. Preachers preach about being honest, don't they? Thou shalt not lie. That's in the Bible, isn't it, Preacher?" Mr. Jacobson said.

"It is," David said.

"But I'll bet you lie sometimes. You'll probably tell a few tonight. Polite little lies like it's so good to meet you. Well, that's not me. I believe in telling the truth whatever."

"Good," David said. "I like a man who says things straight out. You don't have to try to guess what he's thinking that way. You know."

"Is that one of your polite little lies, Reverend?"

"No. Just the truth straight out the way you like it."

Mr. Jacobson smiled. "Well, well, Leigh. Maybe you know how to pick them after all. As long as he doesn't try to convert me."

"I always wait until the second visit for that," David said.

"So, you're one of those preachers who likes to crack jokes, huh?" The man slapped David on the shoulder and laughed again. Then he looked at Mrs. Jacobson. "All right, Catherine, everybody knows you're not happy. Now I'm hungry. Let's eat."

Mrs. Jacobson sat up and glared at him. "That's all you think about. What you want. Never the first thought about how I'm feeling."

"Please, Mother. Don't start," Leigh said.

"Me? He's the one who started it," Mrs. Jacobson said.

"All I said was let's eat." Mr. Jacobson feigned an innocent look. "I thought you were always ready to eat."

One thing for sure, the man knew how to push his wife's buttons. But the anger seemed to help her pull herself together as she fought her way free of the soft couch cushions. On her feet, her voice was icy as she said, "It's ready to put on the table."

The dinner conversation was stilted. They talked a lot about how good the food was and about how much it was snowing or had snowed on past Christmases. They didn't talk about the engagement at all. After they ate Mrs. Jacobson's delicious stack pie, they opened presents. There was no excitement, no paper ripped and tossed on the floor the way it had been at David's house on Christmas morning. Mr. Jacobson carefully cut each piece of tape with a small silver pocketknife before folding the paper back from his presents. Mrs. Jacobson managed to open her presents just as neatly using her fingernails to cut the tape. They both seemed more interested in preserving the wrappings than what was inside any of the boxes.

At last all the presents were opened. There was a sense of relief as Mrs. Jacobson folded up the last scraps of paper. David sat outside their family circle and wondered how a girl so full of laughter and love could have come from this house of bickering.

"Well, that's over," Mr. Jacobson said. "Now how about some more of that stack pie, Catherine, and some coffee? Maybe the preacher here might want some too."

"Coffee would be great, but I couldn't eat another bite," David said.

"We might need to just get some to take with us, Mother," Leigh said. She went over and turned on the porch light to peer out the window. "The snow's not letting up. We probably should start back before the roads get too bad."

"You could always spend the night," Mrs. Jacobson said with a look at David that said she wished he'd go get lost in a snowdrift somewhere.

"That's sweet of you, Mother, but we have to get back. We both have to go to work tomorrow, you know. And I think if we leave now, the roads will be okay. Don't you, David?"

"My car goes good on the snow," David said. The roads could have been drifted fence-post high and he would have said the same. One of those little lies Mr. Jacobson had talked about earlier, but this one didn't have the first thing to do with politeness. It was pure survival.

When Mrs. Jacobson started to say more, Mr. Jacobson cut in. "They don't want to stay, Catherine. They slide off the road into a ditch, then the preacher here will just have to pray his way out of it."

Mrs. Jacobson clamped her lips together and went to pack up the parcels of food she was sending home with Leigh. At least they'd have plenty to eat if they got snowbound. After they got their coats on and Leigh hugged her mother and father, David shook Mr. Jacobson's hand and then took Mrs. Jacobson's hand. He tried to look her in the eyes, but she was staring holes into the middle of his chest.

"I love your daughter, Mrs. Jacobson, and I'll do everything within my power to make her happy."

The woman's eyes came up to his then. "She won't be happy unless she has babies. No woman is."

"Mother," Leigh gasped.

David kept smiling. "That's something Leigh and I will have to decide, but I can certainly understand your desire to have a grandchild."

"I guess you can. Since you already have one," Mrs. Jacobson said.

"And he is precious. A gift from the Lord. Just as your daughter is to me."

When Mrs. Jacobson seemed to not know what to say to that, Leigh jumped between them to give her mother another hug. "It was wonderful, Mother. This is a Christmas I'll never forget."

And then they were out the door, stepping through snow over their shoe tops to the car. The snow crunched under the car's wheels as David backed carefully out of the driveway. He didn't want to have to pray himself out of the ditch right in front of their house. Once they were back on the main highway, the roads were still fairly clear. There wasn't much traffic. Just a car now and again. Some other idiot trying to escape his future in-laws' house.

David was concentrating on driving, feeling every slip of the wheels, but he was keenly aware of Leigh's silence in the dark beside him. He glanced over at her. "You okay?"

"I'm sorry, David. They were even worse than I thought they would be."

"Your mother wasn't too happy about our news, but you know, I'm not marrying your mother. I'm marrying you and you're happy about our news."

"I am." Suddenly Leigh started laughing.

"What's so funny?" David asked.

"I don't know. Us. Them. The snow. Everything. I always have to laugh when I leave their house. All that laughter that I couldn't spill there gets piled up inside me and I have to let it out."

And so they laughed and prayed their way through the snow back to Hollyhill.

## 22

Zella didn't like snow. Not even at Christmastime. The only good thing about a white Christmas was the song. Besides, it wasn't Christmas now. It was the Sunday after. Thank goodness. People got way too carried away by Christmas.

Not that it wasn't something a Christian should mark, but she'd read somewhere that Bible scholars said Jesus wasn't even born on Christmas Day. No snow on the stable roof. They claimed somebody just picked that date. Something about there already being some kind of holiday to celebrate the sun starting back closer to the earth. As if the people way back then even knew what the sun was doing. After all, they thought the world was flat as a pancake.

So who knew, and as David said, what difference did it make when they celebrated? The important thing was that Jesus had been born. Some people were always coming up with something to try to mess up a good Christian's head. A person had to decide what was right. By reading the Bible and praying, of course, but then they just had to stick to it.

One thing for sure, every snowflake outside was sticking to it. To the ground, that is. There had to already be two inches of the white stuff on her front walk. It was plain inconvenient. Not that First Baptist canceled services because of a little snow. Or because families were having Christmas get-togethers. That's what David's church had done today. Just called off night services without a second thought. What about getting together as a church family? People should go to services twice on Sunday. It was a person's Christian duty.

But she couldn't really wade through all that snow to church, and heaven knew she couldn't drive. She'd never seen the need of buying snow tires. It didn't snow all that often, and she could always walk wherever she needed to go in Hollyhill. The way the snow was coming down, though, it might be over her boot tops by the time services were over and she had to walk home.

That's why she'd called Gertie. Gertie drove a Volkswagen. It looked like some kind of yellow beetle, and a person didn't have room for her knees inside it, but it scooted along on top of the snow without the first bit of problem. Gertie was going on eighty years old and sometimes turned the wrong way down one-way streets, but Hollyhill had no business having one-way streets anyhow. People could just back up out of the way if the street was too narrow to pass on. That's what they'd done for years before Buzz Palmor got to be mayor and decided Hollyhill needed to go modern.

Not that she didn't vote for him. She almost had to. She'd gone to school with his sister and known Buzz ever since he used to wipe his nose on his sleeve back before he started school. And they could always count on him buying ads in the *Banner* during election years even when nobody was running against him. Still, that didn't mean she had to be for everything he did.

Zella looked at the clock. It was almost time to go stand by the door and watch for Gertie. She rinsed out her teacup in the sink and left it to drain. She was getting her coat and boots out of the closet when there was a knock on the door. She frowned. That was odd. Gertie never came to the door. She always just tooted her horn umpteen times until Zella came out. Her horn must be on the blink.

Zella normally peeked out the window to see who was standing on her doorstep before she opened the door, but she was right beside the door and poor Gertie would be getting covered up with snow. So she just pulled open the door.

It wasn't Gertie. Zella was too surprised to slam the door shut. A young man stood on her doorstep. Not much more than a boy really. He didn't have on a hat and snow was clinging to his short brown hair. His ears were red from the cold. He had his hands in his pockets as he stood there shivering. Zella looked down at his feet. No boots either. Young people were so foolish sometimes. Willing to freeze rather than wear sensible clothes. But other than not having the sense to wear proper clothes, he looked harmless enough.

"Mrs. Curtsinger?" he said.

She knew at once who he was, but she wasn't ready to admit it. "*Miss* Curtsinger," she said pointedly. "Is there something I can do for you?"

"I hope so," he said.

"Are you stuck in the snow?" Zella peered past him at the strange car out on the street parked right where Gertie would be pulling up any minute now. "I could call somebody for you."

171

"No, no. I'm not stuck. I've come about Wesley Green. Can I come in?"

She wanted to say no. Just tell him to go back to Pelphrey, Ohio, or wherever he came from. That she didn't even know a Wesley Green. And then she could shut the door. But the poor boy did look half frozen. And Gertie would be driving up any minute. No telling what Gertie might tell him if he started talking to her. She might even recognize Wesley's eyes staring out of the boy's face. Better to get him inside out of sight. Of course the car was there, but it could be anybody's car. The snow would be covering up the license plate that would reveal the car was from out of state.

"Certainly. Step inside so I can shut the door. It's cold." She reached out and pulled him over the threshold before slamming the door shut. Lights were coming down the street, but thank heavens it wasn't Gertie. Zella had a few minutes to figure out what to do.

The boy stood on the scatter rug inside her door and dripped snow. "Have I come at a bad time? Were you going somewhere?" he asked. He looked at her coat on the chair by the door.

"Church. It's Sunday night. I was going to church."

"Oh, then I have come at a bad time, but if you've got a couple of minutes, I'd like to explain why I'm here. I'm Robert Green. I wrote to you a few weeks ago, remember?"

"Of course I remember. You don't think I'd let just anybody in my house, do you?" Zella's mind was racing a mile a minute, but she wasn't coming up with any solutions. She'd just have to go out and tell Gertie it was snowing too much for her to go to church, but Gertie would never believe that. It hadn't snowed too much for forty years.

Maybe she could tell her she'd caught Leigh's cold. That might even be true. She could feel a headache coming on.

172

Then once she got rid of Gertie she could think of a way to hide out this boy long enough to give her time to figure out how to tell Wesley he had a grandson. In Hollyhill.

She shouldn't have put off answering the boy's letter so long. She'd had every intention of writing him. Had gotten out her stationery a couple of times, but it took time to come up with the best words for a letter like that. And she was just so busy before Christmas with all that was going on. She never thought about him just up and appearing on her doorstep. Young people had no patience.

"No, of course not," the boy was saying. "You look like a very sensible woman. If you could just tell me how I could find this Wesley Green you wrote and told us about? Then I can go talk to him. Find out if he's my grandfather."

"He's your grandfather." Zella didn't have time for niceties.

The boy's face was a mixture of surprise and confusion as if he'd just opened up a present he'd been wanting, but now that he had it, he wasn't sure what to do with it. "How can you be so sure?"

"You're the spitting image of him."

"Oh, well, great. So does he live nearby?"

"It's not that easy," Zella said. "You can't just go show up on his doorstep. He might have a stroke."

"So he's still not recovered from his accident?"

"Not totally." Of course Wesley wouldn't have a stroke. That had just been a figure of speech, but Wesley was still limping from that tree falling on him. So it wasn't completely a lie.

"I'm sorry to hear that." The boy looked concerned.

Zella couldn't worry about that. She had plenty of other things to worry about. Like Gertie sitting on her horn out by the curb.

"Is that somebody coming to pick you up?" the boy asked.

"It is."

"I can come back later, I suppose." He looked toward the window out at the snow. "Is there a motel in town?"

"In Hollyhill? Hardly. You're not in Lexington." Zella let out a long sigh. "Just stay put here and give me a minute to get rid of Gertie. Then I'll figure out something."

She didn't even take time to put on her coat and boots. She just ran down the walk stepping in the boy's footprints to the curb. When Gertie rolled down the window, Zella told her she thought she might be catching something.

"I don't wonder." Gertie gave her a disapproving look. "Out here with no coat and nothing on your head. You'll catch your death."

"I should have called you. I'm sorry," Zella told her. She was feeling a little breathless and not just from the run to the curb. She was beginning to feel like one of those silly characters in the novels she read who acted as if they didn't have a lick of sense and were always running pell-mell into trouble of some sort or another. Not that she was in any kind of danger. The boy inside her house didn't look a bit dangerous. And she wasn't afraid of Wesley. Even if it did turn out he was running from the law the way she'd always thought.

"That's okay. I go right by here anyway." Gertie shifted the gears on her little car. "Whose car is that?"

"I'm not sure," Zella said. Again not exactly a lie. She didn't know for sure that it was the boy's car. "Maybe somebody got stuck. You be sure you don't."

"Don't worry about me and old Millie here." Gertie hit her steering wheel. "We've handled lots worse than this little skiff of snow." She started rolling up her window. "You go on back inside before you freeze."

It wasn't until Zella turned and started back up the walk that she saw she hadn't pulled her drapes over her double front windows. The boy was standing there in the middle of her living room plain as day.

Zella looked over her shoulder at Gertie, but Gertie had her eyes on the road as she pulled away from the curb. Maybe Gertie hadn't noticed the boy. After all, it was snowing pretty hard and Gertie didn't see far off as well as she used to. She might not have even looked toward the house. She'd been looking at Zella with no coat or hat on out in the snow. Zella should have at least grabbed some kind of hat or scarf. The snow was surely melting her curls.

Zella held her hands over her head like an umbrella and rushed back up the walk. The boy must have been watching out the window because he opened the door for her. When had that ever happened? Somebody opening her own front door to let her in her own house.

"Are you okay, Miss Curtsinger?" he asked when she pushed past him and slammed the door shut.

"I'm fine," she said, panting a little as she brushed the snow off her shoulders and slipped her feet out of her felt house shoes. They were probably ruined. The toes of her hose were soaked and faded blue from the house shoes. Even before she worried about shaking the snow off her hair, she went over and yanked the drapes shut. Then she carefully touched her hair and tried to brush off the snow without destroying her curls, but the curls felt wet and sort of flat. Things were definitely going from bad to worse.

"So do you think you could call my grandfather and tell him I'm in town and would like to see him? Maybe that would soften the shock of my showing up out of the blue."

"Blue? It looks all white out there to me." She made the halfhearted attempt at a joke just to stall for time, but it made her feel better when he smiled. He was a nice-looking boy. Friendly eyes even if they were like Wesley's.

"I've got to admit you're right about that, Miss Curtsinger. It's some storm. When I left home this morning, it wasn't snowing a bit and the weathermen weren't even calling for snow at home or here. I checked."

"You can't depend on the weather forecast," Zella said. "Come on in the kitchen and I'll fix you some cocoa. You do like cocoa, don't you?"

"That sounds wonderful," the boy said.

"And take your shoes off so your feet can dry out. You don't want to get some kind of fungus," Zella said as she led the way to the kitchen.

He was a nice boy. Wesley would want to meet him. If only she could figure out a way for him to be there in Hollyhill without her having to admit she had anything to do with it. Not that she thought it was wrong what she'd done. Somebody had needed to find out about Wesley's family in case he had died after that tree fell on him. It was certainly a possibility. Him dying. It was a possibility for anybody. Dying. Nobody had any guarantees of another day.

She was putting mustard on some bread to make the boy a ham sandwich because weren't boys his age always hungry, when David's name popped in her head. David. Of course. David would know how to handle it. David could talk to Wesley. The boy could even go to David's house and spend the night. David wouldn't care. After all, wasn't he always saying Wesley was the same as family to him? If

176

Wesley was family, then so was this boy. And a person had to make room for family.

She left the boy eating the sandwich and drinking the hot cocoa and went to the living room to call David. She didn't know why she'd been so worried. When a person was doing what she knew was best, things always worked out. She felt a little warm glow inside as if she'd been drinking some of the hot cocoa herself. Maybe she would sit down at the table with the boy and drink a cup after she talked to David. She might even put in two marshmallows.

ocie had just come in from outside when the phone rang. She'd taken Stephen Lee out to introduce him to snow. Aunt Love had made her put so many clothes on the poor baby that nothing but a small circle around his eyes even showed, so he hadn't really gotten much feel of the snow. He liked looking at Zeb more than the snowflakes. When Jocie held him down by the dog, Stephen Lee bounced his mitten-covered hands on top of Zeb's head. Zeb didn't seem to mind especially after Jocie gave the dog a biscuit left over from breakfast as a reward.

It had been a fun Christmas weekend and the unexpected snow piling up outside was an extra bonus. She doubted if her dad was enjoying it all that much since he and Leigh were out on the roads somewhere. Then again, he might like getting snowbound with Leigh. Jocie didn't know whether Leigh liked snow or not, but she probably wouldn't mind being stuck in the snow with Jocie's dad.

Jocie loved snow. She guessed they might have three inches on the ground already. She'd take out a ruler later to measure for sure. At least they'd have snow pictures to put in the *Banner* this week. Snow pictures always sold a few extra papers.

She'd slipped her feet out of her boots at the door but hadn't taken off her coat or gotten Stephen Lee out of his snowsuit when the phone rang. Tabitha and Aunt Love were both off in their rooms taking naps or something since Jocie was entertaining the baby, so she grabbed the phone. She hoped it wouldn't be a church member saying one of his or her sisters, brothers, mothers, fathers, whoever, was sick. She wouldn't be able to write down a message for her dad. It was hard enough trying to keep a good hold on Stephen Lee in his snowsuit. Plus he was beginning to fuss.

It was Zella, of all people. "I need to talk to your father," she said.

"Is everything okay?" Jocie asked. Zella never called. Not unless she needed something right away. Like the time the pipe under her sink had burst and her kitchen had flooded.

"Of course it is. I just need to speak to your father."

"He's not here."

"Well, where is he?" Zella sounded irritated. Or maybe it was just the interference on the line. Sometimes the phones went out when there was a lot of snow or rain.

"He's gone with Leigh to Grundy. I thought Leigh told you." Jocie talked loud to get over the crackling on the line.

"Oh," Zella said. "She did, but I thought they'd have the good sense not to go in all this snow."

"It wasn't snowing much when they left."

"Well, it is now. They should have come home."

"They're probably on the way. Did you need something?" Jocie's arm was getting tired and Stephen Lee was whimpering more. She tried swaying him back and forth.

"Certainly I needed something. I needed to talk to David." Zella was quiet for a minute. The crackling on the line was getting louder. "So if he's left already, he should be there in an hour at the very longest."

"Maybe. I don't know. He may get snowbound somewhere."

"He won't. But that's what I needed. There's this boy here who's got snowbound and he needs a place to stay. I'm sending him to your house because obviously he can't stay here."

"What's he doing at your house?"

"Don't be asking so many questions. You don't have to know everything. Here's just where he ended up. And now he needs a place to stay and David will know what to do."

"To do? What do you mean? And how's he going to get here if he's snowbound?"

"I didn't say he was stuck. Just snowbound. He'll explain it all to your father when he gets there."

"But Dad's not here," Jocie said again. The line went dead. For a minute Jocie thought Zella had hung up on her, but when she pushed the plunger down and let it back up, she didn't get a dial tone. The snow must have gotten to the line.

"Oh well, so much for nutty old Zella," Jocie told the baby as she carried him over to the couch to get him out of his snowsuit. She shrugged off her coat. "Nutty, nutty Zella. She should have just sent him over to Wes. He has an extra couch. That's more than we have around here. Right, baby boo?"

Stephen Lee laughed. Jocie didn't know whether it was because of what she was saying or if he was just glad to get free of the bulky snowsuit. "I'll go get a snowball for you to play with later. That way you can touch the snow. Your mama won't care. She says you need to learn new things. I mean, you're already three and a half months old."

Aunt Love came in the living room. "Was that your father on the phone?"

"Nope. Zella. She's sending some guy out here to spend the night. At least I think she is."

"Who in the world?"

"Beats me. Something about the guy being snowbound but not stuck. I hope Dad doesn't get stuck." Jocie picked up Stephen Lee and kissed his red cheeks.

Aunt Love was frowning. "Call her back and tell her to send whoever it is over to stay with Wesley. That would be closer anyway."

"Can't." Jocie looked around at Aunt Love. "The phone went dead. We can't call anybody."

"Oh well. He surely can't be anybody dangerous if Zella's sending him over," Aunt Love said. "We'll just have to remember what it says in Hebrews. 'Be not forgetful to entertain strangers: for thereby some have entertained angels unawares.'"

The guy did sort of look like an angel when he finally knocked on the door over an hour later. Either that or a snowman. Snow was clinging to his coat and pants and melting on his hair. "Did you walk all the way from Zella's?" Jocie asked when she opened the door.

"Not all the way. I slid off the road about a half mile from here."

"Let him come in, Jocelyn, so he can warm up by the stove," Aunt Love said from the kitchen door. Tabitha had stopped halfway down the steps, carrying Stephen Lee. She was looking at the guy standing in the door as if she'd never seen a man before.

"I'll drip all over your floor," he said.

"It's been dripped on before," Aunt Love said.

The man stomped his feet to get off as much snow as possible and stepped inside. "It is cold out there."

"Too cold to be traipsing around without gloves and boots. Of course you're cold. Hungry too, I'd say. We just finished supper, but we've got plenty of leftovers," Aunt Love said.

"That's okay. Miss Curtsinger fixed me a sandwich and made me some hot chocolate," the man said.

"Zella made you hot chocolate?" Jocie was shocked. "Are you her long-lost son or something?"

"Jocelyn, behave yourself," Aunt Love said. "Run get one of your father's sweaters and some socks."

"I'll get them," Tabitha offered from the stairs.

"I don't want to be any trouble," the man said with a smile at Tabitha.

"No trouble at all." Tabitha looked so ready to swoon that Jocie thought she might ought to run up the stairs and be ready to catch Stephen Lee.

Jocie took a better look at the guy now that some of the snow had melted off his hair. She supposed he was sort of cute and he looked about Tabitha's age. And that smile. It reminded her of somebody.

He was trying to explain why he was there dripping all over their floor. "Miss Curtsinger said she thought it best that I should talk to Mr. Brooke about why I'm in Hollyhill. Or rather, Reverend Brooke. She said he's a preacher. Is he here?"

"Not right now, but he should be soon," Aunt Love said as she stepped over closer to the stranger to get a better look at his face. "You look familiar. Have we met before?"

"No, ma'am. I sort of doubt it. I'm from Ohio, and I've never been down this way before."

"Maybe you just look like somebody I know," Aunt Love said.

"That might be it," the man said. "I guess I should introduce myself. I'm Robert."

Tabitha practically fell down the steps in her hurry to get the sweater and socks to the guy. She handed Stephen Lee off to Jocie as she said breathlessly, "I'm Tabitha and that's Jocie holding Stephen Lee. And that's Aunt Love. All Brookes." Tabitha's eyes were sparkling and her face was almost as pink as the rose in the little tattoo on her upper cheek.

"Except Aunt Love. Her name's Warfield." Jocie frowned a little. She wanted to tell Tabitha to take a deep breath and count to ten before she fell off the deep end. This Robert hadn't even given them his last name. "And your last name?" she asked.

"Miss Curtsinger said it would be better if I just waited and explained everything to Reverend Brooke."

"I didn't ask for the whole story of why you're here in the middle of a snowstorm or how you ended up snowbound at Zella's house, of all places," Jocie said. "Just your name. That ought to be an easy enough question to answer."

Tabitha turned to make a face at Jocie. "Stop being so rude, Jocie. You don't have to always know all the answers. I think it's sort of fun to have a mystery man show up in the middle of a snowstorm." She looked back around at Robert with a big smile as she handed him the sweater. "Here, let me take your wet coat."

Aunt Love was pulling a chair up close to the stove. "Take your shoes off and come over here and warm up," she said, ready to give her best effort to entertain angels.

The man shrugged off his wet coat and pulled on the sweater Tabitha handed him. "That feels great," he said. Before he went over to sit down in the chair Aunt Love offered, he stepped closer to Jocie and looked straight into her eyes. "I'd answer your questions, Jocie, but I promised Miss Curtsinger I'd wait and talk to Reverend Brooke. But you don't have to worry. I'm harmless. You and little Stevie here don't have a thing to worry about."

Stevie. The name echoed in Jocie's head. The only person to ever call Stephen Lee Stevie was Wes. And suddenly staring into the eyes of this man who said his name was Robert, everything was echoing. It was the same as if she might run into Stephen Lee's father someday and look into his eyes and see Stephen Lee. Or some stranger's eyes and see a reflection of herself. But now she was looking into this man's eyes and seeing Wes.

The ship from Jupiter had finally landed. And she wanted to put Stephen Lee down and run out the door and all the way to Hollyhill to make Wes promise that he wouldn't get on it and fly away. She would have too if it hadn't been snowing. But Aunt Love would never let her go at night with it snowing the way it was.

184

# 24

It was after eleven before David and Leigh drove back into Hollyhill. The roads had gotten more hazardous by the mile, and twice they'd slid sideways going down a hill. Luckily no car had been coming from the other direction, or perhaps luck had nothing to do with it. It was prayer, pure and simple.

He and Leigh both breathed sighs of relief when he pulled up to her apartment. "Were you praying as much as I was?" Leigh asked.

"More. At least we didn't have to pray our way out of a ditch."

"Or spend the night at my parents' house."

After he helped Leigh carry her gifts and packages of food up the steps and into the apartment, he kissed her good night. He was amazed afresh every time he put his arms around her how right it felt. How well she fit there in the circle of his arms. She asked him if he wanted to eat another piece of her mother's stack pie before he left, but the snow was still falling. If it got much deeper, his car would belly up in the snow and he'd be stuck for sure.

He tried to call home from Leigh's to let them know he was on the way, but the line kept beeping the busy signal. Nothing to worry about, he told Leigh. The line went out a lot.

Once he drove out of the city limits, the roads got even worse. He crept along staying in the tracks of some other car that had passed along the road some time back. He wasn't too concerned. Even if he got stuck, he was close enough to his house that he could walk the rest of the way if he had to.

Just over the top of one of the hills in a curve, the car that had made the tracks he'd been following was sideways in the ditch. Snow covered it like a blanket, so it had obviously been there awhile. David carefully tapped his brakes to stop his car. He got out and brushed the snow off the driver's side window of the car in the ditch to peer inside. His flashlight's beam was weak, but strong enough to let him see the car was empty. Whoever it was must have deserted the car and walked wherever he was headed.

He had expected the house to be dark and everybody to be asleep when he got home, but instead when he turned into the driveway, the house was ablaze with light. His heart started beating faster as possible reasons for so much light this late at night ran through his head. Stephen Lee might be sick. Aunt Love could have had a stroke. Jocie might have gone out and gotten lost in the snow. The girl loved snow. But there was no reason for her to get lost and there was no reason for him to panic until he knew what was wrong.

Jocie must have been watching for his car because she flicked on the porch light and stepped outside to meet him. His heart felt a little lighter. At least she was okay. "What's wrong?" he asked as he climbed up the porch steps. "Is Stephen Lee sick?"

"No, no. Nothing like that. We have company."

"Company? Oh, did whoever got stuck up on the hill walk down here?"

"Yeah, but here is where he was headed to begin with," Jocie said. "He says his name is Robert. That's all he would tell us. Seems Zella sent him out here to tell you his story and only you."

David frowned as he brushed the snow off his coat and stomped his feet. Maybe he was just tired—it had been a long day—but nothing was making a whole lot of sense. He pulled in a deep breath to try to get his mind working better. "Then I guess I'd better go in and hear what he has to say."

"Wait a minute, Dad." Jocie looked over her shoulder at the crack of light spilling out of the door she hadn't quite pulled shut when she stepped out on the porch. Then she looked back at David. "I know where he's from. He's from Jupiter."

"Jupiter? Jocie, it's too late for this nonsense."

"Well, maybe not really Jupiter, but wherever Wes is from." Suddenly Jocie looked ready to cry. She mashed her mouth together and sniffed before she went on. "He looks like Wes. He must be family. Maybe a son or something."

David reached out and put his arms around Jocie. "That might be. But you don't have to look so worried. Wes could have a hundred sons show up from Jupiter and it wouldn't change how he feels about you."

Jocie kept her face against his coat. There were tears in her voice as she said, "But they might want him to go back to Jupiter with them."

"They might, and he might go. I don't know." David

pushed Jocie back where he could see her face. "We can't keep the people we love captive."

"I don't want to keep Wes captive. I just don't want him to leave."

"He hasn't gone anywhere. He probably won't. But even if he does, I do know one thing for sure. He'll never stop loving you."

Jocie pulled in a shaky breath and rubbed the tears off her cheeks. "I know. But it just seems like I'm always having to borrow family. Sometimes you have to give back stuff you borrow." She kept her eyes down.

For a minute David forgot about the person inside who might or might not be related to Wes. He thought they'd worked through all this after the tornado, but sometimes it was hard to hold on to the truth. "Look at me, Jocie." Slowly her eyes came up to his. "There's nothing borrowed about your family. I am your father. I have always been your father, and I will always be your father. There's nothing you can do to ever change that. And Wes loves you the same way. Whatever you want to call him. Grandfather. Uncle. Friend. He's not going to change how he feels about you. The two of you are tied together by something stronger than mere blood kinship. If you don't believe me, ask him."

Jocie smiled through her tears. "I know, Dad. But sometimes I can't help but worry that everything might change. That something will happen."

"Something has happened. Something is always happening, but love stays. Okay?"

"Okay."

He rubbed the tears off her cheeks with his gloved hand. "Now let's go in before we both freeze."

Jocie was right. The young man who stood up when David came into the room did look like Wes, but he was too young to be the son Wes said he'd left behind when he went out on the road after his wife and daughter had died in the auto accident. A grandson perhaps. But there was no reason for David to play guessing games. The boy would tell him his story. That was why he was there.

"Hello, Reverend Brooke, my name is Robert. I apologize for barging in on your family like this, sir," the young man was saying as he reached to shake David's hand. "But Miss Curtsinger said you'd know how best to handle my situation. I don't want to upset anyone or cause any problems. And she said maybe you could put me up for the night since there isn't a motel in Hollyhill. I realize that might be a terrible imposition. If so, I can always go sleep in my car."

"The one stuck up on the hill, I presume," David said.

"Yes sir."

Aunt Love jumped in. "You aren't going to sleep in your car. You can have the couch. Jocelyn can bunk in with Tabitha."

"I could sleep on the porch the way I did on Christmas Eve," Jocie offered.

"No," Aunt Love said. "It's too cold and I'm not having that dog tracking snow all over the porch. It won't hurt you two sisters to share a bed one night."

David almost laughed at the way Jocie's eyes popped open wide as she looked at Aunt Love. She'd thought her dog coming in to sleep by her bed out on the closed-in porch until winter had pushed her in to the living room couch had been a secret from Aunt Love. "All right," he said. "That's settled. Somebody bring Robert a pillow and blankets, and then everybody to bed."

Tabitha jumped up to fetch the blankets. Her eyes were shining and she was smiling as if Santa Claus had brought her a late gift. The boy looked a bit stunned at being showered with attention by such a beautiful girl, but not at all unhappy. Sometimes the chemistry of attraction worked fast between young people. It could be David should plan to sleep light whenever his head finally did hit his pillow this night. Or morning now.

Finally Tabitha reluctantly followed Jocie up the stairs, and David and the young man were alone. David stretched out his socked feet toward the stove. Outside the wind was picking up, blowing snow against the windows. It sounded cold and his feet were cold, but not as cold as the day he'd baptized Wes. Forevermore he would have a reference for cold. Cold, yes, but not that cold.

He settled his eyes on the boy. "All right, Robert. It's time to tell your story about why you're here. I'm guessing your last name's probably Green."

"Yes sir. Robert Wesley Green Jr. I guess you could see the resemblance the same as Miss Curtsinger."

"You look like Wes. No doubt of that. Even Jocie knew who you were."

"She did?" Robert looked troubled. "Miss Curtsinger told me whatever I did not to tell Jocelyn—Jocie—who I was. That things might get really messed up if that happened."

"I'm a little confused here. Just what has Zella got to do with all this?"

So Robert told him about getting Zella's letter back in the summer. "I was so excited. I just had a feeling about it all. I wrote back to her saying I wanted to come down as soon as possible to see if the Wesley Green she knew could be my grandfather, but she'd said in her letter that he'd been in an accident and might not be strong enough to have some unknown family member just show up without warning.

190

So I waited to hear from her. Then my school started and I couldn't miss classes."

"Did she say how she found you?" David stared at the gas flame in the stove and waited for his answer.

"I didn't ask. I didn't care. I was just glad she had if this turned out to be my grandfather. So I waited until a few weeks ago and then I wrote again. To see if she thought it would be all right if I came now."

"And she wrote back and said you should come?" David looked over at the young man. At least they knew now why Zella had been so on edge around Wes. It was a wonder she hadn't already dumped the problem in David's lap, but sometimes Zella thought she could handle and rearrange everybody's life for the better.

"No, she was pretty surprised when I showed up at her door." The boy smiled a little.

"I can imagine," David said.

"But since I'm on break until the second week of January, I thought now would be as good a time as any. I've seen pictures of him, you know. I was pretty sure I'd know him if I saw him. I never thought about anybody recognizing me even though Dad has always said I looked like his father." Robert Wesley shifted in his chair and looked uneasy as he pushed out his next question. "He's not in trouble, is he? My grandfather, I mean."

"Not that I know of. Why?" David peered over at him.

"Just something Miss Curtsinger asked in her letter. If the police had ever contacted us or anything."

"That's just Zella." David waved his hand in dismissal. "She likes things she can understand, and she's never been able to understand Wes."

"I guess maybe Dad's the same way. He didn't really want me to come. Said it wouldn't be our Wesley Green.

That I'd just end up disappointed. He's always said my grandfather had to be dead. That he wouldn't have stayed away so many years if he hadn't been dead."

"No, not dead in body. In spirit for a while, I think." David massaged his forehead, hoping it would help him think more clearly. He had no idea what Wes was going to think about this boy showing up to claim kinship. Would it make him run again the way he'd run so many years ago? "I suppose you know why he left."

"Right. The wreck where Dad's mother and sister were killed." He waited for David to say something, but David stayed quiet and after a moment the boy went on. "Dad said he and my grandfather both had a hard time accepting their deaths. That instead of leaning on one another, they drew apart to suffer alone. Of course Dad had just gotten married and he had Mom to help him. Still, he was surprised when my grandfather bought a motorcycle and rode off. That's the last he'd seen of him or heard anything about him until Miss Curtsinger's letter. That was over twenty years ago. How long has he been here in Hollyhill?"

"About ten years," David said. "I don't think he meant to stay, but the years just sort of piled up on him. He works for me putting out the local paper."

"I thought Miss Curtsinger said you were a preacher."

"I am. Preacher. Newspaper editor. General problem solver." David smiled. "Although I don't always do so good at that last one."

Robert Wesley didn't smile back. Instead he looked worried. "Do you think I'll be a problem for my grandfather? I mean I don't want to be a problem. I just want to meet him. To find out he's okay so I can tell my father. Dad said they didn't part on very good terms. Dad has never actually said so, but I know that's been eating away at him all these years."

"At your grandfather too, although he doesn't talk about the past. He's always told Jocie he fell out of a spaceship from Jupiter." David looked toward the kitchen where the wind was rattling the kitchen windows. He hadn't gotten around to replacing the putty in them again last summer.

Robert smiled. "Dad said his father was always a great storyteller. When I was a little boy, I made up an imaginary grandfather. We went for walks together. He told me stories. He listened when things went bad."

"It wasn't imaginary for my Jocie. The two of them have a special relationship."

"It sounds like my grandfather has a good life here, and I don't want to do anything to spoil that for him," the young man said. Then he looked sort of wistful as he went on. "But do you think there's any way me and my grandfather might still have a special relationship of our own?"

"I don't know, Robert. I guess that's up to you. And to Wes."

# 25

The next morning Tabitha was out of bed early, taking a shower, brushing her long honey-brown hair till it shone, searching for the green sweater that matched her eyes.

Jocie looked up at her from where she was changing Stephen Lee and said, "He didn't come here to find you, you know. He came to find Wes."

"Wes? What are you talking about?" Tabitha pulled the sweater over her head and yanked her hair free as she turned away from the old dresser mirror to look at Jocie.

"Robert. Robert Green probably. Wes's son, grandson, nephew, or something."

Tabitha frowned. "What makes you think that? Did you sneak out in the hall and eavesdrop on him and Daddy last night?"

"Nope. All you have to do is look at him."

"I looked at him," Tabitha said.

"Yeah." Jocie picked up Stephen Lee and kissed his cheeks before she said, "I guess your mommy must have been swooning too much to use her eyes."

"I wasn't swooning."

"Don't get me wrong." Jocie looked at Tabitha. "I don't care if you were swooning. He is sort of cute."

Tabitha came over to sit on the bed. Stephen Lee reached for her and she took him. She thought maybe that had been the best thing about Robert. He hadn't batted an eye when she'd said Stephen Lee was her baby. He'd still looked at her as though he thought she was pretty. But he might have thought she was married and her husband was just off in the army or somewhere. She'd have to find a way to tell him that wasn't the way it was. "And you think he looks like Wes?"

"He does look like Wes. Taller and lots younger and his hair doesn't stick out in every direction, but you could put pictures of their faces on top of one another and the eyes and mouth would be the same."

"You make that sound like a bad thing."

"I didn't mean to." Jocie stood up and went to the dresser to brush her own hair back away from her face. She didn't look at Tabitha in the mirror.

"Well, it doesn't make any difference to me who he came to find. He came and now maybe I can find him. You think he's awake already? He and Dad talked a long time last night."

"He's up."

"How do you know?"

"He and Dad went out awhile ago. To try to get his car out of the ditch. But the snow's drifted some."

"Have you been outside already?" Tabitha asked. Jocie had been dressed and gone from the room when Tabitha woke up that morning.

"Yeah. I went out real early. I wanted to see the snow before anybody messed it up so I could get some good pictures for the paper. Of course Zeb had already made footprints

195

all over. He must have some malamute or something in him the way he was jumping around and rolling in the snow. Maybe I could teach him to pull a sled."

"Not likely. That dog only does what he wants to do when he wants to do it."

"That's because he's so smart," Jocie said.

"Yeah, whatever." Tabitha carried Stephen Lee over to the window to peer out. Her room faced the back and she couldn't see the road from there, but she could see the snow. Lots of snow on the ground and some still swirling in the air even though the sun was shining in a bright blue sky. "You think they'll be back, don't you? I mean, they won't just head for town."

"Not without breakfast. Plus I doubt if anybody will be able to head for town until the snowplow comes out. And who knows when that will be? Dad took the shovel to dig out the worst drifts between here and Robert's car. Oh, and the phones are still out too."

"Thank goodness we have electricity," Tabitha said.

"Yeah, speaking of which, I'd better go down and make sure Aunt Love doesn't forget the biscuits. You want me to take Stephen Lee while you finish primping?" Jocie reached for the baby. "You know he probably thinks you're married."

"Then I'll just have to tell him I'm not."

"What are you going to tell him about Stephen Lee?" Jocie asked as she swung the baby up in the air and made him giggle.

"That I made a mistake."

"Stephen Lee isn't a mistake."

"No, but Jerome was."

"Maybe Robert is too. What if he's the one who's married instead of you?"

"Go, save the biscuits." Tabitha grabbed a pillow off the bed and threw it at Jocie.

Jocie laughed as she ran out of the bedroom. Tabitha could hear her singing to Stephen Lee all the way down the stairs. "To know, know, know him is to love, love, love him."

That's all Tabitha wanted. To get to know him. She wasn't going to fall in love that easy. She couldn't. She had responsibilities now. But it was fun to talk to a person of the opposite sex again. She was practically living a cloistered life in Hollyhill. There were boys, but none she was interested in. And none who seemed the least bit interested in her even if she had been interested in them. That was probably best until Stephen Lee got older. But still it wasn't half bad to feel that funny flip of her heart again when a boy looked at her. It meant she wasn't dead yet. She hadn't been too sure a few times in the last couple of months.

Jocie wanted to walk to town, but her father wouldn't let her. Said Wes hadn't known about Robert for twenty-one years and that a few more hours wouldn't matter. Of course her father didn't understand why she needed to talk to Wes. She didn't understand why she needed to talk to Wes.

Robert was a grandson. Jocie's father told them that at breakfast. He said Zella had tracked him down somehow after the tornado last summer, but she'd kept it a secret. Guess Wes would know now why Zella had been acting even weirder than usual the last few months.

Later Jocie's father pulled her aside. "It's not a bad thing. Robert Wesley showing up. Wes will be proud to have a grandson like him." But her father hadn't looked all that sure of what he was saying. He had looked sure when he'd told her that under no circumstances was she to walk to town and go see Wes until after he'd had a chance to talk to Wes himself.

So she had to wait. They all had to wait, trapped by the snow. Robert didn't seem to mind all that much. He was enjoying Tabitha making eyes at him. They'd already exchanged addresses. Tabitha must have found a way to tell him she was single and available.

Aunt Love and Jocie's father liked Robert too. And what was not to like? He smiled all the time and had polite cornered. And he was smart. Studying physics and science at a university up in Ohio. Even that was like Wes. The being interested in science and how things worked.

Jocie got her notebook out and tried to write down what was bothering her, but she didn't know how to put it into words. She ended up just writing what her father had told her. *Wes loves me. He may not really be my grandfather, but he loves me.* Then she put the notebook up and pulled her boots back on. She couldn't walk to town, but she could walk somewhere. If she didn't move or do something, the spiders crawling around inside her were going to eat her alive.

She wasn't outside even long enough to decide whether to walk back in the old apple orchard or down the road before Robert followed her out. Jocie was surprised Tabitha wasn't running after him.

"Hey, wait up," he called. "Do you mind if I walk with you?"

She did, but she couldn't very well say so. If only he'd really been from Jupiter instead of Pelphrey, Ohio. If only Zella had minded her own business. Jocie stood in the snow and scratched Zeb around the ears until Robert caught up with her. Then she led the way out to the tumbling down rock fence between the backyard and the old apple orchard. The rocks looked like marshmallow cushions.

Robert picked up a handful of snow and tried to make a snowball, but the snow was too fluffy. "How much do you think is on the ground?"

"Seven inches," Jocie said. "I measured earlier. It's drifted higher in places though. Do you get a lot of snow up where you live in Ohio?"

"Piles of it." He gave his handful of snow a fling. "But that's okay. I like snow. How about you? Do you like snow?"

"As long as it doesn't make us miss too much school. The buses won't run when there's snow and then we end up going to school into June. I hate going to school in the summer. But of course right now we're off for Christmas anyway." Jocie was rambling. She shut her mouth, stepped through the breach in the rock fence and looked up at the sky. It was extra blue. The Lord had known what he was doing when he made snow white and the sky such a vivid blue. *Great is the Lord and greatly to be praised.* Aunt Love was always quoting something like that out of Psalms. Jocie would have said it out loud if she'd been alone, but she wasn't alone.

They walked along without talking for a little ways. Jocie was thinking about claiming she was cold and suggesting they turn around when Robert said, "Your father told me you and my grandfather are real close."

Jocie wasn't sure what he wanted her to say to that, so she just nodded a little and kept walking. They were almost to the end of the apple orchard, but Mr. Crutcher didn't mind her walking in his pasture fields. Her dad walked there all the time when he was praying through something for a sermon or whatever.

Maybe she should be praying through something. She

just wasn't sure what. She wasn't sure why she had that spider crawly feeling inside and tears in her eyes that weren't there just because of the cold wind blowing in her face. Just because proof that Wes wasn't from Jupiter was walking beside her didn't mean Wes had to stop telling her Jupiter stories. And even if he did, so what? She was too old for Jupiter stories anyway.

"Tell me about him," Robert said.

"What about him?"

"I don't know. Tell me why you love him."

"Why do you want to know that?"

"So I can love him the way you do. Like a real grandson would."

It seemed only fair, so she told him about the spaceship from Jupiter. And about the motorcycle and how Wes talked to the press to keep it running. She told him about the tornado and the tree falling on Wes. She didn't tell him why they were out in the tornado. She figured that would just confuse things. Last she told him about Wes being baptized in the river even though it almost made his ears freeze and fall off. They both laughed about that.

By the time they walked back to the house, she'd passed some of her love for Wes over to Robert, but the funny thing was she didn't have a bit less inside her. Maybe love really was like a candle flame that kept burning just as brightly no matter how many other candles were lit from the flame.

The snowplow was coming down the hill when they went back inside.

# 26

The phone woke Leigh. She sat up in bed and looked at the clock. She blinked her eyes and looked again. It said eight thirty. She must have forgotten to set her alarm. And no wonder after the ordeal of visiting her parents and then the wild ride home in the snow. She had been exhausted.

The phone was still ringing. She got out of bed and ran for the kitchen in her bare feet. The cold wooden floor shocked the last of sleep out of her. Leigh dropped a dishtowel on the floor to stand on as she reached for the phone that was still jangling. It was no doubt Judy to check on why Leigh wasn't at work. Or maybe David letting her know his phone line was fixed. Or perhaps her mother to say she was sorry she hadn't acted happier about Leigh's engagement. That—her mother being happy—was about as likely as temperatures in the eighties today.

Leigh picked up the phone and said hello. No one was there. She said hello again. Still nothing. There must be trouble on her line now. She was about to hang up when she thought she heard something. She pushed the receiver up closer to her ear. It sounded like someone breathing on the other end of the line. "Hello. Is somebody there?"

No answer, but the breathing got louder. Definitely someone there. Edwin Hammond. Leigh took the receiver away from her ear and gently hung it back on the phone hook. Why did she think of Edwin Hammond every time something happened that made her uncomfortable? And why in the world would he call her up just to breathe in her ear? But then again, why would anybody?

The phone started ringing again almost at once. She stared at it a minute before she picked it up. "I want to know who this is right now," she said without even bothering with a hello.

"Whoa, Leigh! It's Judy. Judy Mitchell. What ever happened to hello, how are you?"

"Oh, I'm sorry, Judy. I just got a prank call and I thought he was calling back."

"What? Did he say something ugly to you?"

"No. Whoever it was didn't say anything. Just sat there breathing in my ear."

"Maybe it was a bad connection," Judy said. "There's a lot of snow out there. It's probably messing up some of the lines."

"I guess so. I think David's phone is out."

"Hey, I heard about the engagement. Congratulations. Or maybe I'm supposed to tell David congratulations and you best wishes. I never get that straight. He's not there, is he?" Judy's voice changed to a teasing tone. "Maybe that's why you're late to work."

"No, of course not. We got engaged, not married. Yet," Leigh said and felt a lift of her heart. If she hadn't been on the phone, she would have twirled across the kitchen floor in a happy dance. She made herself think about talking to

Judy again. "I'm sorry about being late, but I just woke up. I must have forgotten to set my alarm. Tell Ralph I'll be in as soon as I can get dressed."

"That's why I'm calling. To tell you Ralph said not to bother. We're both down here at the office, but the snow's practically up to your knees out there. Nobody's going to be coming into town this morning. If you want to, you can come in at lunch and I'll take the afternoon off."

"Sounds good. That'll give me time to hunt my snow boots."

"You'd better dress warm. That wind's whipping out there and it is cold with a capital C. I keep telling Ralph he needs to retire so we can go to Florida every year for the winter."

"You can't do that. I need my job," Leigh said.

"Now maybe, but who knows what will happen after you get married? I've heard being a preacher's wife can be a full-time job. Not to mention headache."

"I've got plenty of aspirins," Leigh said. "How in the world did you find out about it so soon? I was looking forward to springing the news on you myself when I came in."

"Are you kidding, kid? The news was all over Hollyhill before three o'clock yesterday afternoon even with a blizzard going on. We have a fine network of news that doesn't depend a bit on your future hubby-to-be's newspaper." Judy laughed. "And that's not the only news going around. You should hear what I heard last night at church."

"I don't know if I want to," Leigh said. "Is it good or bad?"

"More like wild and crazy," Judy said. "Have you talked to Zella today?"

"No, I told you I just got up. Why? Is something wrong

with her? Wasn't she at church?" Leigh had no trouble imagining Judy's face. Her eyes would be wide and she'd have that knowing smile. Judy loved being in the know on the latest gossip going around town.

"No. She asked Gertie to pick her up, but then when Gertie got there, Zella ran out in the snow to tell her she was sick. Didn't even put on a hat. Now can you imagine Zella out in the snow without something protecting her hairdo?"

"Not really," Leigh said. "But I don't know if I'd qualify that wild and crazy."

"You haven't heard everything yet. There was a strange car parked in front of her house. And that's not all." Judy paused to let a little silence gather on the line between them for the dramatic effect. "She had a man in the house. Gertie saw him through the window."

"Gertie's half blind."

"True, but Eldon Johnson who lives across the street isn't. He was outside clearing the snow off his walk when the man got there. Said he was young. Said he asked where Zella Curtsinger lived. Eldon saw the car's license plate. It was Ohio. Now who in the world does Zella know in Ohio? And then she lied to Gertie. Have you ever known Zella to just out and out lie?"

"She could have been sick even if she did have company." Leigh took up for Zella. "He was probably a long-lost relative come to visit."

"That's the story going around. A long-lost relative she never expected to show up in Hollyhill. Like a son she adopted out years ago after an indiscretion."

"An indiscretion? That's crazy," Leigh said. "We're talking about Zella."

"I told you it was wild and crazy, but sometimes wild

and crazy turns out to be true." Judy laughed. "I can't wait to see that ring." Then she hung up.

Leigh put the receiver back on the hook and stared at the phone. She forgot about her cold feet. Should she call Zella? But what was she going to say? *Oh, Zella, I heard you had a man in your house last night and the rumor's going around that it might be your son.* She couldn't say that over the phone. That would be something better said in person. That way when Zella fainted, Leigh would be there to catch her and fan her face.

Or maybe she should just tell David. He'd know what to do. That was one of the things she loved about David. He always knew what to do. Hadn't he been great with her parents the day before even though they'd been far from great?

"How do I love thee? Let me count the ways," Leigh said out loud and twirled happily around the kitchen and back down the hall toward her bedroom. She stopped at the front door and peered out to see how much snow was out there. Hers and David's footprints had been covered up, but a fresh set of prints traced a path up the steps to her door. Narrow, long footprints.

She unlocked her door and peered out almost as if expecting somebody to rise up out of the snow that covered her small stoop. Nothing there but the footprints. Coming up the steps and going down. And the wind was cold the way Judy had said. It was already sweeping away signs of some of the footprints. She was shutting the door when she noticed the tiny roll of paper tucked in her keyhole.

She took it out and slammed the door shut and locked it. Then she unrolled the paper. It was about the size of a playing card. The writing on it was very small, almost tiny, but each letter was perfectly formed in black ink.

Don't throw yourself away on a man without wings. I have wings that will let me soar. Your love will be the wind beneath my wings. So beautiful as you sleep.

Leigh looked at the door and then toward her bedroom. There was no way he could have seen her sleeping. No way. Still, she went to the bathroom and got a towel to drape over top the curtains that covered the window in the door. Then she went back to the bathroom and tore the note into pieces and dropped it into the commode. She watched to be sure every piece disappeared when she flushed the water down the drain.

That helped, but it didn't completely get rid of the vision of Edwin Hammond standing on her stoop, peeking through her window. She shook herself as she filled her teakettle. The man was an English teacher. He wasn't dangerous. He'd just read too many Shakespearian tragedies or whatever. And now he was playing some weird game. Well, she wasn't going to play.

Of course, who knew what Mrs. Simpson might have already told all her telephone friends about him coming to her door so early in the morning. There would be wild and crazy stories circulating about Leigh the way they were about Zella. Only in Hollyhill could anyone ever imagine a woman like Zella had a hidden past. The only things Zella had hidden were a couple of romance novels in her purse.

Still, there had been a strange man hunting for Zella's house the night before. Definitely something Leigh needed to know more about. She'd just walk on down to the *Banner* offices after breakfast and see what was going on. Besides, she'd promised to come by and let Zella see her ring. Could be David might make it through the snow and be at the

*Banner* by the time she got there. That would definitely be worth the walk.

First, just as soon as she got her shoes on, she'd go out and sweep the snow off the stoop outside her door and the steps. She didn't want even a trace left of Edwin Hammond's presence at her door.

## 27

Zella couldn't believe it when she got the first phone call Monday morning even before she left her house to walk to the *Banner*. A person missed church one night in the middle of a blizzard and let a poor boy come in out of that blizzard to keep him from freezing to death and everybody was talking. About her.

Or at least that was what Agnes had told her when she'd rung her up at seven o'clock. Zella hadn't even finished her oatmeal, and Agnes had talked so long she'd had to scrape the rest of it out into the trashcan. By then she'd lost her appetite anyway.

Agnes hadn't even been at church the night before either. Heavens no, she'd said. She couldn't go out in that kind of weather. But she'd talked to Josephine who had talked to Lenora who had talked to Gertie who of course had been there. And who obviously had spotted Robert Wesley Green Jr. standing in the middle of Zella's living room after all.

"It was just somebody needing directions," Zella had told Agnes when she asked about the boy.

"To your house is what they're saying," Agnes had yelled into the phone.

Zella pulled the receiver away from her ear. Agnes thought just because she was hard of hearing everybody else in the world was too. "So I could give him directions somewhere else," Zella said loudly.

"Oh," Agnes said. "Well, that's what I told Josephine. I told her there was bound to be some reasonable explanation and that there was no way on God's green earth he could be your son."

"My son?" Zella squawked. "Who told you that?"

"Eh, what did you say? I can't hear you. I must need a new battery in my hearing aid," Agnes said and hung up without so much as a goodbye.

"A new battery indeed," Zella muttered as she stared at the phone. What Agnes needed was a new brain. That had to be the most outlandish thing the woman had ever said, and she'd said some pretty outlandish things over the years. Zella had hung up the receiver and glared at it as if daring it to ring again. It hadn't.

But her glare didn't work on the phone at the *Banner* offices. It was ringing off the hook when she let herself in the door. Nobody was there. Not even Wesley. That was good. She hoped he wouldn't show up until after David did, and heaven knew when that would be the way the roads were sure to be drifted over out in the country.

Zella let the phone ring. It wasn't eight o'clock. She didn't have to answer it. And she just might not answer it even after eight o'clock. Not until she'd had time to think. Of all days for David to be snowed in. What if that boy hadn't made it through the snow out there? She had no way of knowing. David's phone must still be out because all she could get was a busy signal.

The phone on her desk started shrilling again. She looked at it as if she expected it to fly apart with each ring. It could be David, and she'd like to talk to David. But it could be one of her so-called friends who were passing around a story about that boy, Wesley's grandson, being her son. Her son!

That had to be the wildest, most preposterous story anybody had ever come up with in Hollyhill, and Zella had heard a few over the years. Some of them that turned out to be true. But not this one.

The only person who could come up with this crazy a story might be Wesley, and he didn't even know about Robert Wesley Jr. yet or at least Robert had said he didn't. And then, of course, there was Jocelyn. She knew about Robert if he'd made it to her house the night before. That girl could make up fiction quicker than anything. But she'd been snowed in with no telephone.

By ten o'clock when Leigh came in the *Banner* office, Zella still hadn't answered the phone. Wesley had navigated his steps in the snow and was back in the pressroom. When he had first come downstairs, he'd stuck his head through the pressroom door after the phone rang twenty or so times to see if there was a problem.

There was a problem, all right, but she hadn't told Wesley about it. She'd just looked at him and told him she'd decided to wait until David came in before she started answering the phone. That she didn't have time to write down a message from every person in Hollyhill reporting how deep the snow was in his or her front yard. Both things absolutely true.

"Suits me. Snow news is no news," Wesley had said and disappeared back into the pressroom. Sometimes Wesley could be too clever.

She'd started to yell at him there was news all right. That his past had caught up with him. At least some of his past. The law hadn't found him yet, but who knew? That might be next. If that happened, though, it was going to be because somebody else did some digging. Zella was through digging into other people's pasts. Even if it was for that person's own good.

The phone was ringing when Leigh came in red-cheeked and fairly exploding with her exciting engagement news. Leigh slipped her feet out of her snow boots and snatched off her left glove to hold her hand out for Zella to admire her ring. Zella jumped up and came around the desk to hug Leigh.

For a minute she almost forgot the ridiculous stories circulating Hollyhill. And maybe all the phone ringing didn't have the first thing to do with what Agnes had said. Maybe everybody had been calling to talk about David and Leigh. It could be she should have been answering the phone to make sure they all knew who should get the lion-sized share of the credit for that wonderful diamond on Leigh's finger. Without Zella prodding David to wake up and notice Leigh, this engagement would have never happened.

Leigh said they'd even already set a date. "The first weekend in June. Saturday probably. Don't you think a Saturday would be best?"

"Definitely. Afternoon. Four o'clock. The very best time for a wedding," Zella said. The diamond wasn't big, but it was a diamond. Behind them the phone kept ringing.

"Sounds good. Or maybe a little earlier if we decide to go somewhere for a honeymoon."

"Well, of course you'll go on a honeymoon. Somewhere exotic and romantic."

"I guess David and I will have to decide on that." Leigh

looked from Zella to the phone that kept ringing. "Aren't you going to get that?"

"No."

"Are you all right, Zella?" Leigh's smile was gone and she looked concerned.

Zella frowned at her. "You look like you may have been listening to gossip."

"Judy called to see why I wasn't at work. I overslept. She told me some man was at your house last night, but I told her there had to be a reasonable explanation."

"Well, certainly not the explanation Agnes Calhoun gave me this morning." Zella stomped back around her desk and sat down. "My son, indeed. A poor boy comes to my door to get directions and this is what happens. I just let him in because he was standing there in the snow without the proper coat or hat."

"Where did he need directions to?" Leigh perched in the customer's chair next to Zella's desk. She still looked concerned.

"David's, of course," Zella said. "I don't know if he made it out there. David's phone must be out."

"Why did he need directions to David's?"

"You don't have to look so worried. It doesn't have the first thing to do with you and David. He's not David's long-lost son any more than he's mine. Can you believe the kind of stories people will tell?"

"I was thinking more of maybe Stephen Lee's father."

"He wasn't black," Zella said matter-of-factly. The leaps some people made without the first bit of facts. She looked over her shoulder toward the pressroom and lowered her voice to a whisper. "He's Wesley's grandson."

# 28

Wes would have known the boy anywhere. Looking at him standing there in front of him was like looking in a mirror that could go back in time forty years. Back before his hair turned white and he started letting it sprangle out wherever it wanted. Back before his eyebrows grew in bushy and stiff. Back before the years of riding his motorcycle into the wind had wrinkled his face. The boy looked the way Wes still sometimes imagined he looked when there weren't any mirrors around to prove different.

But he didn't look angry. Wes had thought he might when David had come in the pressroom and told Wes about the boy after the snowplow had cleared the roads into town. David made the boy stay out in the front office with Zell and Jo while he talked to Wes. It was plain that David wasn't sure whether Wes would think he was bringing him good news or bad.

Wes wasn't sure himself. He hadn't ever expected his past to come hunting him. He'd sometimes thought about going back to see what kind of man Robert had become, but then he'd think he should leave things as they were.

Robert had been in his twenties with a new wife and the promise of the rest of his life in front of him when Wes left. He hadn't needed Wes to hold his hand. More to the point, Wes hadn't wanted his son to think he had to stop his life to hold Wes's hand.

Besides, Wes had had to run. He couldn't stand being in the house he and Rosa had lived and loved in. It was Rosa's house. Without Rosa it was a prison cell.

Then after he'd been on the road a few years, he felt like he'd been gone too long to go back. He wasn't the same man who'd left. They wouldn't know one another. They'd never really known one another as adults. Only as father and son.

He had loved his family. He had loved his son. Too much to stay around and be a reason for sorrow. It was himself he had hated. Himself he couldn't live with. That's why he'd gone on the road and invented a new Wesley Green. A man who could be from Jupiter.

And then there was Jo. Wes hadn't invented her. The Lord had dropped her into his path to walk beside him and hold his hand. To tug him back to a place on earth where he could let himself love again. Funny how the Lord worked.

Maybe the Lord was working in this. Maybe the Lord knew the time was right now for him to look straight into the face of his past. Wes would have liked to ask David that, but David went back out in the front offices and sent the boy back alone. Wes saw Jo peering through the press-room door as the boy came through it. She looked worried, and Wes wanted to step past the boy and assure her that Jupiterian love lasted through anything earth could throw at it. Sort of like old Paul wrote in Romans about how nothing—*not death, nor life, nor angels, nor principalities, nor powers, nor things present, nor things to come, nor height, nor depth, nor any other creature*—could separate a person from the love of God.

But the boy stepped through the door, and the door closed, leaving the two of them alone. He looked unsure of himself as he stood there staring at Wes without saying anything. Wes could imagine him groping through the words he'd practiced inside his head and coming up empty. What do you say when you come face-to-face with a man who has been the same as dead to you all your life?

Wes didn't help him out. He just waited for the boy to find words and wondered what he'd say back to him when he did. The boy wasn't going to be interested in any Jupiter stories. The silence built between them until it almost twanged like a guitar string stretched too tight.

"Are you really my grandfather?" the boy finally pushed out.

"From what David tells me, I'm thinking that might be the case," Wes said.

The boy's lips twitched as if he wanted to smile but then thought better of it. "My name is Robert Wesley Green Jr. I'm sorry for showing up like this without letting you know or anything but I've always wanted to meet you and ever since we got Miss Curtsinger's letter, I've been anxious to come. So I just did." Then the boy did smile. Not big and wide, but worried and hesitant.

So Zell was behind this. That was a bigger surprise than the boy showing up in front of him. But then again, she'd always been curious about his past. Had been sure for years that the authorities would show up to cart him away one day. It had probably been a letdown to her that nothing more potent than a grandson had shown up.

The boy was still standing there, waiting for Wes to say or do something, maybe throw open his arms and embrace him or else turn away from him. Wes thought he might ought to ask the Lord to give him the right thing to say, but the truth was, he hadn't gotten that good at praying yet. Not at asking for anything specific. He'd been working on it, but most of the time he just opened up the Scripture and read awhile before he sat quiet in his chair to let the Lord fill his head with whatever he wanted to be in there.

David had told him there wasn't any one set way to pray to the Lord. That the Lord heard all prayers, so maybe the Lord was hearing Wes now and he'd put the right words in Wes's mouth to say to this boy. The only thing Wes was sure of was the way his leg was paining him. "You mind if I sit down?" he asked the boy. "My leg's bothering me some today." Wes sank down in one of the chairs and propped his foot up on a handy box. "You can sit down too."

The boy turned one of the other chairs around and sat in front of Wes. "Jocie told me about you getting hurt in the tornado."

"She did?" For some reason that surprised Wes. He hadn't expected the boy and Jocie to have talked.

"We went for a walk in the snow this morning. She told me about how she'd claimed you for her granddaddy. I think she might have just pushed me over in a snowbank and left me there if I had said anything against that." The boy finally smiled big and full.

Wes smiled too. "That sounds like Jo. She's the reason I'm here. The reason I stopped running."

"But you didn't stop running from us. Why didn't you ever write and tell us where you were?" The boy's smile disappeared.

Wes looked down at his hands in his lap and then over at the press. "I don't know that I can give a good reason for that. It just seemed like once I rode off I couldn't ever go back. Not after what happened." Wes looked back at the boy. He deserved the truth. "Me being the reason your Grandmamma Rosa and your Aunt Lydia were gone and all."

"Dad says it was an accident."

"It was that, but a good many accidents can be prevented if a person is more careful."

"What happened?"

Wes looked back at the press. "I don't know. One minute I was driving down the road in a rainstorm. The next I woke up in an ambulance with my life blown to smithereens. The doctors said I hit my head and that I'd probably never remember exactly what happened."

"Then you don't know if you could have prevented whatever happened or not."

Wes didn't say anything for a minute. Some things couldn't be explained, and the way the tentacles of guilt had wrapped around Wes and strangled out his life was one of them. Finally Wes said, "How's your father?"

"Dad's good. He sold your house a couple of years after you left and used the money to go back to engineering school. Has a good job. Mom, she's a teacher. Third grade. I have a sister younger than me. Her name is Lydia Rose."

Wes felt the tears pushing against his eyes. "Is she pretty like her Aunt Lydia?"

"She's pretty, but she doesn't look much like Aunt Lydia's pictures. She looks like Mom. But Dad says she's like Aunt Lydia in a lot of ways. Smart, sweet tempered, but stubborn too. She just turned seventeen a couple of months ago." The boy reached into his pocket and pulled out his wallet. "I've got pictures. Do you want to see?"

Wes took the pictures the boy pulled out of his wallet. The girl had blonde hair and light blue eyes. Her smile showed perfect teeth and a glowing happiness. There was also a family picture, a few years old since the boy looked to be maybe sixteen in it. Robert was older. His face broader. His hair going gray at the temples. But Wes would have known him anywhere. His son. The son he'd rocked through the nights when he had the colic. The son he'd taught to fish and play baseball. The son he hadn't been able to share his grief with. The son he'd never stopped loving.

His hand shook a little as he tried to hand the pictures back.

"Keep them if you want," the boy said with a wave of his hand. "Mom can hunt up some more copies of them for me when I get home."

Wes stuck the pictures in his shirt pocket. They seemed to almost burn a hole through his shirt into his heart. Still, he couldn't tell this boy he'd go home with him. He was home. There wasn't any use beating around the bush about it. Best to get it out in the open. "Okay, you found me. So what do you want from me, Robert Jr.?"

The question seemed to throw the boy off. Like they'd gone from sweetness and light to the brass tacks of the matter too fast. For a minute it looked as if he might just run out of the room and clear back to Pelphrey, Ohio, but he pulled himself together and said, "I don't know." He stopped and looked puzzled. "I don't even know what to call you. Mr. Green? Grandfather? Wesley?"

"Wesley or Wes will do," Wes said. "I guess as how I haven't earned the name grandfather."

"What does Jocie call you?"

"Wes."

"Then that's what I'll call you too. Since we both claim you as grandfather. I think that's bothering her a little, thinking she might have to share you with me, but maybe she'll decide it's not so bad after she talks to you and sees that nothing's changed." He glanced over at the door and then back at Wes.

"Everything changes. Every day."

"Me being here, me finding you, won't change how you feel about Jocie, will it?" The boy leaned forward in his chair and looked almost like he might be holding his breath as he waited for Wes to answer him.

"No."

"So love doesn't change." The boy looked relieved.

"David out there would tell you God's love won't, but people aren't so divine with their love," Wes said softly as he stared over at Betsy Lou. No need in not being honest with the boy. He was young, but not too young to look straight at the truth. "Love down here on earth can get stronger or maybe weaker. Sometimes it can disappear."

"Did your love for us, for Dad, disappear?"

"No, but I wouldn't blame him if his love for me did." Wes looked back at Robert Jr. "Did he want you to come hunt me?"

"He was afraid it wouldn't be you. That I'd just be disappointed. That we'd all be disappointed. But before I left, he gave me gas money for the trip. And he told me that if it was you, to tell you he was sorry."

"Sorry for what?"

"I don't know. I asked him, but he wouldn't say. Said you'd know."

And Wes did know. He felt the same sorrow inside his chest. Sorrow for the years they'd lost. Sorrow for the way they'd turned away from one another instead of toward each other when they'd both already lost too much. Sorrow for the truth that there was no changing the past. "I can't go back," Wes said.

"Not even for a visit?"

"I don't know. I don't think so. Not yet," Wes said.

The boy was persistent. "All right, but can't we still talk? Get to know one another before I have to go back to school. Do you have a couch I can sleep on? It was sort of crowded out at Reverend Brooke's house."

"I know what you mean. I spent a few weeks there at Brooke Central Station after I got out of the hospital with my leg busted last summer." Wes smiled. "And I don't reckon I'm so coldhearted I'd send a boy back out on these snowy roads. You can stay a day or two, but I can't just sit around and talk. I've got to help David and Jo get the paper out. We're already a half day behind."

"Sure. Maybe I can help too."

"Do you know anything about presses?" Wes peered over at him.

"No, but I like fiddling with stuff, figuring out what makes them work. I'm studying physics and science at the university."

"You don't say. Well, Junior, we'd better open the door and let the others come on back so we can get to work," Wes said.

He stood up and went to open the door. Jocie must have been watching the door for the first sign of motion. She was bursting through into the pressroom before he could get the door pulled back. She wrapped her arms tight around his waist. "I don't care if you are his granddaddy. You were my granddaddy first."

It wasn't exactly true, but it was true enough.

# 29

*riday—January 1, 1965.* Jocie wrote the date at the top of the page in her notebook journal. Then she stared at the blank lines under it and didn't know where to start. Words were exploding in her head so fast that she wasn't sure she could pull them out one by one to put down on paper. So much had happened. Was happening.

She chewed on the end of her pen and looked around the living room. Not that much was actually happening right that moment. Aunt Love was napping in her chair. Tabitha was feeding Stephen Lee his bottle and making eyes at Robert who was talking to Wes and her father about some project he'd done for one of his classes last semester. Leigh was yawning behind her hand and pretending to listen.

Jocie wasn't even pretending. Robert was okay, but sometimes he went on and on about how smart he was. Jocie's dad had told her maybe Robert was trying to impress Wes and that they should cut him a little slack until they got to know him better.

Jocie was willing to do that. She'd gotten over being jealous of him. Had lost that even before Wes had told her that

Jupiter love was stronger than ten grizzly bears, stickier than bubble gum in hair, and had the staying power of a Jupiterian fropple.

When she'd laughed and asked what in the world a Jupiterian fropple was, he'd grinned at her and said, "Nothing in this world, for sure. A fropple is sort of like the frogs you have down here but some bigger with longer jumping legs. Fropples can hop all the way around Jupiter after eating two teeny little bugs. Never get tired. Never wear down. Never quit. Just keep hopping. Around and around."

"But why are they hopping around Jupiter?"

"Now that's something nobody knows. Mr. Jupiter, he's had the scientists up there working on it for years. They can't figure it out. Of course they did figure out that they could make rocket fuel from those little bugs. That's how come I'm here. Bug juice fuel."

Jocie almost giggled out loud thinking about bug juice fuel now as she looked across the room at Wes. He must have felt her eyes on him because he turned his head toward her and winked.

Jocie swallowed her giggle and started writing.

A new year. My fourteenth New Year's Day although I don't remember the first few any more than Stephen Lee will remember this one. But if he ever wants to he can read this and know what was happening on his very first New Year's Day.

We started the New Year out right this year. Invited everybody over. Aunt Love cooked black-eyed peas and cabbage. Yuck! But she says that if you eat those things on New Year's Day then you'll have good fortune all year. I ate hotdogs and applesauce. Everybody else ate the peas and cabbage. Tabitha even mashed up one of the black-eyed peas and fed it to Stephen Lee. He made this awful face and spit it out, so I guess both of us will just have to trust the Lord instead of lucky black-eyed peas for our good fortune this year.

Things have been sort of crazy around here ever since Christmas. Ever since Robert showed up anyway. Robert is Wes's grandson. Remember, I wrote about that last time. How no matter what Wes was still my granddaddy, and he is. But I don't mind him being Robert's too now. Robert has a sister. Lydia Rose. So I guess Wes is her granddaddy too. Robert says she's seventeen. Wes says he might go visit them next summer. Might. He says he needs some more time to think about it.

Dad told me a little about what happened and why Wes was here. It didn't have much to do with bug juice fuel, but I'm glad Wes still wants to tell me his crazy Jupiter stories. If he ever wants to tell me his Pelphrey, Ohio, stories, I'll listen to them too. Maybe we can cry together about them the way we laugh together about the Jupiter ones.

The craziest thing about all this is Zella. Right. Zella! You won't believe the stories that went around town after Robert showed up in the blizzard at her door. Well, it wasn't really a blizzard, but it was a lot of snow. So much that a lot of it is still hanging around. Not enough to keep us from going to school Monday though, unless some new snow starts falling. I'm hoping. That way I won't have to see the teacher from Neptune.

I don't know how I'm going to survive five more months in his class. He's scary weird. Plain and simple. I spotted him hanging around Leigh's place the other day. Just standing out in the snow leaning against a tree staring across the street at one of her windows. It gave me that funky spider crawly feeling. Like I needed to do something. But what? Go over and ask him what the heck he was doing or run back downtown and tell Dad or go on up to Leigh's and tell her to call the police. I wish somebody would arrest him and send him back to Neptune or wherever he came from.

It's no telling what he'll do to me next semester now that he's chasing after Leigh. I don't know what his problem is. He can't catch her no matter how many roses he sends. She's already been caught. By Dad. She has a ring to prove it.

Anyway the creep gave me a look and melted away down the street. Did you like that one? Melted away. Like the snow. I love it when the right words pop up in my head.

But where was I? Oh yeah, creepy teacher spying on Leigh. So after he starts off down the street, I go on in and tell Leigh he was out there. She shivered like somebody had walked over her grave. She tried not to look worried, but she was. And she tried to make excuses for him. Like maybe he was just walking by. Or maybe he was thinking about writing a poem about the snow. She said I had enough trouble with Mr. Teacher Creep from Neptune without hunting more so I should just forget about him. Gladly.

But back to Zella. It's hilarious. She hunts up where Wes is from. She hasn't admitted how yet, but I think she had to have poked around in some of his stuff. Anyway she found out and wrote to them in Pelphrey, Ohio. But she says she never told them to come. Robert just did. Showed up on her doorstep last Sunday night. People saw him on her doorstep and in her living room and bingo! They decided he must be some long-lost relative showing up. Like a son. Zella went almost apoplectic when she heard that. (I just had that word—apoplectic—in my ten-new-words-per-day vocabulary book, and it actually fits. I think.)

Anyway then the stories got even crazier when the news got out about how much Robert looks like Wes. Suddenly everybody was sure they'd figured out why Wes had shown up here years ago. Folks were saying Wes and Zella had a history together. That Robert maybe was their son. Zella's talking about going to visit her cousin in Florida until the stories quit circulating. I think it serves her right—always messing in other people's business.

Still, I almost felt sorry for her last week. She about jumped out of her skin every time the phone rang because she was afraid it was going to be one of her friends ready and eager to fill her in on whatever new version of the story was going around Hollyhill. To let her know for her own good, of course. I even answered the phone

224

one day for her. Told everybody Zella was too busy to talk if it was somebody that wasn't calling for business reasons.

I mean apoplectic didn't even come close to it when she heard that story about her and Wes. She was ready for Dad to run a three-inch headline saying Robert was not related to her in any way. Dad told her that would just make things worse. That the only way to deal with gossip was to tell her friends the truth or as much of the truth as she wanted told and then just ride it out. She said she supposed he should know since he'd had to ride out a few gossipy stories after my mother left town when I was a little kid.

Tabitha hasn't heard from our mother, from DeeDee, even though she's sent her pictures of Stephen Lee. It bothers Tabitha. She says it doesn't but it does. At least it did before Robert came knocking on the door. Now she's so gaga over him that she hasn't got time to think about anything else. Except of course Stephen Lee and she never forgets him. She's a good mother. Stephen Lee's lucky in that.

Tabitha still worries about him having chocolate-colored skin, but I never even think about it anymore. He's just cute and adorable Stephen Lee, and I'd fight bears for him if I had to. We all would. Dad tells her some of the same things he told Zella. That we'll just have to ride out whatever people say. That the Lord sends guardian angels to watch over little babies like Stephen Lee. And over big people too. People like me. My poor guardian angel got a real workout last year. I'm hoping all that kind of stuff is over. Tornadoes. Fires. I mean, what else could happen?

I know what you're thinking. Weddings. But that won't be anywhere close to tragic. Just different. Very different. Having a stepmom, I mean. Still it's six months before the wedding, so I've got time to get used to the idea. Leigh wants to be a June bride, and she wants me to help her pick out her dress. Says she knows I won't lie to her, and that if a dress makes her look fat that I'll tell her straight out. And I would, but she's lost so much weight that I don't think any dress could make her look fat. She's not exactly skinny like me, but then who would want to be skinny like me? Nobody, that's who.

225

Not even me. I haven't started stuffing toilet paper in my bra yet, but I've considered it. But knowing the way things go for me, I figure it would just fall out and then I'd look like a real nut trailing toilet paper everywhere.

Gee, I'm getting writer's cramp and no wonder. So guess I'd better wind this up for now before my fingers give out. I just wanted to count my blessings for 1964. I mean I know I sort of did that when I wrote on Christmas Day, but nobody can count blessings too often. So here goes. Surviving the tornado and the fire. Wes walking and riding his motorcycle again. Tabitha coming home. Stephen Lee. Aunt Love smiling more. Zeb. Wes being baptized and not freezing his ears off. And of course, Dad. Always Dad. The Lord knew what I needed when he gave me to Dad.

I don't know what 1965 will bring. A wedding and a stepmother for starters, I suppose. But who knows what else? I would have never guessed what 1964 was going to bring back last January 1. Aunt Love says it's mostly better not to know what's going to happen before it happens. That we just need to lean on the Lord for strength to get us through whatever comes. But Dad says it's okay to pray about it, to ask the Lord to bless us and keep us from hard trials. So that's what I'm trying to do. Praise the Lord for my blessings and ask him to help me do the things I should do and not do the things I shouldn't do in 1965.

I'll write again soon. They're getting out the Scrabble board and I know I can beat them all, even brilliant Robert, if we don't let Wes use Jupiterian words. Maybe I'll get the letters to spell out "apoplectic." Nope, that won't work. Too many letters. But there's always the chance for "quiz" on a triple letter score.

Jocie smiled as she closed her notebook and stuck her pen down in the wire coil. 1965 lay out in front of her ready and waiting.

# 30

Adrienne sat in her usual spot in the doctor's waiting room. It was anybody's chair, really. First come, first served. But nobody else wanted it this morning in front of the window with the sun streaming through. The April sunshine was warm. Nearly hot now.

She needed the sunshine on her back. Not just for the warmth although that too was good. Ever since the surgery, she stayed chilled. But even more she needed the light. She could feel the darkness reaching for her, so she clung to the light, gathered it around her the way an old woman might pull a shawl close against the chill.

An old woman. That's how she felt. Old. Each time she came into this office they drained more of her life away. They'd taken her breast. They'd hollowed out the muscles under her arm. They'd said it was her only hope. To take it all. To turn her into an invalid, a sorry shadow of the woman she'd been. Her skin had gone pale and translucent like fine bone china. She'd let Francine chop her hair off short since her arm was still so weak. It was devilishly hard to style hair with one hand. Her eyes that once could fasten on any man and get an appreciative look in return had lost their flash and were circled by dark shadows.

She didn't look in mirrors anymore. She'd gotten rid of every mirror in the apartment except the one above the bathroom sink. She only used it to make sure her hair wasn't sticking up in odd angles or to put on her makeup. She didn't know why she bothered. The makeup couldn't cover the truth that the surgery had given age the chance to catch up with her and even tack on extra years. But the lipstick and makeup made it easier for other people to look at her. It didn't hide the truth, but it let people pretend it did.

So she stayed away from mirrors, but every now and again she wouldn't look away fast enough and would catch her reflection in a window or in one of the mirrors at Francine's house. And then she'd wonder who that person reflecting back at her could be. Certainly not her. Not Adrienne Mason. She'd been a lot of things in her life, but she'd never been ugly.

Of course, what was it her mother used to tell her back when she was a teenager? That there were all kinds of ways of being ugly. And beauty was only skin deep. Adrienne had told her that was the reason a girl needed to take such good care of her skin. That good looks took a girl places, and Adrienne intended to go places.

Eventually she'd figured out it took more than looks. It took nerve too. Nerve to just get in the car and drive away from her old life to find a new life. That nerve had carried her all the way to California. But now her looks were gone and her nerve seemed to be leaking out of all those holes they had punched in her when she had let them cut off her breast.

Francine lied to her and told her she didn't look that bad. Dear Francine. She'd sat with Adrienne in the hospital after the surgery, cried for her when the bandages had come off and revealed the hideous scar on her chest, pushed her to do the arm exercises, even slipped her part of her tip money to help Adrienne pay her rent.

The last couple of weeks Francine's husband had started giving her grief. Said she might as well move in with Adrienne since she was over at her apartment so much. He hadn't had much use for Adrienne ever since she told him to take a hike when he'd hit on her at that party for Francine's thirty-fifth birthday last year. He was a bona fide bum, but even so, Francine loved the bozo. Adrienne didn't want her cancer to be the reason he split.

Bad enough that it had made Eddie split. She'd known it would happen. From the moment the doctor had said the C-word, she'd known it was just a matter of time. Eddie had actually stuck with her longer than she'd thought he would. Hadn't left until after the surgery. After they'd mutilated her, smiling all the while and telling her that with a properly fitted prosthesis, she'd be good as new. Once it healed. Once she could lift her hand back over her head. Once she stopped worrying about the way the scar on her chest looked. Once she regained her appetite for food. Good as new.

Eddie couldn't wait till then. He had good as new, better than new, hitting on him at the club every night. He didn't have to come home to a one-breasted old woman who could barely summon a smile most days.

Francine said Adrienne should say good riddance, that Eddie couldn't have loved her very much to desert her at a time like this. And of course Francine was right. Eddie hadn't loved her very much. Eddie didn't love the pretty young thing he was with now. Eddie loved Eddie. Adri-

229

enne knew that. Had always known that. The trouble was, Adrienne also loved Eddie.

Who could explain love? She sometimes thought about that in the middle of the night when her arm was aching and she couldn't sleep. David had claimed to love her all those years ago, but he'd loved his God more. She'd met many men who had claimed to love her since then. Maybe some of them had. She'd pretended to love some of them back, but until Eddie, it had just been a game she'd played.

Love. Eddie had changed her. Love had changed her. Made her willing to forgive the unforgivable. Made her forget her pride. Pierced the hard shell that had made her invulnerable over so many years. And even while she was hurting, while her heart was breaking, she wasn't sorry she had loved Eddie. Still loved Eddie.

Love was a mystery. Unexplainable. Unreasonable. Made no sense. There could be no sensible reason to explain why she loved a baby clear across the country she'd never even seen except in pictures. She hadn't properly loved his mother. Yet she loved that little baby in the pictures.

In the night when the darkness threatened to overtake her in spite of the lamps she left burning all the time, she would hold a picture of Tabitha's baby and stare at his little round face until it seemed to almost lift off the photo and come alive. He was getting bigger, but his eyes hadn't changed. They were her eyes peering up at her. It didn't matter that the color wasn't the same. The eyes were. She recognized them. She'd stare at the picture until she dozed off or the darkness gave way to the morning sun.

"Adrienne Brooke." The nurse held open the swinging door with her plump shoulder while she waited for Adrienne to stand up and venture forward. They hadn't changed the name on her file even though Adrienne had told them she didn't use the name Brooke. They'd said it would be too confusing to have a different name on her insurance card and her file. Now Adrienne was glad they hadn't. She could turn into someone else while she was in the doctor's office. Someone who had very little to do with the real Adrienne Mason.

She didn't bother ignoring the first call of her name as she'd been wont to do when she first started coming to this doctor's office. Still, as she stood up she left the sunshine with reluctance. She wished she could gather handfuls of it to stuff in her pockets to carry back into the sterile room awaiting her beyond the swinging door.

The nurse's name was Candace. She was married, had two little boys, Joshua and John. Good Bible names. She sometimes showed Adrienne pictures and laughed about the naughty things they did. The little boys had big smiles and shining eyes full of mischief, and once or twice, Adrienne had considered bringing one of the pictures of Stephen to show the nurse. Trading cute for cute. But she hadn't. She might have to explain how she'd never actually seen Stephen. How she might never see him.

Candace chatted cheerfully about the weather as she led the way down the hall past closed doors with other thick files in clear bins on the doors. She stopped beside the scales. "Let's see how your weight's doing. You should be rebounding after the surgery by now." The nurse waited for Adrienne to step up on the scales.

Adrienne shoved her hands hard into her pockets as if that would help the pointer go up higher. Barely over a hundred. Fashionably thin. That starving look that was so popular with models.

Candace made a tsking noise with her tongue as she wrote down the number on Adrienne's chart. "You've lost two more pounds. You have to eat, Adrienne. Your body can't fight without fuel."

"I haven't had an appetite." She didn't know why she bothered making excuses to the nurse. She'd have to say it all again for the doctor. Dr. Mike. She knew his last name. Rollingsworth. But he said she should call him Dr. Mike. That they were in this fight together and so should be on a first-name basis while they were battling the enemy.

Today he was supposed to tell her which side was winning. They'd done blood tests, every kind of test to tell if carving her left side down to her rib bones had done the job and gotten the cancer before it had a chance to escape to another place in her body.

A radical mastectomy. Radical. She used to imagine being radical while she was back in Hollyhill. Radically different. Radically wild. The word had seemed exotic and desirable then. Not now. Not when paired with mastectomy.

Candace went away to fetch another patient and left Adrienne sitting on the examining table in the paper gown. White, of course, just like the rest of the room. Once she'd hit her shoe against the wall to make a scuff mark just because she couldn't stand the unending white. The next time she was in that room, the mark had been cleaned off the wall or painted over.

Adrienne shivered. She was cold to her roots. If only she had that sunshine in her pockets to warm her as she waited for Dr. Mike's news. She yearned for good news. The yearning was like a bubble inside her growing bigger with each breath until it was pushing so hard against her heart that she knew something was bound to burst. Either her heart or the bubble.

Dr. Mike was smiling when he came in the room, but it wasn't the right smile. She'd come to know him too well in the months since Christmas. He was still good-looking. Vibrantly young. Seeming to get younger every week while she was aging years.

"And so, Adrienne, how have you been feeling this week?" He took a quick look down at her chart. "You'd been having trouble with nausea. Perhaps stress related. Is the nausea better?"

She looked at him and wanted to ask how nausea could be better, but he wouldn't understand, and it did no good for her to pretend she didn't know what he meant. "Not yet," she said. If she'd had anything in her stomach, she could have emptied it out on his pristine white doctor's coat to prove it.

"It will be," he said as if he could control the universe and her stomach. He sat down on the stool with rollers and stared down at her chart. "The weight's still going down, I see."

"Heck of a diet plan you guys have," she said.

"It's good you can still crack a joke." He smiled, but it was a small smile, an almost sad smile.

She tried to hold on to her smile in return, but it drained away when the bubble burst inside her. The truth was in his eyes.

"So we didn't beat it?" She didn't know why she said "we." She was the one who was still harboring a killer inside her. Not him.

He stood up and adjusted his stethoscope. "Let's do the examination first. Then we'll talk."

As if it mattered whether she had her shirt on when he told her she was going to die. She let him poke and prod on her and took the deep breaths he ordered as he listened to her heart rattling around loosely in her chest now that the bubble of hope had burst inside her.

Later she let herself into her apartment. First, the same as every time she came in the door, her eyes went to the spot on the wall where Eddie's guitar had hung as if she expected the guitar to be back. The nail was still there in the wall. Still as empty as she felt inside.

She flicked on every light and lamp in the apartment on her way to the kitchen. Francine had been there, brought her some soup before she went to work at the restaurant. She'd left a note on top of a stack of mail on the table.

> Hope the doc visit went OK. Chicken soup in pan on the stove. EAT some of it. Carried your mail in for you. Remember, I'm here if you need anything. Anything. F.

She needed something all right. Another twenty years. Dr. Mike hadn't promised her another twenty months. He hadn't promised anything even when, sitting there with her fake breast poking out her shirt properly, she'd pushed him. "How long?"

"That's impossible to say," he'd said, no longer avoiding her eyes. She wouldn't have been surprised if he had reached over and taken her hand. No doubt delivering unwanted news was something he had to do often in those cold, sterile rooms. The fact was, most women died of breast cancer when it was as advanced as hers had been. He'd told her that early on when he'd talked her into letting him hack off her breast as her only hope of survival. Perhaps it would have been better to die as a whole woman.

He kept looking straight at her as he went on. "Every case is different. Sometimes even when the surgery doesn't eradicate the cancer, it still goes into remission for a while."

"Miracles happen," she said. She hadn't expected him

234

to take her seriously. She entertained no illusions about miracles.

But he had looked relieved that she might think a miracle was possible. "They do," he said. "Every day. As a doctor I'm constantly seeing things I can't explain. That no one could explain."

"I'll bet you do," she said. "But I shouldn't count on it, right? So how long?"

He'd never really given her a time. Just told her that if there was anything she wanted to do, that she should consider doing it soon. Just in case the miracle didn't come through, Adrienne supposed. Then he'd said she would need someone to help her in the latter stages. And did she have anyone she could depend on?

Adrienne looked through the mail. Advertisements for things she couldn't buy. Bills she couldn't pay. A get-well card with a verse she didn't even bother to read from that silly little waitress they'd hired on down at the restaurant a few weeks ago. A letter from her mother in Florida. Then there was what she'd been looking for. Tabitha's handwriting on an envelope.

Adrienne still hadn't written Tabitha back, but the girl had always been persistent to a fault. She'd sent at least one picture every month even as the notes along with the pictures had gotten shorter and shorter. Tabitha had only scribbled a few lines with this one.

Hope you are well. Thought you might like seeing how Stephen Lee is growing. He's crawling everywhere now. I'm doing fine. Tell Eddie hi. Love, Tabitha.

Adrienne stared at the photograph. Tabitha must have gotten down on the floor to snap the picture of the baby crawling toward her. His eyes looked determined as if he already knew that whatever he wanted in life he was going to have to get on his own. His eyes that were so like hers even if they were brown instead of green.

*If there's anything you want to do.* The doctor's words echoed in Adrienne's head as she stared at the baby who seemed to be trying to crawl out of the picture right into her arms. She lifted her left arm until the pain stopped her and wondered if she'd be able to hold him if he did magically appear in front of her.

## 31

*T hursday, April 8, 1965. I can't believe spring break is almost over. I'm ready for school to be over. Two more months. I surely can survive that. I survived January and February and March. That was three months.*

Jocie was sitting in Leigh's car in the parking lot waiting for Leigh to get off at lunch. Leigh had taken the afternoon off so Jocie could go with her to Lexington to shop for a wedding dress. Leigh was nearly in panic mode. The wedding was less than two months away and she didn't have her dress.

They'd dabbled at shopping a couple of Saturdays in February, but Leigh hadn't found anything she liked. She hadn't been worried. She had plenty of time. Weeks and weeks before June. March had passed with no time for shopping. Leigh said everybody and his brother in Hollyhill put off getting his or her new license plates until the last minute and then showed up at the courthouse and groused about standing in line. Leigh couldn't take off work until after that madness was over. Besides, she said she figured she might lose another pound or two.

Jocie's dad kept telling Leigh not to worry about losing any more weight, that she looked perfect the way she was, and she did look pretty. Glowing all the time. Like she was walking around on air. Zella said that was the way brides-to-be were supposed to look. But Zella did think it was high time Leigh had her dress. That a person shouldn't procrastinate about something that important.

Leigh hadn't exactly been procrastinating. She just couldn't find the right dress. The perfect dress. When Jocie asked her what the perfect dress looked like, Leigh couldn't tell her. Just said she'd know when she saw it.

Jocie checked her watch and rolled the car window down. It was warm with the sunshine coming through the windows. Leigh had told her she might be late getting off at lunch, but Jocie didn't mind waiting. She liked having time to write in her journal.

I'm going with Leigh shopping again. I told her maybe she should take Tabitha and let me stay home with Stephen Lee, but then Tabitha started working at the Family Diner Thursdays, Fridays, and Saturdays. Aunt Love has Stephen Lee for about an hour before I get home from school and she still takes care of him even after I'm there. But it makes Tabitha feel better with both of us around. She worries about Aunt Love leaving the door open or forgetting something on the stove and catching the house on fire or letting Stephen Lee climb up the stairs. Of course when it comes to Stephen Lee, Tabitha worries about everything. She goes a little nuts every time he pulls on his ear with an earache or falls down and bumps his head.

I think she's going overboard. Half the time when Stephen Lee bumps his head he doesn't even cry. He's a tough little rascal. You can look him in the eye and tell that. He's more likely to cry because he's mad than because he's hurt. But you should see the list of what me and Aunt Love have to watch out for that she leaves us every day. Aunt Love just laughs about it. And I don't think Tabitha has to worry for a minute about Aunt Love forgetting to take care of Stephen Lee. He's in there in her brain along with all those Bible verses she's always throwing out at me.

I've got so I don't mind her Bible verses that much. "Great is the Lord, and greatly to be praised." Psalm 48:1. She says that one nearly every morning now when I go in the kitchen for breakfast. I'm back out sleeping on the porch again. I love it out there where I can see the stars through the windows and Zeb can sleep on the floor beside me. Anyway how could anybody be upset by a verse like that? Great is the Lord. I mean a person ought to be ready to shout that one out whenever. Off the rooftops or wherever. Dad just preached about that—getting up on the roof to tell the good news of the Lord. That's in the Bible somewhere.

Aunt Love doesn't shout out her verses much anymore. Most of the time she's singing the Psalms to Stephen Lee these days instead of using them to try to control my unruly behavior. Maybe I'm just growing up and getting less unruly. Wes says it happens to the best of us. Just look at him and how he's been earthed and goes to church every Sunday now. That he's just getting rulier and rulier. When I asked him what rulier meant he said he guessed it was the opposite of unrulier and meant a body noticed there was a rule here and there that might make sense.

He and Robert have been writing some. Not as much as Robert and Tabitha. Those two keep the mailman busy. Tabitha has a whole stack of Robert's letters hidden away in her dresser drawer. Says if she catches me trying to read them she'll tear all the pages out of my journal notebooks and mail them to Zella. I don't know why she thinks I care if Zella reads what's in my notebooks. There's nothing secret here. Not secret like those letters. I think they're in love.

Everybody's in love, I guess. Believe it or not, Paulette and Ronnie are still going strong. And Charissa is still swooning over Noah every time she sees him or thinks about him. Noah hasn't asked her out yet, which I tell Charissa is just as well since there's no way her daddy is going to let her go on a date. Not till she's sixteen and we've got two years to wait for that. Of course I couldn't care less about going on a date with anybody. I guess I still have a problem with arrested development.

Charissa tells me if I'd spend half as much time thinking about boys as I do worrying about what Mr. Teacher Creep is going to do next, I'd be better off. And more normal. She starts rolling her eyes if I so much as say the first word about Mr. Creep. That's one reason I have to write it all down in here. I mean she knows he's a creep and that he does pick on me, but she says so what? That happens to a lot of kids in school when they get on the wrong side of this teacher or that. That black kids like her have that problem all the time just because they don't have white skin and they just have to learn to get along with it.

Thank goodness I can still talk to Wes about it. I don't talk about it to Dad because of the weirdness with Mr. Creep still chasing after Leigh as if he didn't know she was engaged. He sent her more roses that ended up at the nursing home again on Valentine's Day and wrote her a poem. I saw it. It stunk. Didn't make the first bit of sense. Then just last Friday before spring break he even tried to get me to carry a note to her. Can you believe that? You should have seen the look on his face when I told him they still sold stamps at the Post Office. I'll have to pay for that one when we go back next Monday.

The man is weird. Definitely weird. Me and Wes are pretty much in agreement on that. Still, I have to go to English class. Mr. Madison told me I did. Yeah, I actually asked. I mean, you've got to know how bad things are if I went to the principal's office. Students don't voluntarily go to the principal's office.

But when I got my last theme back and Mr. Teacher Creep had marked a big red F on it, I'd had enough. I went right up and asked him about it, and he sort of laughed and said I should have picked a better subject. That nobody could write a proper paper about dogs. I reminded him he'd said we could write about anything we wanted, and he said that didn't mean he had to approve of whatever we decided to write about. But Joe Masterson wrote about horses and he got a B. I saw his paper. Had red marks all over it where he'd misspelled this or that word. Probably misspelled horse. Then Mr. Creep had written "Good Effort" on top of it. My paper didn't have a red mark on it. Not one. Except, of course, the big F. That was because there weren't any mistakes. Not one. And what I'd written was interesting too. I might get Dad to run it in the *Banner* if we have some space to fill. Dogs have universal appeal. Except I suppose with Mr. Creep. Maybe they don't have dogs on Neptune.

Anyway I didn't give myself time to think. I marched right down to Mr. Madison's office and sat down in a chair and refused to move until Miss Gilbert let me in to see him. I was so mad. I mean I plan to go to college someday and how's it going to look if I get an F in freshman English? Bad, that's how. And I'll need scholarships. A person has to get A's to get scholarships.

Anyway once Miss Gilbert saw I meant business and let me go talk to Mr. Madison, I showed him the paper and told him how I'd tried to talk to Mr. Creep about the grade he'd given me, but that he'd just laughed at me. Well, I didn't say Mr. Creep, but I wanted to. I told Mr. Madison how I was trying to be a perfect student in that class. On time, quiet, homework turned in, every answer on the tests right. I told him how Mr. Creep kept making me stand in front of the class and do humiliating things like hop on one foot while repeating whatever stupid poem he told me to and how once he'd hit me on the back of the head with a book.

But I didn't tell him everything. I didn't tell him how Mr. Creep keeps lurking around Leigh's apartment and calling her. I didn't tell him how Mr. Creep makes fun of the stories in the *Banner*. I didn't tell him how I have to go to my locker and stick my head inside it nearly every day after English class so nobody will see me crying. I didn't tell him how I prayed every day to be invisible when I went in there. I've even been desperate enough to pray for Mr. Creep a few times. And no, I don't pray that he'd fall in a hole and break both his legs. I just wish that sometimes.

Well, you know how it is with teachers. They form a solid wall in front of you no matter what they actually think. So Mr. Madison said I couldn't switch out of that class because Mr. Creep is the only freshman English teacher. He kept my paper and suggested I send my dad in to talk to him about my problems. My problems? What about somebody talking to Mr. Creep? He's the one with problems.

So now I have to talk to Dad about talking to Mr. Madison. And I'll have to tell him some of what's been going on and he'll get that look on his face like he'd rather not include Mr. Creep in his prayers either. I've been putting it off, but I'll have to do it before Monday. Maybe Sunday night after church. Dad will be too tired to go rushing out of the house to throttle Mr. Creep then. Or maybe I can get by with talking to Wes and letting him go talk to Mr. Madison. That ought to be interesting. Wes could share his Jupiterian theory that no one from Neptune should ever be a teacher. Or for that matter, even allowed on earth. I like the way Jupiterians think.

"What are you writing about that's got you smiling?" Leigh asked as she opened the car door and slid under the wheel.

"Oh, nothing much," Jocie said and shut her notebook. "Just silly stuff."

"That's the best kind of stuff to write in a journal." Leigh stuck the key in the ignition and turned it. "You ready to go find that dress?"

"Sure."

"We're going to do it today. We have to do it today. How's that for pressure?"

"You don't have to have a fancy dress to get married. Sometimes people tie the knot in whatever they happen to have on. Don't even dress up a bit."

"I know. I see them at the courthouse when they get Uncle Howie to marry them since he's the judge and all. He comes and grabs me to be one of the witnesses if they don't bring someone with them. But I've been waiting a long time for this, and I want everything to be perfect. I mean, I already have the perfect groom. It's not too much to want the perfect dress too, is it?"

"I don't know. But I'll say a wedding-dress prayer for you if you want me to. Dad says it's okay to pray about everything." Jocie looked down at her journal and thought maybe she should be praying more about what to do about Mr. Creep instead of just griping all the time.

"It couldn't hurt. I've been praying about lots of things about the wedding. About being married. Like please let my new stepdaughters like me." Leigh looked over at Jocie as she pulled out of the parking lot.

"You don't have to pray that one. We already like you, and nothing will be all that different even after you're officially our stepmom. That is, unless you want us to start calling you mom or something."

"You can call me whatever you want. But for sure, I'd be proud to be your mom." Leigh reached over to touch Jocie's hand.

"Gee, that's so nice you're liable to make me cry or something, Leigh. Thanks. I guess that's more than DeeDee ever was. She wasn't too happy when I came along."

"Her loss." Leigh's voice changed a little, got carefully casual. "Does she know your father is getting remarried?" She kept her eyes on the road.

"I don't know. Tabitha writes her sometimes, sends her pictures of Stephen Lee, but I don't know what she tells her about what's going on here. She might have told her, but DeeDee never writes back. So who knows? She might have moved and not even be getting Tabitha's letters." Jocie studied Leigh's profile a moment before she asked, "You aren't worried about her, are you?"

"No, no, of course not. I was just curious, I guess. The

first wife and all, you know." Leigh glanced over at Jocie. Leigh's face was a little red, but that could have been because of the sun shining through the car windows.

"I used to be curious about her too. But then I found out she never wanted me, and so I don't worry that much about her anymore. The Lord gave me Dad and Wes and I'm happy."

"Me too. I'm happy, I mean," Leigh said. "I have to be the luckiest girl in the world or will be just as soon as we find that perfect dress today."

They went to three different shops. Leigh tried on dozens of dresses. Some of them were really pretty. All very white. Some had long flowing trains. A lot of them had puffy sleeves that did make Leigh look a little top heavy. Others had high tight necks that Leigh yanked on so she could breathe. The fluffy chiffon skirts over the satin underskirts just weren't Leigh's style. A few times Leigh stood in front of the mirror and considered a bit longer on this or that dress, but she always ended up shaking her head. None of them were perfect.

They started for home, leaving behind them a trail of chiffon and satin and lace for the frustrated salesladies to put back in their plastic dress bags. Jocie's feet hurt and she felt almost snow-blind from so much white. Her ears were ringing from all the clerks chirping about how beautiful this or that looked. One of the clerks had even looked at Jocie and said she was a beautiful child. As if that would make Leigh decide one of that clerk's dresses was the perfect one.

"I'm sorry, Jocie," Leigh said with a sigh as they pulled out into traffic after leaving the last store. "Maybe I should have gone on and taken that last one. It was nice enough."

"But not perfect."

"No, but maybe I shouldn't expect perfection." Leigh sighed again.

Just then a car pulled out in front of them and Leigh slammed on her brakes. Jocie held her breath and braced for the crash as the tires squealed. Leigh's car stopped with bare inches to spare. Before he drove off, the man in the other car shook his fist at Leigh as though she'd been the one to pull out in front of him.

Leigh's knuckles were white where she was gripping the steering wheel and her eyes were wide. "Oh my gosh!" Her voice sounded shaky. Horns started blowing behind them, but Leigh just sat there.

"Are you okay?" Jocie asked.

"I think I need to park a minute to give myself time to quit shaking. You see a place?"

"How about over there in front of that dress shop? What's it say? Vintage dresses. Wonder what that means."

"A fancy way to say 'used,' I'd guess." Leigh pulled her car out of traffic into the parking spot. She took a couple of deep breaths. "I hate driving in Lexington. Everybody over here drives like a maniac."

"Look, Leigh." Jocie pointed toward the dress shop. "That dress in the window, it's pretty fancy. Maybe they have some vintage wedding dresses in there."

"They'll probably look vintage."

"Come on. Can't hurt to look. And vintage sounds interesting to me." Jocie pulled up on the door handle to get out.

"You're not the bride," Leigh said, but she turned off the key and scooted across the seat to get out of the car after Jocie.

The store was sort of dark and had a closed-up closet smell. The clerk barely looked up from the thick textbook she was studying and waved them toward the back when Leigh asked about wedding dresses.

There hanging on the wall was an antique ivory wedding dress with a lace-covered bodice that dipped down in a point at the waistline with the satin skirt flowing gracefully away from it. The lace sleeves had the same point to lie against the back of Leigh's hands. Real-looking pearl buttons ran partway up the sleeves and all the way up the back and took forever for Jocie to button. But once Leigh had the dress on, it looked as if it had been made for her. The right size. The right length. The right everything.

Leigh whirled the skirt back and forth in the tiny space in front of the one mirror. The whispery sound was like music. Nobody said the dress was beautiful. No clerk told Leigh what a beautiful bride she would be in it. But it was beautiful. Leigh was beautiful. But even better, it was perfect.

Sometimes it was almost scary the way the Lord answered prayers.

# 32

David had no idea getting married was going to be so crazy. When he'd done it the first time, it had been simple enough. He and Adrienne had driven a couple of hours to Tennessee, stood up in front of a judge, and come home Mr. and Mrs. Brooke. It might not have been a wise thing to do, but it hadn't been hard. Or complicated.

Of course, the day after they'd come home from Tennessee, he'd caught a plane to go back to the submarine and finish out the war. He'd missed out on the wedding showers and all the newlywed advice.

No such luck this time. He'd always thought showers were just for ladies, but the women at church insisted he had to be at the one they were having on Saturday afternoon. David looked at his calendar on his desk. Wednesday, May 19. Not quite two weeks until he and Leigh were tying the knot. A happy feeling soaked through him and settled in his bones. He was willing to go through a little craziness to make that happen.

His calendar for the next few days certainly looked crazy enough. He had things scribbled in everywhere. A visit to

Willie Jefferson who'd just found out he had lung cancer. An interview with Andrew Webster who was opening up a new feed and farm supply store on Center Street. A reminder in red to pick up his new suit and get a haircut before the wedding. A doctor's appointment for Stephen Lee to be sure his ear infection had cleared up. Prayer with Jimmy Byrd who was home on leave before being shipped out to Vietnam.

David frowned when he read that entry. Nobody knew what was going to happen over there, but ever since the North Vietnamese had summarily rejected President Johnson's peace offer, none of the news had been good. Air strikes had been going on for a while, but now the president had sent in an Army combat troop to join the Special Forces already there. Jimmy's mom and dad were worried sick about Jimmy. David wrote himself another reminder to say extra prayers for Jimmy and all the other young men who were graduating high school or college and facing the likelihood of being drafted into the service.

Graduation. David had that on his to-do list already. The *Banner* needed pictures of the graduates. And of the Little League ballplayers. Pictures sold the *Banner* better than anything he could write. At least this week's issue was already on the stands and in the mailmen's packs.

And praise the Lord, circulation was increasing again. It helped to be the only paper in town. People could get mad, people could get morally outraged, people could decide David was doing everything wrong, but if they wanted to read about what was happening in Hollyhill, they had to buy the *Banner*. And most people did.

The *Banner* might not always be totally accurate, but it was more often than not and certainly more often than the rumor mill. Take the rumors that had gone around after

248

Christmas about Zella. For a while there, the poor woman had practically slid down under her desk every time the bell had rung over the office door.

David didn't know if Zella would ever get over people imagining her anything but morally upright and then having the incredible gall to pair her up with Wes. To her that went beyond ridiculous to insane. In fact the stories still kept popping up as irrepressibly as dandelions springing back up out of the grass after a lawn was mowed.

Wes hadn't been worried about it at all. Hadn't even been all that upset at Zella for poking unasked into his business. "I don't know how she did it, but you got to give Zell credit. She's a regular Miss Marple," he'd said with a shake of his head. "But fact is, I'm thinking some of this just might be the good Lord's doing. He must have known now was a good time for me to stop running from what happened. Rosa wouldn't have ever wanted me to leave Robbie on his own the way I did."

"From the looks of Robert Wesley, your son must have done all right for himself," David said.

"Yeah, Robbie Jr. is okay. A little full of himself, but then so was I at his age. Thought I was smarter than the average joe. Something to do with being twenty, I think," Wes said. "He's bringing his dad down next visit."

"His dad? Maybe you should think of him not as Robert Wesley's dad but as your son."

"Maybe I should," Wes agreed, but he looked worried as he massaged his injured leg.

In spite of Wes's misgivings, the visit had gone well. Wes and his son had circled each other like wary dogs not sure of the other dog's welcome, but once they decided neither of them were anxious to bite or growl, they sat down and started talking. They had no way of ever getting back the years they'd lost, but they had gotten a good start for the years ahead of them. The son's wife and daughter hadn't come. Something about shopping for a prom dress.

David had found out, what with Leigh's anxiety over finding the perfect wedding dress, that shopping could be serious business. Thank the Lord Leigh had finally found a dress she liked. Jocie hadn't told him what the dress looked like. Seemed that was taboo in wedding rules and regulations. But she'd seemed to be as relieved as he was that Leigh had found what Jocie called the perfect dress. Said that when or if she ever got married, she was wearing blue jeans. That she was having a Jupiterian wedding.

When she'd made the pronouncement in the pressroom, Wes had looked at her and said, "I can't recall ever telling you about Jupiterian weddings."

"And I don't want you to," Jocie said. "When and, as I said, *if* I ever get married, I'll figure out what a Jupiterian wedding is then. It might just be whatever I decide to make up."

"Sounds Jupiterian enough for me." Wes laughed.

"Let's not be talking about any more weddings for a while," David said.

Jocie looked from Wes to him and smiled. "It's not me you need to be telling that. It's Tabitha. I think she'd like to have a double wedding this summer."

"I'm not sure she and Robert Wesley are quite ready for that. I know I'm not," David said.

And he wasn't. His own wedding was enough to worry about right now. Of course he'd seen Tabitha falling for Robert Wesley, and he'd been happy to see Robert Wesley returning her interest. The girl needed to feel attractive again after Stephen Lee had been born. But surely it was way too early to even be thinking about anything serious between the two of them. They'd only seen each other a few times.

He had filed the idea away in his head along with all the other things he needed to worry about. Like whether Jocie could make it through another week of school with that teacher making her life miserable. At least the man had quit giving her bad grades. Carl Madison somehow made sure of that after David had gone to school to talk to the principal. But Jocie still had to go to English class. She was still at Edwin Hammond's mercy, and it appeared the man didn't have much of that.

Or much sense either the way he was still chasing after Leigh. Leigh had told him she was engaged and uninterested, but he kept calling her, kept sending her flowers, kept mailing her poems, kept hanging around. Kept David seeing how much older he was than Leigh. But she said she loved him—David—and as amazingly hard to believe as that was, he did believe her. He wasn't worrying about that.

And truly the Lord said worrying was the wrong use of a Christian's energy. The Bible was pretty clear on that. A worry in the mind just meant a person was neglecting his prayer life and not turning over worries and problems to the great problem solver.

David had been praying. Every day. About the wedding. About being a good husband. About finding a way to convince his future mother-in-law that Leigh wasn't completely ruining her life by becoming Mrs. David Brooke. About how they were going to find enough seats at Mt. Pleasant Church for everybody planning to come to the wedding. You'd think it was the social event of the century in Hollyhill.

Every time he walked up the street or went to the Grill

or out to take pictures of the end-of-school activities, somebody came up to him and said they were looking forward to coming to his wedding. Leigh said the same thing was happening to her every day at the courthouse.

As great as it was that everybody was smiling and wanting to share in his and Leigh's happiness, the fact was Mt. Pleasant Church might hold 120 people tops and that was with chairs in the aisles. That wasn't going to leave much room for Leigh to walk down the aisle in her perfect wedding dress.

David looked at his watch and closed his calendar book. He wasn't going to be able to solve anything by staring at all the things he needed to do. Besides, Leigh was coming up from the courthouse any minute now to go to lunch with him. Maybe they could figure out a way to tell half of Hollyhill they couldn't come to the wedding.

Zella threw up her hands with a squawk when David told her that as he sat down in the chair beside her desk to wait for Leigh. "You can't do that."

"We have to do that. Mt. Pleasant can't hold that many people."

"Well, of course not," Zella said as she began folding her tissue into little squares. She peeked up at David. "Didn't I tell you I had it worked out?"

"You had what worked out?" David was almost afraid to ask.

"You're not getting married at Mt. Pleasant."

"We're not?"

"Be realistic, David." She sounded like she was selling him an ad for the *Banner* as she looked up at him and went on. "Your church is way too small. I know. I've been there. They had some kind of Women's Missionary Union program out there years ago. As best I recall, there was barely enough room for the WMU members then. And the basement where you'd have to have the reception isn't any bigger than this front office. My heavens, David, sometimes I think you must walk around with your eyes shut."

David frowned a little. "All right. My eyes are wide open right now. What am I supposed to be seeing?"

"That you have to have a little common sense about all this. Everybody wants to come to your wedding. You're in the public eye. What with being the editor of the *Banner* and a preacher. And of course, everybody knows Leigh from going in the courthouse and buying their car tags from her. You can't be telling people now they can't come to your wedding. You put a big announcement in the paper two weeks ago saying all friends were invited. What are you planning to do? Tell some of them they aren't your friends? I don't think so." Zella rolled her eyes and shook her head until her black curls bounced. "I mean, do you want half of them to cancel their subscriptions?"

"No, definitely not that," David said. "But didn't the announcement also say that the wedding was on June fifth at Mt. Pleasant Church?"

"A minor problem," Zella said with a dismissive wave of her hand. "I've already given a correction to Wesley to set up for next week's paper. And you can announce it to your church people Sunday."

"So where are we having the wedding? The football field at the high school? There should be plenty of seats there."

"True. But it would be sure to rain. Sure to. I don't care how much you prayed. Poor Leigh would be frazzled with worry about the weather. Plus who wants to climb up on bleachers in heels and Sunday dresses. Certainly not me. And think of Leigh's poor mother. No way could she climb up on any bleachers." Zella grabbed another tissue and dabbed it against her forehead and then her nose. "Honestly, David, sometimes I don't know what you would do without me."

David sighed. He really didn't know what he'd do without Zella either, but right at that moment he thought he might like to try to find out for a few days. "All right. What have you done?"

"You make it sound like I've done something bad. Well, not at all. I've been taking care of you the way I always do. I talked to Pastor Vance weeks ago about keeping that date open at First Baptist. It's the only thing to do. Get married there where there will be plenty of seats. We do have a balcony, you know. And it has a great center aisle. Leigh will look so beautiful coming down the aisle in her dress. A beautiful bride needs a beautiful church to get married in." Zella put her hands together under her chin as her eyes went dreamy.

David didn't know what to say.

The dreamy look disappeared. Zella gave him a very pleased-with-herself smile as she said, "Now don't bother thanking me. And don't be worried about your people out there at Mt. Pleasant. They agreed with me that it was the only thing to do. I talked to Sally McMurtry. She thought it was a wonderful idea. She said she and the McDermotts and some others would handle things on that end. She said nobody would be the first bit upset. Said there wouldn't have been nearly enough parking space out there anyway for all the folks that would want to come from town."

David felt a little as if somebody had just run over him with a truck. Maybe he had been walking around with his eyes shut. "You know Myra Hearndon is singing in the wedding."

"Well, of course I do. I probably know more about what's happening at your wedding than you do."

"Obviously," David said.

"And it's not like Myra will be the only person of color there. Reverend Boyer and his family will be there, and of course, Noah has to be there."

"Not to mention Stephen Lee," David said.

"Right," Zella said. "First Baptist is every bit as forward thinking as Mt. Pleasant. We don't shut our doors to people with colored skin."

"Good. Just didn't want to cause any problems for Reverend Vance."

"Brother Vance is a wonderful man," Zella said. "You're just upset because he wouldn't marry you, what with you being divorced and all. Lots of preachers are that way, and it's going to be nice to have the judge do the ceremony since he's Leigh's uncle and all."

"The Lord works things out," David admitted. He had been upset when every preacher he'd asked had looked apologetic but had refused to marry him. It was pretty surprising Reverend Vance even agreed to let them be married in his church. Zella's force of character must have steamrollered his objections. Or maybe she hadn't asked. She hadn't bothered to ask David.

"What has the Lord worked out?" Leigh asked as she came in the front door in time to hear David's last comment.

"Our wedding, it appears. The Lord and Zella, I might add."

"Uh-oh. What's going on that I don't know about?" Leigh looked at Zella.

"Nothing much," Zella said quickly. "Just a change of venue. I was going to tell you both just as soon as everything was arranged."

Leigh frowned a little. "A change of venue? You mean we're not getting married at the church?"

"Of course you're getting married at the church. Just not the Mt. Pleasant Church. There is so much more space at First Baptist and think of the longer aisle. It's going to be wonderful. You'll see," Zella said.

"Shouldn't somebody have asked us about this?" Leigh asked.

"Apparently not," David said.

Zella stood up and leaned toward them with her hands on her desk. "I can't see why the two of you are getting in such a snit about it all. You have to admit this will be better. So just enjoy."

"Enjoy," David echoed and looked at Leigh. She was biting her lip to keep from smiling, and then suddenly they were both laughing. Enjoy. It was the best advice he'd had for days. Advice he planned to take.

## 33

The car was packed, ready to go. Adrienne had never thought she'd leave California. The place had been home from the moment she'd crossed over the state line five years ago. She'd never stayed in one place so long, not counting Hollyhill. And Hollyhill had never been home for her. It had just been the place where she'd been born. Surely by mistake.

Now she was going to die. Surely that was a mistake too. But then everybody died. It was a fact of life. People lots younger than her walked over death's bridge. All she had to do to realize that was read the papers about what was happening in Vietnam. The president was sending boys half her age to a jungle on the other side of the world to cross that bridge into eternity. Most of them didn't want to go hunting that bridge any more than she liked being pushed toward it by the disease spreading through her and into her bones.

Some of them, like Eddie, were refusing to go, draft or no draft.

Maybe driving across country to spend her last months

with her mother in Florida was a mistake too. She hadn't even seen her mother for over five years. But there was some kind of unwritten rule that said a person should be with family when that person breathed her last. And her mother was family.

Those boys in Vietnam had no mama, daddy, sister, brother holding their hands when those bullets or the shrapnel ripped into their bodies and sent them out into the great beyond. But that was different. They didn't have a choice. She did. Maybe not about dying, but about where it happened. And Florida would be a better place for dying than California. Lots of practice there with all the snow-birds going down there to live out their last days in the sunshine.

Her mother promised the sun was just as bright in Florida as it was in California. Still, it would be different. Adrienne knew that, but she didn't know what else she could do. Francine had tried to get Adrienne to stay in California, had promised to be her family. She'd even cried as she'd helped Adrienne sell her furniture and pack up her car, but then Francine had crying down to an art. She teared up when she heard the theme music for *Lassie* reruns on television.

Adrienne didn't have any more tears. Her tear ducts were as dry as the Mojave Desert she'd soon be driving through. What was it people were always saying? No need crying over spilt milk. Cancer wasn't exactly spilt milk, but whatever it was, those ravenously hungry mutant cells were piling up inside her and sucking away her life. There wasn't any way to sop it up and put it back in whatever bottle it had come out of.

Besides, she'd done her crying. Was still crying inside. Silently. Painfully behind the smile. At least that was the

258

way it had been the day Eddie came by to say goodbye before he headed to Canada to keep from being drafted.

"I'm not waiting until they pull my name up," he'd said. "I'm out of here."

"But what will you do up there?" Adrienne had hated the way she'd sounded maternal. She'd never wanted to be Eddie's mother, but that had been the way she felt as she watched him that day. He looked so young next to her disease-aged body.

"Get a new club to sing at. A couple of the guys are going with me. We'll make out."

And Gina, Adrienne thought, but didn't say aloud. She'd even heard Gina was saying they might get married once they got settled in Canada.

Eddie noticed her frown and got defensive for all the wrong reasons. Nothing was new about that either. "What do you want me to do?" he almost shouted. "Let them send me over there to get shot? I'm not cut out to be a soldier. I'm a singer. I mean, it's not like anybody's attacking us over here."

"The enemy lies within." Adrienne shouldn't have said it out loud. She knew that as soon as the words were hanging out there in the air between them.

"You're not going to get all maudlin on me, are you?" Eddie looked worried as he moved a couple of steps closer to the door. "I mean, Francine told me you were handling everything really well. And you know doctors can be wrong."

Adrienne smiled even though she'd lost count of the times people had told her that very same thing while they stared off past her head or down at the floor to keep from looking into her eyes. She tried to hold on to him for another minute. The last minutes. "They can. Of course they can. And we were talking about you, not me. You'll make it, Eddie. To the big time someday."

"You really think so?" He stopped looking uncomfortable as he shifted back to his own problems easily enough. "It won't be as easy in Canada."

"The war can't last long. Maybe your draft number won't ever come up and you won't have to stay north. It's bound to be cold up there."

"Yeah, that's what Gina says too." He didn't even seem to realize how talking about his current girl was twisting a knife in Adrienne's gut. "She says we should get married, have a kid or two fast as we can and then I'll be 4-F or something."

"That's a plan," Adrienne managed to say.

He had the grace then to look a little shamefaced. "Well, hers not mine." He shuffled another step closer to the door even as he said, "Hey, you want me to stay over tonight? To, you know, talk and stuff before I take off tomorrow."

It was all she could do to force herself to keep smiling. "I don't think tonight will work out."

"You don't have to worry about Gina," he said. "I mean, I do whatever I want. She's cool with that."

"Good, then maybe things will work out for the two of you." She forced another smile and felt even more maternal. "But I'm not feeling the best today. You understand."

He was surprised. He hadn't expected her to chase him out the door. For a minute he didn't know what to say even as a bit of relief sneaked into his eyes. She'd always known him so well. And loved him in spite of that. In his way, as much as he was able, Eddie had loved her back. That had been the difference between her and Eddie and her and David. While she had never loved David, at the same time

260

he had never loved her. Not the real her. He'd wanted to love the person he had imagined her to be.

Eddie stopped with his hand on the doorknob and turned back to grab her in a hug. She tried to pull back from him. She wasn't wearing her prosthesis. She hadn't known he was coming by and the thing was so infernally heavy that it seemed to drag her into the ground when she wore it. But he kept his arms tight around her, not seeming to notice her bosom imbalance. "Just a hug," he said. "A hug can't hurt."

That had just shown how young he was. The hug had hurt. Her ribs had been tender to the touch ever since the surgery, and even more, her heart had felt as if it was splintering into a thousand pieces. But she'd managed to hang on to her smile as she'd watched him out the door. "Sing a song for me sometimes, Eddie."

He'd promised he would even as he'd run away from her toward his future.

Now he was gone. A new band was playing at the club. Green Grass Trees or some silly name like that. She'd never bothered to go hear them. Francine said they were okay. Not as good as Eddie B. and the Bugs, but okay. Of course, Francine liked everybody. Even Adrienne.

Francine was standing on the sidewalk, tears running down her cheeks as she watched Adrienne start up her car and shift it into gear. "Don't forget to call when you get there so I'll know you're okay," she yelled after Adrienne.

As if there was ever any chance of Adrienne being okay again. But Adrienne nodded and waved at her as she pulled away from the curb. Behind her, Francine was jogging up the sidewalk after her, still waving. "Have a good life, girl," Adrienne whispered at Francine's image in her rearview mirror and then stepped on the gas and left her behind.

It didn't take long to leave California behind as well. Then the rest of the country lay between her and Florida. But there was something restful about being in the car moving down the road. Being alone. Being closed away from the world in her car. She could scream. She could talk to herself. She could turn the radio up loud when she heard a good song and sing along while dreaming the next song might be by Eddie B. and the Bugs. She could imagine the hot desert sun was burning away the cancer inside her the same way her tears had been burned away weeks ago by grief. She could pretend she believed there was a heaven and she might find it.

And when the road glare got too strong or her thoughts got too lonely, she looked at the picture of little Stephen that she had stuck on the dash.

It wasn't until she actually crossed into Arkansas and took a turn toward the northeast that she admitted to herself why she was driving across country to Florida instead of flying. It wasn't because she had stuff she couldn't bear to part with. She didn't have any stuff like that. Not even clothes, since none of them fit any more. She didn't have photo albums or cherished keepsakes. She only had the pictures Tabitha had sent her of Stephen. Ten snapshots altogether. They would have fit in her pocket.

Dr. Mike had said if she wanted to do anything, to plan on doing it soon. And she wanted to hold Stephen in her arms. She wanted to look into his little face and see herself in his beautiful brown eyes.

It didn't matter that she'd tried to talk Tabitha into not having the baby. That had been then. This was now. A detour through Hollyhill would make the trip to Florida longer. Lots longer. But it wasn't as if Adrienne had anything else to do. Nothing to do but die.

# 34

Saturday morning Leigh woke up to birds singing in the tree outside her bedroom window. The last Saturday in May. In exactly one week she would walk down the aisle of the Hollyhill First Baptist Church and stand beside David Brooke and say *I do*. She'd be Mrs. David Brooke. Leigh Jacobson Brooke.

She spoke the names out loud softly. They sounded right. Good. Perfect. Amazingly perfect. Just like her wedding dress.

She lay still and imagined walking down the red-carpeted aisle in the dress. She'd tried it on again after it came back from the cleaners. She had to get it cleaned even though she worried about the lace maybe disintegrating or something. But the lace survived intact, and the dress came back smelling fresh instead of like that musty dress shop where she and Jocie had found it after the idiot driver of that other car had pulled out right in front of her. Thank the Lord, she was able to slam on her brakes and keep from hitting him, and thank the Lord, they ended up stopped right in front of the Vintage Dress Shop. She'd never noticed it there until then—she didn't drive to Lexington all that often to shop. Most of the time she did her shopping in Grundy so she could drop by and see her parents.

Another thank the Lord. Her mother was beginning to come around. She still wasn't exactly excited about the prospect of Leigh becoming Mrs. David Brooke, but at the shower Aunt Wilma had given for Leigh a few weeks back, Leigh's mother had actually laughed and joined in with everybody teasing Leigh about having kids. Leigh was hoping her mother had finally opened her eyes and looked at David and seen he wasn't all that old even if he did have a daughter who had a baby.

And what a sweet baby too. Leigh didn't mind a bit being his stepgrandmother. Jocie had even started calling Leigh Grams to Stephen Lee. Of course Stephen Lee was still too little to say much but ma-ma and da-da, but his beautiful brown eyes lit up every time he saw her. Leigh didn't care what the baby learned to call her as long as he kept smiling when he saw her.

Leigh loved babies. She had always loved babies. And she didn't deny she would like to have a baby. She and David had even almost talked about it a couple of times. David said there wasn't anything they shouldn't be able to talk about, but babies came close. That and Edwin Hammond.

Leigh frowned and tried to push that thought away. But she couldn't. Edwin Hammond had a way of edging into her head like an unwanted weed in a flower garden. Leigh hadn't figured out what his problem was other than he must have a few screws loose in his head. She'd told him plain out more than once to leave her alone, to never call her again, to get lost. Then there he would be again, standing in her path. The thorn on the rose of her happiness.

She didn't know why. She'd never once encouraged him.

And while she had lost weight and gotten a new hairstyle and looked surprisingly good when she looked at herself in the mirror, she didn't think she looked that good. Not to have some strange man chase after her when she not only hadn't given him the first bit of encouragement but had done everything she could think of to discourage him.

Jocie was right when she called him Mr. Creep. Not that Leigh would tell Jocie that. It wasn't exactly respectful to call a teacher a creep even if it was true. So instead she kept telling Jocie school was almost over and that the man would be gone then. The school board hadn't hired him for the next year.

Jocie had already known that. She'd said the man had actually cornered her outside the school building and yelled at her.

"What did he say?" Leigh had asked her. She was giving Jocie a ride out to the park to take pictures of some Little Leaguers playing ball.

Jocie stared down at the camera in her lap and ran her finger over its edges. She didn't seem to want to answer Leigh, but she finally said, "Nothing that made much sense. Something about me being the reason he wasn't being hired back. That he knew I went and talked to Mr. Madison about him. And I did do that, but I don't think Mr. Madison paid much attention to anything I said."

"So what did you tell him?"

"I didn't want to tell him anything, but he kept stepping in front of me when I tried to leave." Jocie's voice trembled a little as if even thinking about the man in front of her scared her.

Leigh reached over and touched Jocie's arm. "He didn't hurt you, did he?"

"He didn't hit me or anything, if that's what you mean, but I got the feeling he might. I mean, Dad told me to pray about it all, and I have. I've tried every kind of prayer you can think of. Let me get sick and have to study at home. Let some miracle happen that they let school out early. Give me courage to sit in English for an hour every day. Help me survive the year. And I guess the Lord did answer those last ones. School will be over in a couple of weeks and so far I've survived."

"Maybe you should tell your father more about what's going on."

"No, he'd just get too upset." Jocie looked over at Leigh. "And you have to promise not to tell him either. Please."

It wasn't a promise Leigh should have made. David had already told her they shouldn't keep secrets from one another. But she was already not telling David some things. She hadn't seen the need to tell him about all the notes Edwin Hammond kept sticking in the keyhole of her door. She tore them up without reading them, so what was there to tell? And maybe when she kept spotting the man hanging around her street, it was just coincidence. Hollyhill was a small place and the man lived a couple of streets over. He could just be out taking a walk or something.

So when Jocie had begged her, Leigh had said, "All right. But you should tell him yourself. Your father can't help you if he doesn't know what's going on."

"Nothing's going on. Nothing that I can't survive. With the Lord's help. Maybe you could pray about it too sometimes," Jocie said. "Both of us praying will surely make the days go faster so school will be out. And that way it'll be June. You'll be walking down the aisle in that dress the Lord helped us find. You and Dad will be married. Summer will stretch out wonderfully in front of us. And Mr. Creep will disappear back to wherever he came from."

Now Leigh shut her eyes and said that very prayer. Two more days until school was out. Seven more days until she became Mrs. David Brooke. "Please, Lord, let the days go fast and then let next Saturday be the best day of all," she whispered. She moved her hand down the sheet beside her. She'd be sharing a bed next Saturday night.

The thought made tingles run through her and a flush climb up into her cheeks. She wanted to be married in every way. Heart and mind. Body and soul. But at the same time she was nervous that she might turn out to be totally inept at certain aspects of marriage. What if she did everything all wrong?

She stood up and went to the bathroom to splash cold water on her face. It was a natural thing. Hadn't she been able to kiss David without the first bit of trouble when she'd been worried about that back when David first started coming to the park to walk with her? But they'd kissed and it had been easy and now wasn't it like second nature to just put her arms around David and kiss him?

That's how Wes had told her the other would be too. Easy. Natural. Wes, of all people, had been the one to look at her and know she needed advice even though she'd been way too embarrassed to ask for any. She'd thought about asking, but hadn't known who to ask. Zella certainly wouldn't have been any help. Not only had she never been married, but she'd probably come up with some wild ideas she'd gleaned from all those romance novels she read that weren't a bit like real life.

She'd thought about talking to Miss Sally out at the church. A person could talk to Miss Sally about anything without ever having the first worry of her laughing at you or of anybody else knowing about what was worrying you. But Miss Sally had never been married either. Leigh figured she'd just make both of them blush.

So she hadn't talked to anybody, but Wes had caught her off to herself last Tuesday after they'd folded the paper for delivery on Wednesday. "Looks like something might be worrying you, Miss Leigh," he said.

"What makes you say that?" she asked.

"Oh, just a hunch." He looked at her with that slow smile of his. "Maybe something about getting married."

"Not exactly getting married. More being married." Leigh blushed scarlet.

"I sort of thought that might be the case." Wes put his hand on her shoulder. "Don't you worry one minute about any of that. It'll come as natural as a frog hopping off a lily pad into a pond."

"But I don't have the first bit of experience." Leigh picked up a piece of paper to fan her burning cheeks. She kept her eyes away from Wes as she said, "In hopping, I mean."

Wes chuckled and squeezed her shoulder. "That's good. No experience needed for this job the Lord has given you. The good Lord designed a man and woman to want to be together, and when both parties want to be together, there ain't an easier thing in the world to do. You know to go hopping in a pond somewhere together."

Leigh peeked over at Wes. "Then you don't think I'll be a disappointment to David? I mean everybody says Adrienne was so pretty, so, so . . ." Leigh hesitated as she tried to come up with a word she could say to Wes without totally melting down with embarrassment. "So enthralling."

"She was pretty, best I recall, but truth is, David never seemed all that enamored with her, at least not after I was around. Not like he is with you. He loves you. And you love him. Love makes a difference. A big difference. David won't be a bit disappointed. Not one bit." Wes had grinned at her. "And neither will you. Just trust your old Uncle Wes on this one."

*Love makes a difference.* It would, Leigh decided as she stared into her eyes in the mirror. Then she picked her watch up off the sink and checked the time. She should have time for a quick walk in the park before she had to get ready for the big shower at the church that afternoon. David wouldn't be at the park to walk with her. He'd told her he'd have to work on his sermon this morning since the shower would take up most of the afternoon.

The people at Mt. Pleasant had been looking forward to throwing them the shower for weeks. David said no telling what his deacons were going to do to try to embarrass him, but that no matter what, they'd have to keep smiling and let the church people have their fun. Thank goodness the sun was shining because they'd invited way more people than could fit in the basement of the church. Dorothy McDermott had told Leigh they'd borrowed folding chairs from one of the other country churches to be sure they would have enough seats for everybody.

Leigh's mother and father were even supposed to drive down to attend. Her father had been complaining about missing his golf game every time Leigh talked to him. Not only this Saturday, but the next one as well for her wedding. Two Saturdays without golf at the best time of the year to play the game before the weather got too hot. Couldn't she have gotten married in March when it would be raining or something?

Leigh had just laughed at him and hadn't let him off the hook. She'd told him he had to come and bring her mother. They needed to see where she was going to live. They needed to see the church that loved David and now her. They needed to get used to how happy she was.

When Leigh went out the door, a rolled-up note fell out of the keyhole. Leigh just picked it up and crumpled it in her hand without unrolling the first curl. She pitched it in the trashcan at the bottom of the stairs. Nothing was going to spoil this day for her. Nothing.

## 35

Early Saturday morning, Jocie rode her bike to town to help Wes clean the press and sweep out the pressroom. Her father usually helped with the cleanup chores, but he had to stay home to work on his sermon for the next day. He was still closed up in his bedroom when Jocie got home around noon, but he'd have to come out soon, whether or not the Scripture had spoken to him. The people at church might forgive a bad sermon but they'd never forgive him not showing up for the shower.

Jocie had her present all wrapped and safely out of Stephen Lee's reach. The baby was pulling up to everything, and he liked tearing paper above all else. Besides, her present was breakable. She'd found some great iced tea glasses decorated with strawberries on special sale at the ten-cent store. She figured she couldn't go wrong with glasses, since they averaged at least one broken glass a week and sometimes were reduced to drinking their iced tea out of pint mason jars. Jocie couldn't wait to see all the presents the church people were going to give her father and Leigh. It felt almost like Christmas.

Leigh must have been feeling the same way. When she showed up after lunch to see who was riding with her to the shower, she looked ready to explode with happiness. She gave Jocie a hug before she grabbed up Stephen Lee and headed up the stairs to see Jocie's dad. Jocie started to say her dad didn't like to be disturbed when he was working on his sermon, but Leigh was up the steps before Jocie could get the words out. From the sound of the laughter from her dad's bedroom, he didn't mind a bit Leigh disturbing him.

Things were going to be different around the Brookes' house after next Saturday, but different in a good way. Leigh already felt like one of the family. Next week would just make that official, and Jocie couldn't remember ever seeing her father smile so much. Even when he was complaining about all the fuss going on over the wedding, he was smiling. Happy was good. Jocie liked happy.

She was going to be especially happy after next Tuesday when school was finally over for the summer and she no longer had to spend an hour a day in Mr. Creep's class. He'd head back to Neptune and she'd say a thank-you prayer as she erased all memory of him from her mind. Wes said some people were just past understanding and that there wasn't any reason straining a body's brain trying to figure them out. That if a person wanted to strain his brain, he should read Plato or study calculus.

Leigh had warned Jocie the night before that Leigh's parents sort of fit in that category—the past-understanding category—but that she hoped Jocie would try to like them anyway. She'd said that Jocie didn't have to worry about them wanting to be her grandparents or anything. That they probably wouldn't drive to Hollyhill to visit more than once or twice a year, if that.

"I'll be lucky to get them here for the rehearsal dinner and the wedding. I guess I shouldn't have asked them to come to the shower, but the people out at the church kept saying they had to come." Leigh had looked worried.

"I'll be good," Jocie told her. "I promise."

"I wasn't worried about you being good. I was worried about them being good," Leigh said with a sigh. "But you know, you can't make the whole world be happy and get along, can you?"

"Nope," Jocie agreed. "But we can pray about it. I'll do a happy-mom-and-pop prayer for you."

"My mother and dad happy? That would surely be a miracle," Leigh muttered. Then she laughed. "But then again, look at me. Last year this time I would have said it would take a miracle for me to be getting married to such a wonderful man. And I am. Oh truly, I am." Leigh had grabbed hold of Jocie and spun her in a circle. Joy sparkles had practically exploded off her.

Leigh was happy. Jocie's father was happy. Tabitha was happy now that she had Robert writing her love notes. Stephen Lee was always happy as long as he got his bottle and a cookie now and again. Even Aunt Love was happy these days. Sometimes Jocie went in to talk to Zella just to get her frowning and fussing. It made Jocie feel better to know she wasn't the only one who couldn't hang on to happiness every minute of the day. But after Tuesday, maybe Jocie could do a better job of it. No school. No Mr. Teacher Creep.

When there was a knock on the door, Jocie figured it must be Leigh's parents showing up early to check out where Leigh would be living after next week. Jocie whispered her happy-mom-and-pop prayer and hurried to the door. It might not help with the happiness department if Zeb came around the house and started barking at them. Zeb's barks could practically shatter a person's eardrums.

Jocie pulled open the door. It wasn't Leigh's parents. She stared at the woman standing there on the porch with a half smile on her face and knew her at once—she was much slimmer and older than in the photo that had sat on the piano up until her dad had got engaged to Leigh. Then Aunt Love had put it away in a closet somewhere.

The woman, her mother, DeeDee, smiled a little more and opened her mouth to say something. Jocie slammed the door shut in her face. Jocie stood there and stared at the door and remembered her father's sermon a few weeks ago about the Bible story of how the angel led Peter out of jail, and then when he knocked on the door where all the followers were praying for him to be released, the servant girl thought he was a ghost and shut the door in his face. His sermon had been about how sometimes people didn't expect the Lord to answer their prayers.

But this was different. DeeDee standing on the porch wasn't an answer to prayer. Not now. Not today with the wedding shower hours away. More a reason for prayer.

Jocie stared at the door and waited. She wasn't sure for what. Divine inspiration perhaps. Her father's and Leigh's voices drifted down from the room upstairs, mixed in with Stephen Lee's happy squeals. Tabitha was singing as she got ready upstairs. Aunt Love was banging pans in the kitchen. Jocie was hoping DeeDee was disappearing off the porch. Going back to her car. Driving back to California.

Funny. For years Jocie had hoped to open the door and see her mother and Tabitha standing there. She'd wanted a mother desperately. A mother who would brush Jocie's hair and make cupcakes for her school parties and laugh at her silly songs.

273

It had never happened, and slowly over the years she'd realized it would never happen. Finally after Tabitha had come home, Jocie had quit even wanting it to happen. She had Wes to laugh with her. They didn't have class parties at high school so she didn't need cupcakes anymore. She could brush her own hair. She had her father to love her. But now it had happened. Her mother was standing on the other side of the door.

There was another knock. Louder this time. Determined. Aunt Love stopped rattling pans and came to the kitchen door to peer out at Jocie staring at the door. Another knock. Aunt Love frowned and said, "Well, gracious sakes, Jocelyn, can't you hear that knocking? Somebody's at the door. Open it up and see who it is."

Jocie glanced over her shoulder at Aunt Love. "I know who it is. It's DeeDee."

Aunt Love's frown got deeper, but Jocie didn't wait for her to say anything. She just reached over and pulled open the door again.

Her mother was still smiling. Not a big smile. Not a particularly happy smile. More a whatever-happens-keep-on-smiling type smile. "Hello," Jocie said.

"Are you Jocie?" her mother asked.

"I am."

"I'm—"

Jocie jumped in front of her words before she could say she was Jocie's mother. She wasn't her mother. She didn't have a mother. Had never had a mother. "I know who you are. You're DeeDee."

"Yes," her mother said, the smile still firmly on her face. "I thought you might not recognize me. May I come in?"

"It's not really a good time," Jocie said.

Behind Jocie, Aunt Love was whispering a Bible verse.

274

"'I will have mercy on her that had not obtained mercy.'" But Jocie wasn't feeling merciful. Just worried that DeeDee showing up at the door was going to ruin everything. Make the happiness in their house drain away.

DeeDee put her hand flat against the door to keep Jocie from shutting it. "I drove all the way from California."

"Why?"

"Because I wanted to." DeeDee's smile got a bit larger. "Is your father here? And Tabitha?" DeeDee's eyes pushed past her to search the room behind Jocie.

Aunt Love stepped up beside Jocie and took hold of the door and pulled it open wider. "Of course you can come in. You must be tired from your trip. Can I get you a glass of tea? Maybe something to eat?"

"The tea would be nice. You're Lovella, Mae's sister, aren't you?"

"That's right," Aunt Love said.

"You look different," DeeDee said.

"I am different. It's been a lot of years since you saw me," Aunt Love said.

"It's more than just being older. You look changed." DeeDee studied Aunt Love for a moment before she went on. "Maybe it's the smile. I never remember you looking happy."

"'This is the Lord's doing; it is marvelous in our eyes.'"

"Scripture, I suppose. I do remember that about you. How you quoted Scripture at me whenever you came around."

"You just laughed at me," Aunt Love said.

"Did I? Oh well, I probably laughed at everybody then. Things aren't so funny these days."

"I'll get your tea. Please sit down." Aunt Love headed

275

toward the kitchen before Jocie could offer to go instead and escape standing there alone with her mother.

Then her father and Leigh still holding Stephen Lee came out of her father's room to look down at them from the top of the stairs. Her father's smile disappeared, and just as Jocie had feared, the happiness seemed to drain away with his smile. Leigh looked puzzled, then worried. Jocie had no idea what to say or do. Neither from all appearances did her father.

Tabitha pushed past them and came running down the steps. "DeeDee! Is that really you? I heard your voice, but I couldn't believe you were really here. Oh my gosh! Why didn't you write and tell me you were coming?" She grabbed her mother in a hug. "Did you see Stephen Lee? He is so precious. You won't believe."

# 36

eigh watched Tabitha embrace her mother and felt as if the house was collapsing around her. Her hopes and dreams were crystallizing in her mind and then shattering into a million pieces. Had the Lord just been playing a game with her, letting her get her hopes up, only to bring David's first wife, his first love, home to show Leigh how foolish she'd been? Thinking a man like David could love her. Imagining being married to such a man. Even dreaming of having his babies.

Tabitha ran back up the stairs and grabbed Stephen Lee out of Leigh's arms. The baby laughed when Tabitha bounced back down the stairs with him.

Leigh struggled desperately to hold on to her smile as she looked at David who was staring down at the woman at the bottom of the stairs. He looked stunned. Stunned by her return to his house. Stunned by her beauty.

Leigh made herself look at the woman again. She was reaching long, graceful arms for Stephen Lee and the baby was reaching for her. Stephen Lee loved everybody and was used to being passed around at church. Still, Leigh felt somehow betrayed by the smile the baby was bestowing on this woman, this person who was really his Grams. Not just a pretender the way Leigh was.

Adrienne didn't look like a grandmother. She didn't look all that much different than she'd looked in the picture that used to sit on David's piano. Leigh looked at the piano. The picture wasn't there now. But the woman was. She was still beautiful. Exotic almost. And very, very slim. Suddenly Leigh felt like a cow. An awkward, stupid cow. She wished she were closer to the door so she could just slip outside and drive away.

"What in the name of heaven is she doing here?" David said.

Leigh wasn't sure if he was talking to himself or to her. She didn't have an answer anyway. Not a good answer. But she found her voice and said, "I don't know. Maybe you should ask her."

David looked over at Leigh almost as if he had forgotten she was there. Then his face softened as he said, "It's okay, Leigh. Everything will be okay."

"Okay," Leigh repeated.

"Adrienne always did have an almost uncanny sense of timing," David muttered as he moved past Leigh to head down the stairs.

Leigh followed him down. What else could she do? She couldn't just stay there at the top of the stairs watching the family reunion. Halfway down the stairs, Leigh looked over at Jocie. She looked as confused and unsure of herself as Leigh felt.

David could hardly believe Adrienne was standing there in his living room. He had long given up her ever returning to Hollyhill. He wasn't happy to see her there now. She would have a reason for coming. And whatever that reason was, it would mean trouble for him. He didn't want trouble this week. He wanted to simply rejoice in the gift of love the Lord had presented to him and feel joyful as the days passed until his wedding next week. It would have been better if his past had stayed on the other side of the country.

"Hello, David," Adrienne said as she swept her eyes up and down him. "You're looking good. Very good."

"Thank you. So are you," he said.

"You never were a good liar," she said.

He let that pass. Truth was, she didn't look good. She was too pale. Nothing but skin and bones. She looked sick. Was that the reason she'd come home? To find someone to take care of her? He mentally shook his head. This wasn't her home. She'd deserted it years ago. She couldn't just show up and decide it was home again. She *wouldn't* just show up and decide it was home again. Not Adrienne.

"Jocie says I've come at a bad time," Adrienne said with that smile he'd once so dreaded seeing on her face. The smile that meant she was glad to be causing him problems.

"A busy time," David said. "We have a wedding shower out at the church in a couple of hours."

"A shower? Who's getting married?"

Before David could answer her, Jocie jumped in. "Dad's getting married. Next Saturday."

Adrienne didn't look at Jocie but kept her eyes on David. "You? You're getting married again?" She let out a laugh. "Oh, this is too much. After all these years and then I show up just in time to wish you well. Or perhaps not to wish you well. Who's the lucky lady? Anybody I know?"

279

"No." David reached back to put his arm around Leigh and pull her up beside him. She felt stiff, unwilling, in spite of the smile plastered on her face. It took David by surprise to realize she was worried about Adrienne standing there in front of them, but hadn't he told Leigh how much he loved her, how much he wanted to be married to her? He smiled at her to remind her of that, but her eyes were on Adrienne. He tightened his arm around her as he said, "This is Leigh Jacobson, soon to be Mrs. David Brooke."

"How do you do," Leigh said and held out her hand toward Adrienne.

"You're kidding?" Adrienne said, not bothering to acknowledge Leigh's greeting. "She looks almost as young as Tabitha."

"DeeDee!" Tabitha said. "You're one to talk about somebody being too young for you. What about Eddie?"

"Ah yes, dear sweet little Eddie. Vanished into Canada ahead of the draft. No Vietnam in his future."

"I'm surprised you didn't follow him north," Tabitha said.

"Too cold up there."

"In other words, he didn't ask," Tabitha said.

"There were complications." Adrienne pulled Stephen Lee up closer to her and dropped a kiss on his cheek. The baby started screaming as if Adrienne had pinched him instead. She looked truly distressed as she let Tabitha take the baby from her arms.

"Sorry. He'll hug you all day, but he's not much on kisses." Tabitha held the baby close and rubbed her hand up and down his back.

"Smart kid. You shouldn't let just any strange woman kiss on you," Adrienne said, but she looked sad as she dropped her hands down to her sides and pulled her eyes away from Stephen Lee. She glanced around the room. "Some things never change."

"And some things do," David said.

"Right. You're getting married." Adrienne looked at him with that smile again. "Am I invited?"

"The wedding isn't until next Saturday."

"Oh yeah. The shower's today. Well, don't let me make you late for the fun. It'll take awhile to open all those dish towels and act happy and pleased. Been there. Done that. Don't envy you a bit on that one. But I was driving through so I thought I'd stop in for a minute. Could be my minute is up."

"You can't leave already, DeeDee. You just got here." Tabitha looked from Adrienne to David. "Tell her she can't go yet, Dad. Please."

David looked at Tabitha. Of course the girl would want to see her mother more than five minutes. And Adrienne had driven all the way across the country to see Tabitha. She could say she was just passing through, but Adrienne never did anything she didn't want to do. He couldn't exactly chase her away without giving them the chance to visit, even if that was what he wanted to do. He shut his eyes and said a quick prayer for wisdom, for charity, for understanding. Then he looked at Adrienne and said, "Maybe we should talk alone for a minute."

"Just like old times. Your place or mine?" Adrienne smiled and raised her eyebrows as she peered at him. "Your bedroom or my car? Of course my car might be a little warm. Then again so might your bedroom. Too warm."

David had never felt much colder in his life, but he wasn't about to start playing games with Adrienne. "The back porch will do," he said. "The rest of you finish getting ready. We'll need to leave in a half hour." David put his hand on Leigh's arm and said, "Don't worry, Leigh. It will be okay."

She blinked and echoed him. "Okay."

He wanted to put his arms around her and make sure she understood that he could never love anyone the way he loved her. That he had never loved anyone the way he loved her. And he needed to talk to Jocie too. She looked just as mixed-up as Leigh did. But first he had to find out why Adrienne was there. What she wanted. He led the way to the back porch and shut the door after Adrienne stepped down into the room.

"This hasn't changed either," Adrienne said. "It's as if I left yesterday instead of years ago."

"Jocie's changed."

"True. I barely recognized her when she opened the door. She didn't want to let me in, you know."

"Jocie has sort of had a rough year."

"Yeah, haven't we all?" Adrienne said.

That too was the same Adrienne. Not worrying about anybody's trouble but her own. She'd certainly never spent any time worrying about Jocie. Or him. David made himself push that thought aside. That was past and gone. He didn't care anymore what Adrienne did. He just wished she'd get in her car and drive away. He closed his eyes and tried not to pray that.

"Are you praying?" Adrienne asked. "I was always good at enriching your prayer life. Giving you something to pray about, wasn't I? One of the Lord's little unexpected blessings, I suppose."

"What do you want, Adrienne?"

"Why do you think I want something?"

"You're here."

"I am, aren't I? Actually I'm almost as surprised as you are. Not quite since I did deliberately turn north in Arkansas. I was headed to Florida. My mother's still living down there, you know. In a cute little retirement trailer. At least she says it's cute. Who knows with Mother? That probably means it's got pink ruffles on all the curtains and a plush rug." Adrienne seemed to be having trouble holding on to her smile. She looked away out the window. "I never liked ruffles, you know."

"I remember." But he didn't want to remember. He wanted to forget everything about this woman standing in front of him. Even if she was sick. Even if she obviously needed help. Even if she was the mother of his daughters. He mashed down the resentment rising inside him and made himself tune into what the Lord might want him to do. The Lord didn't say to be kind and caring to everybody except his ex-wife. Perhaps the Lord had turned her car toward Hollyhill for a purpose.

David pushed away thoughts of Leigh in the next room worrying about whether his love for her was strong enough. He pushed away thoughts of Jocie who had looked betrayed by this woman in front of him. Who *had* been betrayed by her. He pushed it all away. He was a man of God and this person in front of him was a child of God. It was that simple. And that hard.

He pulled in a deep breath and prayed without words. "Would you like me to pray for you?"

"A simple run-of-the-mill prayer won't be much help. You'd have to pray for a miracle. My doctor says that's what I have to have to make it to another year. A bona fide miracle."

"What's wrong with you?" He tried to care. He asked the Lord to help him care.

Adrienne licked her lips and then pushed out the word. "Cancer."

"They couldn't treat it?"

"Oh, they treated it. Sliced off my breast. Turned me into an invalid. Left a hideous scar." Adrienne eyed him. "You want to see it?" She reached toward the buttons on her shirt.

"No."

She dropped her hands and shrugged. "I just thought it might help your girlfriend out there not feel so threatened. I'm sure she has two beautiful, ample breasts."

David's voice turned cold. "We're not talking about Leigh."

"Sorry," Adrienne said. "Just trying to be helpful."

"I thought you were the one who needed help."

Adrienne's wicked smile disappeared. "All right, David. I'll be straight with you. There's no reason not to be. I didn't come here to get you to pray for me. I've been past prayer too many years to expect your Lord to look on me with favor now." She held up her hand to stop him from saying anything. "And I don't want to hear about it never being too late. I didn't come here to be preached at either. I came for one reason and one reason only. To see Stephen. Tabitha's been sending me pictures."

"I see."

"No, you probably don't. But that's okay. You don't have to understand. Just let me stay a couple of days. Let me play with the baby. Let me look into his eyes."

"You never wanted to play with a baby before."

"I was never dying before." Adrienne looked straight at David. "It's not a big thing. Just the gift of a couple of days out of your life. I realize it might not be the best time, but it's the only time I have." When David didn't answer right

284

away, she went on. "And I've given you gifts. You've said so yourself. Think of Jocie."

"You didn't want to."

"But I did. She's standing out there in the living room hating me, but loving you. I spent nine miserable months making that possible. All I'm asking now is a couple of days. Then I promise to disappear from your life forever. Finis."

He had to let her. What else could he do? "That's not the promise I want."

"Oh? What promise do I have to make?"

"That you won't tell Tabitha you're dying."

She stared at him a long minute before she shook her head sadly. "You're afraid that will make her want to go with me. Poor David. You always did try to hang on to what can't be held. Tabitha is an adult. She can go where and when she wants. You can't hold on to her any more than you could hold on to me."

"Just promise me."

"All right. I promise." She made a cross mark over her heart.

It probably wasn't much of a promise, but it was the best he could hope for. Adrienne was right. He couldn't hold on to what didn't want to be held. But that didn't mean he couldn't pray the ones he loved would make good decisions and stay where they were loved and safe.

David looked at his watch as he went back into the living room. He'd tell Tabitha she could stay there with Adrienne if she wanted to, but the rest of them were going to have to move. It was almost time for them to meet Mr. and Mrs. Jacobson out at the highway. They were supposed to follow David and Leigh to the church. He didn't want to add being late to their list of his faults.

The living room was too quiet when he came into it. There was no chatter. No smiles. No Leigh. "Where is Leigh?" he asked. "Did she go on to meet her parents?"

"I don't think she was thinking about her parents when she left," Jocie said. "I think she was thinking about her." Jocie nodded her head toward Adrienne who had followed David back into the room.

David's heart sank. "What did she say?"

"That some things were too good to be true," Jocie said. "I followed her outside and told her to wait. To talk to you. I told her DeeDee being here wouldn't make the first bit of difference. But she said she couldn't talk. That she had to go."

Adrienne's car was blocking his in the driveway. "Move your car," David ordered her.

"Sure. Just give me a minute," Adrienne said. "Where did I set my purse?"

"I don't have a minute." David ran out to his car. He flattened two rosebushes going through the yard to get around Adrienne's car, but Aunt Love would understand.

He drove like a maniac out the road. He had to catch Leigh. But then he realized he didn't even know how long she'd been gone. How long had he talked to Adrienne? Too long. He got to the end of the road and didn't know which way to turn. Right toward Hollyhill or left toward the parkway where Leigh was supposed to meet her parents.

He sat there without turning either way. He didn't know what to do. *Oh, dear Lord. Help me. Bring her back to me.*

## 37

ears dripped off Leigh's cheeks as she drove back to Hollyhill. She kept seeing David and that woman, his first wife, stepping down into the porch. She kept seeing the door closing behind them, shutting her out. She couldn't just stand there and act like everything was okay. Jocie had wanted her to. Had begged her to. But the tears had been building inside Leigh, and if she was going to cry, she wasn't going to do it where that woman could see her.

And things weren't okay. Even if David said they were. At least that's what she thought he'd said. Her mind had been spinning so much the words might have come through to her wrong. Everything had been wrong. She had to get away where she could think things through. Figure out what to do. Where she could cry without anybody seeing.

She did. She no more than pulled out of David's driveway than she started wailing. Just the way the Bible said the mourners did back in Bible times. In one of his sermons, David had said those women were professional mourners. It was their job to cry and wail and be in sorrow. What a terrible job, Leigh had thought at the time. To be a griever.

That was what David's sermon had been about. How some Christians seemed to want to be chronic grievers, always ready to see a slight, always seeing the dark side of every situation, always moaning and wailing that things weren't fair.

But he hadn't been preaching at her. Not then, but maybe he would be now. Still, this was different. It wasn't fair that Adrienne had picked now, this very week, to show up after all these years. Leigh had reason to wail, didn't she?

She angrily swiped the tears out of her eyes and mashed her mouth together. She'd never been a wailer. She'd always been a good girl. Always kept smiling when the kids at school made fun of her for being fat. Always kept smiling when her father stared at her with that puzzled frown as if wondering how a child so inept could be his child. Always kept smiling when her mother held her in her lap so long Leigh felt as if she might smother. Always kept smiling no matter what happened. Good girls smiled. Good girls didn't misbehave. Good girls didn't complain. Good girls certainly didn't wail. Not even if they were watching every hope and dream they'd ever had pop like soap bubbles in the air.

She didn't want to give up hope. In her mind she reached for the bubbles to gather them softly to her. She couldn't let them all burst. What was life without hope? And who was the source of hope? Just two weeks ago her Sunday school class had a lesson about hope. Leigh had memorized the focal verse from Romans. *Now the God of hope fill you with all joy and peace in believing, that ye may abound in hope, through the power of the Holy Ghost.*

At the time she'd already been filled with joy and peace as she contemplated being Mrs. David Brooke. She had abounded in hope. Hope for her and David's future. Had she given it up so easily? Was that what the Lord wanted?

For her to just open her hands and turn loose of that hope? Surely if she could do that, the hope that had been in her heart had been shallow with no power. As easy to pop as those soap bubbles in her head. Not true hope.

Of course she still had the hope of the Lord. The Lord hadn't deserted her. He was standing there waiting for her to stop wailing, to stop letting her thoughts shoot in every direction. He was standing there reaching for her. When she was a child afraid of the dark, she had often imagined Jesus standing in the room with her, promising to stay with her through the dark. He was with her now too.

Leigh stared at the road as she came to Hollyhill and turned down the street to her apartment, but she wasn't seeing the familiar buildings and trees. Instead she was trying to picture Jesus in her mind, promising her peace and joy. But it wasn't the Lord she saw reaching for her. It was David.

Leigh pulled into her driveway. What was she doing there? She had a shower to go to. Her parents would be waiting at the parkway. She looked over at the stairs up to her apartment. Edwin Hammond was standing on the bottom step. When he saw her, he smiled. As if he thought she'd come back just to see him.

The man started across the yard toward her, his smile getting broader as he must have seen the distress on her face. "Are you all right, Leigh? What has that man done to you?"

She started rolling up her window. She didn't want to talk to Edwin Hammond. She didn't want to see Edwin Hammond.

"Don't shut me out. You and I were meant to be together," Edwin said as he ran toward the car. He put his hands on top of the window glass before she got it all the way up.

"Go away, Edwin," she said flatly. "Let go of my window and leave."

"Truly I cannot. For you need me. I need you," he said.

"Why?" Leigh asked.

"Why what?" Edwin looked puzzled.

"Why do you need me? You barely know me."

"But I do know you, my dear. I know when you rise in the morning and when you retire at night. I know the songs you sing before breakfast. I know the way you dance in the rain. I know the things you throw away and the things you keep. You should have kept my roses. You should have stored my poems in your heart. Then you would have no need for these tears." He reached through the small space left at the top of the window toward her cheek.

She jerked back before he could touch her. She didn't want him to touch her. She didn't want him to watch her. She didn't want him anywhere near her. She was repulsed by his words in her ears, by his nearness.

"Don't fight it, my dear. You know you love me. It was destined by the stars." Edwin leaned closer to the window until she could feel his breath coming through the opening.

"You don't know the first thing about my destiny. Turn loose of my window and leave me alone." She stared at him coldly.

He stared back at her with that smile that made her cringe inside. "You fear you have no destiny."

"The Lord is in control of my destiny."

"The Lord?" Edwin laughed. "How parochial. You people are so totally and unendingly amusing. And I suppose you think David Brooke is part of your destiny? Has he told you that? Is that why you're here? Running away from that destiny? If so, I applaud you for that."

"I'm not running away from anything, but I do have somewhere I need to be, so let go of my window." Leigh put her car in reverse.

He kept smiling at her without moving away from the car. She took her foot off the brake and began pushing down the gas pedal. For a few seconds he ran alongside the car, but then he jerked his hands free and fell back. Leigh didn't look toward him as she backed out into the street, shifted into drive, and mashed down on the gas. She didn't want to see him.

She was looking ahead toward where David was waiting for her. She couldn't believe she'd been so foolish as to run away. To so have doubted the wonderful love David had promised her. Not for a day. Not for a week. But for the rest of their lives. How could she have run from that? Without even trying to hold on to it.

She dug a tissue out of her purse as she drove and wiped the last of the tears off her cheeks. She blew her nose and fluffed back her hair. She pulled the rearview mirror down and peeked at her face. She had looked better. But that was okay. Her nose had been redder when David had proposed. He wasn't going to turn his back on her because of a red nose.

She was surprised when she saw his car off the side of the road where he either had to turn right to go toward Hollyhill or left to go to the church or to the parkway where her parents were no doubt in a tizzy by now as they argued about whether to wait for Leigh to show up or go on back home. She couldn't believe she had forgotten all about meeting them. But right now she was more worried about meeting David.

She drove over on the wrong side of the road to pull up beside him, window to window. There weren't any other cars around and even if there were, she didn't care. They could just go around her. Still, after she was there beside David, she was afraid to look at him. Afraid of what she might see. Disappointment? Anger? Regret? Could she possibly hope to see what she most wanted to see? Love.

*That ye may abound in hope.* The bit of Scripture ran through her mind again as she kept her eyes away from his face and instead studied the hairs on his arm laying in the sun in the open car window. She found her voice. "I'm sorry, David."

"Look at me, Leigh. Please." His voice was gentle, kind, and his hand was reaching across the divide between them toward hers.

She raised her eyes to his and felt the hope bounding up inside her. Knew her prayers were being answered even though she'd been too distraught to offer them in words. Her hand went out to his even as she repeated, "I'm sorry."

"You don't have to be sorry," he said. "You came back."

"But I shouldn't have left. Not without talking to you."

He caressed her hand with his fingers. "No, you should have trusted my love. You should have remembered how I told you we could talk about anything and how nothing could ever keep me from loving you."

"I'm glad because I'll probably do some other dumb things," Leigh said.

He tightened his hand around hers. "As long as you don't think it was a dumb thing saying you'd marry this preacher man."

Her eyes flew open wide as she realized he was feeling as vulnerable and open to hurt as she had felt earlier. "Oh no, David. Surely you'd never believe that was possible."

"I didn't know what to believe. You were gone and I came after you, but I didn't know which way to turn. I've been sitting here trying to say the right prayers, trying to believe you'd come back. Hoping beyond hope that you hadn't decided being Mrs. David Brooke was going to be too hard. Hoping my love would be enough."

"That's what I asked the Lord for too when I got back to town and realized how sorry I was that I'd run from your love. And he gave me a verse, made me remember that he is the God of hope."

"'Now the God of hope fill you with all joy and peace in believing, that ye may abound in hope, through the power of the Holy Ghost.' Romans 15:13." David's eyes burned into hers as he said the verse.

It was better than a mere physical embrace. As they held hands, every part of their minds and hearts and souls embraced. The heat of the sun was forgotten. The time was forgotten. Her waiting parents were forgotten. The church people preparing their shower were forgotten. Adrienne was forgotten. It was just Leigh and David becoming one. Forever.

She almost started crying again. Happy tears this time. But then a horn was blasting beside her as a car went around them. "Maybe I should get out of the road before somebody hits me," Leigh said.

"Good thinking," David said, but he didn't turn loose of her hand.

"And my parents will be wondering where we are."

"They will." His grip tightened on her hand for a second. "I love you, Leigh Catherine Jacobson."

"And I love you, David Enoch Brooke."

David smiled. "I didn't know you knew my middle name."

Leigh laughed. "A girl always knows the name of the man she loves."

She followed David back to the house. Jocie was out at the edge of the yard watching for them. Leigh waved at her and Jocie smiled all the way across her face before she ran back to the house. Abounding in hope. *Oh dear Lord, help them all to be abounding in hope*, Leigh prayed as she stopped her car and got out. David was waiting for her.

"What happened to Aunt Love's rosebushes?" Leigh asked as they walked toward the porch.

"I sort of ran over them," David said.

"Aunt Love will never forgive me," Leigh said with a groan.

"Those old rosebushes are tough just like Aunt Love. They'll be okay. We're all going to be okay."

"Okay," Leigh echoed him, and this time she believed it.

# 38

ocie woke up early Wednesday morning. She lay still on her back porch bed and listened to the mockingbird outside. It felt strange not having to jump up to get ready to go to school. School was over. Complete. Finished. She'd made it through her freshman year in high school in spite of Mr. Teacher Creep. Three more years and she'd really be finished with it all.

Then it would be time to do something else. Maybe go on to school somewhere else. She'd have to leave Hollyhill to do that. Jocie didn't like to think about that. It made those spiders start crawling around on the inside of her ribs.

So she didn't think about it except in a way-off wondering kind of way. Someday this or that might happen. Someday, but not right now. That's the way she used to think about her mother. Someday she might see her again. Someday she might come home. Someday she'd tell Jocie why she'd left her behind without so much as a goodbye.

If it was strange waking up and not going to school, it was even stranger waking up knowing her mother was sleeping in the house. Not on the couch. Not in Tabitha's room. She'd taken over Jocie's father's room. Jocie's dad was bunking in with Wes until she left.

Maybe that was the strangest of all. Waking up and knowing that her father wasn't sleeping in the house. It bothered Jocie. She didn't like thinking her father was miles away. Not that Hollyhill was that far. She rode her bike to town all the time. But what if something happened? What if her mother did something?

She didn't know what she expected her mother to do. But whatever it was, it wouldn't be good. Her showing up unannounced on their front porch hadn't been good. Talk about bad timing. DeeDee had practically scared Leigh silly. Jocie wasn't sure why. There was no way Jocie's father was going to forget about Leigh and fall in love with DeeDee again. No way. He'd just been irritated when he'd seen DeeDee at the bottom of the stairs. Jocie had seen that plain as day in his face.

Leigh must not have figured out Jocie's dad's expressions as well yet. Maybe because she'd been too busy going into full-scale panic. First wife back. Wedding one week away. Trouble for sure.

Leigh had no reason to think trouble, but Jocie knew about panic. Sometimes it made a person do things that didn't make the first bit of sense. Like running when that person should be talking to find out the truth. That's what she'd done last summer. Run away instead of talking to her father after Ronnie Martin had said those hateful things. And look what kind of fix that had gotten her into. Landed her and Wes right in the path of a tornado.

Thank goodness Leigh hadn't needed to get almost blown away to come to her senses and turn around and come back. When Jocie had seen Leigh's '59 Chevy coming back down the road, she'd been so happy she'd jumped up and down. Until that afternoon, Jocie hadn't realized how much she depended on Leigh being around. She'd thought she was just happy about the wedding for her father because he seemed to be so happy about it all. She'd thought she didn't really care one way or another whether her dad and Leigh got married. It was all what they wanted.

Then when Leigh had looked so ready to cry as she'd gone out the door, Jocie's heart had gotten heavy inside her and she'd wanted to wrap her arms around Leigh and make her stay. And not just for her dad. She wanted Leigh to stay for her. She even thought about calling her Mom, but she was afraid that might make Leigh run away faster. Still, the word Mom had been in Jocie's head. It was still there.

Jocie had written about it in her journal late Saturday night after they'd gotten back from the shower and her dad had left to stay with Wes.

I don't guess I've ever had a mom. Certainly not DeeDee. She may have been my mother, but never my mom. And then all of a sudden I'm looking at Leigh and thinking Mom. I guess that has to take the weird award for the year. Me wanting to call Leigh Mom when my actual mother was standing in the next room after being gone all these years. I never thought either thing would ever happen.

So now I have a granddaddy I call Wes and a mom I call Leigh. Maybe I'll tell Leigh that after the wedding. After DeeDee has left. After things have settled down a little. I wouldn't want to scare Leigh. While I think she really might like having a kid of her own, I'm sure she has in mind some sweet little baby like Stephen Lee, not some ugly duckling like me who's fourteen, going on fifteen. Mom might be the last word she wants to hear me say.

*That's certainly the way DeeDee was,* Jocie thought now as she got out of bed. She hadn't wanted to hear Mom, Mama, Mother, or anything from Jocie. Jocie tiptoed to the back door and carefully opened it to keep it from squeaking when she let Zeb out. It was early. Aunt Love wasn't even up yet. And here Jocie was wide awake.

She hadn't slept very well since DeeDee had shown up. Jocie kept jerking awake and listening. She wasn't sure for what. Maybe so she'd know if her mother got up and drove away in the middle of the night. Maybe so she could be sure DeeDee didn't try to pack up Stephen Lee and take him with her. She seemed almost obsessed by the baby.

Tabitha had thought Jocie was way wrong when Jocie said something about how maybe they should watch their mother so she couldn't carry off Stephen Lee. "DeeDee wouldn't do that," Tabitha had said. "She never wanted a baby. She doesn't even like babies."

"She may not like babies, but she likes Stephen Lee. A lot," Jocie had said.

Tabitha couldn't argue against that, and Jocie had noticed that she had started sticking close by when DeeDee had Stephen Lee.

But Jocie knew how Tabitha liked to sleep in the mornings as long as Stephen Lee wasn't being too loud. Plenty of times Jocie or Aunt Love had fetched the baby out of his crib without Tabitha even knowing they were in her room. So that's why Jocie was awake and listening. She was on guard. Who knew what DeeDee might do?

She looked like she might have a secret. Of course everything about DeeDee was a mystery to Jocie. She didn't know her mother. Jocie used to care. She used to want to know what her mother was like. What her mother liked. What her mother did. Now she didn't care.

She did know her mother was sick. Jocie had known that even before Aunt Love had told her they should be kind to DeeDee because she was recovering from surgery for cancer. Jocie still hadn't been able to find any caring in her heart. That was cold and mean of her and certainly not very Christian-like. Jocie was ashamed of how she was feeling, but even though she was praying about it, she still hadn't been able to dredge up one scrap of caring.

And cancer was bad. Jocie knew that. People at church were always having special prayer for somebody who had cancer. Maybe Jocie would remind Aunt Love to ask for special prayer for DeeDee next Sunday. Maybe the whole church praying for her would make up for Jocie's own halfhearted prayers.

Tabitha would have to drive them to church on Sunday. Jocie's dad and Leigh would be somewhere enjoying their first day as Mr. and Mrs. Brooke. Tabitha said maybe Robert could drive them since he was coming in for the wedding.

Somehow Tabitha had talked their dad into letting Robert be one of his groomsmen. He'd needed two since Leigh wanted both Tabitha and Jocie to be bridesmaids and the number of bridesmaids and groomsmen had to match. It was some kind of wedding rule. So he'd asked Robert. After all, he couldn't really ask any of the men out at church, because then all the other men might feel slighted.

Of course Wes was his best man. So Jocie would be walking out with Wes after the ceremony and Tabitha would be walking out with Robert. Tabitha could hardly wait. She was dreaming about when maybe Robert would ask her to walk down the aisle with him in the other direction. She'd told Jocie she'd been praying for a man like Robert to come into her life. Someone good and decent. Someone who could love her and be a father to Stephen Lee. Someone for her to love.

That was why Jocie wasn't worried about Tabitha taking

off in the middle of the night with DeeDee again. Tabitha wouldn't miss the wedding. She could hardly wait to put on the periwinkle blue dress and see Robert in his black suit.

Wes had had to buy a matching suit to be in the wedding. He'd groused about it, but he bought it. For her dad and Leigh, he said. "But I ain't putting none of that slick stuff on my hair to make it lay down. Not even for Miss Leigh. If folks don't want to see Jupiter hair, they can look the other way."

Jocie heard something in the living room and forgot about Jupiter hair. It wasn't Aunt Love. Aunt Love always went straight to the kitchen when she got up. She might forget to take the biscuits out of the oven, but she never forgot to put them in. Jocie stood up and went to the door. She pulled it open a few inches and peeked through.

DeeDee was on the couch holding Stephen Lee. The baby was asleep. DeeDee was rubbing his back and whispering close to his ear. Jocie couldn't hear what she was saying. DeeDee's suitcase was on the floor by her feet. Stephen Lee's diaper bag was beside it.

DeeDee was so focused on Stephen Lee that Jocie was almost right in front of DeeDee before she noticed her. "You can't take him," Jocie said.

DeeDee looked up and smiled at her, but her eyes were sad. "Poor Jocie. You're as bad as your father. So afraid of losing your grip on what can't be held. Don't you know that the only true way to hold someone is by opening your hand and giving them the freedom to go?"

"Stephen Lee is too little to go anywhere. He has to be held. And he's staying here."

"I know." DeeDee kissed the baby's hair. She kept her voice soft. "I wasn't going to take him anywhere. I was just saying goodbye."

"You're leaving?"

"I planned to be already gone, but he felt so good sleeping on my shoulder. His breath warm on my neck. So full of life." She shut her eyes and laid her cheek against his head.

"You didn't tell me goodbye."

DeeDee opened her eyes and looked at Jocie. "I haven't left yet."

"You left the other time. You could have said goodbye."

"Oh, but I did."

"No, you didn't. I remember when you left. I would have known if you had told me goodbye."

"Not then. Not when I left Hollyhill. I told you goodbye when you were three days old. I gave you to your father. A gift. A total, complete gift."

"Why didn't you love me?" Jocie felt an ache that went all the way down to her toes. "Was I too ugly? Did I cry too much?"

"You weren't ugly. At least no uglier than any newborn baby. And all babies cry." DeeDee ran her hand up and down Stephen Lee's back.

"Then what was wrong with me that you couldn't love me?"

"Your father loved you. Wasn't that enough?" DeeDee didn't wait for her to answer. "Love isn't something that a person can conjure up. It's either there or it isn't. I didn't want to carry you, Jocie. I didn't want to be a mother. I can give you nothing now that will make that any different. All I can give you is the truth."

"I've always wanted to know the truth."

DeeDee stared at her. "You're more like me than either of us will ever want to admit."

"I don't want to be like you."

DeeDee smiled a little. "Whether you want to be or not,

you are. You're tough. You know what you want and you go after it. And someday you'll have to leave this place behind just as I did."

"No," Jocie started.

DeeDee took one of her hands off Stephen Lee's back and held it up to stop Jocie. "Only time will tell, I suppose, which of us is right. Don't worry. I won't be around to say I told you so. I'm dying, you know."

"Not everybody who has cancer dies."

"No, not everybody, but the monster is running rampant inside me. It's just a matter of time." She said it matter-of-factly. Then she smiled a little again. "I promised David I wouldn't tell Tabitha, but he didn't ask me not to tell you."

"How long?"

"I don't suppose anyone ever knows how long they have. People die every day without expecting to. Heart attacks. Plane wrecks. Cancer just gives you more time to dwell on it." Stephen Lee stirred a bit and she started rubbing his back again. "And time to hold one child you love. He has my eyes, you know."

Jocie frowned and shook her head as she stared at her mother's face. "Your eyes are green. Stephen Lee's are brown. Tabitha says like his father's."

"True enough, but nevertheless they're like mine too. I saw that in the first picture Tabitha sent me."

"And that's why you love him?" The ache was fading inside Jocie. Now she was just curious.

"I don't know, Jocie. Love is a strange animal. You can't always tame it and make it behave the way you want it to. For years, I thought I could. I thought I could use love the way I used lipstick and perfume. Just to get what I wanted. But real love isn't that way. Real love bangs you around and makes you do things you never thought you would do." DeeDee glanced around the room. "Like be sitting in this house again."

"I'm sorry you're dying." Jocie was surprised to realize she wasn't just saying that to be nice.

"Yeah, me too. Me too." DeeDee tightened her arms around Stephen Lee for a moment before she stood up and handed the baby to Jocie. "Here, Jocie. Take good care of him for me."

The baby barely stirred before he settled his head on Jocie's shoulder and kept sleeping. "I will, but not for you. I love him myself."

"Too much like me." She smiled and shook her head. "This time you will have your goodbye. A final goodbye." DeeDee picked up her suitcase. She looked directly into Jocie's face. "Goodbye, Jocelyn."

Jocie didn't say goodbye back as she watched DeeDee turn and walk out the front door. She wanted her to go, to be gone, yet at the same time she wanted to call her back. Tell her that maybe she could try to love her, and that if she did, maybe DeeDee could try to love her back. She looked around as if she expected to see her father there so he could tell her what she should do. But of course he wasn't there.

Aunt Love was. She was standing in the doorway to the kitchen watching Jocie. She reached for Stephen Lee. "Go, child, run after her and tell her the Lord loves her. That's the least we can do for her."

Jocie ran out the door and down the steps. DeeDee's car was already rolling down the drive, but Jocie yelled at her to stop. DeeDee put on the brakes and waited.

Jocie didn't give herself time to think about what she was saying. She just ran right up to DeeDee's window and said, "The Lord loves you."

DeeDee smiled her sad smile. "Does he? How do you know?"

"The Bible says the Lord loves everybody. And you can still love him."

"And how about you, Jocie? Can you still love me? Doesn't the Bible say we're supposed to love everybody too?"

"It does. And I do, Mother. I hate you, but I love you at the same time."

"See, just like me." DeeDee smiled sadly and took her foot off the brake. "Always telling the truth even when it tears a hole right through you."

Jocie watched her mother drive away. She never looked back. Not once.

# 39

It was a long drive to Florida, but the hardest part for Adrienne had been getting out of Holly County without turning around. She hadn't wanted to leave Stephen behind. She'd wanted to just sit there on that couch or in the rocker on the porch and hold him until she died.

But then again, sometimes she felt as if the real Adrienne Mason had already died and left behind this pathetic shell of a woman to mark her place for a few more months. It didn't really matter all that much where that place was. David, who had been born with a corner on good and noble, would have helped her find a place to live in Hollyhill. He'd have let her keep holding Stephen even though she had certainly never done anything to earn that privilege. Nothing except give birth to his mother. Perhaps that was enough.

That silly girl of a woman, Leigh whatever her name was, seemed well suited to David. Nothing at all like Adrienne. The girl would have probably even helped David take care of Adrienne if she had stayed. It would have been her ticket to sainthood. Her good deed of the century.

Adrienne didn't want to be a good deed. She'd always made it on her own, under her own terms. She'd finish like that. One way or another. She had the memory of Stephen's soft curls against her cheek and the smell of his baby body to carry her through. Once that was no longer enough, the doctor had given her a prescription to help her walk down the final road through the pain that would come and that Dr. Mike had warned her might be brutal. Dr. Mike told her not to worry about the pills being addictive. No time for that. And even if there was, she wouldn't be addicted long.

The Florida sunshine wasn't much different than California sunshine. Hotter maybe. Adrienne didn't mind that. She liked hot. But she missed the California feeling of youth and opportunity. Florida felt old, where people went when they were finished, unlike California where people went to become stars, to get rich, to begin.

The curtains in her mother's trailer did have ruffles, but they weren't pink. They were yellow and the carpet was a smooth, flat tan. Easier to sweep the sand off it, her mother said, and lizards couldn't hide in the nap.

Adrienne barely recognized her mother. She'd gone blonde instead of gray. She wore bright-colored shorts and sleeveless tees. She was part of a group of friends who did everything together. Not unlike how things were in high school way back when, her mother said. And even more fun because nobody was fighting over who was prettiest anymore. They were just playing. She did shuffleboard on Tuesdays and Thursdays. She played bingo on Mondays and Saturdays. They got together for cards on Friday. She went out to eat every day. She had a big tricycle that she rode around the block for exercise and a boyfriend who rode with her.

She looked relieved when Adrienne said none of those games appealed that much to her and that she planned to just sit on the beach and watch the ocean. So Adrienne sat in the sun and watched the waves sweep in and out. Sometimes she put her chair close enough to the ocean so the highest tides washed over her feet and swept the sand under her chair until it was smooth and new looking.

She gathered the sunlight around her like a blanket and let her mind wander wherever it wanted. She liked to imagine Stephen sitting at the edge of the ocean and how he might laugh when the waves touched his toes. His baby laughter would echo in her head, and she would smile. Other times she wished Francine were there to cry for her. And sometimes she thought about Jocie running after her to tell her the Lord loved her.

# 40

Leigh was awake before the sun came up on Saturday morning. She didn't want to miss a minute of June 5, 1965, the day she was going to become Mrs. David Brooke. It was a beautiful day. Even before the sun came creeping over the eastern horizon and climbed above the trees across the street to start pushing its light through her bedroom window, she knew it was going to be a beautiful day.

The sky could have been clouded over and rain falling in buckets, and it still would have been a beautiful day. But it wasn't raining. The sky was a cloudless blue. Almost the same color as the dresses Tabitha and Jocie would be wearing that afternoon in the wedding. The weatherman had promised low humidity and a nice breeze with eighty for a high. It was almost enough to make Leigh wish she'd decided to get married outside at the park.

But First Baptist would be nice. There would be plenty of seats and Zella was overseeing the decorations. She'd wanted roses, but Leigh told her she couldn't afford that many roses. She'd have to go with something cheaper like daisies.

"Daisies?" Zella had practically squawked. "I guess you just want me to go out in the field and pick them. Honestly, Leigh, this isn't the time to be pinching pennies. You only get married once."

"I like daisies. And sunflowers. Sunflowers just look like they're shouting out joy, don't you think? The way they reach for the sun." Leigh held her arms up over her head to demonstrate and smiled.

Zella didn't smile back. "They're messy. They drip pollen all over. Roses are better. Besides, sunflowers aren't blooming yet."

"They'll be blooming somewhere. Blanche over at the flower shop can get them. I want daisies and sunflowers of joy," Leigh said. "Big bunches of them."

"That might be better suited at Mt. Pleasant than First Baptist," Zella said with a sniff.

"Then maybe we should move the wedding back to Mt. Pleasant."

"I guess you expect people to stand outside and peek through the windows once all the pews are full."

"If they want to," Leigh said. She didn't really care. All she cared about was how she was going to look in her perfect wedding dress and how David was going to look as he stood at the front of the church watching her walk down the aisle. Whichever aisle it was.

Zella mashed her lips together into a thin line before she said, "All right. Daisies and sunflowers it is. With one bouquet of roses on the reception table where the cake is going to sit in the fellowship hall. You don't want pollen all over your cake and in the punch, do you?" Zella didn't wait for an answer. "I'll pick those roses out of my garden. And Lovella's. She has some yellow ones. That won't cost you anything."

"Thank you, Zella. For everything. Without you, we might not be talking about roses or sunflowers," Leigh said as she gave Zella a little hug.

"True enough. Sometimes people have to be shoved toward their destiny."

Destiny. A marriage written in the stars. A match made in heaven. A blessed event. A reason for celebration. And she was celebrating as the sun began to rise on her wedding day.

Leigh sang a few hallelujahs as she danced across her bedroom, through the living room, and into the kitchen. She didn't even mind when Mrs. Simpson hit her broom handle against her ceiling below Leigh's feet. After today, Mrs. Simpson's too-sensitive ears would be somebody else's problem.

Nearly all of Leigh's stuff was in boxes, ready to move. She hadn't figured out exactly where she would put any of it at David's house. His house was already full of stuff and people. David was talking about building on a couple of rooms. Some of the men at church had volunteered to help. Thank goodness, they weren't having to make extra room for Adrienne. She'd left.

David hadn't asked her to. Leigh hadn't asked David to ask her to, but Leigh was still relieved Adrienne had decided to leave before the wedding. Leigh did feel bad for her. Not just because of the cancer, but because she'd never realized the blessing of her family. A blessing that was now Leigh's.

Leigh filled the teakettle and put it on to heat. She had so many butterflies in her stomach that she wasn't sure she'd be able to eat a thing, but she stuck some bread in the toaster. Maybe the butterflies were hungry and would settle down if she fed them.

She picked up a paper plate covered with ribbons off the table. Jessica Sanderson had carefully threaded all the ribbons from Leigh's shower gifts through a slit in the paper plate so Leigh could use it for her wedding bouquet at the rehearsal. Leigh fingered the long, streaming ribbons. They'd had the rehearsal at Mt. Pleasant Church the night before. Zella had said that couldn't happen, but David told Zella not only that it could happen. It would happen.

"One church is not that much different from another," he'd said and held up his hand to stop her protests. "So First Baptist does have a longer aisle, but that just means more walking. We don't need any practice walking. And right or wrong, we're having the rehearsal at Mt. Pleasant because the good people out there have been planning for months to have the rehearsal dinner for us in the church basement. So we're going to enjoy."

Enjoy. She and David had kept whispering that word to one another all through what surely had to be the zaniest wedding rehearsal on record. Tabitha and Robert Wesley were making eyes at one another in a little world all their own. Stephen Lee was crawling under the pews. Myra Hearndon's twins had crawled under the pews after him while Myra sang "The Lord's Prayer." Jocie had to leave her spot beside Tabitha and Leigh at the altar to corral them and sit them down on the pew beside Miss Sally who thankfully pulled a sack of graham crackers out of her purse to keep the babies still for a few minutes. The ring bearer and flower girl, Leigh's cousin's kids, took turns banging each other in the head with the ring pillow in spite of their mother's loudly whispered reprimands.

As if all that hadn't been bad enough, her Uncle Howie had said he wasn't really sure he could do the preacher's version of the wedding. As a judge he always just used a civil ceremony to marry people. Zella got right in his face and told him he'd say the ceremony the way they told him to and that was it. When Zella had paused for breath, Wes had offered to do the Jupiter version. Zella hadn't been amused. Neither were Leigh's parents if their glum expressions were any indication as they sat on the second row and watched the madness.

But then the rehearsal dinner made up for it all. Miss Sally took Leigh's mother in hand and had her smiling and laughing before she'd downed her first glass of iced tea. Matt McDermott sat down by her father and talked tractors. Leigh hadn't even known her father knew the first thing about tractors, but before long the two men were agreeing on which make was best at pulling a hay baler.

Zella had cornered Leigh before Leigh even had a chance to fill her plate. "A bad rehearsal always means a smooth wedding. If the wedding is as good as the rehearsal was bad, then the ceremony should go off without a hitch." Zella patted her curls that were looking a little limp in the heat of the overcrowded basement and fanned herself with a paper plate. The whole church congregation had obviously decided they were close enough family to be part of the rehearsal dinner.

"I don't care, Zella. Not as long as I end up hitched. To David."

Zella had rolled her eyes at Leigh. "Horses get hitched. Not people."

Leigh had mashed down a giggle. Giggling was probably something prospective brides her age shouldn't do either. But then David stepped up beside her and whispered in her ear. "Enjoy."

So Leigh had laughed and done just that. Enjoyed. And she was going to enjoy today. Rejoice and enjoy. And count her blessings. Number one, David. Number two, David. Number three, David. Number five hundred and six, David.

She had just poured the boiling water over her tea bag and sat down with her toast when she heard something out on her stoop. She sat very still without making a sound and hoped it was David coming by to say good morning before he went in to put in a few hours working on next week's issue of the *Banner*. But of course it wasn't. She knew who it was even before she saw the edge of white pushing through her keyhole.

The man just would not leave her alone. Even after she'd practically run over his feet getting away from him the week before. Even after David had called him and told him to stay away from her. Even after he no longer had a job or a reason to be in Hollyhill. Even after she and David had gone together to talk to Randy Simmons, the chief of police, about the man bothering Leigh.

"He's a strange one," Chief Simmons had agreed with them on that. "But I don't know that anything you've told me is against the law. He calls you on the phone. You see him hanging around out on the street around your place. I can't arrest him for that. I need some proof of some wrongdoing."

"What about the notes in my door? That's proof he was there," Leigh said. "When I didn't want him to be there."

"I understand, Leigh. Really I do. But did he do anything illegal? That's what I have to think about as an officer of the law. He's at your door, but he's not breaking and entering." The chief looked at them across his desk.

"God forbid," David said as he reached over to hold Leigh's hand.

"Well, see, that's what I mean," the chief said. "He may

be bothersome and a pain in the neck, but he's not dangerous. He's just trying to get your attention, Leigh. Change your mind about getting married to David here."

"But I've asked him to leave me alone. Over and over."

"Is he threatening you in any way? Saying anything obscene?" The chief picked up a pencil and a little notebook and waited for something to write down.

"No," Leigh admitted.

"Then I don't think there's really anything I can do. Except maybe give him an earful if he bothers you again. Tell him to take a hike, but I can't arrest him for trying to catch your eye." Chief Simmons looked sorry about that as he put the notebook down and sat back in his chair. "Like I said, the man's a strange one. He was in here himself just last week."

"What about?" David asked.

"Research, he said. For that great American novel he's writing. Asked me if I'd ever shot anybody in the line of duty. Then he sort of laughed and added 'or not in the line of duty.' And when I said I hadn't ever found it necessary, he asked me if I thought I could if it was necessary. If I even knew how to get my gun out of my holster."

"Did you tell him you saw action in France during the war, Randy?" David asked.

"I didn't see how that was anything he needed to know. Course he does appear to be drafting age. Single and all like he is, I'm surprised he hasn't already been called up. Could be he might have to serve some time in 'Nam if things don't settle down over there. I wouldn't envy the man that."

They'd ended up with Leigh promising to call the chief if Edwin Hammond showed up in her yard or on her doorstep again, and David promising to let the chief handle it if that happened.

314

Chief Simmons had walked with them to the door of his office. "What is it now? Not even a week till the two of you tie the knot. Once you're married, legal and all, this Hammond nut will give up on it and head back north to wherever he came from. One thing sure, nobody in Hollyhill will be sorry to see the heels of his shoes leaving town."

Now Leigh looked at the phone on the wall across the table from her. Too far away for her to reach without getting up. She didn't want to move or make any kind of noise that might let Edwin Hammond know she was awake and listening to him out on her stoop. She had a thick bath towel draped over the window in the door. He couldn't see inside even if he did try to make her believe he could.

Leigh held her breath as the doorknob turned and the door rattled. She said a thanksgiving prayer that she'd gotten up and double-checked to be sure the door was locked the night before.

"I know you're in there, Leigh. I know you're awake. I know you're listening."

He wasn't shouting, but his voice slid easily through the cracks around the old door. She wanted to put her hands over her ears. She wanted to scream until he went away. She bit her lip and sat very still instead. Maybe the chief was right. Maybe after today, after she was officially and finally Mrs. David Brooke, Edwin Hammond would give up and go away. She wanted him to go away right now. She didn't need him trying to spoil the most wonderful day of her life.

He was talking a little louder now. Leigh could almost see Mrs. Simpson downstairs peeking out her kitchen window trying to see what was happening. At least Leigh would have a witness if Edwin did cross the line from legally driving Leigh crazy to something Chief Simmons might consider illegal.

"You can still make the better choice. You can still love me. I'll take you away from here. I'll make you soar to the heavens."

Funny, Leigh thought. The man had never said the first thing about loving her. It was always her loving him.

"Let me in," he said and began shaking the door. "I'll make you mine."

Leigh stopped sitting there like one of the three little pigs while the wolf tried to tear down her door. She stood up and grabbed the phone, but she didn't know the police department's number. Back in Grundy, her mother had always kept the telephone number of the police taped to their phone. The strip of paper was brown with age with the tape curling up on the edges. Never once had her mother had the occasion to use it.

Leigh knew that number by heart from seeing it a thousand or two times. A lot of good that did her. The Grundy police weren't going to come run Edwin Hammond off. She started frantically searching for her telephone book under the piles of newspapers she'd been using to wrap her dishes. There was something to say for paranoia. At least then she'd know the number for the Hollyhill police.

"Are you afraid to talk to me, Leigh Jacobson? Hiding like a little mouse in a hole? That's what living here is doing to you. You're a tiger, not a mouse."

Leigh dropped the stack of papers. She knew the county clerk's number. She dialed it and asked Judy to call Chief Simmons. Then she went right to the door and pulled the bath towel off the curtain rod. She stared through the window at Edwin Hammond who started smiling at her.

She kept her face blank. "Go away."

316

"The door's old. I could break it." His smile got wider. "Just a little harder push. That's all it would take."

"Go away."

"You don't really want me to go away. Not really. Your future is at stake. My future is at stake."

"Go away. Now." A few streets away, Leigh heard a siren. Not a common sound in Hollyhill. Half the town would be running to their doors to see if it was the ambulance or the police stopping a speeder. No one would think it was a mentally unbalanced man at her door.

"Never," Edwin said. "I'm here to rescue you."

The siren was getting closer. Leigh didn't say anything more as she very deliberately hung the towel back over the window in the door. Then she went back into the kitchen and sat down to drink her tea. Nothing, not even Edwin Hammond, was going to mess up this day for her.

Outside she could hear Chief Simmons talking to the man, but she didn't try to hear what either of them said. She got a piece of paper and began making a list of things she needed to take to the church. Her suitcase packed for their weekend at Cumberland Falls. Her dress and veil. Miss Sally's handkerchief she was going to carry in the wedding for the something borrowed. The garter Zella had given her for the something blue. Her grandmother's gold locket for the something old. Her white slippers would do for the something new.

Something old, something new, something borrowed, something blue was supposed to bring luck. But she and David didn't have to depend on making luck. The Lord had blessed them by giving them love. She was just going to depend on the Lord to take care of them and to keep blessing them.

There was a knock on her door. "Are you all right, Leigh?" Chief Simmons called.

"I'm fine." Leigh went to the door and opened it. She didn't even look around to see if Edwin Hammond was gone. "I'm better than fine."

The chief smiled at her. "I can believe that. And you don't have to worry about that joker anymore. I've sent him packing. You just enjoy the day."

"Oh yes, indeed." One of the verses Aunt Love was always saying bubbled up inside Leigh so she just said it out loud. "'This is the day which the Lord hath made; we will rejoice and be glad in it.'"

"You sound like a preacher's wife already." The chief laughed and turned to start down the steps. He glanced back over his shoulder to say, "I'll see you this afternoon. Me and the wife are looking forward to the big event. If you need any more help before then, you just give me another holler."

# 41

Jocie was glad it wasn't too hot as she carried her brides-maid dress into the First Baptist Church. She didn't want to make sweat circles under her arms on the beautiful dress. First Baptist was air-conditioned, so the temperature out-side really didn't matter all that much. Still, the weather being so near perfect was nice. As if the Lord was smiling down on them, celebrating the day with them. And she hadn't once thought to say a good-wedding-day-weather prayer, but her father said the Lord sometimes answered prayers a person didn't even think to pray.

Of course she wasn't the only person who might be pray-ing for the day's big event. The Mt. Pleasant people had put the wedding on their prayer list months ago. They were a praying church. Jocie's father said so. Said he could feel when the people were praying for him. That it lifted him up. If so, he might be floating today.

He might be floating anyway. He was that happy. And Jocie was that happy for him. And herself. It was going to be good having Leigh living with them. A little more crowded, but good. Jocie had never had a mom, but that's what she wanted Leigh to be. Her mom.

Jocie still cringed inside when she thought about her last words to DeeDee. She should have just told her she loved her and left off the hating part. She didn't always have to tell the complete truth. She could mash her lips together and keep some of it inside. And those crazy spiders not only crawled around inside her ribs, they started biting on her when she thought about her mother saying Jocie was like her. Jocie didn't want to be like DeeDee. She wanted to be like her father. Or Leigh. She wanted to be someone who cared about other people and not just herself.

Her father had assured her she was when Jocie told him what DeeDee had said to her. "She said I was like her. Too much like her."

"She is your mother," her father had said.

"But I want to pick a new mother. I want Leigh to be my mother now."

Her father smiled. "That will make Leigh happy. And me. But Adrienne isn't and never was all bad. She has force of character. She always knew what she wanted and went after it. She always looked for her own answers. Those are good traits to have, and some that you share for sure."

"But she hurt people doing that. I don't want to hurt people."

Her father put his arms around her. "Just because you are like your mother in some ways doesn't mean you're like her in every way. We all make choices, and a big difference between you and your mother is that she never made the choice to step into the circle of the Lord's love. You have. You know about how the Lord can walk along beside you and lift you out of troubles. You've trusted your life to him. But your mother was always afraid she'd have to give up too much to have that kind of trust. What she refused to believe is that when a person turns over his life to the Lord, he is set free."

"I told her the Lord loved her before she left. He does, doesn't he?" Jocie raised her head off her father's chest to peer up at him.

"The Bible tells us the Lord loves us all. God is love. For God so loved the world. The world pretty much includes everyone, don't you think?"

Jocie had nodded and her father's arms had tightened around her. "I'm so proud of you, Jocie. And so glad you are my daughter."

Jocie was glad about that too. And she was glad about her father marrying Leigh, but she wasn't as glad about the whole wedding business. People just got too carried away about the smallest details when they had wedding fever. A fever Zella had obviously contracted weeks ago. When Jocie came through the church door, Zella dropped the bunch of sunflowers she was holding and practically ran up the church aisle to confront her.

"My heavens, Jocelyn. Your hair. It looks the same as always. I thought Pamela was fixing it for you."

"She did. She worked on it early this morning." Pamela at the beauty shop had set aside the whole morning to do everybody's hair for the wedding. She'd even offered to do Aunt Love's, but Aunt Love said her usual bun would be fine. She'd just put an extra flower on her hat.

"Well, mercy sakes, she should have used hair spray." Zella touched her own curls that were cemented in place.

"She did that too. Really. I almost choked on the fumes. But my hair just won't hold curls. Tabitha says she can do some kind of little braids on top of my hair in the back and twine ribbons in with the braids. She found some ribbons the same blue as our dresses. That'll dress my hair up a little."

"I guess it'll have to do," Zella said with a heavy sigh. "Now don't be doing anything to mess things up today."

Jocie managed to not roll her eyes until she turned away from Zella. She'd promised her father she'd go along with whatever Zella said because this was probably the biggest day in the woman's life since who knew what had happened.

"But she's not even family," Jocie had protested.

"Close enough," Jocie's dad had said. "And in ways this wedding, Leigh and me getting together, is a gift she feels she gave us. To be honest, without her prodding I might not have noticed Leigh and Leigh might have given up on me."

"I think the Lord had more to do with that than Zella," Jocie had mumbled.

"Could be, but letting her have such a big part in helping with the wedding is kind of our gift back to Zella. And you have to promise not to spoil her fun."

So Jocie bit her tongue and headed back to the Sunday school room where Leigh was sitting in one of the folding chairs in her slip and stockings, fanning herself while Pamela fussed over her hair. "You're gonna look just beautiful, honey," the woman said as she pulled a curl free with the pointed end of her comb.

Actually Leigh already looked beautiful. Her cheeks were rosy and her eyes were sparkling. She was glowing all over. That was what Jocie told her. "You look fantastic, Leigh."

"I don't even have my dress on yet. Or my makeup."

"You don't need it," Jocie said. "The makeup, I mean. I guess you'd better put on the dress. We wouldn't want

322

to have to print the headline 'Bride Forgets Dress' in next week's *Banner*."

"I'm so excited, nervous, whatever, that I've probably forgotten something." Leigh slapped her forehead. "Oh no! I did forget something."

"What'd you forget? Your shoes? Your veil?" Jocie asked. "I can run over to your place and get it for you. Tabitha's not here yet anyway to fix my hair. She's going to do some little braids in the back."

Pamela looked up from Leigh's hair. "I'm real sorry, Jocie. I did my best to get those curls to stick." She reached over and touched Jocie's hair. "You've got pretty hair, but it is bound and determined to be straight."

"It looks great just the way it is, Jocie. You look great just the way you are. Don't you worry about it for a minute," Leigh said. "And I don't want you to have to go back to the apartment. I can just not use it."

"What?" Jocie asked.

"The fancy garter Zella bought me for the something blue. I had it out there on the dresser, but then I walked right off and forgot to pick it up. I've got Miss Sally's hankie for the something borrowed and Grandma Wilson's locket for the something old and my shoes for the something new."

"Well, honey, you've got to have the something blue to make it all work," Pamela said.

"And Zella will get upset big time if she bought it for you and you don't wear it in the wedding. She wants everything to be perfect." Jocie draped her dress across the back of a chair and headed for the door. "I'll go get it. I can probably run over there and be back before Tabitha even gets here. Robert just left to go pick up her and Aunt Love."

"Don't run. You'll get all sweaty," Leigh yelled after her.

323

So Jocie walked and wished for her bike, but it was home. Still, it wasn't that far and the day had a special glow to it just like Leigh. It was good to be out in the sunshine, to have everybody she met on the street smile and tell her they'd see her later at the wedding. Everybody in Hollyhill was acting as happy as her father and Leigh. It was almost enough to make Jocie reconsider eloping Jupiter style if she ever went crazy enough to think about getting married.

Jocie stuck Leigh's key back in her pocket when she got to the apartment. She wasn't going to need it. Leigh's door was ajar. Jocie smiled as she crossed the yard thinking Leigh must have really been in a spin when she left for the church. To leave her door standing open.

Before she started up the steps to the door, Jocie looked over toward Mrs. Simpson's kitchen window to wave, but Mrs. Simpson wasn't there peeking out from behind the curtains. She was probably getting dressed to go to the wedding or maybe she was already at the church to stake out the best seat. She'd want to get a good view of everything and everybody.

The apartment was sort of dark after the bright sunlight outside. For some reason Leigh had pulled all the shades. Jocie frowned. She couldn't imagine Leigh pulling the shades down and shutting out the sunlight. Not this morning. Not any morning. Leigh liked the sun coming through her windows. She kept her curtains tied back to let in the most light. But maybe she was closing out her old life to start her new. Taking her light with her. Or maybe Mrs. Simpson had been up there to shut up the place since Leigh was moving out.

It didn't really matter. Jocie was just there to get the blue garter Zella had bought for Leigh. Tabitha would probably be at the church by now waiting to fix the braids in Jocie's hair. Leigh had said she left the garter on her dresser. Jocie hoped it was still there, because if it wasn't, she'd never find it in all the boxes sitting around.

Jocie pushed open the bedroom door. The light in the bedroom was even dimmer than in the living room. Jocie hesitated. For some reason her heart was beating a little faster and she felt the way she sometimes did when she had to go get a jar of beans or tomatoes out of the cellar for Aunt Love. As if spiders were about to drop on her head and snakes crawl up around her legs. Jocie wanted to turn around and run, leave it to the ghosts or whatever was spooking her, but then she spotted the garter on the dresser.

She couldn't leave without that. What would she tell Leigh? That she was too scared to walk into the bedroom and pick up the garter? Then somebody else would have to come get it and they'd be teasing Jocie about it forever.

She wasn't afraid of ghosts. She didn't believe in ghosts. She believed in the Lord. He'd walk across the floor with her. He'd even run across the floor with her and she could snatch the garter and be out of the room before the spiders got her. Besides, Jocie had never seen the first spider in Leigh's apartment.

She was picking up the garter when she caught sight of a face staring at her out of the mirror. Her heart bounded up in her throat as she whirled around to stare at Mr. Teacher Creep sitting in the chair by Leigh's bed. He was smiling at her. Not a good smile.

"Well, well," he said. "Look who we have here."

She swallowed hard and found her voice. "Mr. Hammond!"

"Yes indeed. Mr. Hammond himself."

The sound of his voice walked cold fingers up her spine.

"What are you doing in here?" She tried to keep her voice from shaking but failed.

"An interesting question. But then you're always full of interesting questions, aren't you, Jocie Brooke?"

She didn't care if he answered her or not. She just wanted to be out of this room and away from him. She could worry about why he was there later. After she was back at the church. She wrapped her hand around the garter. "I just came to get something for Leigh. I'll be going now."

"I don't think so." Mr. Hammond raised his hand up out of his lap. In his hand he had a gun. A gun he pointed straight at Jocie.

# 42

ocie couldn't move. Even her breath froze inside her as she stared at the gun. It was a small gun. Black. Not new. The end of the barrel was nicked. But there was no doubt it was real as Mr. Hammond cradled it in his hand with one finger caressing the trigger. Outside a bird was singing. A car went past on the road. Inside, a fly was buzzing and hitting against one of the windows, and the clock beside the bed kept ticking. But time for Jocie screeched to a halt.

"You act as if you'd never seen a gun before." Mr. Hammond laughed. It was a terrible sound. "I suppose that's not something your reverend father has. A gun. He probably wouldn't even shoot a snake. A bit unlike my own dear departed father who lived and died by the gun. They say a gun very like this one dispatched him to his just rewards."

Jocie had thought she knew what it was like to be afraid. She'd been afraid during the tornado and even more afraid after the tornado when she saw Wes trapped under the tree limb. She had been afraid when Miss Sally's house was on fire and they'd had to crawl out the upstairs window. She'd been afraid, but there had been something to do.

Some action to take. A way out of the danger. The Lord had helped her then. She sent up a silent plea for help now. *Show me a way out, Lord.*

She kept her eyes on the gun as she slid one of her feet backward. Her heart was pounding so hard that she could barely hear the man when he spoke, but she did see his finger tightening on the trigger. "Stay where you are. I'm not ready for you to leave yet."

"But I'm ready to leave," Jocie managed to say.

"I'd wager you are." Again the laugh. "I'd wager you're about to wet your pants. But let's talk first."

"What about?" Jocie pulled in a slow breath and tried not to think about it maybe being her last. She tore her eyes away from the barrel of the gun pointed toward her and stared at the man's face.

"About the good fortune that brought you here at just this moment. Do you believe that some things are meant to be? Ordained. Predestined." He waved the gun back and forth. "But of course you do. You believe in the Bible."

"Why is it meant to be that I'm here?" Jocie asked even as she was frantically praying silently. *Lord, help me ask the right questions. Help somebody miss me at church and come hunt me. Let Mrs. Simpson hear us downstairs and call the police.*

"Your father took something from me. Now I have the opportunity to take something from him."

"My father didn't take anything away from you. You never had Leigh."

"But if not for your father, who knows what might have been. Your father." Mr. Hammond spat out the two words. "Everybody thinks he's so wonderful. Practically the second coming here in Hollyhill." He shook the gun at her.

Jocie held her breath. The gun didn't go off. But then she wondered if it might have been better if it had. Mrs.

Simpson would have heard it and called for help. Maybe any noise would do. Jocie could stomp the floor or knock over something. Without moving her head, she looked to the side where a couple of boxes were piled. All she had to do was stumble a bit and bang into them. She did her best to pretend she'd just lost her balance. The top box fell to the floor with a heavy thud.

"Always thinking, aren't you, Jocie Brooke?" Mr. Hammond said as he leveled the gun at her again. "But never listening."

"I listen." She was really listening right then. Surely Mrs. Simpson had heard that and would know that nobody was supposed to be in the apartment over her head.

"You think noise will help you? Here, then, how about a little extra noise?" He jerked the gun up and shot over the top of Jocie's head.

Jocie's heart tried to jump out of her chest as she put her hands over her ears and screamed.

He brought the gun back down to point at her. "Now that's too noisy. But the point is, I've taken care of the snoopy old lady downstairs. All the noise in the world isn't going to bring you any help from that quarter."

"Taken care of her?" Jocie was surprised she could speak. She was surprised she was still standing the way her legs had turned to jelly. She should have run out the door when he shot the gun. Maybe she should even now run out the door. That might be a good idea if she could trust her legs to work.

"Oh, don't look so worried. I didn't shoot her. Just tied her to her kitchen chair where she can't spy out her window for a while. I actually didn't plan to shoot anybody but myself until you showed up."

Relief shot through her. At least he hadn't already shot

somebody. Even himself. He'd had time before she had shown up. So maybe he was having second thoughts. "I don't think you should shoot yourself."

"Oh? You think I should only shoot you then?" He raised his eyebrows at her.

"No. If you shoot me, you'll go to prison. You wouldn't like prison."

"How could you know that? But that's the way you are, isn't it? A veritable fountain of knowledge." His mouth twisted in disgust as he looked at her.

"Nobody likes prison," Jocie said in a small voice.

"It might be better than Vietnam. I got my draft notice." He waved the gun toward an envelope on the table beside him. "They found me even out here in Nowhereville. You can't hide from Uncle Sam. It appears he wants me, but I'm not going to Vietnam. No matter what I have to do." He had the gun steady on her again.

"You might not have to go to Vietnam."

"Oh, I'm pretty sure I won't now. Not after tying up Mrs. Snoop downstairs and scaring the socks off you. But then there is that little matter of prison." He grimaced. "Remember, even you were of the opinion that I wouldn't like it there."

"You haven't done anything that bad yet. You might get off with probation or something."

"Might. Ah, that is the operative word."

Jocie tried desperately to think of something more to say, but nothing came to mind. Instead, she sent up silent prayers.

Mr. Hammond didn't seem to have as much problem finding words. "You know, I've never seen one word of mine in print. Not one word. It's always rejection after rejection. So sorry your poem is not quite right for our

330

publication. So sorry your story isn't what we're looking for this month. So sorry we're not accepting submissions. So sorry but your words stink. Your exalted father wouldn't even print my letters to the editor."

"You sent something in to the *Banner*?" Jocie was surprised.

"I did. Opinion pieces that would have elevated your small town rag from its mediocrity."

Jocie frowned. "I don't remember ever seeing anything from you come into the paper."

"No, you wouldn't have. I didn't sign my name. Opinions are sometimes best expressed anonymously."

"Dad doesn't print anybody's letters or whatever unless they sign them. It's just policy." Funny, Jocie thought, how talking about the *Banner* was helping her not be so terrified. Maybe a person could only be totally and completely terrified for so long.

"So you're saying your father might have printed my pieces if I'd put my name on them." He gave her an incredulous look. "I rather doubt that. I have the distinct feeling that your father dislikes me. I doubt he would even pray for me."

"That's not true. I know for a fact he has prayed for you and he said I should pray for you too."

"And did you send up prayers to your God for me, Jocie Brooke?" Mr. Hammond lowered his wrist down to rest it on his knee, but he still held the gun pointed at her. He looked amused as he asked, "Are you praying for me right now or for yourself?"

"Both."

"What are you praying?" His smile got bigger.

"I don't want to die," Jocie said.

"I would have said the same thing last week. But things

331

change." He lost his smile as he began stroking the gun barrel with his free hand.

"Not that much. What if you shoot yourself today when in another week you would have wanted to live again? And then it would be too late."

"Too late. Such sad words. Your father may have missed you by now. He may be running here, not knowing the danger you are in. Not knowing how if he'd run a bit faster he might have been in time. But now all his life he'll have to say he was too late." He raised the gun up.

*And lo, I am with you always, even unto the end of the world.* The words came into her mind and with them a great stillness. Her heart quit pounding so hard and her thoughts were crystal clear. She was not going to die on her father's wedding day. Not without trying to live.

# 43

f you don't stand still, Wes, I'll never get this knot straight,"
David said as he worked on his best man's tie.

Wes quit shifting back and forth on his feet and held his
chin up out of David's way. "I don't guess I've worn a tie
since, well, since I started motorcycle riding some years
back. I plumb forgot how to work the things."

"I could have tied it for you, Wes," Robert Wesley said.
Robert Wesley was looking very handsome in his black
suit with his sky blue tie that matched the bridesmaid's
dresses. David hoped Tabitha wouldn't swoon when she
saw him.

"That's okay, Junior. We'll make the groom do the work.
We keep him busy enough, he might not notice how shaky
he's feeling," Wes said.

David smiled and jerked the tie a little tighter than necessary. "I'm not the least bit shaky."

"I don't know why not," Robert Wesley said. "I'm nervous, and I'm not even the one getting married."

"Not yet anyhow," Wes said.

The boy's face turned pink as he said, "I do hope to
marry someday."

"Good. I highly recommend it," Wes said. "For the two of you. I'll save my suit for the occasion. Better a wedding suit than a funeral suit. Come to think of it, if I were to meet an untimely end, make sure they don't bury me in it just because it's handy. I don't want to go to the hereafter dressed like this. The good Lord might not recognize me."

David finished tying the tie and handed Wes the gold tie clip he'd bought for him. "Don't be talking funerals on my wedding day."

"I've heard some men say they were one and the same," Wes said with a grin.

"But not for me," David said. "Me, I'm the most blessed man in the world."

"Miss Leigh is a prize. That's for certain," Wes said.

There was a tap on the Sunday school room door. "Is it time?" David asked.

Robert Wesley looked at his watch. "Not yet. It's still fifteen minutes before we're supposed to go out according to Miss Curtsinger's schedule."

There was another knock before the door opened a crack. Tabitha whispered through the opening, "Dad, we've got a problem."

"It's okay, Tabitha. You can come in. We're all suited up," David said.

Tabitha stepped through the door in her blue bridesmaid dress. She looked beautiful with her hair tied back and ribbons falling down among the long tresses. David didn't really get worried about whatever problem she had come to tell him about until Tabitha hardly even glanced toward Robert Wesley. "What's wrong?" David asked. "Is Leigh sick?"

"No, no. Just a little frantic. Jocie's not here."

David frowned. "What do you mean, Jocie's not here?

334

I dropped her off here myself over an hour ago. She said you were going to fix her hair since whatever Pamela did didn't work."

"Yeah, she was here. But Leigh forgot the blue garter Zella gave her, and Jocie went to get it and she hasn't come back. I don't know where she could be." Tabitha looked worried. "You don't think she decided to run away again? She didn't seem upset or anything about you getting married today, did she?"

"Not a bit. She's looking forward to having a stepmom. And she definitely hasn't run away. She promised me she would never do that again." David's chest felt tight. Something was wrong.

Wes must have felt the same thing because every hint of smile was gone as he asked Tabitha, "How long has she been gone?"

"Leigh couldn't remember for sure, but it was before I got here and I've been here awhile."

"I'll go after her," Wes said. "Maybe she just forgot the time and is lollygagging."

"I'll go too," David said.

"You need to stay here. That way you can go on with the ceremony," Wes said.

"It's supposed to start in fifteen minutes." Robert Wesley looked at his watch. "Fourteen now."

"Leigh says she's not getting married without Jocie here. She told Zella she didn't care if the church was full of kings and queens. She wasn't budging out of that room until Jocie showed up and had time to put on her dress. The people could just go on home if they didn't want to wait." Tears popped up in Tabitha's eyes. "Something's wrong. Jocie wouldn't do this to you and Leigh if something wasn't wrong."

335

"Easy, baby," David said. "What could be wrong?"

"With Jocie, who knows? Tornadoes. Fires. Something's always happening to her," Tabitha said. Robert Wesley went over to put his arms around her and she leaned against him.

"There's not a storm cloud in the sky. And no smoke. She's probably just hunting for the garter and doesn't realize it's so late," David said. He wished he could believe that himself. "Tell Leigh we'll be right back."

They went out the side door of the church. "I didn't bring the keys to my car," David said.

"Wouldn't have done you any good no how. Your car's blocked in." Wes waved his hand at the packed parking lot. "My motorcycle's over there on the grass. We can take it over to Miss Leigh's. Once we get Jo, I'll bring her on back to the church and then come back for you."

"What if she isn't at Leigh's?"

"No need worrying about that till we get there," Wes said as he climbed on his motorcycle. "I mean, what could happen to the girl in Hollyhill?"

"I don't know." David climbed on behind him. "But I've got a bad feeling."

"Ditto. Could be we should be praying. Hang on." Wes kicked the motorcycle to life. Some late arrivers turned to stare at them.

David was praying as they bumped across the sidewalk and curb out onto the street. *Dear Lord, watch over my child. Stand with her and protect her. And help me not to yell at her if nothing's really wrong. I want nothing to be wrong. Oh please, dear Lord, let nothing be wrong.* But in his head he seemed to hear the whispered word "hurry."

The streets were unnaturally still. Nobody was out mowing the yard. No kids were roller-skating on the sidewalks.

Surely not everybody in Hollyhill was at the church for his wedding, but the parking lot had been jam-packed. It could be that if Jocie had had some sort of accident, there hadn't been anybody to help her. But what kind of accident could she have just walking three or four blocks to Leigh's apartment?

During the last year Jocie had stumbled into one problem after another. Had she somehow stumbled into a new problem? David ordered himself to stop playing guessing games. To pray instead. Prayers would be more valuable than guesses if something did turn out to be wrong.

The door to Leigh's apartment was standing open. Wes bounced the motorcycle across the sidewalk and through the yard right up to the bottom of the steps. David thought Wes would have ridden straight up into the apartment if he could have made the motorcycle climb the stairs. When Wes cut the motor, the silence was deafening. David took a quick look toward Mrs. Simpson's kitchen window, but of course the old lady wasn't there peeking out at them. She would be at the church waiting for the wedding music to start.

Something popped like a car backfiring or a firecracker on the Fourth of July. It came from the apartment over their heads.

Wes didn't even look around as he started up the steps, two at a time. "That sounded like a pistol."

David pushed past Wes at the top of the stairs and went into the apartment first. "Jocie!"

## 44

ocie heard the motorcycle coming, but so did Edwin Hammond. "You think your weird old friend is going to rush in and rescue you. But remember what I said about it being too late."

"You don't want to do this." Jocie's mind was racing five hundred miles a minute. He was right. Wes was still too far away, but there had to be something she could use, some way out. She stepped back and bumped into the box she'd stumbled against minutes earlier. She slipped her hand behind her back to feel down inside it. Blankets and pillows. Nothing hard she could use for a weapon.

"Why not?" His voice was calm, almost bored sounding, as if he wasn't talking about anything more important than verb tenses. "Think of the headline. 'MAN SHOOTS GIRL ON FATHER'S WEDDING DAY.' My ticket to fame."

"It won't be much fun being famous in prison."

"No prison. You first. Then me. Two shots and we're through. Finished. We'll both be famous." His voice changed, became dramatic as he flung out the hand not holding the gun. "The whole town will wail and mourn at your funeral. Such a tragedy. It would make a great story. The *New Yorker* would take it in a minute." He sighed and went on. "But alas, time has run out. The rescuer draweth nigh."

"Are you ready to die?" Jocie was amazed that she could still talk, still think. The Lord had to be helping her. She just had to trust in his power the way David in the Bible had trusted in the Lord's power when he had faced Goliath. But at least he'd had a slingshot and lots of practice using it. What did she have? Blankets and the throw pillows Leigh had made just a couple of months ago to decorate her bed. Jocie had helped her stuff them with old stockings.

"Are you?" He looked at her with raised eyebrows.

"No." She stared at him and tried desperately to think of something to keep him talking long enough for Wes to get there. The motorcycle was getting closer. "But if I do, I know the Lord is waiting to take me to heaven."

"How childishly sweet. I'll wager you don't think he's waiting for me."

"He could be. He loves you the same as me." Outside the motorcycle roared up into the yard. For a minute Jocie thought it might come on up the steps, but then the motor stopped.

"Well, what do you say we go see?" Mr. Hammond straightened out his arm and aimed the gun at her head.

Jocie gripped the edge of one of the throw pillows. She dropped to the floor and threw the pillow in the same motion. The pillow hit his arm just as the gun went off. The bullet shattered the mirror on Leigh's dresser.

Jocie grabbed another pillow and threw it as hard as she could. He ducked to the side and came after her as she scrambled toward the bedroom door. Her hand touched a can of hair spray that had fallen out of the box she'd

339

knocked over. She grabbed it and came up spraying toward Mr. Hammond's eyes. He yelled and shot wildly up into the air.

Then both Wes and her father were there, grabbing Mr. Hammond, pushing him down on the bed, knocking the gun out of his hand. Jocie scooted over into the corner, pulled her knees up against her chest, and burst into tears.

David wanted to kill the man. With his bare hands. He had never felt such rage. It consumed him as he knocked Edwin Hammond down on the bed and wrapped his hands around his throat.

Hammond didn't fight him. He just smiled up at David and said, "It's her fault. She came here asking to die."

Behind David, Wes made a growling sound. "Let me at him, David."

David's hands tightened on Hammond's throat. The man kept smiling. His voice sounded funny as he said, "Go ahead. Kill me if you have the nerve."

"Daddy, don't."

Jocie's voice penetrated through the fog of David's rage. He pulled in a slow breath and lifted his hands away from the man's throat.

Hammond put his hand to his throat and gasped. Then the gasp turned to a laugh as he said, "Just as I thought. No nerve."

David didn't say anything as he jerked him to a sitting position. Wes yanked Hammond's arms behind him as they stood him up. "What are we going to do with him?" Wes asked.

"Not what he wants," David said. He looked around. Jocie was huddled in the corner watching him with big eyes, but he couldn't turn loose of the man to go to her. Wes might not be strong enough to hold him by himself. "Get that sash off the curtains. We'll tie him up."

"Don't you have a wedding to get to?" Hammond shifted on his feet until his face was right in front of David's. The man's glasses sat sideways on his head to add to the demented look in his eyes as he smiled and said, "I daresay we're late already, aren't we?"

"Not too late," David said as he pushed him back.

"That's what he said you'd be," Jocie spoke up in a shaky voice. "Too late."

"As you would have been if I hadn't misfired. My father would be disappointed in me. He was always a crack shot." Hammond's laugh was like fingernails raking against a chalkboard.

"Keep your mouth shut or we'll find a gag for you," Wes said as he started tying up the man's hands.

"He tied Mrs. Simpson up," Jocie said. "Downstairs."

"Attacking old ladies and little girls. What a man." Wes jerked the sash tight around Hammond's hands.

Hammond ignored Wes as he kept talking to David. "It rather spoils the wedding, doesn't it? Leaving the bride at the altar."

David stopped listening to the man. Hammond was just a problem to get out of the way now so he could go comfort Jocie. He saw the open closet door. Leigh had already packed up all the stuff in it. "Put him in there until we can get hold of the chief," David told Wes.

Hammond's smile drained away as he looked at the closet and started struggling to get away from Wes and David. "You can't do that. I don't like dark places."

"That's too bad," Wes said as they pushed the man into the closet and shoved the dresser over in front of the door.

The man started pounding his body against the door and screaming. Wes looked at David and said, "That might not hold him. We'd better move the bed over here too."

After they scooted the heavy oak bed across the floor up against the dresser, David picked Jocie up like a baby and carried her out of the bedroom. Hammond was still screaming. Jocie wrapped her arms around David's neck and held on. She was crying again.

"Are you okay, honey? Did he hurt you?" David pulled back from her a little to look into her face.

"I'm okay, but I'm sorry, Daddy. I didn't aim to ruin your wedding day."

"I'm not worried a bit about that. I'm just thankful. Very thankful." David held her close against him and kissed her hair.

"Amen to that," Wes said as he tried to hug Jocie too. "But from now on we aren't letting you out of our sight. Ever. Not even to go to the little girls' room." When Jocie turned her head to look at Wes, he swiped away some of her tears with his tie.

Jocie giggled through her tears. "You're ruining your tie."

"Folks never wear ties on Jupiter anyhow. If they want to dress up special, they just paste a blue spot on their foreheads."

"Yeah, but remember you've been earthed," Jocie said.

"Don't I know it. That's how come I'm wearing this blasted thing." Wes smiled and put his hand on her head.

Jocie looked back up at David. "I prayed, Daddy, and the Lord helped me find a way out. I'm glad. I didn't want to die on your wedding day."

David hugged her against him again. He didn't want to ever turn her loose.

"Dad, I can't breathe."

He reluctantly loosened his hold on her. She pushed away from him. "I really am okay, Dad. Honest. Can we go back and have the wedding? Please. After we untie poor Mrs. Simpson."

"Right. Mrs. Simpson."

As soon as David took the gag out of Mrs. Simpson's mouth, she started talking nonstop. "What happened to that man? Where is he? Is that him making all that racket upstairs?" Her gray hair was standing out in every direction and her eyes were so wide open they looked about ready to pop out. Her wrists and ankles were red and swollen where the cord Hammond had used to tie her to one of her kitchen chairs had cut into her skin.

"I'll call the ambulance to take you to the hospital," David said. "You've been through quite an ordeal."

"Have I ever, but you can't call anybody. Not even the police. That man cut the wires. I saw him."

"Wes can go next door and call," David said.

"I think not. I'm not about to go off to any hospital right now. I've got a wedding to go to." She frowned at him as if she'd just realized who he was. "What on earth are you doing here instead of being at the church anyway?"

"We couldn't get married without Jocie." David reached over to touch Jocie who was standing as close to Wes as she could get.

"What has Jocie got to do with any of this?" Mrs. Simpson's frown got deeper as she peered over at Jocie.

"It's sort of a long story," Jocie said.

"Then save it. I'll read about it in the paper next week. Right now we have a wedding to get to." She looked back at David. "Don't we?"

"That we do," David said.

343

Mrs. Simpson stopped frowning. "Good. Then I can still be there to see the bride come down the aisle, although heaven knows all the good seats will be taken, and of course, I couldn't possibly drive myself to the church. Not after what I've been through." She poked her finger against David's chest. "So you'll have to wait until I get ready. Then you can drive me."

"Yes, ma'am. One thing sure, they won't start without me."

Above their heads, Edwin Hammond was still banging around in the closet. Mrs. Simpson's frown came back. "Pipe down up there," she shouted as she grabbed her broomstick and banged it against the ceiling. "For mercy's sake, and I thought Leigh was noisy. I'll have to apologize to that girl."

# 45

It was already more than a half hour past the time the wedding was supposed to start when Wes and Jocie got back to the church. Her father was still waiting for Mrs. Simpson to get ready.

"Oh my heavenly days," Zella said when Wes ushered Jocie through the back door. "Where on earth have you been, Jocelyn?"

"Not one word," Wes warned Zella. "Not one. She's here now and we're going to wait until she gets ready."

Zella stared at him a moment before she said, "And dare I ask where David is?"

"He'll be here," Wes said.

"Well, that's comforting," Zella said. "Soon, I hope."

"As soon as he can," Wes said.

"I'm sorry, Zella," Jocie said. "I really didn't aim to mess things up. And I hope you won't be too upset about Leigh not wearing the garter you bought her for the blue part. I had it, but I dropped it and then forgot to pick it up before we got out of there."

"The garter? My stars, that's not what this is all about, is it?"

"That's what I went after, but then things happened," Jocie said.

"Don't they always when you're around. But I don't have time to hear it now. Go wash your face and get dressed. I'll have the judge tell everybody to just sit tight. Again. I suppose Myra Hearndon can sing another song." Zella turned to look at Wes with narrowed eyes. "And what happened to your tie, Wesley? Go let that sweet grandson of yours try to straighten it up so you'll be ready whenever David does finally get here. You're sure he's on the way?"

"He'll be here. But meantime I need you to go get Chief Simmons," Wes said.

Zella's face went pale. "You can't ask the police chief to come out right now. The whole church is in a buzz already about what could be holding things up. They see Randy leave, they'll panic and bolt for the doors." Zella shook her head. "We can't have that, Wesley. We just can't. I don't care what's happened."

"Could be you're right on this one, Zell. Guess we'll just have to wait till after the blessed event."

Jocie didn't have ribbons in her hair when she walked down the aisle carrying her bouquet of sunflowers and daisies, but she celebrated each step. She had never felt so alive or so loved. When Wes had escorted her down to the room where Leigh was waiting, Leigh had come out in the hall risking being seen in her wedding dress to grab Jocie and pull her close before they stepped back into the room.

Jocie had told Leigh and Tabitha what had happened as briefly as possible. "Mr. Hammond was in your apartment. He had a gun. He shot at me but missed. Dad and Wes got there. They locked him in your closet. Dad's okay. But I forgot the garter. I'm sorry."

"Oh, my dear child," Leigh had said as she hugged Jocie as tightly as Jocie's dad had earlier. "I'm the one who's sorry. You want us to postpone the wedding?"

"No way. I want you to be my mom. The sooner the better. Me and Tabitha will be your something blue in our dresses."

"Sounds like my lucky day or better yet my most blessed day," Leigh had said.

Now Leigh and Jocie's dad were standing together in front of the packed church promising to love one another forever. "Till death do us part."

Then they were putting the wedding rings on each other's finger. "With this ring, I thee wed."

Judge Wilson smiled at Jocie's dad and said, "You may kiss the bride."

Jocie's dad lifted Leigh's wedding veil and kissed her. Leigh was crying. Her happy tears. Jocie wanted to shout she was so happy.

Judge Wilson looked up at the people in the pews and said, "I present to you Mr. and Mrs. David Brooke."

Jessica Sanderson started playing the going-out music and Zella jumped up on her feet in her front row seat on the groom's side and started clapping. Jocie laughed out loud. Then everybody was standing up clapping as the bride and groom swept past them down the aisle.

Wes tucked Jocie's hand up under his arm as they followed them out. Jocie leaned over close to Wes and said, "Maybe I'll pass on that Jupiter wedding and have an earth wedding after all. If I ever get married."

"I'll be there, Jo. Blue spots on my forehead and all."

**Ann H. Gabhart** and her husband live on a farm just over the hill from where she grew up in central Kentucky. She's active in her country church, and her husband sings bass in a southern gospel quartet. Ann is the author of over a dozen novels for adults and young adults. Her first inspirational novel, *The Scent of Lilacs*, was one of Booklist's top ten inspirational novels of 2006.

# Looking for more good books to read?

# Discover unexpected love, fear, and forgiveness *with the* Brooke family

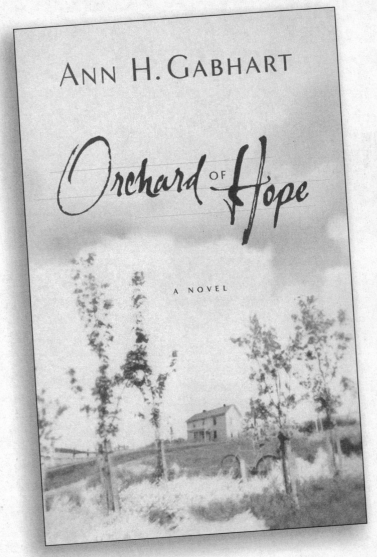